THIRTY LOVE

THIRTY LOVE

A Novel

TOM VELLNER

Published in the United States by Alcove Press, an imprint of The Quick Brown Fox & Company LLC.

Alcove Press and its logo are trademarks of The Quick Brown Fox & Company LLC.

Library of Congress Catalog-in-Publication data available upon request.

ISBN (hardcover): 979-8-89242-477-6
ISBN (paperback): 979-8-89242-478-3
ISBN (ebook): 979-8-89242-479-0

Cover design by Débora Islas

Printed in the United States.

www.alcovepress.com

Alcove Press
34 West 27th St., 10th Floor
New York, NY 10001

First Edition: March 2026

The authorized representative in the EU for product safety and compliance is eucomply OÜPärnu mnt 139b-14, 11317 Tallinn, Estonia, hello@eucompliancepartner.com, +33757690241

10 9 8 7 6 5 4 3 2 1

For Danny

"Pressure is a privilege."

—Billie Jean King

Grand Slam: US Open
Surface: Hard
Where: Queens, New York
When: August 27–September 10, 2023

CHAPTER ONE

Time never runs out in tennis. It's one of the few sports in which the clock ticks up instead of down. As long as the match is still in action, it's never too late to win. And yet, Leo Chambers, tennis's top-ranked American man, has an innate fear of time running out.

At the moment, though, in a podcast studio with a mic staring him in the face, Leo is tucked inside a memory from when time still felt limitless. He's thinking about the big piece of blue confetti that landed on his shoulder at the US Open men's final in 2003. It stuck to his T-shirt while he was cheering his lungs out alongside his dad, both of them clapping their hands until their palms were raw. The twenty-one-year-old American superstar Andy Roddick was hoisting what would be his first and only Grand Slam trophy into the muggy September air. Leo glanced down at the confetti resting on his shoulder and then back up at the thousands of pieces swirling around Arthur Ashe Stadium, applause and whistles reverberating in his ears. He was only nine years old, but he remembers it distinctly: This was the day he fell in love with tennis.

But he's not going to talk about a big piece of blue confetti on *What a Racket*. His dad's friend and fellow retired tennis star, Paul Davis, has hosted this podcast for over a decade as part of the Tennis Network and chats with lots of different players about their careers, including Leo—who's been featured, what? About 8,724 times now? Fine, it's more like eight, but he's never particularly enjoyed being a guest on this show, or speaking with most interviewers. For all the hours he logs at the gym and at practice, talking with the media is actually one of the most draining parts of being a tennis pro. He's only here now, in the studio, yet again, because his dad asked and because Paul's at least a decent guy.

"What will you be thinking about or, you know, reminding yourself of, as you hit the court at the US Open next week?" That's the question Paul has just asked Leo, no doubt hoping that he'll talk about being aggressive on court, playing first-strike tennis, the typical stuff. Leo wants to scream, "I'll be thinking about that big blue piece of confetti! The moment that made me want to win the goddamn US Open in the first place!"

"I'll be thinking about how I need to stay aggressive out there," Leo says, his voice polite and measured, "and how I'll have to play first-strike tennis if I want to get the win."

"I hear you, Leo, I hear you," Paul says. "And I know your dad has been working you hard to get that second serve percentage up, right? Johnny had a pretty good one himself back in the day. Tripped this guy up a few times, in fact!"

Lost in his own nostalgia, Paul doesn't wait for Leo's response before pressing on: "How's your dad doing, Leo, with the MS? He still hanging in there?" He adjusts his round wireframe glasses that, alongside his graying mustache, look like they were teleported from 1985.

"Yeah, he's been feeling fine, just fine, thanks for asking," Leo says, providing his boilerplate response to this question—one that people often ask him with a certain tone of pity or because they can't ask what they really want to: *Should he still be coaching you?* "He's got me working hard on my second serve, like you said. It's been failing me a little too often this season. But I wish he would take a break sometimes. I've barely gotten to go out and enjoy New York this year!" He forces a smile, rumpling his face, freckled from the summer sun.

"Well, we're just days away from the start of the action, so the Statue of Liberty will have to wait, my friend," Paul says. "I'm glad to hear you're gearing up. As always, you're a home favorite to lift the trophy. You've been having a solid season. But it's been an elusive thing for you, hasn't it? Securing your first Grand Slam title, that is."

It sure has, Paul!!!

"It sure has, Paul," Leo says. "But I've had my heart set on winning the US Open since I was a kid, so I'm going to take what I learned during my semifinal run last year and hopefully use that to go all the way this time. It was really tough to get that close and not clinch it."

Leo, who turned twenty-nine last month, has been on the ATP Tour (Association of Tennis Professionals) since he was eighteen and has fifteen singles titles to his name. He's had a stellar career, no doubt about it. But for Leo, and for all tennis players, the year revolves around the four Grand Slams, the most esteemed titles of the season: the Australian Open, Roland-Garros (a.k.a. the French Open), Wimbledon, and the US Open. To win a Grand Slam is to cement yourself in tennis history, to announce yourself as one of the greatest athletes on the planet. And Leo wants that more than anything. Like most players, he spends at least forty weeks a year traveling and competing on the ATP Tour, chasing his dream of winning the US Open. So, while he's managed to rack up those fifteen singles titles at other tournaments, he still can't call himself a Grand Slam champion, and he still can't sleep at night when he thinks about that fact.

"I have to be honest, it reminded me of when your dad came close to winning the US Open in '90! Boy, was that final a heartbreaker," Paul says, shaking his head. "Okay, now, I know you're probably tired of being asked this, but it's been twenty years since Andy Roddick won the US Open in '03, and no American man has done it since. You've been compared to Andy a lot throughout your career. Do you feel pressure coming in as the American favorite?"

It's true. From the moment Leo started winning matches on tour, the press started likening the two, from their serves to their smiles, nicknaming Leo "Baby Rod" and printing headlines like "LEO CHAMBERS: AMERICA'S ANDY RODDICK 2.0."

"I'd be lying if I said it doesn't add more pressure," Leo says. "I think all the American men want to be the next one to win it. It pushes us to bring our best out there."

"Well, you've got a lot of fans cheering for you, lots of admirers," Paul says. "You frequently pop up on, um, well . . . to be honest, my producer insisted I bring this up . . . an Instagram account called Serving Looks." Paul practically chokes on those two words as they come out of his mouth. "Can't say I understand the name, but it's essentially a tennis gossip page, isn't it?"

"Oh God," Leo says, flustered while thinking of how to explain that people on the internet think he's hot. "I mean, sort of. It's, like, news and pictures of players, especially ones they think are, uh, attractive. They talk about who players are dating, which ones are having the best season, that type of thing. But yeah, I get tagged once in a while."

"And, so, I guess I should ask: *Are* you dating anyone, Leo? Some of my listeners might want to know if you'll have a *special lady* rooting for you in your player's box at the Open."

Jesus Christ, Paul.

"Jesus Christ, Paul," Leo says, then realizes he just said that out loud. "Oh. Oh my God. Sorry. That just slipped out. Sorry. I think I'm just really tired from pract—"

Through muffled laughter, the podcast's producer, cute and curly-haired Jesse, interjects over the speaker: "Don't worry, Leo, we can cut that in post."

"Okay. Okay, thanks, Jesse. Sorry again," Leo says. "Um, no, no, I'm not seeing anyone at the moment. Just focusing on my game." His other boilerplate response.

"Good man," Paul says, looking only slightly agitated. "I look forward to watching you play, as always. It's going to be a thrilling two weeks of tennis."

Leo forces a smile and shifts in his swivel chair.

"I'm sure I'll be seeing you around the grounds, Leo. And I'm sure I'll be seeing many of *you*, my listeners, around the grounds too!" Paul's face is back to looking bright and confident. "You can always feel free to stop me and say hello or talk match picks. Well, folks, I'm Davis, Paul Davis, and this has been another episode of *What a Racket.*"

Why does Paul always state his name like James Bond during sign-off? Who can say.

"Sorry about that," Leo says, lifting off his headphones, further ruffling his already messy hair. "My brain is just—"

"Focused on the Open! I get it," Paul says. "It's really no problem, Leo. It's really no problem. Right, Jesse?"

"No problem!" Jesse says, waving from the sound booth, smiling at Leo.

"Okay, well, thanks, guys, and yeah, I'll see you around the grounds next week," Leo says, reaching for the doorknob.

"Tell your dad I say hey, and send in the next guy, will you? Gabriel's out there," Paul says, shuffling through some papers.

"Gabriel? You mean Gabe? Montoya?" Leo asks, turning around, brow furrowed.

"No, Leo. Peter Gabriel, from Genesis."

Leo blinks. "Who?"

"Yes, Gabriel Montoya! You know, the guy who knocked you out of Wimbledon this year?" Paul says with a smirk. "Send him in. He's recording a clip for an episode, too."

Leo steps into the next room and there he is. Gabriel. Gabe. Gabe fucking Montoya. Sitting on the fucking sofa in the fucking lounge. Is there anybody worse Leo could bump into while trying to keep himself centered ahead of the Open? Look at this guy! Look at his loose, black curls, perfectly coiffed! Look at his tight gray T-shirt, barely stretching over his broad shoulders! Look at his jawline, likely able to saw wood! Oh, ha ha, no, just kidding, Leo doesn't notice any of that. Hold on, is Gabe reading a *book* while he waits? Leo can't quite make out the cover, but he's probably reading up on Bitcoin or Brooklyn sex clubs or something. This man is the living worst.

Leo and Gabe first met as teenagers, back when they were junior players at Break Point Tennis, a premier tennis academy in Boca Raton, Florida. It should be noted that, for tennis players at least, Florida is heaven. It's an elite hub for the sport, offering gorgeous weather year-round and an endless supply of world-renowned coaches and facilities. The expansive grounds of Break Point are lush—lined with palm trees and flowered shrubbery, all hugging a Tetris-like grid of thirty tennis courts as cerulean as the South Florida sky or Leo's own eyes. Those eyes caught sight of Gabe a year after Leo first started training at Break Point. Playing there every day after school for months at a time, he considered the academy a second home. Growing up a short drive away in the small, tennis-obsessed town of Delray Beach, he spent as much time at Break Point as he could, making sure he could "become one with the court," as his dad told him all pros must. But the familiarity of his life at Break Point shifted seismically when Gabe arrived one sticky August afternoon.

Leo was really cool about it from the beginning.

"Who is that? Do you know who that kid is? I haven't seen him at BP before. Who is that over there? On court three," he asked his dad during their practice session, oblivious to how rapidly he was now bouncing the ball with his cherry-red Wilson racket.

Square-faced Gabe, who must've come out of the womb with that perfectly coiffed black hair, was doing some stretches before starting his practice session a couple courts over. It's not that things of a sexual nature hadn't ever crossed Leo's mind before. He was a hormonal fifteen-year-old with dial-up internet access, after all. But he had developed such narrow tennis tunnel vision that he never thought too critically about his own sexuality. Not to mention, it was the early aughts, in Florida. "Your swing is so gay" and "Don't be such a fag" and "You're playing like a pussy" weren't exactly uncommon remarks he'd hear other guys toss around at school or BP, sometimes directed at Leo himself.

Whenever he would notice another guy was cute, he would pretend it was nothing—just a blip, a glitch—and continue thinking about his next match. He was usually able to push it aside. But he had never felt his breath catch in his throat like this before. He had never felt his mind fixate on a person like this before. Not until Gabe showed up and cracked his concentration right down the middle.

But, hey, it was probably just the humidity. Right?

"Did you hear me?" his dad asked. "His name is Gabe. He's the same year as you."

Leo continued to bounce the ball—and stare.

"Go ahead and serve!" his dad shouted. "Leo?"

Bounce. Bounce. Bounce. Bounce. Stare. Stare. Stare. Stare.

"Hello? Leo?" Gabe says, rising from the couch in the studio lounge.

"Oh. Didn't notice you there," Leo says curtly, snapping out of it. His breath? Definitely not caught in his throat. "The doctor will see you now." He gestures toward the recording booth, immediately regretting this joke.

"What did you and Paul talk about this time?" Gabe asks. "How I'm going to kick your ass at the Open like I did at Wimbledon?"

The tension is building in Leo's body, and he can see Gabe feeding off it.

"That makes it, hmm, let's see . . . a 10–0 record against *the* Leo Chambers? The number nine player in the world? Damn, I'm good." Gabe winks.

"That's some big talk for somebody who won't even be seeded at the Open. You're what, number forty-seven now? Too busy partying, perhaps?"

"Quit talking about your seed," Gabe says. "It's gross." He winks again.

"Hilarious," Leo says. "And *stop wink—*"

He doesn't quite get this sentence out before Gabe closes the door in his face, tilting his head as it shuts, flashing him a smirk.

Leo stands there for a second. The air still holds a little of Gabe's scent. Fresh, crisp, like cedar . . . Wait, what? No. This trip to *What a Racket* needs to end.

Sufficiently rattled from his awkward morning, Leo is relieved when he finally steps onto one of the practice courts at the Open. Jogging onto the court, in the shadow of the hulking Arthur Ashe Stadium—the largest tennis stadium in the world, named for the first Black US Open champion—he spins his racket in his hand (still cherry-red, still Wilson), ready to lose himself and the sound of Paul's voice and the smell of Gabe's body in the rhythm of his routine. The Open starts in just a few days, and while Paul called his season "solid" on the podcast, Leo knows all too well that he's been feeling tight on the court this year.

Uninspired, even. He can't seem to get out of his own way. And if he doesn't make another deep run at the Open, he'll lose the ranking points from his semifinal appearance last year—and watch his spot in the top ten disappear. So, it's time to compartmentalize the bullshit and focus on his game.

Leo smacks a forehand crosscourt.
"Footwork, Leo," Johnny says.

He rockets a backhand down the line.
"Swing through."

Another forehand.
"Take that earlier!"

Shuffling side to side, Leo returns each shot from his assistant coach, Brian Wilkins, with power and precision. Backhand, forehand, backhand, forehand. One of the best players in the world and the number one American player right now, Leo is powerful in his shot-making and swift on his feet. You'd be forgiven for thinking you're at a shooting range upon hearing the forceful pops of his groundstrokes. Groups of fans looking to glimpse their favorite players ahead of the tournament press up against the court's fence and pack into the elevated stands behind him, their eyes glued to Leo's every move. His forehand, flat and fast like a bullet, is a sight to behold. And it helps that he's shirtless. Is one of the fans sending a photo of him to Instagram sensation Serving Looks as we speak? Most likely. Leo wipes his wristband across his sweaty, scruffy face.

Leo's dad, who's been observing from the wall behind him during practice, makes his way onto the court, his right leg taking a moment longer to lift off the ground than his left.

Johnny was diagnosed with multiple sclerosis in 1991, just a year after he was the runner-up at the US Open. Even though his symptoms are manageable, they impact his mobility and energy, and they ended his career as a pro player before he got another chance to go for the US Open title. So, Leo's dream of winning it? It's as much for himself as it is for his dad.

"Looking pretty good," Johnny says. "But remember to keep that—"

"Elbow up on the backhand, I know, I know."

Leo has an elegant one-handed backhand modeled after his dad's that, like any player with a somewhat uncommon one-handed backhand, is a major point of pride for him.

"Everything okay?" Johnny asks.

"Oh, yeah, just a weird morning," Leo says.

"Don't tell me Davis, Paul Davis, didn't treat you right," Johnny says.

Paul and Johnny go way back.

"Don't make me bring up our doubles run at Wimbledon '87," Johnny always says.

"I never would," Leo likes to say in response.

"No, no, he was fine," Leo says now. "I mean, I wasn't the ideal guest but—wait, yeah, why does he talk like James Bond at the end?"

"Leo, I have never understood that man," Johnny says, deadpan.

Leo knocks his head back with a laugh.

Click click click. The fans immediately take photos. Perfect content.

"But I appreciate you going on there again," Johnny says. "Between you and me, I think he's been scrambling to get the best players on that show of his."

"Well, that can't be true. Gabe Montoya went in after me."

"Gabriel! Ah, what a good guy. I don't know what you have against that kid, Leo. Other than your losing streak against him, I guess." He grins.

Leo ignores his dad's quip. He's all too aware he's never won a match against Gabe, starting with their very first one, when Gabe stole the winning point from him.

Leo's game is all about overpowering his opponent. It's a straightforward approach, a classic strategy. The problem is that Gabe's game absolutely dismantles it. He has a wicked slice and a mean drop shot that Leo never sees coming. Gabe also comes into the net to volley. A lot. The tempo and finesse of Gabe's game throws Leo out of his rhythm every time they meet, causing him to make errors left and right. It doesn't help that the mere sight of Gabe's face doesn't just dismantle Leo's game but his entire existence.

For Leo, in every sense, Gabe hits different.

"Hey! Speaking of good guys," Johnny says, holding out his hand to shake Ollie's, who has just arrived for their practice session. A Canadian player, Olivier Tremblay—Ollie—grew up in Montreal but moved to Florida to pursue tennis as a teen and remains Leo's best friend to this day.

"Don't go easy on him, okay?" Johnny says to Ollie with a knowing smile. "Remember your footwork, Leo. Your footwork." Johnny turns and begins to walk toward the back of the court again, more slowly now, his breathing a little heavier.

"Dad, you can just watch from here," Leo says, quickly moving his stuff from one of the benches, which is positioned in the shade of a big white umbrella.

"No, I'm good," he says, his right foot dragging a bit.

Leo looks at him concernedly. "Please?"

"All right, all right, I'll sit with Brian," he says, and takes a seat with a quiet groan and his clipboard. "I do need to make some notes for us to go over later, Leo."

"Sure," Leo says.

"I thought we were practicing on Ashe," Ollie says, pulling a neon-yellow racket from his giant black Babolat bag.

"Didn't you see the schedule?" Leo says. "Sascha already has it booked all afternoon."

"Of *course* he does," Ollie says, his subtle French accent coming out more, as it always does whenever he raises his voice. As does his favorite Quebecois swear: "Tabarnak!"

Over the course of another two-hour session, Leo rockets the ball back and forth with Ollie, Johnny looking up from his clipboard occasionally to yell to Leo about his elbow or his pronation or his topspin. Leo has always loved hitting with Ollie. Lanky, loyal Ollie, whose blond hair has been in a buzzcut for as long as Leo can remember. He's probably the most disciplined guy on tour—consistently a top twenty player for years now—but he also makes Leo laugh more than anyone else, a delightful curmudgeon.

"Did you hear him on *What a Racket* the other day?" Ollie says. The two of them are chatting at the net now, drenched in sweat.

"Who?"

"Sascha," Ollie says. "His advice to kids who want to make it in tennis? 'A little less focus on pronouns and a little more focus on practice.'"

"I saw that on Instagram! What the fuck?" Leo says, his brow furrowing.

"So, let's see. Sascha Volkov, he/him/his," Ollie says. "I wonder if *he* will break *his* racket when I beat *him* again this year."

"I can't with you," Leo says, chuckling, and heads for the benches to start packing up. "Ah, I forgot—"

"How to hit a second serve?"

"Hilarious! Everyone's hilarious today!" Leo says, looking up from his phone. "No, I forgot that I'm meeting up with Tess tomorrow after practice with my team, so I won't be able to hit with you. Sorry. Tess and I are playing mixed doubles again this year, so we need to figure out our game plan."

"Ah, okay, I see who the favorite is," Ollie says, inserting his rackets back into his bag. "You two better win it this year."

"I mean, I'd prefer to win singles, but—"

Ollie gasps. "No! *Leo Chambers* wants to win the US Open? Mon dieu, I had no idea."

Leo stares at him, straight-faced.

"Okay, but I'm glad you're playing mixed again, dude. Tess always helps you loosen up. She helps you play more fearlessly, more like you used to," Ollie says.

"Well, thanks. I think."

"Anytime!" Ollie says, and starts heading for the exit. He's walking backward, facing Leo. "Let's just hope you don't draw Gabe!"

The draw—the tournament's bracket—for men's singles will be released tonight, and Leo will most likely pass away if he's forced to play Gabe in the first round.

"If you wink right now, I swear to God," Leo says.

"Why would I wink at you?" Ollie asks.

"Never mind," Leo says. "I'll text you once the draw is out!"

Ollie throws up a peace sign to Leo as he turns to greet a group of fans outside the court who rushed over when they saw him leaving.

"I gotta make a call, LC," Brian says, and tosses Leo a banana to keep his strength up.

A forty-three-year-old bald and built Black man, Brian joined Leo's team at the start of this season. A former pro himself, Brian has a collection of nine titles and a career-high ranking of number five. After struggling to come back from a serious ankle injury, he retired at thirty-three, and has since coached some of the best players in the world. His crowning achievement, however, as he's told Leo on many occasions, was earning the Arthur Ashe Humanitarian Award for his work supporting the Crown Heights Junior Tennis Program in Brooklyn.

It's always a good idea for players to have additional voices on their team to offer perspective beyond the head coach's, especially when that head coach is the player's dad. Leo knew that bringing Brian on board would improve the team dynamic exponentially, and it was an anticipatory move, too, to provide support as his dad pushes sixty and MS pushes his limits, even if Johnny won't admit that.

"We'll hit the gym in a few?" Brian asks, pointing to Leo.

Even when practice is over, practice isn't really over. Leo will hit the gym for an extensive fitness session, followed by an appointment with his physiotherapist, where he'll work out any pain or knots in his body.

"Yeah, see you in a bit," Leo says.

"Wait up," Johnny says to Brian, trailing behind him. "Let's walk and talk."

For now, Leo is by himself, catching his breath before heading to the gym. Beads of sweat cover his forehead and stomach as he performs his instinctive scan of the fans still gathered by the court, monitoring whether they're watching or judging his dad's careful steps. He knows he should be relaxing during these free minutes before diving back into his packed schedule, but the knot that always forms in his stomach while looking out for his dad is one that can't be worked out.

Leo's hotel room in Midtown Manhattan is enormous and sterile. His match clothes from his Nike kit and extra Wilson rackets in plastic wrapping are scattered across the California king bed and the concrete floor. With his full team—Johnny, Brian, his physio, his agent—in a half-circle behind him, he's hunched over his laptop at the desk, watching a livestream of the US Open draw announcement.

Leg bouncing up and down like the tennis ball before his serve, he's waiting excitedly to see what his route to the final will look like this year. Who will his first-round opponent be? Will Gabe fall in his path? Who else will be in his quarter of the draw? Unseeded players, like Gabe, are randomly positioned within the draw. Will Gabe fall in his path? Will there be any potential blockbuster matches along the way? Will Gabe fall in his path? These questions ricochet off the walls of his brain ahead of every tournament, but especially ahead of the Grand Slams, and especially the US Open.

Just after seven PM, it's out. The draw is finally released for the field of 128 hopefuls, all the men in the midst of this exact same ritual in their hotel rooms across the city. Hunching even closer to the screen now, Leo scans down the bracket carefully, eyes squinted as he hunts for his name among the list of players. When he reaches the third quarter of the draw, he finds this:

1st Round

Leo Chambers 9
Gabriel Montoya

CHAPTER TWO

Leo's heart plunges into the depths of his belly. In the first round of the Open, Leo Chambers will face off against Gabriel Montoya. The man he's never beaten. Ten straight losses. Of course. Of course this would happen. At least it took until the third round for them to meet at Wimbledon. But the *first round*? This is cruel. It feels like the tennis gods have dropped Gabe here just to fuck with him. Making it to the semifinals again—let alone winning the whole goddamn Slam—has just gotten much more complicated.

"It's okay. This is okay," Johnny says, his hand on Leo's shoulder. "We can work with this."

Leo can't deal with his dad's optimism right now. He needs a second. He gets up from the desk and heads into the bathroom. He slides the heavy pocket door into place and flips the lock, which is distinctly less satisfying than slamming it behind him, and this sets him off even more. Standing over the sink, he splashes some water on his face and then takes a gulp, trying to clear that pesky breath caught in his throat. He stares in the mirror and attempts to do the 4-7-8 breathing exercise his sports psychologist taught him.

It's okay, I can do this,
I can beat him.

Except, you never have.

I've come close.

You can't handle his slice.

It's fine, I'll find a way.

Sure, sweetie.

His phone vibrates in his pocket and breaks him out of the conversation that all the voices in his head are having with each other right now.

I think I jinxed you, Ollie's text reads.

Yeah, thanks for that, Leo responds.

Ollie sends an angel emoji.

Leo closes their conversation and decides to distract himself by opening Instagram. Rookie mistake. The first thing on his feed is a post from Serving Looks, which is already sharing reactions to the men's draw. What's worse, the post staring back at him shows side-by-side photos of him and Gabe. On the left is Leo and—shocker—it's a fan's photo of him from today's practice. His six-foot frame is twisting as he hits a forehand. His body, toned but not chiseled, is glistening in the oppressive sun, light brown hair covering his chest, his happy trail leading down into his navy-blue shorts. On the right is Gabe, also practicing for the Open. A couple inches taller than Leo, he's wearing a black tank that highlights his powerful arms as he tosses a ball into the air. The caption reads:

> **servinglooks** SPICY. Our two favorite American heartthrobs are set for a first-round showdown at the @usopen. Can @leochambers finally solve the @gabemontoya riddle? Their head-to-head is 10–0 Montoya.

He scrolls down to the next post on his feed, another side-by-side of him and Gabe:

espn Grab your popcorn, tennis fans. It's an 11th career meeting for @leochambers and @gabemontoya, America's greatest hopes for a new home champ at the @usopen. You won't want to miss this round-one battle on Monday.

He keeps scrolling and finds a photo of Gabe with sunglasses on, turning to the camera as he walks the US Open grounds:

gabemontoya LFG, NYC! Ready for a show?? I know I am.

Ughhhhh. Leo locks his phone and shoves it back in his pocket, nearly tearing a hole in it. He lets out a frustrated sigh. There's a knock at the door.

"Leo? You all right?" Johnny says.

He hears his dad and the rest of his team gathered and pacing outside the bathroom, eager to talk to him about the game plan for this first-round showdown. It's like they're all backstage, outside a Broadway dressing room, delicately trying to convince the lead actor to get over their jitters and get out on stage. It may seem dramatic and, yes, it is, but this is how it works with tennis players. It's one of the most individual sports in the world. No matter how important the coach, physio, trainer, and hitting partner are in molding them for success, it all comes down to that one person who walks onto the court at match time, relying only on themselves to get the win. And they're walking onto that court up to 150 times a year. So, yeah. There might not be an "i" in "team"—but there certainly is in "tennis."

Leo steps out of the bathroom. "Yeah, I'm good," he says, nodding. "I got this."

At practice the next day, Leo turns midstretch to see Johnny hauling over a ball hopper.

"It's that time again!" Johnny says.

Leo groans. "I hate how much you love this."

"Hey, what do I always say? You're only as good as your second serve," Johnny tells him, placing a hand on Leo's shoulder. "I didn't coin that phrase for nothing."

"Dad, you literally didn't coin that phrase."

For the next hour, Johnny stands at the corner of the court, watching Leo practice his second serve over and over and over again. He bounces the ball five times with his left hand, then presses it to the center of the racket, leaning over and swinging his arms a couple times. He tosses the ball high into the air, somewhat resembling the Statue of Liberty (which Paul seems to think he's dying to visit?), puts his feet together, and launches his body upward. His right arm rotates around and he skids the racket strings along the ball to give it a bit of extra kick. It flies over the net, lands in the box, and bounces with a tall arch.

"You'll have to give it to him good," Johnny says.

Leo lands back on the ground and whips his head around toward his dad. "Sorry?" he says, suddenly dizzy.

"I just mean, I think you'll have to give that second serve as much kick as you can with Gabe," Johnny says. "Really get it up."

"Oh. Right," Leo says. "What do you think about me going for the slice out wide? I feel like I need to throw him off balance more."

"You're much more comfortable with the kick, you know that," Johnny says.

"I know, but Gabe knows that, too. He won't be expecting it out wide," Leo says. "I never go for the slice with him."

"Ooh, all this talk of slices. I gotta get some New York pizza while we're here," Johnny says, zooming right by Leo's strategizing. "Okay, let's keep it going."

Johnny claps as Leo steps up to the line for about the billionth time today, and Leo can't help but roll his eyes.

Meanwhile, the episode of *What a Racket* featuring Leo has been released. As always, Paul is churning them out practically every other day ahead of the Open, his social team sharing each episode link on the podcast's Instagram.

As he makes his way into the men's locker room after finishing what feels like ten thousand practice serves with his dad, Leo sees he's been tagged in a post.

> **servinglooks** "No, no, I'm not seeing anyone at the moment."—@leochambers on the latest "What a Racket." I'm, like, dropping hints that I'm single!!!

The caption rests below another shirtless photo of Leo, this time during a changeover at Wimbledon. He's sitting down, wide-legged, pulling on a fresh white shirt.

He's not particularly fazed by posts about his looks anymore. It comes with the territory of being one of the world's top tennis players. Serving Looks has reached 200K followers and draws a ton of new young fans to the sport. Leo is just relieved that good ol' Jesse must have cut the whole "Jesus Christ, Paul" moment like he said he would; otherwise, that definitely would've made its way into this caption.

Leo listens to the episode just to make sure.

Phew. Jesse kept his word.

He knows he shouldn't keep listening. The final part of the episode features the interview with Gabe. It's not worth it. Really. Gabe will just spout some pompous bullshit. Leo will put his phone away now. Yep. Here he goes. In 3, 2 . . . Putting his phone away.

"So, it's not your first rodeo here, Gabriel," Paul says. "But I want to ask you the same question I asked Leo. It's been twenty years since Andy Roddick won the Open. Coming into this Slam, do you feel any pressure being an American favorite?"

"I don't," Gabe says, cool as ever. "Leave that to Leo. He's the chosen one, right?"

Leo's hand grips his phone tighter.

"Well, not to put too fine a point on it, but straight out of juniors, you both became the biggest hopes for American tennis. It's been you two vying for the glory," Paul says. "Leo may be ranked higher, but I think fans have always been pulling for you, too."

"That's definitely true. I have a special connection with the fans here, maybe even more so than Leo. I think they like to root for somebody who can actually put on a show."

He can't listen to any more of this. Leo shoves his phone into his Wilson bag and plops it down onto the bench. Sticky from the humidity and planning to head straight to Tess's hotel for dinner, he desperately needs a rinse. He peels off his shirt and rummages through his locker for his toiletries. When he shuts the door a few moments later, he spots Gabe standing at his own locker across the aisle.

Leo jumps. "Shit," he says, and his tone turns sarcastic. "Wow, lucky me. I keep bumping into you."

"Just like in the draw, huh?" Gabe says with a wry smile. He has nothing on but a towel wrapped around his waist, some droplets of water from the shower still hugging his body. His hair is soaking wet and slicked back. Before Leo can even make a quippy response, Gabe is now taking off the towel, draping it over the bench behind him. Leo makes a point of not looking over at him, or his sculpted back, or his bubble butt, or—oh my God, okay, enough. He pretends he needs to rummage through his locker again to avert his eyes.

"Sorry to have to knock you out in the first round," Leo says, doing nothing in his locker but picking up his bottle of sunscreen and putting it down to look busy.

Gabe laughs as he pulls on his briefs: Calvin Klein, white, the kind he wore in the company's campaign earlier this year, which Serving Looks reposted at the speed of light:

> **servinglooks** SHEESH, warn us next time, @gabemontoya. The American star is the latest ATP player to strip down for @calvinklein's #mycalvins campaign and, uh, DAMN.

Did Leo linger on that post for a few seconds? Nah, not really. Scrolled *right* on by that one for sure. He's seeing these white Calvins on Gabe for the first time. Now. Here. In the locker room. Yup, yup, yup.

"The numbers don't lie, friend," Gabe says. He's still standing there in his briefs, sliding on some deodorant now.

"If you want to talk numbers, I've seen your win–loss record this season and it's, uh, not looking so good," Leo says, flashing a grimace at Gabe, while still picking up his sunscreen and putting it down.

"Whatever you need to tell yourself," Gabe says.

"Chambers!" A new, booming voice echoes through the locker room as the man approaches. Sascha Volkov.

"Hey, Sascha," Leo says, trying to keep his voice steady, as always, even though he despises this man even more than Gabe. But Leo's learned throughout his career that you *do not* mess with him.

A thirty-five-year-old Russian legend, Sascha has held the number one ranking on and off for two decades and has twenty Grand Slam titles to his name. That number has awarded him GOAT status among the fans. It's also awarded him the ability to do anything he fucking wants and still have those fans' adoration. Over the years, his temper has often spiraled out of control on the court. He once smashed his racket over and over against an ump's chair when he disagreed with a call. Another time, he pummeled a ball at the wall behind him and accidentally hit a ball boy in the stomach. He even threw his racket at his player's bench and when it bounced off the court, it crashed into a spectator in the front row. But his violent outbursts have only ever led to an occasional fine or a default from a tournament. They have hardly tarnished his reputation. When you have twenty Slam titles and conservative "family values" (read: bigotry) behind you, you can get away with anything. His fellow players fall in line, the commentators fawn over his game, and the fans swarm him for autographs and selfies everywhere he goes. Everyone is too distracted by the shine of twenty Slam trophies to see this man for who he really is: a bully.

"How's it hanging, man? A little to the left for you, I see, Gabriel," Sascha says, glancing down at Gabe's crotch as he passes by, heading for his locker in the next row. "Have you always had that tattoo?"

Gabe touches his ribs, brushing his fingers over the intricate crest on the right side of his body. "Nope, got it this summer," he says, monotone.

"What's that from? The, uh, Mexican flag?" Sascha asks, scrunching his slim, sharp face, terrifying but refined.

"Peruvian," Gabe says, shutting his eyes.

"Ah, right, Peru," Sascha says. "That's the island you're from."

Leo tries to choke down his anger but shoots Sascha a frustrated glance.

"What?" Sascha asks sternly, blue-gray eyes as icy as ever.

"Nothing," Leo says, suddenly making himself smaller, like he's back at his locker in middle school, afraid of bringing too much attention to himself.

Sascha looks at them, amused, confident. "I'll leave you two to get ready for your cat fight on Monday," he says, and takes his shirt off. He's still ghostly pale despite it being the end of summer. He then walks toward the shower with a towel thrown over his shoulder.

"Fuck that guy," Gabe says into his locker once Sascha is out of earshot.

"Pass," Leo says.

Gabe huffs out a laugh, and Leo catches himself smiling at him.

"Okay, well, see you on Monday for the cat fight," Leo says, shutting his locker door. He passes by Gabe, mustering all his energy to stare straight ahead. "Better bring your A game."

"Never needed to before," Gabe says confidently as Leo turns the corner into the showers. "By the way, you've got some white stuff on your shorts."

Leo looks down so fast his neck almost snaps clean off. He didn't realize he was squeezing the bottle while glaring at Sascha. There's sunscreen all over his lap.

"Miss! Top!! Ten!!!" Leo says through cupped hands as Tess opens the door to her hotel room.

She takes a royal bow before pretending to catch some roses.

"Cincinnati champion!" Leo shouts, walking into her room, floor-to-ceiling windows letting in some waning sun and the lights of Midtown beginning to shine. "And cracking the top ten right before the Open? You're living the dream."

"Thank you, sweet angel," she says, wrapping her arms around him. "God, but have you seen some of the articles? All everyone can talk about is how *astounding* it is that I made the top ten for the first time at—I'm not sure you're ready for this, Leo—thirty years old."

Leo fakes a gasp as he falls onto the king bed.

"The headlines are like, CORPSE BRIDE MAKES TOP TEN DEBUT," she says. "Sascha Volkov could still be playing at eighty-five and people wouldn't blink. I make moves after I turn thirty and they want to study my body for science."

"Just wait until they see you win the Open this year," Leo says.

"Oh my God," Tess says, redoing her messy bun, her cropped white Nike tee lifting a little. "Can you imagine if I somehow pulled that off? The front page of the *Times*: GERIATRIC WOMAN WINS US OPEN."

"GRANDMOTHER OF TWELVE TAKES US OPEN BY STORM," Leo says, swiping his palm across the air. Tess cackles.

"And, you know, the real news is that I'm the first Filipino American woman to be ranked in the top ten. Ever. But that's just a footnote, I guess."

"That fucking sucks. I'm sorry," Leo says. "I did see some amazing posts about it on Instagram, at least."

"Yes, oh my God! Did you see the one from Serving Looks? They were so sweet," she says, placing her hands on the sides of her heart-shaped face. "You should've seen me straight-up sobbing at some of the DMs I got from all these Filipino kids, too."

"That's incredible!" Leo says.

"I kinda feel like I should be doing more for them," Tess says, fidgeting with the thin gold ring on her right hand. "I just want them to know they really do belong in tennis. I want to find a way to get my voice out there more, show them that a Filipino player can really rep this sport."

"Tess, at the risk of sounding cheesy as hell, you do so much every time you step onto the court," Leo says. "But I'm sure you'll think of something. I'm always here if you ever want to brainstorm."

"Thank you, angel," she says, her face scrunching bashfully. "Okay, let's order food before I start crying about those messages again."

They order poké bowls before getting down to business. After a half hour of mixed doubles strategizing, they switch to the topic they—and all players—really want to talk about: winning. Mixed doubles doesn't start for another few days, anyway.

"You know, you could win the whole thing," Leo says. He's sitting cross-legged on the fluffy white duvet. "You've got a pretty good path to the finals. Just saying."

"You sound like my coach!" Tess says, getting up from the bed. She answers the knock at the door and thanks the delivery man profusely. "I just don't want to think that far ahead right now. I'm taking it one round at a time."

She pulls their bowls out of the brown paper bag and sets them down on the desk—bright, beautiful palettes of salmon, tuna, edamame, avocado, radish, and sriracha.

"Sure, sure," Leo says, drizzling a little extra sriracha onto the sushi rice in his bowl. "Well, I've got my money on you."

"And what about you? You could go all the way, too," she says, taking her first bite, brow furrowing. "Huh, this is actually pretty good for a place called Hokey Poké."

"Yeah, maybe, if I can even—"

"Do *not* start with the Gabe stuff," Tess groans, driving her chopsticks into the rice. "I can't handle it, Leo. I know he's been, like, your kryptonite since birth, but you and I both know you could beat him."

"You sound like you're describing my superhero origin story," Leo says. He takes a big bite and then wipes some sriracha off his mouth with a napkin.

"Well, I'm serious, Clark Kent," she says, and takes another bite. "I don't even get what you're so hung up on."

"Oh, come on, you must see it, too," Leo says. "He thinks he's this golden boy. It's so smarmy. Always smirking, always running a hand through his hair. The Calvin Klein ads, the Head ads, the Head and Shoulders ads. You know, the one where he's literally smirking and running a hand through his hair in the shower? I mean, at least we know he has dandruff."

Tess is searching for her next bite with her chopsticks and shaking her head. "I don't think the people in those ads actually have dandruff."

"Whatever! It's the way he talks about our matches at the press conferences after, too, like he didn't even break a sweat," Leo says, and begins mimicking Gabe's slightly deeper voice, bobbing his head back and forth. "*I know Leo's game well, so I just went out there and gave him all the shots I know he hates.* And then he smirks, of course. He's an asshole."

"Well, all that may be true, but if you're going to win, you better find a way to put it out of your mind come Monday. If it were me, I would try and beat him at his own game. I know you have a killer drop shot in there somewhere," she says, tapping his forehead with a freshly manicured blush-pink nail.

"Yeah, I think my coach would disagree."

"Oh my God, I miss your dad," she says, putting a hand over her heart. "I need to see him while we're in New York. How *is* the sweetest man on Earth?"

"Hmm, right, you mean the stubbornest?" he asks. "Most stubborn? I don't know. He's good. But we haven't been seeing eye-to-eye on my game for a while now. He has one idea of how I should play and that's it. No discussion." He scarfs down another bite before continuing. "He just pushes me so hard. He pushes himself too hard, too. It can be a lot."

"Do you think you'll ever say something to him?"

"At this point? I don't think that's gonna happen. We've been at this for so long. It's not worth rocking the boat," he says. "Maybe next year I'll bring it up, but for now, I'm just going to ride out the rest of the season."

Tess gives him a concerned look. She has a sesame seed stuck to her upper lip.

"He still knows his stuff," he says. "He's still one of the best, obviously. I just . . . I don't know."

"Yes, you do," Tess says, arching an eyebrow.

Leo sighs. "He just doesn't hear me anymore," he says. "But he works so hard for me. He puts up with all the shit people say about him or ask me about him in interviews. I would feel silly pushing back, you know?"

"Oh, angel. I've never pretended to know exactly what it's like between you two," she says. "But I *do* know that you guys have an amazing bond. You always have. And I hope you can . . . honor that? By talking about how unhappy you are with his approach?"

"Yeah," Leo says, letting out a long sigh. "Maybe. I guess I'm afraid of hurting him. I can't imagine doing this without him."

Tess nods and offers a sympathetic smile.

"Anyway, sorry," Leo says, reapplying his smile. "I didn't mean for our mixed doubles dinner to get so heavy. Back to talking about serve formations."

"BREAKING NEWS: AMERICAN TENNIS STAR LEO CHAMBERS HAS DADDY ISSUES," Tess yells.

"You're the worst," Leo says, throwing a piece of edamame at her.

"WHITE MAN THROWS EDAMAME AT ASIAN WOMAN AT US OPEN," she yells, wheezing from laughter.

"I'm *leaving*," Leo jokes, storming toward the door. "Oooh, hold up, is this your kit for the Open?" he asks, stopping in his tracks to pick up one of her match shirts.

"So cute, right?" Tess says. "Nike hooked your girl up this year."

"These are sick," he says, holding up a varsity-style tank top, kelly green with white trim.

"Speaking of sick, can you stay for a horror movie?" she says. "I decided I'm watching this absolutely disgusting French slasher tonight called *High Tension*."

"As appealing as *that* sounds," Leo says, head turning toward the door, "I should probably get back for my own nighttime ritual."

"Ew," Tess says.

"Not *that*," Leo says, blushing a little.

"I mean, whatever helps relieve your stress, my dude," Tess says. "You have your thing, and I have mine."

"First of all that's not my *thing*, and I don't get why you always watch these gory-ass movies right before tournaments."

"It's controlled anxiety," Tess explains, shrugging. "I read it somewhere. Horror movies give you a chance to focus your attention and release your stress through something unrelated to your own life. I don't know, I find it helpful."

"That's . . . actually kind of brilliant," Leo says.

"I know," Tess says, looking pleased with herself. "You want to stay now, don't you?"

"Still no!" he says, tossing his empty bowl in the trash.

"Your loss."

"All right, freak, I'm gonna go so you can watch people get hacked up."

"Yum," she says, and gets up from the bed. She gives him a big hug, then puts her hands on both sides of his head. "If I don't see you before your match—remember, it's all up here. Dig deep."

"Thanks," he says, his smile starting to curl.

"God, Gabe is so hot, though," she says, staring off into the distance.

"*Okay*, I'm leaving for real now," he says, pulling his face away and turning for the door.

"He is!" she shouts, rolling her eyes. "Ugh, straight men. You're all so fragile."

Leo clears his throat. "Okay, bye, corpse bride! Good luck at your match!"

"Love you!" she says as the door clicks shut.

Waiting at the elevator bank, Leo is stuck on Tess's words: "dig deep." She's right. He needs to find it in himself to get over this Gabe hurdle, once and for all. The other words he's stuck on: "straight men." Tess and Ollie and his parents may still see him this way—at least, he assumes they do, because he's never told them otherwise—but he knows other people wonder about him. He's never dated anyone publicly (okay, or privately), and he's seen the chatter online.

Ok but is he gay?!
My dream mannn I want him to come out ugh
CLOWN. he's not going to beat Montoya
Gay tho???
He HAS to be queer
Paying $5,300 rn to 15 people who msg me "STRUGGLING" stay blessed y'all
DADDY

This is the only thing that *does* faze him about these types of posts: all the people who track the details of his love life (or lack thereof), speculate about his sexuality, push him to share his identity with them. It's been drilled into his brain that dating on tour is a distraction and that tennis players should keep their personal lives personal. He's shared this plenty of times in interviews—how it's too difficult to maintain a relationship when he's in a new city every couple weeks, how his focus is only on tennis—but it doesn't stop the rumor mill from churning.

He can't even imagine coming out as gay when—in this, the year of our Lord 2023—not *one* active male tennis player has *ever* done so. Not one! *Ever.* The women's tour has had gay icons like Billie Jean King to pave the way for others to come out, but the men's tour? None. Zero. Zilch. Blame it on the expectation of hypermasculinity in sports, plus the homophobic reindeer games in the locker room. This bleak fact is the mortar that holds together each brick in the wall of privacy he's built up since he realized he was gay in his early twenties. *Keep your personal life personal. Don't rock the boat. Don't get distracted.*

So, yeah. What Leo Chambers does behind closed doors is nobody's business but his own, thank you very much.

Behind closed doors, Leo Chambers is watching *The Golden Girls* in bed. He's back in his hotel room now and, yes, this is how he decompresses after a long day and, no, he has never told a soul. His paternal grandmother, Eleanor, was the one who got him into *The Golden Girls*. She lived with Leo's family when he was growing up and, being a woman of a certain age living in Florida, the show was an obvious favorite of hers. Every day, when he got home from tennis practice, he would take a shower as quickly as possible and then plop himself down on the big white couch next to her, moving in close, chilly from the air conditioning set to high.

Listening to his grandmother hum along to the theme song night after night, her gold bangles clanking along to the beat, it became a sort of lullaby, relaxing and comforting him after he'd spent most of the day pushing his growing body on the court. Watching the campy antics of Dorothy, Blanche, Rose, and Sophia was one of his only breaks from his nonstop tennis schedule. He held onto those evenings with Eleanor and her giddy laughter until the day she died, when he was a sophomore in high school. Sometimes he swears he smells her floral perfume when he's watching an episode.

Does he hide this nighttime ritual out of embarrassment? Maybe. But it's also out of protection. There isn't much he can have just for himself while he's on tour. As individual as tennis is, when he's not playing a match, he's nearly always with his team, his dad by his side every day, coaching him through life. They share stats and meals and flights and advice. But this show—these lovable ladies of Miami—it's sacred. It's like an heirloom that Eleanor passed down to him, and he's keeping it close to his chest.

That's why Leo is in bed now, chilly from the air conditioning set to high, tucked under the white duvet, drinking a gin and tonic he made from the mini bar, and watching an episode of *The Golden Girls*. Blanche, the self-proclaimed "slut" of the foursome, has just arrived at her latest date's swanky condo.

"You certainly have a nice place here," Blanche says.

"I took it because I spend so much time in Miami, and I do hate hotels," he says.

"Oh, yeah, I know," Blache says. "The way they charge you for the whole night when you're only there for a few hours."

Leo cracks up as if he hasn't seen this scene seventeen times before—his laugh bouncing off the walls of the cavernous suite—and takes a sip of his G&T. And then he takes another, and another, and another, and before he knows it, he's finished his drink and another episode. He's a bit tipsy and, unlike Blanche, he's staying at this hotel for more than a few hours. And when Leo is tipsy and alone in his hotel room, wherever that room might be—Rome, Seoul, New York—he sometimes slips into his other nighttime routine.

Grindr.

"Hey, what's up?" he sends, his message appearing in a yellow bubble.

"Hey, just in for the night, you?" the blue bubble reads.

"In the city for work," Leo replies.

"Cool cool. I live in the West Village."

Leo clicks on the profile pic to see it closer again. A fair-skinned, toned torso, just like his own pic.

"Do you watch any sports?" Leo asks. He taps his fingers nervously on the outside of the sweating glass, only a sip of gin left.

A few moments later, the torso responds: "Lol no."

"Perfect," Leo types, relieved this guy probably won't recognize him, and takes the final sip. "Can you host?"

"Sure can," the reply reads.

Leo hops out of bed and pulls off his loose boxers, revealing the stark tan lines on his thighs. He digs through one of his duffles for a pair of briefs he thinks his hookup will like.

Knock, knock, knock.

Leo jumps up, pulls his boxers back on, and looks through the peephole. It's his dad. Of course.

"Hey, just came to say goodni—" His dad sniffs. "You smell like a distillery."

"I had one gin and tonic, Dad, chill," Leo says.

"I'm chill, I'm chill. I just want you to be ready for tomorrow."

"I will be. I only have media stuff in the morning. We're not practicing until the afternoon," Leo says, then pauses. "And, you know, it's going to be hot out tomorrow. If you need to skip practice, I totally understand. Brian and I will be fine."

"Trying to get rid of me, huh?" Johnny jokes. "I'm not missing practice now! Your first match is in a couple days."

"No, I know, I just . . ." Leo tries. "Okay. Never mind."

"You need your rest," Johnny says. "Get to bed soon."

"Yes, Dad," Leo says, shutting the door slowly. "Good night."

Once he takes a shower and puts on something more presentable, he makes sure the coast is clear in the hallway and heads down to the car he's just called.

"Leo?" the shirtless man at the door asks.

"Hey," Leo says, noting that the man's torso matches the one in the profile pic. The triangle tattoo above his left hip corroborates it.

"Cool, come on in. I'm Gabe," he says.

Leo knocks his head back with a laugh. He's still buzzed. "Of course you are."

"Sorry?" the man says. His angular, clean-shaven face looks confused.

"No, nothing, I just, uh, knew a Gabe as a kid that I hated. One of those childhood associations, you know?"

"Ah, got it. I have those, too. Never met a Josh I liked."

"Hmm, yeah, never met a Gabe I liked," Leo says, smirking.

"Well," the man says, smiling coyly, "hopefully I can change that for you."

Other Gabe pulls Leo into a long kiss, then takes his hand and leads him down the hall into the living room.

"You have a nice place here," Leo says, shutting his eyes as he realizes he sounds just like Blanche.

"Oh, thanks. Here, come sit," Other Gabe says, gesturing toward the green velvet couch. "Do you want a drink or anything?"

"No, I'm good," Leo says, and settles into the couch.

Other Gabe sits down next to him and, wasting no time, Leo climbs on top of his lap, picking up where they left off, tongues tangled.

For the rest of the night, he makes sure *not* to moan the name *Gabe.*

CHAPTER THREE

It's Kids' Day at the US Open, the day before the tournament begins, and like a handful of other American players, Leo is on a side court with about a couple dozen elementary school kids and their rainbow of colorful rackets.

"Everybody ready to play?" he asks brightly.

The kids race to get in line to play with him, their sneakers making small scuff marks as they go. Leo spins his racket. "Let's go three at a time, okay?"

As he turns to take his spot midcourt, his eye catches Gabe a couple courts over, playing with his racket upside-down, smacking the ball clumsily with the handle, making the little kids laugh as he yells, "What am I doing wrong?"

Leo finds himself smiling, but before his own laughter escapes, he clears his throat and forces his attention back to the kids across the net.

A few of the parents step in to help keep the kids organized, sending the next ones onto the court after Leo has spent a sufficient amount of time with each trio. He's hitting much more softly than he usually does, tapping the ball over the net, and he's beaming as the kids swat at the ball as if they're holding a butterfly net.

There's one boy in the group who actually seems to be getting the hang of it as his trio rotates onto the court throughout the session. A mop of light brown hair on his head and a glint of youthful determination in his blue eyes, he reminds Leo of himself when he was a kid. He's spunky, going after the ball without fear, like he's right at home on the court.

That's exactly how Leo was from the start: meant to be there. And it was there he stayed. Before he even finished first grade, he was spending nearly every afternoon at the Delray Beach Tennis Center with his dad. He can remember being five years old and going for the first time. It felt like a scene from a secret tropical garden—covered by a canopy of sloping palm leaves above, the row of courts the color of the ocean, adults scattered across them in their tennis whites as if they were specks of foam on the ocean's waves, moving in and out like the tides. His dad knew everyone at the center and they all knew him, too—a former American star. Johnny shuffled Leo up to each one of them, his voice overflowing with pride as he said, over and over around the grounds, "This is my boy, Leo. He plays tennis now, too."

It's wild to Leo how much he's grown to look like his dad today: the same blue eyes, the same high cheekbones, the same thick, light brown hair and scruff, the same ears sticking out. Eventually, he inherited the same power on the court, too, the same glorious one-handed backhand. It's as if Leo were born to carry on the torch in tennis that his dad was forced to prematurely snuff out after his MS diagnosis.

Three years after that diagnosis, Leo was born. He has never known his dad without MS. He has never known his life without this sport. These two things are intrinsic to his existence. While his dad's MS wasn't severe enough to keep him from coaching, there were still symptoms that wedged their way into Leo's comprehension of it: a brief spasm in his dad's right leg, a short dizzy spell during which his dad would have to pause their practice, the increased fatigue that cut his time on the court with Leo little by little throughout his life. He watched the steady decline of his dad's health in painstaking detail while his childhood marched onward, a firsthand witness to the way his dad moved and functioned and adapted on the other side of the net each day, each year, as the nerve damage continued to break down the communication between his brain and body.

Leo wasn't the only witness, however. Other people playing on the courts next to them would sometimes whisper or hold their side-eyed glances at his dad in moments of struggle, long enough that Leo would notice. *Please stop staring at him*, he would think. *He's fine.* He thought they must have never met anyone with a disability like this, how eager they must have been to gawk at a man who was different from them. And not just any man, either. This was Johnny Chambers, one of the greats. What are tennis players without their strength? Their speed? Their endurance? *This man is not invincible, after all*, he imagined they were all thinking. *He is sick.*

Though he didn't have the words for it then, Leo could sense that, for other people, Johnny was either an object of pity or, what sometimes felt even worse to him, an object of inspiration. If he and his dad were talking off court over a snack, for example, sometimes another player would pass by them and, with overly sympathetic eyes, make a comment about how "amazing" Johnny's story is or how "remarkable" it is that he was still able to play, if only recreationally. They often had their hand placed over their chest. But Leo didn't see his dad the way others did. He only saw someone he wanted to grow up to be just like, whose skill and experience and patience he could learn from endlessly. Still, it didn't take much time for him to internalize the message being sent: When confronted with something unfamiliar, people will reach for their fear before their understanding.

Just play tennis, he would tell himself, and focus all his attention on the next point, channeling his emotion into the yellow ball flying toward him. Hearing "good" and "nice hit" and "keep it up" coming from his dad would center him in the moment and block out the negativity threatening to unbalance him. His favorite comment from his dad usually came when they were in the outdoor dining area after hitting. If Leo, then in middle school, was beating himself up for losing his latest match or playing poorly at practice, sulking over his turkey burger at the table, his dad would lower his head, put a hand on his shoulder, and tell him in a soft voice: "Remember what I always say? Hold your own. I don't just mean hold your serve. I mean stay strong, no matter what." The two of them never talked much about how his dad was feeling or the toll the MS took on both of them, but this one comment, shared every so often, told Leo everything he needed to know.

Today, on the practice court, hitting with this boy who takes him back to when he was a kid in Delray, Leo hears himself saying "good" and "nice hit" and "keep it up." Once they're finished playing, the kids all gather around him, looking up at him gleefully and asking him questions about being a pro. He pulls out his phone and takes a selfie with them, bending his knees to meet them at their level.

There aren't many places to hide on the US Open grounds. But after so many years practicing and playing here, Leo eventually found one reliable spot that he can duck into when, on days like today, the fans and photographers and selfies are relentless. So, feeling overstimulated by all the activity and weighed down by all the memories clouding his mind, he sneaks off to a supply closet at the southernmost end of the grounds that he's never once seen a member of the staff using, and shuts himself inside to catch his breath.

Atop a giant box of jumbo-roll toilet paper in the dark, he uses his 4-7-8 breathing technique, attempting to exhale the pangs of childhood shame. After a few minutes, he finds his way back to himself. As he rises and reaches for the door, it suddenly swings open, and Gabe comes flying in without looking and knocks into Leo. Leo's ankle hooks onto Gabe's in the process and sends them both flying onto the boxes of toilet paper and rolls of paper towels. A bottle of spray cleaner falls from a shelf above and bonks Leo on the head.

"What the fuck?" Leo yells at Gabe, who's now fully on top of him.

"What the fuck?" Gabe yells back, staring down at Leo.

"You're in my hiding spot," Leo says, realizing he sounds seven years old.

"You're in *my* hiding spot," Gabe says.

"I've never seen you in here," Leo says.

"No shit," Gabe says.

For a moment, they lock eyes, and neither speaks. Their lips are dangerously close. With their bodies pressed together, Leo's senses betray him, taking in Gabe's musk from playing in the sun, his soft skin that's also slightly sticky from sunscreen. Gabe's body feels warm and heavy on top of Leo's, and he can feel Gabe's heart pounding, just like his own.

"Your hand is on my ass," Gabe finally says.

"Your entire body is on my body!" Leo quips, yanking his hand away.

Gabe tries to stand, but his hand slips on a roll of paper towels, and he loses his balance, flopping back down.

An *oof* sound comes out of Leo.

"Sorry, sorry," Gabe says impatiently, and scrambles to his feet. "What are you doing in here, anyway?"

"Getting away from all that," Leo says, nodding toward the world outside the closet as he gets back on his feet. "I just needed a break. Like I said, this is my hiding spot. Usually, there's no one else in here."

"Yeah, same," Gabe says, and his eyes shift down to the floor.

Again, neither of them speaks for a moment. There's a small, tiny, minuscule part of Leo that wants to ask Gabe if he's okay, ask him why he's hiding.

"Well," Leo starts. "Let's . . . not do this again sometime." He rushes out of the closet.

Later that day, determined to show Gabe that their literal run-in is not on his mind, he posts a selfie that he took with the kids earlier. In the background, fans have filled the bleachers and Ashe looms large.

leochambers My favorite part of the year, every year. See you on Armstrong tomorrow night, NYC!

CHAPTER FOUR

On Monday at six forty-five PM, Leo is leisurely pedaling on a stationary bike in the players' workout room, staying in motion to keep his muscles warm. In fifteen minutes, he'll walk onto the court inside Louis Armstrong Stadium to play Gabe Montoya in the first round of the Open. They're the headlining match on night one of the year's final Grand Slam, which will unfold over the next two weeks. Though he's not playing on Ashe—the largest and most revered stadium is set aside for the number one seed—he's honored to be playing on the second largest, Armstrong, no matter how many times he's done so before. He knows that all fourteen thousand seats will be filled on opening night, especially for an all-American battle. Even now, inside the workout room, he can hear a faint rumbling out in the stadium starting to grow louder as fans make their way inside.

He spent the day compartmentalizing his anxiety about playing Gabe—after tennis, his greatest talent is compartmentalizing his emotions—and practicing, of course, which today included many sets of short sprints from the baseline to the service box so he could prepare his body to react swiftly to Gabe's inevitable drop shots throughout the match. If he wants to get up to a drop shot in time, his first step out of the gate is crucial—exploding his body into motion toward the ball before it can bounce twice. He has to be ready for anything with Gabe, who can certainly hit with power, but will mostly be throwing in plenty of variety to trip Leo up, as usual. When faced with a tricky opponent like Gabe, Leo's plan has always been to focus on the basics: pick his targets, hit through the ball with pace, and make as many first serves as possible. And maybe don't look directly into Gabe's dreamy eyes or at the way his butt bounces while he jogs in place before his service motion. Not that those things are what have kept Leo from beating Gabe before. Of course not. Promise.

Leo and his dad are now standing facing each other, Leo shifting his weight from one leg to the other, his dad holding a ball and suddenly dropping it either to Leo's left or right, having him grab it as quickly as he can, practicing his reaction time some more.

"All right, Johnny, we need to get to the box," Brian says, and turns to Leo. It's five minutes until showtime. "You got this, LC. Play without fear."

Leo nods at him and they bump fists.

Then Johnny puts a hand on Leo's right shoulder. "Hold your own."

"Thanks, Dad."

They go to take their reserved seats in Leo's player box. Each player has a designated area, front row, at one end of the court where their team sits and, after a change of rules in the last couple years, they're allowed to give bits of advice to their player between points if they want. Alongside his dad, his physio, his agent, and Brian, Leo's mom, Sheryl, will be in the box too, having just flown up from Delray Beach, where she still lives with Johnny and works as a real estate agent. A former sports journalist (she met Johnny at a press conference—a real-life meet-cute),

Sheryl only comes up to Leo's chest and has thick, wavy, shoulder-length hair that frames her round face and is a bit darker than his. She's too anxious to watch Leo play—even after all these years—but she still shows up in his box at the Open and a few other tournaments throughout the year anyway, her face buried in her hands for about 80 percent of the match.

Alone in the hallway that leads onto the court, alone with his thoughts, alone until the end of the match, Leo is now staring straight ahead—his enormous red Wilson bag on his back and his equally enormous headphones on, which are playing his favorite pre-match song: "Don't Stop Me Now" by Queen. For what it's worth, he knows he looks good in his all-Nike outfit, his sponsor since he first went pro. His polo is white with navy-blue and mustard-yellow piping on the collar and sleeves, his midthigh shorts are also navy-blue, and his sneakers are white with just the heel in mustard-yellow. His racket is still cherry-red, Wilson.

Looking good can certainly help a player feel good, and it's not exactly a secret when Leo looks good out there, eliciting whistles from fans in whatever stadium he's playing in—and eliciting posts from Serving Looks. The account has surely been posting Instagram stories all day leading up to tonight's Chambers–Montoya showdown: video highlights from their best matches this season, video highlights from their matches against each other over the last decade, polls on whether Leo or Gabe will win and in how many sets, and, obviously, shirtless pics galore. Leo never goes on Instagram the day of a match, though; more "DADDY" comments aren't going to help him win this match.

Besides, he doesn't need to see more photos of Gabe's tall, lean frame when he has the real thing, right in front of him now. Gabe has just taken his spot at the mouth of the hallway, just out of sight of the fans, as the lower-ranked player is always announced to the crowd first. He's in an all-maroon Adidas outfit, which, naturally, hugs him in all the right places, with white sneakers and his signature backward hat, also white. For once, here, just like in the locker room a half hour ago, they say nothing to each other. The two of them stay focused, simply waiting for their names to be called.

And that wait is now over.

"ALLLLL RIGHT, TENNIS FANS," the announcer growls over the microphone, "it's time for tonight's first-round matchup on Louis Armstrong Stadium."

Even with Freddie Mercury belting in his ears, Leo can hear the crowd erupt in cheers and whistles and applause.

"Please welcome to the US Open, from the United States: GAAAAABRIEL MONTOYAAAAA."

Leo can hear the crowd explode again as Gabe gives a wave and walks across the court to take the bench to the right of the umpire, who sits in an elevated chair like a lifeguard beside the court, calling the score and issuing warnings if necessary.

"And his opponent, also from the United States, your ninth seed and a semifinalist here last year: LEOOOOO CHAMBERRRRRS."

He can't help it. This first walk-on at the Open is the peak of Leo's entire season, every season. There's nothing like the electric atmosphere here, a testament to the constant, radiant buzz of New York. He makes his way into Louis Armstrong Stadium and looks around at the raucous crowd as he holds up a hand and flashes a smile. As he suspected, just about every seat is already full, fans jumping up and down as their cups of beer slosh from side to side, while others are clutching a Honey Deuce in one hand—the Open's signature pink drink with Grey Goose, lemonade, Chambord, and three honeydew melon balls sticking out to look like tennis balls—and pointing to Leo with the other. He sees a few fans around the stadium waving American flags, and there are a few Peruvian flags, too, for Gabe. The roof is wide open on this clear August night, and while it's still muggy, the temperature is beginning to drop with the sun. The subway rattles and clunks down the aboveground track nearby, adding another layer to the stadium's swelling music: "Back in the New York Groove" by Ace Frehley.

Once their bags and towels are settled on their benches and their various bottles of water and protein concoctions are lined up beside them, Leo and Gabe each grab their rackets and meet the ump at the net for an explanation of what towel box to use, where the serve clocks are located (the serving player has twenty-five seconds to towel off and serve), and that they cannot challenge line calls, as the Open now uses an electronic system that instantly and loudly calls "out" for shots that miss and "fault" for serves that miss. All the while, Leo and Gabe, on opposite sides of the net, are jogging in place, squatting, lunging, practicing their swings, and rotating their necks. This is so they stay warm and loose, sure, but it's also a form of peacocking, their attempt to psych out their opponent by showing them how amped up and focused and limber they are ahead of their match.

They pose for a photo, smiling ear to ear, and the moment the photo is taken, their smiles disappear—and so do they, bolting back to the baseline on their sides of the court so they can begin warming up together, hitting groundstrokes, volleys, and serves. Leo ensures his face doesn't betray the nervous energy coursing through his body.

A few minutes later, it's finally match time. The crowd explodes with more applause and whistles as Leo steps up to the line to serve.

"First set. Leo Chambers to serve. Ready?" the ump says into his mic. The stadium falls into silence. "Play."

In that moment, the world fades away. Under the blazing fluorescent lights, Leo sees nothing but Gabe at the other end of the court, knees bent, swaying his body from side to side, waiting for the first serve like a jungle cat. He hears nothing but his own heartbeat pounding on his eardrums. He holds up the ball to signal to Gabe that he's ready. Then: *Bounce. Bounce. Bounce. Bounce. Bounce.* He tosses the ball into the air and the fluorescent lights surround the ball like a halo. He pushes his body upward and smacks the ball as hard as he can, sending it speeding over the net into the far corner of the service box. Gabe lunges to his right to try and get his racket on it—but misses. It's an ace. 133 mph. A perfect start.

Leo clenches a fist as the stadium erupts in cheers.

"15–love," the ump says.

Bounce. Bounce. Bounce. Bounce. Bounce. Leo sends another massive serve straight at Gabe's body and he can barely react in time, merely bunting the ball back. It flies high and lands short over the net—Leo is all over it, hitting a screaming forehand past Gabe before he can reach it, his first winner of the match. He clenches a fist again in celebration.

"30–love," the ump says over all the *WOOOOO*s coming from every direction.

Leo serves the ball out wide.

Gabe hits a forehand back
across the court.

Leo sends a forehand right back.

Another.

Another.

Gabe hits his first drop shot.

Leo's sneakers squeak as he slides up
to the ball and slices it hard the opposite way, out
of Gabe's reach.

"40–love."

"Let's go," Leo says, pumping his fist. The fans do the same.

Leo steadies his breath. Game point. *Bounce. Bounce. Bounce. Bounce. Bounce.* He serves and the ball lands just beyond the service box.

"FAULT," the line-calling system shouts.

Leo wipes his wristband across his forehead. Okay. It's time for a second serve. He looks at Gabe, who's moved a couple steps in, ready to pounce. *God, he does look obscenely hot.*

Leo exhales and hits a gentler serve with some kick on it and it bounces high, but it's not enough: Gabe pummels it past him for a winner. The handful of Peruvian flags around the stadium are waving in excitement.

"40–15."

Leo looks over to his box and gives his dad a brief glare, as if to say, *I told you so.* He moves on, nodding to the ball boy, who tosses him another ball.

WHACK. It's another ace—and it's also the game.

"Game: Chambers," the ump says over the screaming fans. "First game."

He holds up a fist to his team and they all pump theirs back, except for Sheryl, who gives him an encouraging smile but also looks like she already wants to puke three minutes into the match. With the first game under his belt, he's settling in, and he's ready for Gabe.

"Gabriel Montoya to serve," the ump says as Leo watches Gabe step up to the line and jog in place for a few moments. Another wave of whistles and claps engulfs the stadium. Leo bounces from one foot to the other as he watches Gabe hold up the ball, quieting the crowd. A lone "Vamos!" echoes from behind Gabe.

Leo studies Gabe's toss for a split second, trying to guess which way he's going to serve—out wide or down the middle (the "T")—and leans a little to the right. He guesses correctly. The ball comes careening over the net, heading out wide, and

Leo cracks the ball back to Gabe. They get into a crosscourt rhythm, hitting it to each other over and over and over until Gabe mixes up the pace with a backhand slice. Leo steadies himself and slices it back. Gabe slices it back again. Leo doesn't want to get into a slice battle with a guy who, he's reluctant to admit, is a master of the shot, so he attempts to eject himself from the rally with a strong shot the opposite way. It lands a bit long.

"15–love," the umps says, and the fans let out a victory cry for Gabe, the Peruvian flags shaking faster yet.

Leo silences Gabe's supporters, though, when he smacks a return winner down the line off his next serve.

"15–all."

The next rally is even longer than the first—twenty-eight shots, to be exact, sending both of them gliding along the baseline to meet each forehand and backhand—and this time, Leo is the victor when Gabe hits a forehand into the net.

"15–30."

Leo feels pumped now as he puts some early pressure on Gabe. He's bouncing around with a real pep in his step and muttering, "Come on" to himself, keeping his thoughts positive and away from the fact that Gabe never looks better than when he lifts his shirt a little after a big point, airing out the heat and the tension, Leo's favorite habit of his.

His least favorite habit of Gabe's, however, shows up in the next point, when he pushes Leo farther and farther off the court with his forehand, and then unleashes a gentle drop shot that Leo has no hope of reaching in time.

"30–all."

The next point is over before it even begins, Leo mishitting a rocket of a serve from Gabe and sending it flying.

"40–30."

Leo's step? A little less pep in it now. Then it's completely snuffed out when Gabe curves his next serve down the T and, again, Leo has no hope of getting his racket on it.

"Game: Montoya," the ump says. "One game all."

Beads of sweat sliding down the bridge of nose already, Leo glances at Gabe and their eyes meet briefly, Gabe raising one of his thick eyebrows, daring Leo to bring his best. Two games in and Leo can already sense that this is going to be a tense first set. He looks to his box for encouragement as the stadium rumbles louder than the subway.

"Point by point," his dad says as he claps emphatically. "Let's go."

Quite literally digging his heels in, Leo refuses to blink first, to allow Gabe to break him—not just his spirit, but his serve. If Leo loses a service game, if he gets broken, Gabe will move that much closer to winning the six games he needs to take the first set. Leo will not let that happen tonight. It's happened far too often in meetings past.

The games tick by in smooth succession. Neither player has stolen the momentum just yet—both of them in a tug-of-war to earn the upper hand, back and forth, back and forth, back and forth, like the fans' heads moving side to side as they watch the ball fly from end to end. Leo holds, then Gabe holds. Leo holds, then Gabe holds. Leo holds, then Gabe holds.

The crowd is enthralled, putting their drinks down and their hands together every time Leo serves an ace or crushes a forehand winner or—their favorite and his—hits a smooth one-handed backhand winner down the line, arms stretched wide, his full wingspan on display. Much to Leo's chagrin, a chorus of *oohhs* and *aahhs* also fills Armstrong whenever Gabe lands a perfect drop shot that Leo can't sprint to before its second bounce, or slices the ball so finely over the net that it dips viciously at the baseline, too low for Leo to spin it back over.

An hour passes by like this, Leo's soaked-through shirt a testament to both the humidity and his effort, and the set reaches what feels like an inevitable conclusion.

"Six games all," the ump announces. "Tiebreak."

It's the first to seven points, win by two.

It's no surprise to Leo that the tiebreak is just as tight as the rest of the set. In a flash of powerful serves and forehand winners from both players, Leo finds himself down 5-6—a set point for Gabe.

He can feel every pair of eyes in the stadium watching him. Okay. He can do this.

He can do this.

He can do this.

He—his first serve lands long.

Okay, okay, okay. He shakes out his body. But the nerves don't go anywhere. He looks across the court at Gabe, who's moving in and keeping his eyes locked on Leo, prepared to pummel another of his second serves. *Don't get the yips. Don't get the yips. Don't lose to Gabe. Don't lose to Gabe.* His internal monologue is still going. The crowd is still roaring. They know this could be it for the first set.

"Please," the ump says firmly into the mic. "Ladies and gentlemen, players are ready."

They settle down.

Leo does not.

His toss isn't as precise as it should be.

His arm comes down. The ball flies over the net and—

"FAULT," the system shouts.

It misses the service box out wide.

Leo hears Gabe yell "Vamos!" as the crowd erupts and the ump calls it: "Game and first set: Montoya, 7–6."

Fuck. Fuck. Fuck. A double fault? Seriously? He grips his racket tighter and stares straight ahead as he makes his way back to his bench, more beads of sweat making their way down his face.

The noise from the crowd is too loud for Leo to hear any of the surely optimistic words wafting over from his box, so he grabs his things, tells the ump he's taking a bathroom break, and heads off the court. Despite his having lost the first set, some of his fans are hunched dangerously over the tunnel on his way out, dangling T-shirts and tennis balls in hopes he'll stop and sign some during the break. He has to stay focused, though, so he keeps his gaze fixed ahead and attempts to block out "Shake It Off" by Taylor Swift blasting in the stadium, mocking him.

In the bathroom, he changes into new, fresh match clothes and leans over the sink, using the five minutes he has to practice the 4-7-8 breathing exercise again and give himself a pep talk: *Play without fear. Pick your targets, Swing through the ball. It's not Gabe on the other side of the net. It's just some opponent. Don't think about his face. Don't think about his butt. Pick your targets. Swing through the ball.*

Leo would very much like to be beamed up into space right now, considering that his pep talk is having approximately zero effect on his level of play after that nail-biter of a first set. Gabe continues to take hold of the momentum in this match, chipping drop shots like magic tricks, punching volleys at the net like a brick wall, and keeping that fucking smarmy look on his smarmy face that always burrows its way into Leo's mind. And after another thirty-five minutes, Gabe takes the second set 6–3, and Leo finds himself down two sets to love. There is nothing to love about this. He's now a set away from being knocked out in round one of his favorite Slam by his least favorite person.

Except, then, Leo starts to read Gabe's drop shots a little more quickly in the third set. He notices a crack in the disguise Gabe has been putting on them. At three games all, neither of them has broken the other yet. The crowd is getting behind him even more now, cheering louder each time he steps up to the line to serve, sensing that he needs an extra push to keep himself in this contest. A New York crowd, so loud you can practically reach out and touch the noise, always has the ability to influence a match. If they want another set, they can will it to happen. If they want more tennis, they can manifest more tennis. Okay. He's still in this. He's still Leo Chambers. He's still a fifteen-time title winner. He's still—

He gives away another break, putting Gabe up 5–4 in the third set, giving Gabe a chance to serve for a straight-sets win and a ticket into round two. After Gabe wins the game with a devastating slice that barely jumped off the court, Leo looks at his box in total frustration, mouthing, "What am I supposed to do with that?" His team is seemingly out of answers, other than gesturing with their hands for Leo to lower his temper and raise his focus. Considering the scoreboard, Leo feels it's maybe a bit too late for that, and it only aggravates him more. During the next changeover, the two of them sitting on their benches on either side of the ump, Leo peeks over at Gabe, who's pulling on a new shirt, and it raises his blood pressure even higher. Between his rising anger and the fact that he truly has nothing left to lose at this point, Leo starts ripping forehands and backhands harder than ever into both corners, and he's got Gabe on a string now. He manages to take him to 30–all.

"Come on," Leo says to himself, shaking a fist after the last point.

The fans' cheers and whistles and claps reach a crescendo now, the entire stadium understanding that the next point will either be a break point for Leo or a match point for Gabe.

"Thank you," the ump says, raising his voice to meet their volume. "Thank you, ladies and gentlemen. Please. Players are ready."

The stadium is completely silent now except for the scuffing of Leo's feet as he bounces from one to the other, waiting for Gabe to serve.

Gabe's first serve careens toward Leo.

Leo pummels a forehand return.

Gabe hits a forehand and rushes the net.

Leo goes for another forehand.

Gabe hits a backhand volley.

Leo smacks a backhand.

The ball soars in the direction of Gabe, who pulls his racket out of the way to let the ball pass, and, from Leo's perspective, it then diverges from its initial path, just marginally.

"OUT," the system calls as the ball lands in the doubles alley.

The crowd can finally stop holding their collective breath and goes wild for Gabe, who's just earned a match point.

"It touched his racket!" Leo yells over the noise to the ump, who's just called the 40–30 score. "It tipped the top of his frame!"

This can't be happening again, Leo thinks, all at once flashing back to the final point of his first match with Gabe, fourteen years ago.

The ump points to his ear, signaling that he can't hear Leo over the noise. Leo jogs over to the ump's chair, as does Gabe after he's finished pumping his fist and notices that there's a conversation happening between the two.

"Leo, I've already called the score," the ump says. "We cannot replay the point."

"Just watch the replay," Leo argues, knowing this point should be his. "You'll see the ball change direction!"

"It's my call, Leo, and I didn't see it. I'm sorry."

"But the replay will show you that it—"

"What happened?" Gabe asks as he approaches them.

"Leo thinks your racket touched the ball, but as I've told him—"

"Whoa, whoa, I did not touch the ball," Gabe says, shooting Leo a defensive look.

"Then why did it change direction? It tipped your frame as you brought your racket down. I saw it."

"Gentlemen, we cannot replay the point," the ump repeats. "It's 40–30."

They both ignore him. There's murmuring across the stadium, the fans unable to hear what's transpiring below.

"Leo, I wouldn't lie about this," Gabe says. "Get a grip."

Leo steps closer to him, fuming at the attitude in Gabe's voice. Leo needs to get a grip? Gabe needs to get a grip!

"Gentlemen," the ump says more firmly now. "I will be forced to issue *both* of you a warning if this continues."

There's nothing left for Leo to say and, to be honest, arguing with an ump like this isn't usually his MO—like his technical tennis skills, he also inherited his dad's calm and collected nature on the court—so he turns and walks back to his side, spinning his racket furiously the whole way. He begins bouncing again behind the baseline, waiting to see if Gabe can serve out the match, right here, right now.

The ball comes careening toward him. Leo swings with force. It soars across the net and for a moment Leo thinks he may have hit a winner, until he hears it. "OUT." Like a punch in the gut, it lands just long. He feels the air leave his body.

It's over. He lost.

"Game, set, and match: Montoya," the ump declares. "7–6, 6–3, 6–4."

Gabe shakes his racket, his right bicep bulging, and screams, "VAMOS!" at his team. And the crowd rises from their chairs, applauding, roaring. Peruvian flags wave in different sections of the stadium.

Letting out a heavy sigh, Leo walks up to the net to shake Gabe's hand and, frankly, book it the fuck off this court. He braces himself, mustering what's left of his energy to congratulate

Gabe, and instead of his typical "Great match," something else comes out.

"You're welcome for that match point, asshole," he says.

"Yeah, sure," Gabe says, gripping Leo's hand a little tighter now as they walk in tandem to the ump's chair.

"I think we both know you tipped the ball," Leo says, removing his hand from Gabe's.

"I didn't, but I guess you'll just have to go cry to Daddy about it, huh?" Gabe shakes the ump's hand and jogs over to his bench so he can wipe his face and step back onto the court.

"YOUR WINNER TONIGHT," the announcer yells joyfully into his microphone, "GABRIEL MONTOYA!"

The stadium roars again as Gabe walks in a circle, pumping his fist in every direction and pointing to the Peruvian flags that he spots.

Leo can barely watch. He's fuming, visibly vibrating. He packs up his stuff in a hurry and walks toward the tunnel, ready to chill his muscles and his temper in an ice bath.

"AND LET'S GIVE IT UP FOR LEO CHAMBERS," the announcer says. A round of thunderous applause and whistles surrounds him, and he puts up a hand and mouths "Thank you." Leo's not just crushed to have another loss in his record against Gabe. He's also crushed to be ending another US Open bid—and this early in the tournament. A round one exit? He feels like an idiot for thinking he could have won the whole thing. It stings even worse when he remembers that he'll be thirty this time next year. Tess might be able to brush off age as simply a number in this sport, but it's hard for him to do the same. Right now, winning the Open at thirty feels like an impossible feat. Roddick won it at twenty-one and, oh yeah, announced his retirement *on his thirtieth birthday*.

Leo's dying to get into the locker room and find his way out of this anxiety spiral—perhaps with a good cry in the shower—but he stops to sign some tennis balls and hats for kids reaching their hands over the railing, and he tosses his wristbands into the crowd as souvenirs. He hears someone shout, "We love you, Leo!" as he disappears into the tunnel.

He doesn't know it yet, but tonight is the last time he'll see the fans for quite a while.

CHAPTER FIVE

Leo is in Miami, sunken into his comfy king bed in his tasteful, mostly West Elm-filled condo. Decorating credit should be given to his mom, who, as a successful realtor, has learned a thing or two about staging a home, and that's essentially what his place is—a staged home—considering he's only there for brief stints throughout the year.

It's been two and a half weeks since he lost to Gabe at the US Open, and he's still feeling his way out of the funk. Gabe lost in the second round (a slight consolation) and, after knocking Ollie out in the semifinals, Sascha went on to win the whole thing. Gross. Leo did win a few mixed doubles matches with Tess, but the pair decided to pull out so Tess could focus on singles—she couldn't risk any distraction in the midst of what was becoming a deep run, one that ultimately ended in the semis, her best result at the Open yet. Just as well, with mixed doubles off his plate, Leo was free and eager to head back to Miami, hole up at his place, and let all the articles and posts and chatter about his, uh, exchange of words with Gabe at the net die down.

GAME, SET, AWKWARD: MONTOYA CALLS CHAMBERS A DADDY'S BOY (WATCH)
We knew Montoya had a good slice, but OUCH he cut Chambers deep with that diss!
CHAMBERS GOT SERVED IN MONTOYA MATCH (VIDEO)
Yikes, Montoya hit hard in that match—and we're talking about the dig at Chambers.
JUST THE TIP: CHAMBERS AND MONTOYA SPUR OVER TIPPED BALL

Scrolling through these takes, Leo mostly felt like he could've written better puns. Actually, that last one was pretty funny. At least the articles all agree that the footage does seem to show Gabe tipping the ball. Still, he hates all this salt in his wound, all this attention surrounding their tiff, which he should've known the cameras would pick up, even over all the hooting and hollering from the fans in the stands. What's worse, everyone's making it sound like Gabe is some master of sass, like he won their smackdown at the net. But then again, maybe it's good that people will see how brazen Gabe can be. It's time they knew this about him. Maybe they'll start catching on to what Leo has known since he was fifteen years old: Gabe Montoya is an asshole. On *What a Racket*, Paul brushed it off as two players letting their tempers get the best of them and, of course, used it as an opportunity to harken back to his own era, when he was playing against the likes of John McEnroe, the biggest hothead ever to grace a tennis court: "Leo and Gabe's cat fight was nothing!"

Could people stop saying "cat fight," please?

The only post that seemed to get it somewhat right was Serving Looks, which shared a close-up shot of Leo and Gabe locking eyes at the net.

servinglooks Hooooo boy. This is a tough one, y'all. TBH, I think Gabe, whether he knew it or not, did tip the ball. Either way, did he go too far with that daddy's boy comment?? Don't bring *the* Johnny Chambers into this!

The next image in the post was the "Don't talk to me or my son ever again" meme. It did make Leo chuckle and, against his better judgment, he then clicked into the comments, saw way too many instances of "NOW KISS," and promptly closed Instagram. He hasn't logged in since.

Leo has the day off from his usual four-hour practice session, so he's stopping by Break Point for a visit today instead. Patrick Norton, a retired pro and friend of Johnny's, still runs the academy, and he invited one of his favorite former students and success stories—that would be Leo—to spend the day catching up and showing the current trainees some pointers. Leo jumped at the chance. He's always had a great relationship with Patrick and Break Point and younger players. This is a perfect chance to snap out of his Gabe funk for good.

On the way out of his condo, suited up in more casual Nike gear, he grabs the Rack-O box from one of his bookshelves. He plans to head to his parents' house after Break Point since he'll be up near Delray Beach anyway, and Rack-O, a strategic score card game, is his family's favorite. Leo has always been a fan of board games and cards. They're a fun and easy way to pass the time on tour and, a tennis player through and through, he's a nerd for anything involving numbers and strategy. He's quick to talk about how "legendary" his game nights are during the Miami Open, when he's able to stay at his own place during the tournament and invite Ollie and Tess and other friends over not just for Rack-O but also Monopoly and Catan and Rummikub. His many board games help keep his condo from feeling entirely unlived in.

"You know, you didn't play that poorly against Gabe," Patrick says, glancing down at Leo, as he's always done at six-foot-six.

Patrick is almost sixty years old now, and with a career spent under the South Florida sun, he's much more wrinkled than when Leo first met him fifteen years ago, his perpetually tan skin crumpling on his rugged face.

"I don't know about that," Leo says. All around them are the sounds of tennis balls popping off rackets and sneakers squeaking on courts.

"You didn't play the big points all that great. That double fault down set point? Ouch," he says. "But for most of the match, you held your own against somebody whose game you've never quite grooved with."

"His slice—"

"It still throws you off your rhythm. I could see it. Some things never change, I guess, especially with you two."

"Please, Patrick, don't bring up what happened," Leo pleads.

"No, no, you know I don't believe in rehashing that stuff. You brush it off and you move on," Patrick says, waving away Leo's request. "But I will say—"

"Here we go," Leo says, eyes crossing.

"This isn't how I thought you and Gabe would end up, picking on each other."

"Wait, what do you mean?" Leo asks, suddenly more alert.

"When I brought both of you guys on at BP, I was confident you'd become each other's supporters. You still have that with Ollie, I know. But what you've been through with your dad, it's always made you a gentler guy. I saw that in you and I saw that in Gabe, too. He was a little quieter, more sensitive, when he first got here, at least. I thought you'd click, that's all."

Leo's not sure how to respond.

"Anyway," Patrick says, and he pivots both the conversation and his step to the next court on their right. "Here's somebody I want you to meet, Leo."

Patrick introduces him to a fifteen-year-old phenom from Atlanta, Chris Robinson, who's already been winning some matches on the ATP Tour.

"Hey, I'm Leo, so great to meet you," Leo says, extending his hand.

"I know," he says, his eyes widening. "I'm Chris."

"I know," Leo says, smiling. And he does. How could he not? Chris has been making a name for himself on tour before he's even gotten his driver's license. Not to mention, he also has a stellar one-handed backhand, which Patrick wastes no time bringing up.

"It reminds me of somebody else who perfected their one-hander when they were at BP," Patrick says.

Chris shoots him a look that says, *Be cool, man!*

"It's a sick shot," Leo tells Chris. He doesn't usually say things like "sick shot," but for God's sake, the kid's barely in high school. Leo feels ancient.

"Thanks," Chris says. "It's sort of, uh, because of yours? I watched your matches a lot when I was kid."

"Oh wow," Leo says. "Thank you so much." He also thinks, *You still are a kid.*

"I tried it out when I was first playing, and it just felt right," Chris says.

"That's how I felt when I first started, too," Leo says.

Right now, Leo feels like an idiot. He's been so caught up in losing the match and his temper with Gabe that he was beginning to forget how much he loves this sport and the way it can inspire and unite people. He spends the next half hour hitting with Chris, both of their backhands painting the air, and trying to hold onto this feeling he's been missing. It even starts to unearth a good memory with Gabe at Break Point that otherwise seemed lost to history. There might have been the beginnings of a clicking between them, the clicking that Patrick apparently envisioned back then. Leo, not one to be unfriendly to someone new, tried at first to push through the breath that caught in his throat whenever Gabe stood before him. He tried to simply ignore this unfamiliar sensation and welcome Gabe to the academy anyway.

"Hey!" Leo practically screamed at Gabe on his second day, playing it cool, as always. "I'm, um, Leo. You're new, right?"

"Nice to meet you, Um Leo," Gabe said. It was the first time Leo witnessed that smirk he would grow to hate. "Yeah, I just started training here. I'm Gabe."

The two of them shook hands—a perfect, if clammy, fit. Warm, soft, safe. Leo couldn't help but notice it.

"You wanna hit?" Leo asked, pulling his hand away.

"Yeah, definitely," Gabe said.

Over the next hour, Leo felt like he had never picked up a racket before. His trusty forehand sent ball after ball into the net and his trademark swooping backhand looked more like a broken wing on a baby bird. Meanwhile, Gabe was slicing the ball with ease, Leo's first introduction to the shot that would become his downfall. First the breath in his throat and now this? No, thank you. Leo's subtle resentment of Gabe began to take root.

"Amazing slice," Leo said afterward, still trying to push through this new feeling spreading from his throat down into his stomach.

"Thanks!" Gabe said as he removed his backward cap and ran a hand through his damp but somehow elegantly disheveled hair. "I want to play like Alex Olmedo Rodríguez. He's one of my favorite players. He was Peruvian, but he played for the United States."

"Oh, yeah, he was big back in the fifties, right?"

"Uh, yeah, he was," Gabe said, looking a bit confused.

"What?" Leo asked, praying he didn't say something wrong on top of flubbing their entire practice session.

"No, just, not many people usually know who he is," Gabe said.

"He won Wimbledon, didn't he?" Leo asked, relieved.

"And AO, both in '59," Gabe said, his brown eyes sparkling. "I'm Peruvian, too. That's also why I like him so much."

"That's awesome," Leo said.

They held each other's gaze for a moment—a moment too long for Leo, evidently, who turned away, saw that his dad had arrived and was talking with Patrick, and said, "All right, well, my dad's here, gotta go," and darted off.

See? It wasn't all bad with Gabe. They even had a few other conversations and sessions like this first one. But Leo could only push through the fluttering in his stomach and the flubbing at practice for so long.

For his entire young life, he had learned to be focused and steady and determined. And he was good at it. He was committed to tennis and to his routine, and he was clearly progressing. Until Gabe. Gabe threw him off his game, both literally and figuratively. He made Leo look clumsy on *and* off the court. Worst of all, he made Leo really question his sexuality for the first time. For a type-A teenager with a vision of his US Open victory, this wasn't okay. At best, it was confusing. At worst, it was maddening. His resentment of Gabe grew and grew, so he pushed him away more and more, refusing to acknowledge his obvious attraction to him. He couldn't risk anything derailing his road to success.

Then, on an especially hot day later that fall, Leo was practicing with his dad, who, back then, could act as his hitting partner more often. But Johnny had been hitting for too long on such a sweltering day—the heat only worsens his symptoms—and he lost his balance. He fell onto the court, dropping his racket before hitting the ground in order to avoid injury, like a pro knows to do. Leo and the other coach working with them ran over to Johnny, as did Patrick, who must have been observing nearby.

"Dad, you okay?" Leo asked, getting down on one knee to check on him.

"Oh, I'm all right, I'm all right," Johnny said, trying to pick himself back up. "Don't worry. I just tripped going for that backhand of yours."

Leo scanned the courts to see if anyone was staring, gawking. Gabe was far enough away that he didn't notice. But Ollie caught Leo's eye and mouthed, "Is he okay?"

Leo nodded quickly to Ollie and then continued helping his dad up, who had scraped his knee and was bleeding a little.

"I can't have you bleeding on my courts, Chambers," Patrick joked, and then turned to the other coach with them. "Can you bring Johnny over to the first aid kit and help him get cleaned up? I can hit with you for a bit, Leo, if that's okay."

"Uh, yeah, sure," Leo said, trying his best to seem unfazed by the incident.

He and Patrick rallied for a while longer, which, after the initial anxiety about his dad had passed, Leo was actually pretty excited about. He was still getting to know Patrick at that point, but he was already well aware that Patrick was a former top ten player and, as the owner and operator of Break Point, didn't always have this much time to dedicate to one player among the many who needed attention at the academy. Leo felt lucky to have this opportunity to hit with the head honcho himself. But his mood turned sour when he heard Gabe and another junior player behind him, walking by the court and talking not quite softly enough.

"Figures. Little Leo gets whatever he wants," Gabe said. "Daddy makes sure he gets special attention."

Leo whipped his head over his shoulder, his heart pounding now, but Gabe was already continuing down the path. When Leo turned back to Patrick, he saw the ball coming toward him and rocketed a forehand over the net—a clean winner into the corner.

"Nice hit, Leo!" Patrick yelled.

Normally, he would've leaped at this compliment. But not now. Not after what he just heard. Leo had certainly felt Gabe acting more coldly toward him lately, a natural response to Leo snubbing him over and over. But how could he talk about Leo like that? He hadn't seen Johnny's fall, but didn't Gabe know that Johnny had MS? Who in tennis *didn't* know? Leo wasn't just some spoiled daddy's boy. It was more complicated than that. Gabe should've known.

That comment gave Leo a reason to continue resenting Gabe. It gave him something to latch onto, an excuse for why he didn't like Gabe—one that could bury the truth. The truth that he was into Gabe. The truth that he was gay.

Things only escalated from there. Picture it: the Junior Boys' Delray Beach Open, 2010. Leo and Gabe faced off against each other in the final—for all the glory of their hometown juniors' tournament. Back then, they were the two young players already causing buzz around their futures in American tennis. This was the first time they met in a final, and for Leo, it felt like this would propel one of them to the forefront of that conversation. He needed to win.

The thing about juniors, though, is that the players have to call their own lines. There aren't any umps or electronic line-calling systems to determine if a ball lands in or out. It's an honor system, upheld by teenage boys who call each other "faggot" in the locker room. So.

Leo fought his way through his anxiety during the final, doing his best to compartmentalize his resentment of Gabe, steady his breathing, and focus on his game. But, as would happen time and time again in the years to come, Leo couldn't find his footing. He felt like they were playing on an ice-skating rink, with him falling all over himself to keep up with Gabe's slices.

With his family, friends, and fellow Break Point players watching, Leo was humiliated. By the time they reached match point—Gabe serving at 6–2, 5–3—he was actually relieved it would all be over soon and he could go home and soothe his embarrassment with an episode of *The Golden Girls*.

Still, not one to give up until it's officially over, he gave it his all during that final point, firing back shots as hard as he could, hoping that somehow he might do enough to get back on serve at 5–4. When he drove one particular ball crosscourt into the corner, he knew it was a winner the moment it came off his strings. As he saw the ball clip the line, he knew this could be his opportunity to shift the momentum in his direction. But the next thing he knew, Gabe's arms were flying up into the air as he yelled, "OUT!" and turned excitedly to his parents and older brother, who were rising to their feet.

"You've got to be kidding!" Leo shouted as he jogged over to meet Gabe at the net for their handshake.

"Better believe it!" Gabe shouted back, smirking and running a hand through his hair.

"No! No! That ball was in! I saw it clip the line!" Leo felt his heart rate climbing.

"Oh, gimme a break," Gabe said, rolling his eyes. "It was long by a mile."

Gabe put out his hand, but Leo wasn't having it. He rushed over to see if the ball had left a mark, and there it was: a faint scuff just barely overlapping the line.

"Patrick!" Leo yelled incredulously toward the bleachers, calling for reinforcement as he pointed down to the scuff, circling it with his finger.

"Mierda. Here we go," Gabe said. "Want to call Daddy over, too?"

Before Leo could even make his case, Patrick put his hands up—refusing to take sides—and then gestured for Leo to shake Gabe's hand.

With the heaviest sigh in human history, Leo took Gabe's hand in his, trying desperately to ignore the perfect fit, and muttered, "Congratulations."

"Thank you, Leo," Gabe said, smiling widely like the fucking Grinch, and scurried away to celebrate with his family and friends.

So, yes. Gabe Montoya was an asshole. An asshole and a cheat. Leo sensed it from the beginning—so much so that his breath caught in his throat whenever he was near him. Yes, that was it. Screw this guy and screw his slice. Leo wasn't going to let Gabe get to him.

"Go cry to Daddy about it," Leo mutters now in a mocking voice, hands at ten and two on the steering wheel, driving to his parents' house.

He was in a great mood at Break Point. He really was! He loved rallying with Chris. But thinking about good memories with Gabe only led him to think about the bad ones. And now, of course, he's back to ruminating on their argument from a couple weeks ago on the court. It wasn't just any argument—it immediately opened that wound right back up, and it was taking its sweet time closing.

How could Gabe still think of Leo that way? How, fourteen years later, could he still take that type of swipe at him? How could he cheat at the end of a match *again*? Leo will beat Gabe next time if it's the last thing he does. He'll make him look like a junior. He'll wipe the court with him. He'll—

"Leonardo!" Sheryl calls out her nickname for Leo as he walks through the arched front door of his Mediterranean-style childhood home. He removes his sunglasses and sees her standing at the foot of the staircase, squinting at her phone, which is held about two feet away from her face. Her wavy hair is pulled back into a loose ponytail.

"Ready to lose at Rack-O?" Leo says, pulling her into a hug. "Which might happen more quickly than usual, it looks like. Where are your glasses?"

"Oh, upstairs somewhere, I'll find them before we start," she says. "I'm just trying to look at this post from Linda. You remember Linda, from my realtors' book club."

Leo does not.

"Look at this. She already has pumpkins out at her house. She put a bottle of pumpkin ale next to this one and it's throwing up its insides."

"Where did she even find that many pumpkins in Florida right now?" Leo says. He's happy to be home, looking at a silly picture on his mom's phone and, as he enters the kitchen, his mood lifts even more as sees the spread of takeout tacos on the large marble-top island.

"Oh, also, did I tell you who's in a coma?" Sheryl says, following behind him.

"Jesus, Mom, I got here like thirty seconds ago."

"Amber, from your high school. You remember Amber."

Leo does not. He only went to that high school for a semester before his parents decided to have him learn at home and on the road as he started to travel more frequently for junior tournaments across the country.

"A boating accident, if you can believe it."

"Oh my God," Leo says, spooning some pico de gallo onto the taco he's been building. He desperately wants to change the subject. "Where's Dad?"

"Probably on the phone with Brian, at least he was when I got home from work. You guys head to Astana next, right?"

"Yeah, in a few days. Then it's Stockholm and Vienna before the Paris Masters. You're coming to that one again, yeah?"

"Me? Miss a Paris tournament? Please, Leonardo," she says, wiping some guacamole from the corner of her mouth.

Leo glances at the fridge and sees that there's *still* a fingerpainting of a beach with a rainbow over it displayed from kindergarten. In clumsy handwriting, the corner of the crinkled paper reads: *Leo, age four*. That's why his mom started calling him Leonardo. When he was little, before he started playing tennis, he was always drawing. He would spread his art supplies out on the coffee table and draw pictures for hours. And then he would come home from preschool and kindergarten with even more drawings. His mom would put as many as she could on the fridge, but honestly, she could've wallpapered the whole house with them.

Leo glances back at his mom, who's noticed him admiring the fingerpainting.

"You were my little da Vinci back then," she says, staring at him lovingly. "I always have to keep one of your paintings up there."

"Maybe I could've been a famous artist instead of a tennis player," Leo says.

"I didn't say the paintings were *good*," Sheryl jokes. "You drew some of the worst dinosaurs I've ever seen, to be honest."

"*Wow*," Leo says, cracking up, as his dad, finally off the phone with Brian, comes into the kitchen and puts his hand on Leo's shoulder.

"The dinosaurs?" he asks Sheryl, who nods, fake-grimacing. "The brontosauruses. Oof. They were sad."

"Okay, I was gonna go easy on you both in Rack-O for once, but now?" Leo shakes his head as he takes the last bite of his second taco.

It's times like these, though few and far between, when Leo wonders what his life would look like if it didn't revolve around tennis. The sport means everything to him. Chasing the high of winning a tough match or taking home a title in a faraway city is addictive. Nothing else in life even comes close to that feeling. But who would he be without tennis? Would he be in real estate, like his mom? A dentist? Maybe an art teacher? (Apparently not. The brontosauruses.) Would his nights be filled with more moments like this one, sitting around the kitchen island with his parents talking about childhood memories over takeout? Would he be sitting there with a boyfriend? A husband? That question still floats across his mind, despite how much he's tried to stamp it out over the course of his career.

What if he came out to his parents, right here, right now? He doesn't think they would have any problem with his being queer. They've always voted blue, anyway. But when he thinks about the conversation it would lead to, particularly with his dad—*Are you sure? Is that a good idea? Will you go public? What about countries you visit that aren't as accepting? What about your sponsors? What about homophobic fans?*—it immediately flattens the idea of sharing that part of himself with them. It all just feels too messy, too uncomfortable, too uncharted. He'll keep it to himself, not just to hide it, but to protect it from the unknown. It's not like he'd be coming out because of someone special in his life, either. So, he flips over his next Rack-O card and leaves that thought behind. Tonight, as the September sky twists into pinks and purples out the kitchen window, he just wants to savor how easy, how normal, how nice this is.

After lacing up his sneakers before leaving for practice the following morning—despite the slew of luxurious options available, Leo still only wants to practice at the Delray Beach Tennis Center whenever he's home—he searches for his sunglasses. He checks on top of his dresser—nope, just a small stack of books, including Andre Agassi's memoir, and a couple framed photos of him with his dad at the tennis center as a kid and with Ollie and Tess during one of his game nights. He checks inside his nightstand—nope, just a couple condoms, headphones, and some plane tickets he's saved over the years, specifically the ones to and from the cities where he won his fifteen titles. He's just about to give up the hunt when he feels his phone vibrate in his pocket.

"Mom! Perfect timing. Really quick—did I leave my sunglasses there last night? I can't find them and want to make sure I didn't drop them at Break Point or something."

"Leo," Sheryl says softly.

"They're those black Nike ones, they're polarized?"

"Leo—"

"Sorry, yeah, what's up?"

"Leo, it's about Dad."

The quiver in her voice suddenly becomes more apparent to him.

"What? What happened?"

"He, um. Honey, he had a stroke this morning," she says. "We're at the hospital."

CHAPTER SIX

Johnny is awake. As Leo enters his hospital room, his mom by his side, he sees his dad sitting up in bed, talking to a doctor. As Sheryl told Leo on their walk down the hallway, Johnny isn't totally himself yet. He's misremembering things and speaking incoherently at times, but he's also lucky to be alive. When she came downstairs for breakfast that morning, he was slumped over in his seat at the kitchen island, unaware of who she was. She called 911. When they arrived at the hospital, the ER staff immediately administered the medication needed to dissolve the clot blocking his blood flow and did so within the window of time that makes recovery possible.

"He knows he's in the hospital, and he knows who we are," Sheryl tells Leo, holding his hand. "But he doesn't remember what happened. I know he'll be happy to see you."

The doctor takes his mom back into the hallway to give her an update, so Leo is alone with his dad now. The morning sun is pouring into the stark hospital room through the half-closed blinds, leaving stripes of light across his dad's face. Leo doesn't quite know what to say, especially when he notices that there's a slight droop to his dad's mouth, so he just asks, "You're not doing this to get out of practice, are you?" The same question Johnny would always ask whenever Leo told him he wasn't feeling well as a kid.

His dad lets out a belly laugh, and Leo almost expects this to cure him. But he'll settle for his dad at least knowing they should be at practice together right now.

"How are you feeling, Dad?"

"I'm okay," he says, his speech slightly slurred. "Tired. Sorry we can't be at BP today."

They wouldn't be at Break Point today. They don't practice there anymore. But Leo doesn't correct him. "Oh my God, Dad, don't apologize. Don't even worry about tennis right now. I'm just so glad you're awake."

"Ah, barely," he says, his eyes looking heavy. He tries to say something else, something about Christmas presents, but the words mostly get lost on the way out.

"You should get some rest, Mr. Chambers," the doctor says from behind Leo. He turns to look at her—a tall, slender woman with thick brown eyebrows and olive skin—and she gives him such a comforting, encouraging look that it practically sends Leo crying into her arms. But he's too skilled at compartmentalizing his emotions to collapse that easily.

"I can give you the update I just gave your mom, if you want to follow me into the hall?" she says gently. "He really needs his rest."

When Leo glances back at his dad, he's sleeping again, so he nods to the doctor and heads into the hallway with her.

"I'm Dr. Mennies," she says. "Your mom just went to get some tea."

"I'm Leo," he says, shaking her hand.

"We'll need to continue monitoring your dad, testing his memory and speech and motor skills. It's a good sign that he's able to communicate a little. But it could take a few more days to really understand how much of an effect the stroke has had on him. Do you have any questions for me? I know how difficult this can be."

He wants to sob in her arms again. Instead, he asks, "Was it because of the MS?"

"No, that isn't what caused the stroke. It was likely high blood pressure. But I want to be transparent. I do expect that because of the MS, the physical part of the recovery process may be more challenging."

He can't think of anything else to ask, so he just thanks her and shakes her hand again.

When he and his mom finally get back to the house hours later—after Dr. Mennies tells them that they need to let themselves and Johnny rest, that she'll call if anything changes—they sit at the kitchen island, and Johnny's plate of half-eaten scrambled eggs from breakfast is still there. His mug of coffee is now cold. It feels like a movie set, a scene from another life, before things were irrevocably altered. Leo knows Sheryl feels this, too, because she begins to cry, putting a hand over her eyes.

"I don't think I've let myself really feel it until now," she says when she's finally caught her breath enough to speak.

Leo wraps his arms around her, getting some of her hair, which is barely held together in a ponytail by this point, in his mouth. He spits it out, and it makes her laugh a little. "I'll go get some sushi," he says. His body on autopilot, he drives to pick up dinner, the palm trees waving to him obliviously with their branches in the breeze along the way.

When he arrives back home, he turns off the car and just sits, wondering if staying still for a moment will allow it to sink in that when he enters the house, his dad won't be there, because he's in the hospital, after having a stroke.

But no, nothing. Leo still feels numb. The windows of the car are down, and he can hear the faint sound of his mom's laughter coming from the kitchen. He assumes she's watching some funny cat video on her phone to distract herself. But inside, like some kind of mirage, Leo sees Tess sitting at the island with Sheryl. She's telling a story about how, during her quarterfinals match at the Open, her opponent was using some kind of smiling technique to remain positive, and the size of her grin was downright deranged.

"She looked like she was in that horror movie *Smile*," she says to Sheryl.

Ollie is at the sink, cleaning off the plate and mug Johnny left behind that morning. It's this image laid before Leo that does it. He walks into the kitchen and sets the takeout bag down and his tears follow, splattering onto the marble one by one. Tess jumps up and envelops him in a hug, and Ollie can't wait his turn. He comes over and joins the hug, hands still sudsy from the dishes, getting bubbles all over their backs. Their bodies on his, Leo feels like they're physically keeping his own from falling apart into a million pieces on the floor.

"I'm so sorry," Ollie says, pulling out of the cluster of limbs to face Leo.

"We both are," Tess says, putting a hand on his cheek to wipe away a tear.

"I can't believe this happened." Ollie had joined Leo and his team at the Delray Beach Tennis Center earlier this week, which is why he adds, "He seemed fine the other day."

"I know," Leo says, shaking his head and shrugging. "And I can't believe you're both here right now. I didn't even know you were in Miami, Tess."

"I just got here yesterday," she says. "I stayed in New York for a few days after the Open, but I wanted to come practice down here before fall, get some sunshine before rainy Europe. Now I'm really glad I came."

"So are we," Sheryl says, getting up and putting a hand on Tess's shoulder. "I'll let you all talk. I could really use a shower after today." Her mascara is smudged and the hair tie at the end of her ponytail is now holding on for dear life.

"Mom, you should eat."

"I'm not very hungry," she says. "I'll just put it in the fridge. I'm sure I won't be able to sleep later, so I'll need a snack."

Leo gives her a hug before she makes her way upstairs, and he leads Ollie and Tess over to the couch, the same one on which he used to curl up with his grandmother to watch *The Golden Girls*. They all sink into the cushy cream-colored fabric and Leo feels like a balloon emptying its air. They sit there for a minute in silence before Leo speaks.

"He barely knew what was going on," he tells them. "He thought we were supposed to be at BP. We haven't practiced there in years."

Ollie and Tess look at him with large, compassionate eyes.

"I just keep thinking," Leo says, staring at nothing in particular, "I've spent my whole life with him. He's been everywhere with me. Practices, matches, dinners, flights. And after all that, he might not remember any of it. You spend every day with someone just for it to be wiped clean."

There's a heavy silence.

"Shit. Sorry," Leo says, the weight of his words landing on him. "I know that sounds so dark, but I can't stop thinking about it. What if I walk into the hospital tomorrow and he still doesn't know what's going on?"

Ollie and Tess continue looking at him, clearly at a loss for how to respond.

"You don't have to say anything," Leo assures them. "I just had to get that out."

Finally, Ollie comes up with what is really the only appropriate response in this situation: "This fucking sucks."

"Yeah," Leo says. "It really fucking sucks."

Then, Tess, sitting up, poses what is really the only appropriate question in this situation: "You could walk into the hospital tomorrow and he *will* remember—but until you find out, does your mom have any wine?"

There are only a couple bottles of every mom's choice, white zinfandel, in the fridge, but it's wine, and they pour it.

Tess turns on the TV, and an episode of *The Golden Girls* is on—the one where Dorothy and Rose believe they've witnessed a UFO fly over their house.

Leo laughs. "I love this one."

"You know this show?" Ollie asks.

"I fucking *love* this show. I watch it all the time," Leo says. Right now, he doesn't care about how embarrassing it might sound. "I started watching it with my grandma when I was a kid. It's still so good."

"Okay," Tess says. "It's official. We need to have a *Golden Girls* night in Leo's hotel room whenever we're all in the same city."

"Sure," Ollie says, puckering. "But can we please have a different wine next time? Tabarnak. I feel like I'm sneaking wine coolers at a high school party."

"We never even did that," Leo says, smiling harder than he has in days. "The most we ever did was sneak, like, one beer at that juniors tournament in San Diego. And, if I remember correctly, you threw up during your match the next day."

"It was because of the humidity!"

"Awww, sweetie," Tess says, putting a hand on Ollie's knee.

"He had to call a medical timeout," Leo says through laughter. "It was so hard to clean off the court that play was suspended for the afternoon."

The three of them continue telling stories, laughing on the couch, Tess banging her fist on the cushion. On the TV across the room, Dorothy, Rose, and Blanche are having a laugh, too, as they tell stories around the kitchen table.

When Leo wakes up, the first thing he notices is that he has a headache. He didn't even drink that much. He never has more than two drinks in a night while he's on tour. But the sweetness of the wine is still stinging in his temples. The second thing he notices is that he can't feel his feet. That certainly can't be the wine. He lifts his head and realizes that he's still on the couch, Tess curled up against his legs, Ollie on hers. They're a bundle of limbs resembling the aftermath of a childhood slumber party. Blankets tangled around them, dirty wine glasses on the coffee table. It eases his terror, if only slightly, as he prepares himself for the visit to the hospital that awaits.

Ollie has to leave for Kazakhstan tonight, Tess for Austria tomorrow morning, but they both insist on accompanying him and his mom to the hospital.

Leo first sees Dr. Mennies by his dad's bed, and she turns and smiles at him. "Guess who's remembering more today," she says, clutching her clipboard in delight.

"You brought the whole crew!" Johnny says, seeing Ollie and Tess. He's sitting up and looking much more alert today, his eyes more focused, his mouth no longer drooping.

Leo and his mom melt into a puddle of tears. The relief he feels is so powerful, it's like a priest has just exorcised a demonic entity from his body. He keeps that feeling to himself, though, because, honestly, Tess would probably bring up how much she loves *The Exorcist* and he doesn't exactly want to think about anyone speaking tongues—or Catholicism, for that matter—in this joyful moment.

"The difference a day makes," Dr. Mennies says brightly. "He's doing much better."

"I am," Johnny says confidently.

"He still has a long road ahead with physical and occupational therapy."

"I do," Johnny says less confidently.

"But I'll explain more later and just let you all have a moment."

As the doctor leaves, Leo and Sheryl lean down and wrap Johnny in a big hug, and suddenly Ollie and Tess are piled on top of them, too.

"We should also give you all a moment," Tess says after a couple more seconds of hugging. She looks at Ollie and nods toward the doorway.

"Thank God you're okay," Sheryl says, her hands on the sides of Johnny's face. "Don't ever scare me like that again." She sounds like she's scolding a child who wandered off at the mall. She gives him a long kiss on his forehead.

Over the next half hour, the three of them together, talking like they do around the kitchen island, Leo feels complete again. And he knows he doesn't want to let this go. He can't let this go. Not yet.

"I'm taking the rest of the season off," Leo says without hesitation. "I'm staying here with you both and helping out while you recover."

"Whoa, Leo, come on," Johnny says, sounding sure he can convince Leo otherwise. But he's wrong. "You don't need to do that. There's still three months to go."

"I don't care," Leo says. "I'm not jetting off and leaving you and Mom to figure this all out. We almost lost you."

"You didn't—"

"Yes, we did. Maybe you weren't going to die, but we almost lost *you*. We almost lost the *real* you. You've come with me around the world for the last fifteen years. I can stay with you and mom in Delray for the next fifteen weeks."

Sheryl is teary again, but smiling ever so slightly. Johnny, on the other hand, looks at a loss. But Leo isn't giving up any ground on this. Anything his dad could say about the ranking points Leo will lose by missing all the fall tournaments doesn't hold any weight for him, not after the last twenty-four hours of uncertainty.

"You're sure about this?" Johnny asks. "This will be the longest break you've ever taken. You really don't need to do this."

"I'm positive, Dad. Brian already pulled me out of Kazakhstan, told them it was a family thing. I'll talk to him about how to announce my hiatus for the rest of the season. I want to do this. I want to be with you and Mom right now. I need to."

Johnny sighs, and they stare at each other for a few seconds, a silent standoff between a dad with a stubborn streak and the son he passed it down to. "Okay."

"Okay," Leo says, feeling clearer and more in control than he has in a long time.

"Okay," Sheryl says, her shoulders less hunched than they've been in hours.

"Damn, I really wanted to finish out this season with you," Johnny says, shaking his head in disappointment. "I'm sorry."

"Dad, it's fine, this is so not your fault."

"I know, but—"

"Dad."

Johnny nods. "Thank you, Leo. Really. Hopefully, I'll be back out there with you sooner than we think, sooner than the doctor thinks," Johnny says, covering that last part with a hand next to his mouth. Then he turns a bit more serious. "Because, Leo, I'm gonna be honest, I don't know how many more seasons on tour I've got left in me. I hate to say that, but I can't lie to you."

The words land like an anchor in Leo's stomach. But it's hard not to understand where his dad's coming from, seeing him like this, in a hospital bed. So, Leo just nods, trying to focus on the good: His dad is still here.

CHAPTER SEVEN

Leo spends most of his time at his parents' house these days, driving his dad to physical and occupational therapy and running errands while his mom is at her office. He still tries to keep up with training so his game isn't completely off the rails when he gets back to his regular off-season schedule in December. Sure, he wants to get back on tour because, you know, it's his entire life, but tucked inside the pit of his stomach is also the nagging desire to get back on tour and win the US Open while his dad can still remember it.

What if he has another stroke? Isn't he more prone to have another now? What if it's worse next time? Johnny has stayed on tour with him for so long now, and it's not lost on Leo that he's finishing what his dad started. He's continuing the Chambers legacy, and he doesn't want his dad's hard work to be for nothing, and the same goes for his own hard work to stay at the top of the game for the past decade. Johnny never won the US Open. Winning it for *both* of them would validate all of it and, in a way, let his dad leave the sport with some closure and some peace when it comes time for him to retire, which, suddenly, seems closer than ever. Has Leo expressed any of this crushing personal pressure to his dad or, well, anyone? No. Obviously.

To keep these thoughts at bay during his downtime over the next few weeks, he scrolls through Serving Looks, checking on all the latest news and drama up in his old childhood bedroom or in the waiting area at the physical therapy center. One post, in particular, gets him spiraling. A new couple emerged on tour after the US Open (straight, of course). They are, to be frank, disgustingly hot together—a popular pair of Brazilian players who teamed up for mixed doubles at the Open to hard-launch their relationship. The comments on the photos of them kissing after the match are mostly all gushing observations about how beautiful they are together, but there are still some naysayers in the mix:

> Focus on tennis!!
> No one cares, this isn't a reality show
> This will just make them both soft. Watch they're rankings drop now!

The incorrect usage of "their/they're" would be insulting enough, but Leo is more enraged by the fact that, as always, so many fans expect tennis players to be robots, devoid of emotion and solely focused on the sport. These comments hit a familiar nerve for him. In the days following the announcement of his dad's stroke and Leo's hiatus, there were many articles and posts sharing the news, along with plenty of comments with well wishes for a speedy recovery. There was an outpouring of appreciation for his dad and what he means to the tennis world, plus some notes on how much Leo will be missed at the year's remaining tournaments. They all helped lift his spirits while watching his dad inch through his recovery, gaining just a little strength back in his body, and as he watches the days tick by on the calendar. But his brain is just a brain, and it zeros in on the trolls:

His dad should've stopped coaching him years ago tbh
It's sad but they knew he was sick, he shouldn't have been on tour
Leo should be back out there getting his ranking up! Why is he being a baby??

He's tried to push these jabs out of his mind and remember that the majority of fans aren't total ghouls with an empathy deficiency. But the comments on Hot Brazilian Couple have him fuming again. It's been ingrained in him not to get too personal on social media, but he's finally had enough and now that he's had a few weeks to process everything that's happened, he's ready to share more, on his own terms. He posts a scanned disposable-camera photo of him and his dad on one of the courts at the Delray Beach Tennis Club in 1999. His dad, smiling widely with his 1990 US Open hat on, is pumping a fist with one hand and resting the other on Leo's shoulder. On his right, Leo is sticking his tongue out and holding his tiny cherry-red Wilson racket in the air.

leochambers My dad put a racket in my hand when I was 5, and it was magic. For the last 24 years, he's been coaching me and cheering me on, never missing a match, even on his hard days, even on mine. Most people know, but he has MS and it cut his career short. I don't usually get too personal here, but it can be a lot for our family to handle sometimes. No matter what, though, we're in it together. When tennis players step off the court, we have real lives. And when we step on the court, we carry them with us. There's so much going on in every player's life that none of us can even begin to know or understand. So, I hope you can be patient with us. I hope you can be patient with me as I stay home with my family to help my dad recover from his stroke. I want to be here for him like he's always been there for me. I'm going to miss playing in front of all of you so much over the next few months. It's still magic. See you soon. Love, Leo

He exhales deeply, lets a wave of nausea pass, and leaves his phone on the coffee table. He's at his parents' house and, now that October is here, he heads outside to help his mom construct their own outdoor pumpkin display, in which some of the pumpkins are indeed barfing up their insides with bottles of pumpkin ale leaned against them. In the midst of posting one of the seemingly thousands of photos she took of the display, Sheryl looks up at Leo, teary-eyed.

"Sweetie, this post about your dad. It's—" She doesn't finish the sentence, instead opting to wrap him in the type of hug that only a mom can give. Pulling her glasses back on, she glances at the post again, studying it more closely. "You're getting so many likes! And such wonderful notes from people, too. Oh, wow. And look at that, Gabe just commented."

Wait. What? Gabe commented? *Gabe* commented? GABE? COMMENTED?

"Let me see that," Leo says, ripping Sheryl's phone out of her hand in an extremely cool and inconspicuous way. Through the pumpkin innards he just smudged on the screen, he sees it. There it is. The comment. From Gabe. Well, not really a comment.

An emoji. A single red heart.

Not that it *matters*, but Gabe's heart—er, heart emoji—is on Leo's mind for, one could say, the entirety of fall. Why would he bother to comment? Why would he send a heart after their tiff at the Open? And how many times has Gabe called Leo a daddy's boy? Why would he act like he cares now? Why? He should've stayed out of it! He should've let Leo be!

But, Leo supposes, it was slightly, marginally, *moderately* nice of him to show some support. Leo has known Gabe for half his life, after all. Maybe this was Gabe's olive branch. But then again, maybe that's giving him too much credit.

What's less confusing to Leo—Thanksgiving now upon them, the new season beginning in about six weeks—is that his dad won't be returning to tour next season, at least for the Australian swing. He's still trudging through physical therapy, by no means prepared to travel halfway around the world with Leo's team. They haven't discussed it beyond the plan to have Brian take over in the meantime, and his dad understandably seems defeated, but he still punctuates any mention of next season with: "Don't worry, I'll be back with you by Delray!" The Delray Beach Open, a lower-level event practically held in their backyard, takes place every February, shortly after the Australian Open, an ideal time and place for his dad to slot back in as head coach. His dad still has moments of memory loss or struggles to find his way through a long sentence—something the doctor has assured them is normal—but that one sentence, about the Delray Beach Open, never fails.

When December rolls around and the current season wraps up, Leo is feeling more than ready to get his mind off emotions and that emoji and start his off-season prep. His ranking has dropped to thirty-five after losing all those points from the US Open and subsequent events throughout the fall, so he likely won't be seeded at the Australian Open in January, but he knows it's worth it. Sheryl didn't have to put her real estate schedule on pause; he was always there to take his dad to appointments and help him make his way around the house, and he feels more clear-headed going into a new season than he has in years. Hmm, what's this? He followed his heart and saw positive results? Imagine.

It'll certainly be strange for Leo to travel without his dad, even if it's only for the Australian Open. But he trusts Brian, and he wonders if maybe this is what he needs to start fresh. Brian will no doubt stick to their routine and get him refocused.

It becomes clear, though, that there will be some adjustments, too. At their latest off-season practice, Brian has Christmas carols blaring. In between shouting out notes as Leo moves around the court, Brian is humming out the notes of "Santa Claus Is Comin' to Town" by the Jackson 5.

"What better way to get hyped ahead of next season than with some holiday bangers?"

"Who *are* you?" Leo asks with a chuckle.

He might not recognize this side of Brian, but he's more than okay with it. He wouldn't mind a lighter atmosphere after the heavy months he's had at home with his parents. He hears Brian coaching him about something as he stares down at the new post from—shocker—Serving Looks, but none of Brian's remarks are registering. Leo can't move.

It's a stunning, golden-hour portrait of Gabe, who's sitting oh-so-suavely in a white T-shirt and light jeans on a tennis court, smiling with his back against one of the net posts, one leg out, one knee up. Below it, the caption reads:

> **servinglooks** SCREAMING, CRYING, THROWING UP. Gabe Montoya has just announced that he's gay! This makes him the first active male tennis player EVER to be openly queer on tour. Am I dreaming?! Let's all celebrate Gabe for the incredible trailblazer he is. I can't wait to see what this does for tennis.

Well, fuck.

Grand Slam: Australian Open
Surface: Hard
Where: Melbourne, Australia
When: January 14–28, 2024

CHAPTER EIGHT

He's furry. He's sleepy. And he does have chlamydia. But he's in Leo's arms, and that's what matters. Okay, yes, he's also a koala.

"It's actually a major problem here in Australia," the handler from the wildlife sanctuary says. "Koala chlamydia, that is."

"Oh, for real?" Leo responds, now looking concernedly at the adorable bundle of fuzz clinging to his body.

"Yeah, a real epidemic for these little guys. But don't worry, he can't transmit it to you through cuddling," the handler says with a wink.

Standing on Princes Bridge at the center of Melbourne, Leo, Ollie, Tess, and a handful of other popular players are holding koalas like nervous new parents as they pose for photos arranged by the men's and women's tours. It's the type of cute content the tours' social media teams like to share ahead of the Australian Open, and the local wildlife sanctuary gets to promote their work and spread awareness about protecting these precious creatures. Unfortunately, a not-so-precious creature has joined them, too.

"If Montoya was here, he would probably make two of the male koalas get married," Leo overhears Sascha say to a fellow Russian player. "The fairy."

Sascha hasn't taken a moment off from his crusade against Gabe these past few weeks. Leo couldn't help but click on this headline shortly after Gabe's announcement:

VOLKOV TAKES AIM AT NEWLY OUT MONTOYA

"I'm glad you asked me this. I think this is a distraction," Sascha said firmly, responding to a reporter who showed up at his practice, surely hoping he'd get a juicy quote if he asked the number one player about Gabe's coming out. "This does not have a place in tennis. He is throwing his choices in people's faces. This is inappropriate, especially for all the kids who are watching. I don't care what he does privately, but he does not need to bring it into our sport."

Leo certainly wasn't surprised that Sascha made these comments—after all, he can remember past headlines about Sascha supporting an anti-gay measure in Russia—but he was still shaken. His heart still pounded hearing those words.

It's pounding now, too, after Sascha's latest jab. But before Leo has a chance to push him off the bridge into the river, the photographer shouts, "All right, time for some photos!"

Gabe may not be at this shoot today, but since he came out, he has been *everywhere*. Photos of him—on websites including but not limited to ESPN, Attitude, Out, and the *New York Times*, all just in the last month—have followed Leo around every corner. He hasn't been able to escape them online, in stores, and especially on Serving Looks, which has reposted every last portrait and pull quote possible. A snippet from Out: "'My legacy in tennis isn't going to be the number of Grand Slams I've won, because so far it's none,' Montoya says with that sultry smirk of his. 'But I hope it can be something even greater now.'"

Gabe went on to say in that same interview that what ultimately pushed him to come out was a video Serving Looks reposted.

"They shared a TikTok from this young guy talking about how he's the only out gay player on his high school team, and how alone it makes him feel, how the other guys don't include him. He said he feels like he'll never really belong in tennis because there are no openly gay men playing professionally, either. He loves this sport, but he doesn't see himself in it. How is he supposed to feel accepted if there's no one for him to look up to? I just thought, maybe that could be me."

Ugh. Okay. Fine. That's . . . nice.

Leo has actually learned a lot about Gabe from all these magazine articles, which, to be clear, he's only skimmed in, like, airports.

First off, you know, *GABE IS GAY.* It's something that had maybe, potentially, *fleetingly* crossed Leo's mind before. How could it not? Especially whenever he happened to see Gabe arching his back so expertly while stretching on all fours in the gym. But it never actually seemed like a warranted suspicion—only an underlying hope or desire. Besides, Leo's queerness lives outside the court lines in which he spends most of his life. If the two are separate—tennis and sexuality—why would he waste his time suspecting someone else? Especially Gabe? Gay or not, he's still Leo's nemesis. This doesn't change anything between them. Does it?

Flipping through the seemingly endless articles, Leo has also learned about Gabe's struggles with mental health. He's talked about the immense pressure tennis players feel in general playing an individual sport on a global scale and how hiding his queerness only exacerbated that pressure, leading him to bouts of depression. For him, Gabe has told the press, it felt like he had finally come to a crossroads: retire early under the weight of it all, or continue his career as his authentic self, even if that meant losing some friends and fans along the way. Ultimately, he said, he loves himself and tennis too much to quit that easily, so here he is, starting the new season as an openly gay man.

Well, isn't that just peachy for him, Leo has often found himself thinking over the past several weeks, watching all this unfold from inside the proverbial closet, keeping his own mental health shoved in the very back, behind his old juniors gear. It's nearly impossible for him to admit, but he's . . . jealous of Gabe and his ability to just say *fuck it* and come out to everyone like this, consequences be damned.

In interviews, Gabe has said that he hopes this will encourage other players to feel more comfortable being themselves and even empower them to be open about their own identity, too. But, honestly, Leo feels more frozen than ever. He isn't suddenly prepared to share that part of himself just because one player has come out. He doesn't even feel he owes that information to anyone, especially the fans who constantly poke and prod to uncover it. Not to mention, his body tenses every time he sees the hate Gabe receives online. When, against his better judgment, he scrolls to the comments of those magazine pieces and Instagram posts, he sees things like: *Let's hope this is the first and LAST time a man comes out on tour.* He can't count the number of vomiting emoji he's seen, each one a knife in his stomach. Deep down, he's grateful to Gabe for being the first, for forging this path. He just isn't ready to follow yet.

Gabe will be making his grand return at the Australian Open, having skipped the first couple of warm-up tournaments as part of his plan to play a slimmed-down schedule this year while the media mayhem continues after his announcement. Leo was relieved he didn't have to cross paths with Gabe at those tournaments—and that could be the reason he made the quarterfinals at both—but now he's anxious about their inevitable run-in at the Australian Open and, with all that online hate swirling around his brain, he's even more anxious about how the fans will react to Gabe in person. Not because he *cares* about *Gabe* in particular. He just, you know, cares about *all* players being treated with respect, as an objective, empathetic, non-publicly queer person himself. Yeah.

It doesn't help that Gabe is absolutely glowing in all those new magazine portraits, by the way. He's shining. He's beaming. He's sparkling. He's—

"He's peeing on you," Ollie whispers to Leo as they pose for another group shot and the koala in Leo's arms leaks a warm yellow trail down the front of his gray Nike T-shirt.

"Oh my God," Leo says, just loudly enough that the wildlife handler notices.

"Ah, so sorry about that, mate," he says. "This little fella can be a real bugger. Let's see if we can get you cleaned up for the rest of the shoot."

"Oooh, or Leo could just go shirtless," Tess says, shimmying her shoulders and sticking her tongue out at him. "Ow owww!"

With the other players giggling and Leo blushing as he sneers at Tess, the entire scene resembles a middle school class portrait.

"No, no, we won't make you do that, Leo," the photographer says. "Actually, I think we've got what we need. Thank you for your time, everybody. And thank you, koalas."

Swapping a koala for a towel, Leo pours a little water on his shirt and pats the stain. "I don't think he liked me," he says to Ollie and Tess, who've just finished taking selfies with their little fellas before handing them back to the sanctuary staff.

"The photographer?" Ollie asks. "I really don't think he minded that you didn't want to take off your shirt."

"No, the koala," Leo says through a chuckle, gesturing at the stain.

"Oh. Well, still better than last year's shoot," Ollie says, scrolling through his selfies. "Remember? The kangaroo that tried to punch me?"

Leo and Tess both snort out a laugh.

"I think 'punch' might be a bit of an exaggeration," Leo says, using heavy air quotes.

"Yeah, it, like, grazed your arm with its little paw," Tess says. "You make it sound like you went up against that jacked kangaroo. You know, the famous one. What was his name?"

"Roger," Leo says. "May he rest in peace."

"Okay, whatever, I still liked the koalas better," Ollie says, holding up a selfie of him and his bear both tilting their heads to the side.

"Awww cute, Ol—wait, Roger *died*?!" Tess says, whipping back around to face Leo, her hair catching in her mouth.

"Like, several years ago," Leo says.

"Damn, pour one out for Roger tonight," Tess says, shaking her head.

Before they know it, they've made the short walk back to Melbourne Park, the sunny and meticulously maintained grounds of the Australian Open, which kicks off in just a few days.

"I can't believe it's only nine AM and I've already been peed on by a koala and had to break the news to someone that Roger the Buff Kangaroo passed away," Leo says. "Can't wait for what other fresh hells await today."

"You're practicing with Gabe this morning," Brian says straight-faced after Leo meets up with him in the players' gym.

"Ha ha, very funny," Leo says, starting to increase his speed on the exercise bike.

"Nothing funny about it," Brian says sternly.

Okay, wow, he has a great poker face.

"You'll be on court with him starting at eleven."

Geez, he's not even flinching.

"You know, if you're trying to get my heart rate up, I can just bump this thing up a gear," Leo says, pedaling at a steady pace now.

"Again, not a joke."

"Brian."

"Leo."

"Brian, no. No. Brian. Brian. No."

Leo isn't pedaling anymore.

"As your interim head coach, I'm making this strategic decision on your behalf. I really think this will be good for you. Gabe has gotten the better of you for too many seasons now. It's time you found a new approach. I say, if you can't beat him, join him."

"But—"

"Keep pedaling," Brian says firmly. "Don't you think it would be a smart move to practice with the guy whose game you can't quite figure out? And for y'all to bury the hatchet? Especially since you're both coming into this season under a microscope? I don't need to remind you about your dad's current situation, nor do I need to remind you about Gabe's."

Leo hates when Brian uses words like "nor." And "Gabe." He's always so clear-headed, so reasonable. It makes it impossible to argue with him, not that Leo doesn't try.

"What happened to the other Brian, the Christmas version?" Leo asks. "You know, the fun one? The jolly one! Remember? Can't we keep the good vibes going? Can't we just practice with Ollie?" He flashes a desperate smile.

"Christmas is over," Brian says a bit too ominously. "Sorry, that was dark. And anyway, Ollie's already booked up for the day, and I scheduled this practice with Gabe two weeks ago. You know how far out we have to book these sessions."

"Two *weeks* ago?" Leo shouts. "Why didn't you give me a heads-up? I saw Ollie at the koala thing this morning, and he didn't even mention he's practicing with someone else!"

"Oh yeah, how was that? I love those little guys," Brian says. "You know, a lot of them have chlamydia."

"I've heard that," Leo says. "Don't change the subject."

"Leo, I'm just trying to be the best coach I can be while your dad's at home," Brian says, crossing his bulging arms, which honestly rival those of Roger the Buff Kangaroo. "I'm stepping up here and making this call. I really think hitting with Gabe will improve your game. I wouldn't have set this up if I didn't think it would help you in the long run. And it's just this once."

Leo studies Brian's stern face. He knows he's being a brat about this, that he shouldn't let his grudge match with Gabe get in the way of preparing for his actual round one match on Monday. And Brian, unfortunately, does have a point. He and Gabe are both in vulnerable positions right now. The nice thing to do would be to come together with Gabe in this moment, not create more distance between them. The other nice thing to do would be to trust Brian as he attempts something new in Johnny's absence. But couldn't he have just quit while they were ahead after the whole Christmas carol thing?

"Besides," Brian adds, as Leo continues pedaling his way through this thought process, "don't you want to be a good ally to Gabe?"

If Leo were on a real bike, he would steer it directly off the nearest cliff.

Like all of the courts at Melbourne Park, the practice court on which Leo finds himself this morning is a distinct cornflower blue. The courts on these grounds are like reflecting pools, near mirror images of the bright and clear Australian sky above. It's summer Down Under, and while Leo's never been too affected by the change in time and season on this side of Earth, watching Gabe walk onto the court suddenly has him feeling like he's upside down.

It's not that he's starstruck. No, definitely not! But, admittedly, he is seeing Gabe in a different light now. Yes, Gabe is literally *luminous* in this morning Melbourne light, but it's something more than that. Leo didn't even think it was an option for someone to be openly queer on the men's tour. With absolutely no precedent, no example, no role model, it seemed all too likely that time would simply march on to the beat of the status quo, each of them keeping to themselves. History had shown them that was the way, and so it went. But here is Gabe, setting that precedent, showing that example, serving as that role model for other players, especially young ones. Maybe he . . . *is* a hero? Oh, no. Haha. Gross.

"Hey," Gabe says, meeting Leo by the net.

Why did you put that heart emoji on my post?

"Hey," Leo says.

Then, in unison: "So, I—"

"Oh, sorry, go ahead," Leo says.

"No, no, you were saying something," Gabe says.

"Oh, no, it's okay."

"Oh, okay."

Leo feels sixteen again.

Off to the side, their coaches are chatting before practice begins. Except, Leo doesn't recognize Gabe's coach as the guy he's been working with for the past several years.

"So, uh, who's that?" Leo asks.

"Oh, that's Diego. He's my new coach," Gabe says. "We've been working together since the off-season."

"Oh," Leo says. "New season, new coach, huh?"

"Yeah, all the better to beat you with," Gabe says, and then shakes his head a little, his face turning more serious. "No, um, actually, my old coach wasn't exactly . . . on the same page with me about going public. So, we decided to go our separate ways."

"Shit. That sucks," Leo says, surprised at his sudden sympathy for Gabe. "I—I'm sorry."

"Guess we're both down a coach, aren't we?" Gabe asks a bit too eagerly, then cringes. "Sorry, that came out wrong. I just meant—"

"Let's get started, shall we?" Brian interrupts, approaching them with the usual determined glint in his eye, and leads Leo back to the baseline. "All right, LC, just feel it out. You're not playing for anything here. I just want you to have some time to get used to the pace of his game and start recognizing more patterns of play without the pressure of a real match."

Right, right, just with the pressure of practicing with a longtime rival who recently became a gay sports icon. Got it.

Brian leans a little closer to add, "Don't be afraid to mix it up, either. I want us to keep working on adding more variety, more tools you can use if your A game isn't there. More slices, more volleys, maybe even a drop shot here and there." He pats Leo on the shoulder and jogs to the side of the court. Then, he jogs right back. "Oh, and try to ignore the cameras. We're working on getting rid of them."

Leo's used to fans gathering around the practice courts, iPhones at the ready, but as he scans the crowd that's formed, he sees what Brian's talking about: actual photographers with telephoto lenses have surrounded them now, too. Why didn't he expect this? Of course they would be here, itching to get a photo of newly out Gabe during his Australian Open prep—and with his partner in drama, Leo, too.

He attempts to put the press out of his mind and goes for broke on nearly every one of his shots, using the quickness of the court to his advantage and ripping winners past Gabe. He tries out some slicing to keep Gabe off balance. He attempts a couple drop shots, for better or worse. Brian's right: There's nothing at stake here, so why not swing for the fences? Why not give the photographers some great content?

But Leo knows it's not quite that simple. It's, well—was that a crack in Gabe's facade earlier? When he pivoted from his typical fighting words to an actual moment of vulnerability about losing his coach? It might have been. And it's this one serious moment that seems to be helping Leo clear the breath caught in his throat for the first time. His forehand and backhand are firing at full power—he's even throwing in some backhand slices, albeit with varying success—and Gabe seems vulnerable in his game, too, missing many of his shots long or sending them into the net. Fidgeting with his backward cap after each point, he's looking less and less like the confident cover star Leo's been confronted by on every newsstand and looking more and more . . . nervous? What—and Leo can't stress this enough—the fuck?

After an hour and a half, their session is over, and Leo is technically ahead in their match. It doesn't feel like he's won anything, considering this was just a practice match and, while Gabe did raise his level as the practice continued, he wasn't his usual sinister, slicing self. Leo wants to chalk it up to Gabe simply being a little rusty since he hasn't played any tournaments yet this season, but he knows better than that. Gabe must have a ton on his mind, made worse by the increased presence of journalists and photographers. As freeing as it must be to have finally come out, the new expectations of being The Only Gay Man In Tennis must carry their own type of pressure, not to mention the betrayal he must be feeling after parting ways with his coach. The ATP hasn't even said anything about his coming out, either, let alone celebrated it. *Damn. That really sucks.*

Whoa, hold up. Nope. Gabe is still an asshole until proven otherwise. And the case is still wide open.

But then, why, as he and Gabe make their way through the locker room, is Leo glancing around to see if any of the guys are talking shit about Gabe or giving him dirty looks? Why is he anxiously watching for their reactions like he does with his dad?

Why is he feeling—what's the word—protective? This is not normal. ABORT. ABORT.

"Hey," Gabe says, approaching Leo at his locker.

"Hey!" Leo practically shouts, his left eye on the verge of twitching. "What's up?"

"What I said earlier, about us both being down a coach, I didn't mean to sound so, you know, flippant about it," he says. Leo can sense Gabe carefully choosing his words. That's a first. "I'm sure it's been hard on you. I saw your Instagram post."

Yeah, I know, you commented a heart emoji.

"Oh, yeah, it's fine, I knew what you meant. But thanks," Leo says. *Even though you think I'm a daddy's boy.* "It's been okay, I guess." *It's been traumatic.* "He'll be back at Delray." *But who knows after that.*

"Oh, good. Good. I'm playing Delray, too. All right. Well," Gabe says. Fresh out of nice sentiments, he starts to make his way back to his locker.

"Congrats, by the way," Leo says quickly. "On, you know—"

"Being gay?" Gabe says with a smirk as he turns around.

"No, no," Leo says. "I mean, well, yes, but—"

"I'm fucking with you," Gabe says, sounding like his usual snarky self again. "Thanks, Leo. But don't think this changes anything. That practice match was a fluke. And by the way, you should put more of your legs and hips into your drop shot. I can tell you're focusing on your arm too much."

Did Gabe just reference Leo's legs and hips? *Gulp.*

"A fluke, sure," he says, moving right along. "You just didn't feel like making any of your forehands today."

Gabe shrugs. "Thought you could use a win."

"I won plenty of matches in Sydney and Adelaide this month, thank you very much."

"I know," Gabe says. He gives him a small smile, then turns back to his locker.

CHAPTER NINE

Leo makes his way down the tunnel that leads onto Rod Laver Arena, the biggest of the courts at the Australian Open, named after the Aussie tennis legend. It's opening night of the "Happy Slam," as it's been nicknamed, and, while he may not be seeded (or happy, exactly), Leo has the privilege of playing on center court tonight because his opponent is the number one Australian player and eighteenth seed, Jack Hughes, a mustachioed and tattooed guy who's equally at home on a skateboard as he is on a tennis court. Glowing with blue and white lights, the tunnel is known as the Walk of Champions, lined with the names of each Australian Open winner over the past several decades. As Leo walks through the tunnel, trying to stay focused, he repeats a text he got from his dad earlier today like a mantra. He hasn't heard from his dad as much as he expected over the past few weeks, so he was relieved to get a message from him today.

Keep that elbow up. Remember to attack the Hughes backhand, his weakest shot, the text said. Inexplicably, there was a middle finger emoji at the end. Another text came through: *Sorry, meant to send bicep emoji.*

No "Good luck"? No "Break a leg"?? No "Wish I could be there"??? Leo was peeved at first—until another text came through, a reminder: *Hold your own.*

And he does.

Dressed in white shorts and a shirt with asymmetrical lines and patterns in teal and peach, he plays lights-out tennis in the first set, swinging freely and hitting winners that even get the Australian crowd *oohing* and *ahhing*—not to mention the American expats sprinkled throughout the stadium who make themselves known every time Leo wins a game, whooping it up with their beers lifted high in the air. But the crowd still tries to lift their countryman to victory, chanting, "AUSSIE, AUSSIE, AUSSIE, OI, OI, OI" during each changeover and cheering at full volume whenever Hughes steps up to the line to serve. But their efforts are silenced as soon as Leo sweeps another backhand down the line, his body moving as smoothly as the orange and pink swirls above. With the roof open, a brilliant sherbet sunset presides over the match, and the Melbourne skyline peeks in to watch the action. At set point, Leo crushes a serve out wide at 135 mph, acing Hughes and capturing the second set 6–3.

"Game and second set: Chambers," the ump announces from her high-tech chair, a half-moon that rises and falls with the push of a button. "Chambers leads two sets to love."

Brian is on his feet clapping and saying, "Let's go, LC!" as Leo looks over to him with a clenched fist. The crowd continues applauding politely, despite their hometown hero falling behind significantly now, and the hero himself is less than pleased with the current scoreline. After that ace, Hughes slams his racket on the ground on his way to his bench, outraged that he's down 6–2, 6–3 in what feels like the blink of an eye—a set away from being knocked out in the first round by a player who hasn't been on tour in months.

"Code violation, racket abuse: Hughes," the ump says into her mic, prompting some boos and whistles from around the stands. Hughes rolls his eyes and tells the ump he's taking a bathroom break to change his kit and walks off court. Leo's not surprised he's changing—a fresh set of clothes is always what players think will shift their mindset and help them start anew in the next set.

Leo, on the other hand, isn't going anywhere. He takes a few sips from his water bottle and from one of his protein pouches, staring straight ahead in his sweaty clothes. There's no way he's leaving the court to change them. Altering any detail right now could break his concentration, and he wants to stay in this zone—a zone that has put him a set away from round two. He knows that most people, including Hughes, clearly, have low expectations for him after taking a few months off. At a presser ahead of the Australian Open, plenty of reporters asked him if he was feeling prepared for the first Slam of the year, if he thought he could even get past the first round, if he's in the right place mentally to do so. "I didn't come all this way to fly right home," he replied. Some muffled laughter spread across the press room. He smiled sheepishly. He hadn't meant to sass them; it just kind of slipped out. That needs to stop happening.

Maybe it's everyone's lack of faith in his ability to bounce back. Maybe it's the match wins he was able to put together in Sydney and Adelaide. Maybe it's that practice with Gabe. Maybe it's—and he feels guilty even thinking this—that it feels like a breath of fresh air playing without his dad watching from his player's box. Maybe it's that he's ecstatic just to be playing again. Whatever it is, Leo feels unstoppable tonight. He runs his hand through his damp hair and jogs to his side of the net, ready to claim this match.

It's a yo-yo of a third set, he and Hughes both holding their serve each time, racking up another game, back and forth, back and forth. The change of clothes might have given Hughes the little boost he was looking for, because he manages to take Leo to a tiebreak. There's still nothing between them by the time the tiebreak reaches 5–5. In the middle of an intense rally, the two players smacking the ball like it owes them money, Leo knows he needs to pull the trigger if he's going to earn this point. So, he readies himself, disguises his next shot as a forehand, puts his legs and hips into it, and hits a sneaky little drop shot. It curves over the net and cuts to the right, bouncing just out of reach as Hughes dashes up to it.

"Let's go!" Leo roars to himself. He finds that, without his dad there, he doesn't need to look to his box for approval as often, cheering himself on point by point, his own biggest fan.

"6–5: Chambers," the ump announces, setting off a chorus of cheering and whistling from every corner of the stadium. It's here. Match point. Whether the crowd is for him or against him, Leo doesn't care in this moment. He pushes everything in his periphery away, focusing only on the ball. He steps up to the line, bounces it five times, and tosses it into the air. He smacks it.

"FAULT," the system calls as the serve lands long. A few more whistles from the crowd, who are hoping for a double fault that will keep Hughes alive in this match. The ump asks them to please remain quiet between serves.

A deep breath out. Leo tosses the ball up again, a yellow dot against a pink and orange backdrop, and with a huge kick, it bounces high off the service box. Hughes has to stretch for it, forcing him to hit a weak return that lands short on Leo's side. He shuffles his feet up to the ball, waits for a split second to keep Hughes guessing about which direction he's about to pick—and sends it screaming back behind Hughes, who darted the opposite way.

"Come on!" Leo shouts to his box, where Brian and the rest of his team have jumped up, shaking their fists in victory.

"Game, set, and match: Chambers," the ump says. "6–2, 6–3, 7–6."

And with that, Leo books his ticket to the second round. The two players shake hands at the net and, despite a look of total misery, Hughes wishes him luck.

During a short on-court interview afterward, Leo shares how happy he is to be back on tour and back in Australia. "I love being here so much. The fans are so friendly, you always make the atmosphere amazing. I know I probably wasn't who everyone was rooting for tonight, but, um, if it helps, one of your koalas did pee all over me the other day," he says, and laughter rises from around the stadium.

With a wave to the crowd, he approaches the cameraman and, as the winning player always does, grabs a dry-erase marker to write a message on the camera. Leo leans in close to the screen, writes, "Miss you, Dad" and draws a small koala, which he hopes looks better than his brontosauruses.

Over the next twenty-four hours, Leo is flying high. Brian's pumped about his win, he has another solid practice session (without Gabe, but, for whatever reason, he has a nagging urge to tell him about how successfully he threw in that drop shot), and he's getting ready to go out to dinner with Ollie and Tess in Melbourne. Having all played on day one, they're free after practice today to meet up and take advantage of the city's stellar food scene. Without his dad there advising that he stay in, that they go over notes, that he just have a quick dinner at the hotel, Leo is more than eager to actually have a night on the town with his best friends.

"LC, you're twenty-nine, I'm not going to tell you what to do," Brian had said, looking somewhat confused after Leo asked whether he could go out tonight. "Just don't overdo it."

Unless Brian means don't overdo it on the vegetable samosas, Leo will be just fine, given that all he cares about tonight is gorging on the sensational Indian food at this trendy restaurant Tess knew about.

"Cheers, boys!" she says, holding up her glass of red wine. They all put their glasses in the center and Tess whips out her phone. "I know, I know, I'm such a mom, but put your glasses in again, I want to take a boomerang for Instagram."

"A boomerang! Get it?" Ollie says. "We're in Australia."

"Booooo," Tess and Leo moan in unison.

The three of them are sitting at a corner table in the brick-walled restaurant, a warm and friendly spot with Edison bulbs hanging from the ceiling at varying lengths and bright botanical prints framed on the walls. In a rare occurrence, none of them are wearing athleisure.

Still looking at her phone, Tess calls out, "Oh, Leo! I hadn't seen this!"

"If it's another meme of me and that koala, I don't want to know."

"Oooh, like the one that said, 'Leo Chambers quit tennis, he's into water sports now' and it's a photo of the koala peeing on you? That one was the best," Ollie says, chuckling to himself.

Leo stares at him, blinking slowly.

"Okay, that's incredible, but no, I meant this," Tess says, showing Leo her phone. It's a short clip of him writing on the camera screen after his match, posted by Serving Looks and liked by thousands of fans.

"I thought it might cheer him up," Leo says, shrugging. "I don't know. I feel like he's having a hard time."

"He's coming back on tour soon, right?" Ollie asks.

"I think he'll be at Delray, but after that? I have no idea. I can't get much from his texts, but he doesn't seem like his chipper self, like maybe he knows he won't be ready as soon as he thought he'd be."

"How are you feeling about it?" Tess asks gently.

"I . . ." Leo trails off then grabs his wine glass and stares into the blood-red liquid swirling inside it. "I don't know how much longer he'll be able to be my coach, and that really scares me. I haven't even . . ."

He doesn't let himself say, *I haven't even won the US Open yet.* He's too scared to let that spill out onto the table right now. He'll deal with that fear at a later date. So, he pivots to a different admission instead.

"I didn't . . . hate the way I felt tonight, though. I thought it would suck, not having him at a Slam for the first time," he says, then takes a sip of wine. "Don't get me wrong, it was strange. I really miss having him here. But I also felt a little more . . . free?"

"You did play one of your best matches in a while," Tess says. "I could be wrong, but you didn't expect that, did you?"

Leo shakes his head.

"I can tell you feel guilty about it," she says. "And that completely makes sense. But—"

"But, dude, you're almost thirty," Ollie interjects.

"Ollie!" Tess says, shooting him an impatient look, then sighs in defeat. "I wasn't going to put it exactly like that, but I guess, yeah. You're almost thirty, Leo. It's okay if you want to break away a bit."

"I couldn't even handle being with my parents for two weeks at Christmas," Ollie says. "I don't know how you travel everywhere with your dad."

"That's because your family was in Dubai and you were probably mad at them for cockblocking you on vacation," Tess teases.

"Don't say 'cock' at the dinner table, Tessa," Ollie says, pretending to be aghast. "Tabarnak. Have some manners. But yeah, no, you're absolutely right, I didn't meet anybody on the trip because of them."

"Can I get the check?" Tess jokes, not realizing their waiter is now right behind her balancing a giant tray on her hand.

"You don't want to eat?" she asks, confused.

"Oh, no, oh my God, sorry," Tess says. "You're fine."

Looking confused yet relieved, the waiter sets down their food—a gorgeous spread of curries, tandoori dishes, jumbo prawns, and plenty of garlic naan, all to share. The three of them simply stare at the bounty before them, inhaling deeply and smiling, and then it's a dance of forks and spoons as they reach and scoop and plate the different dishes.

"Well, I didn't meet anybody in California, either," Tess says in between bites. "In fact, I ran into my ex while I was home."

"Oh shit!" Leo says, trying not to open his mouth, which is full of naan. "What happened? Did you talk?"

"He goes, and I quote, 'Are you still playing tennis?'"

Leo almost chokes on his naan.

"Like, yeah, friend, I'm still playing tennis," Tess says. "What did he think, I was home interning at my dad's law firm? He's such a douche nozzle. And there's no way he didn't know I'm still playing. My parents practically told everyone in town when I made the top ten."

"So, you're getting back together?" Ollie asks, deadpan.

Tess and Leo burst out laughing.

"I'm done with men. No offense." Tess grins, then turns to Leo. "*Speaking of which . . .*"

Ah, fuck. Leo was hoping this wouldn't come up.

"We have to talk about the guy at the top of your shit list," she continues. "I didn't know you were going to practice with him!"

"Neither did I," Leo says, glaring at Ollie.

"Hey, I didn't know you were practicing with Gabe," he says, hands up. "All I knew was that we weren't hitting together that day. I didn't think to mention it."

"Well, I saw it on Instagram, surprise," Tess says. "The internet loves to post about you two—they think you're besties now. *Are* you besties now?"

"No, of course not. Brian set it up," Leo says. "But wait, what did the posts say? I didn't see anything. I'm trying to stay off Instagram so I can focus."

That's at least half-true. Leo does want to keep his focus up for the tournament, but he's also been too nervous to look at any news about how Gabe's first match went. What if the crowd turned against him?

"They basically just said there must be no bad blood between y'all anymore," Tess says. "They also said you're both dreamboats, blah blah blah."

"I wonder if he won his match, too. I bet practicing with me helped," Leo jokes, attempting to disguise his genuine curiosity.

"I think he did win," Ollie says, jumping in as Tess chows down on a humongous prawn.

Leo feels his face light up. The first openly gay man to win a match. He has to admit, that's pretty incredible.

"I caught some of the match when I was in the gym," Ollie continues. "It looked like there was extra security and, from what I could tell, there were some hecklers, but I think they had them all removed. A few fans brought Pride flags, too."

"Oh, good!" Tess exclaims. "That must have helped a little."

"He and his coach parted ways last month, too, so he's been going through it," Leo hears himself blurting out. Can he not?

"Fuck, seriously?" Tess says.

"Apparently, his coach wasn't on board with him coming out publicly. He just mentioned it to me at our practice, how we're both down a coach." Okay, enough. Enough sharing now.

"A bit of bonding, huh?" Ollie asks.

"*Interesting*," Tess says, manically tapping her fingers together. "Maybe you are becoming besties. I like this, I like this. New season, new friends."

"Sure, Tess," Leo says, rolling his eyes. "Anyway, let's move on."

"Good, because, dude, I was going to ask if *you* met anybody while you were home all that time. Will there be a *special lady* rooting for you in your box?" Ollie asks in his best Paul Davis voice, even pretending to push up a pair of glasses.

"That was the scariest thing I've ever seen," Leo says, deflecting. "Actually, I did promise to meet with Paul for another podcast recording at Delray in a couple weeks. My dad's joining, too, since he'll be at the tournament. I guess we're finally giving him that inspiring interview he's been wanting." Leo twirls his finger in the air and crosses his eyes.

He supposes he should answer Ollie's question, even vaguely, so, always prepared with a neutral response, he tells him, "But yeah, between helping out my parents and then keeping up with practice and training, I didn't exactly have time to meet anybody. You know how it is."

He really was busy, but he did hook up with someone in the fall. It was another Grindr hookup, this time in Miami, just to blow off some steam in the midst of all the stress.

Deep down, Leo knows he could tell Tess and Ollie the truth. But he already feels so exposed this season. He wants to keep this to himself, just for a little while longer.

Without being seeded and going up against an Italian youngster who only recently cracked the top 100, Leo is playing on a much smaller court compared to Rod Laver Arena in the second round. But he doesn't mind. The side courts can be just as fun and much more intimate—the spectators sitting up close, heads turning side to side with every point, sitting shoulder to shoulder on bleachers instead of stadium seating.

What he does mind, the next day, deep into the third set, is something he and Brian didn't go over during their pre-match analysis of his opponent, Matteo Rossi. Leo has never played him before since Rossi is still fairly new to the tour, so while Leo was prepared to attack his forehand and to hit through the center of the court, he was very much not prepared for how *fucking loud* this guy would be.

UUUNNNNHHH, Rossi groans as he smacks a backhand crosscourt, his prolonged whine trailing off just before Leo returns it, which is *technically* legal. As long as the player isn't still making sound while their opponent is hitting the ball, they can groan and grunt as much as they like during their swing. But, for the love of God, it cannot and should not be legal to sound this much like a dying cow on a tennis court (or in a court of law).

EEENNNGGGHHH.

OOONNNHHH.

UUUNNNHHH.

How can these booming barnyard sounds be coming from this Italian twink? Whatever the science behind it, after a solid two hours, Leo is having a difficult time hiding his facial expressions between points. He'd be more exasperated if it weren't so comical. After Leo's next serve, Rossi swings hard—*OOONNNGGGHHH*—and the ball lands long. "OUT," the system calls. The young ball boy snatches it up, but Leo liked the feel of that one, so he wants to serve with it again. He nods to the boy to toss it back, tucking his lips in to keep from laughing at the latest farm animal sound across the court, and the boy must notice, because he's holding back a smile now, too. He bounces the ball back, and Leo thanks him before crossing his eyes with a goofy smile. The boy giggles quietly before taking his place at the wall again, hands together behind his back, like a toy soldier.

Leo is up 4–3 in the fourth set, two sets to one in the match, and, frankly, he wants to end this one as fast as possible just so he can protect what's left of his eardrums. He goes into lockdown mode, using every molecule in his body to block out the noise, and manages to break Rossi, going up 5–3 and giving himself the chance to serve out the match. He shakes his racket while looking over to Brian, who's squinting and pointing downward, which could be translated to, "Right here, right now, LC."

Unfortunately, Rossi isn't going away that easily. He takes Leo to deuce in the next game, some tension creeping into Leo's limbs as the finish line remains just out of reach. The next point, which will either be match point for Leo or break point for Rossi, might not be the time for a risk, but Leo knows Rossi is expecting him to go for more heavy groundstrokes down the middle, so an idea pops into his head. His dad probably wouldn't advise this at a pressure point, but fuck it. His dad is ten thousand miles away.

After a few deep forehands to the corner, pushing Rossi farther and farther out wide, Leo gets the return shot he's been hunting. He pretends he's going for another heavy forehand, but changes his stroke at the last second to a drop shot, softly chipping the ball over the net. Rossi tries to get his feet in gear fast, but they scramble in place like a cartoon character for a second too long, and he can't make it to the ball in time. He turns away in a huff, gesturing angrily at his box with both hands, and the ump announces, "Advantage: Chambers."

Leo's wasting no time to celebrate. He wants to keep the energy of that last point pumping through him, so he nods for another ball and steps up to the line, the crowd still clapping and whistling at his drop shot. With each bounce of the ball ahead of his next serve, the fans quiet down. They know what time it is. His eyes focused intently on the ball, beads of sweat dripping down his face, he tosses it up with precision and sends it careening down the T at 132 mph. Rossi manages to lob it back, his arm stretched at full length—*UUUNNNHHH*—and Leo rushes up to it. He takes it out of the air with a forehand to the corner. Rossi races over but can only send up a lob again. It soars high as Leo jogs backward, searching for the ball in the sun. He lets it drop, keeps his feet moving in small, quick steps forward, and smashes it as hard as he can. It goes zooming past Rossi, who can't react in time, and it hits the back wall with a triumphant thud.

With all the tension floating out of his body, Leo looks up to the sky with his eyes shut and pumps his fist in joy and relief. "Game, set, and match: Chambers," the ump says, reciting Leo's favorite words. "6–4, 6–3, 5–7, 6–3." He's bound for the third round. After he shakes hands with his opponent, officially dismissing Matteo the Moaner, he waves to everyone on the bleachers and thanks them for their support, and then writes his message on the camera screen: "Not flying home yet!" He adds a small doodle of a plane heading toward "R3."

"Impressive win," Gabe says as Leo walks by. It appears Gabe is about to head into his round two match while Leo cools down from his. He's dressed in a brand-new match kit—a lavender shirt with black shorts and, of course, a backward white hat. When will Leo know peace?

"Oh, thanks," Leo says, half-dressed after a shower, drying his hair off with a towel. At midafternoon, in the early rounds of the Slam, the locker room is bustling with guys heading to and from their assigned courts—dripping with sweat, dripping from the showers—guys who call everywhere from Argentina to New Zealand home.

"Grazie, ciao," Leo hears as his head emerges from the towel. With a freshly done-up pompadour, Rossi is passing by and nodding to him politely as he leaves the locker room, suddenly meek and mouselike. The barn is closed for the day, apparently.

"Hey, great match," Leo says, nodding back. "See you soon."

"He's a really sweet kid," Gabe says after Rossi is out of the room. "But holy shit, who taught him to *moo* like that?"

Leo spits out a little of the Gatorade he just sipped, spraying his locker. He wants to choke down his laughter, but he can't help it. He's cracking up.

"Sorry, I'm such a dick," Gabe continues, grinning. Christ, the way his skin creases around his eyes when he smiles should be illegal. "I played him at a challenger last year, and my ears only stopped ringing yesterday."

Leo wants to tell Gabe a lot of things right now. He wants to tell him that he thought of him while he pulled out that drop shot against Rossi. He wants to tell him congratulations on winning his first match after coming out. He wants to tell him good luck at his next one. But old habits die hard. You have to kill them at least twice. Shoot them in the head, just in case, like in one of Tess's horror movies. So, instead, all that comes out of Leo's mouth is, "Aww, a challenger. That's cute."

"Oh, I know," Gabe responds, no longer grinning. "Chump change for a guy like you. Peasant money at that level, right?"

Aha! See! The spoiled daddy's boy insinuations continue. Asshole alert.

But before Leo can spit out another quip, Gabe cuts him off.

"Actually," he says, waving off his last comment, "let's not do this." He shuts his locker and hoists his bag onto his shoulder, looking a bit flustered. "I've got a match to win, anyway." As he walks by on his way out of the locker room, Leo notices that he has a rainbow ribbon pinned to the side of his hat.

"Well," Sascha says as he passes the opposite way, pointing his thumb back toward Gabe. "I hope everyone kept their towels on."

Chuckles echo around the locker room.

CHAPTER TEN

"Let's not do this," Gabe said.

Let's? Not? Do? This?

It was like he turned and looked the elephant in the room directly in the eye. And it blushed. After all these years of their usual bickering, he just went ahead and acknowledged the hate between them? Just like that? Can he even do that? Can he really just shut down their standard operating routine with a single sentence?

Well, apparently so, and it was clearly messing with Leo's head, because he lost in the third round of the Australian Open to Sascha, who argued with the ump every chance he got and took his sweet time stepping up to the line between serves. Leo knew these were tactics to distract him, and he did his best to stay in the zone, taking the match to a respectable four sets, but he couldn't secure the win. So, he did, unfortunately, have to fly home.

He spent the long flight back to Miami going over each of his three matches in his head, and with Brian, who then spent the remainder of the flight watching the entire Bridget Jones filmography.

Meanwhile, Gabe didn't win his match after their run-in, either, exiting in the second round. It's not exactly rare for Gabe to get knocked out of a Slam early—Leo would be the first to tell anyone that—but he seemed particularly off in his match. Leo would *not* be the first to tell anyone that he was glued to the TV in the gym, watching every point of Gabe's match. Gabe's slices mostly sailed long, and his drop shots didn't quite clear the net. He fidgeted with his backward hat between points, too, like he'd done during their practice session.

Squirming in his seat on the plane, Leo thought about how much Gabe must be struggling with this new phase of his career. How could he not be? People like Sascha are yelling about how he's *throwing his sexuality in their faces*. The hypocrisy of that comment is laughable. Sascha has *always* had girlfriends in his public orbit, pointing up to them in his player's box during matches, posting about them on Instagram, trotting them out at events. And now, he can't stop talking about his new engagement.

"We are so happy, and we can't wait to start a family," Sascha has said over and over in interviews. "This is what matters to me even more than tennis."

Bullshit.

Just two years ago, Sascha was in a relationship with Liv LaRochelle, a Canadian player who, at that point, was still climbing the rankings, but had recently won Indian Wells, officially putting herself on the map. Not long after, the two were spotted everywhere together, and hard-launched their relationship on Instagram with a selfie in Paris. Sascha oozed arrogance whenever he had Liv on his arm, smiling proudly, showing her off like one of his trophies. But that season continued to be a breakout one for her. As soon as she started to win more trophies of her own—including her first Slam, Wimbledon—Leo started to see Sacha's attitude change. Whenever he caught one of Sascha's post-match interviews, Leo noticed that journalists only asked Sascha about Liv. By the end of the season, Liv had won more titles that year than Sascha had. Then came the *Forbes* article that reported she had made more money than he did that year. The next season, about a year into their relationship, it all came to a head.

In another interview, asked about his reaction to his girlfriend's continued success for the umpteenth time, Sascha replied, feigning sincerity, "It is amazing to me, to see her achieve this, especially after all she has been through. The pregnancy with her last boyfriend, then losing the baby, then him leaving her. It was just awful."

The reporters lurched forward in their chairs. No one knew about a pregnancy. Liv must have told Sascha in confidence. This was the beginning of a media frenzy that surrounded her everywhere she went.

Liv didn't play the past two seasons. As far as Leo can tell, she has only said that she's taking an indefinite mental health break from the tour. Her new sponsors dropped her. Her ranking dropped, too.

Sascha went on to win two more Slams.

The rest of the flight home, Leo thought about Liv, and Gabe, and how Sascha can say whatever he wants and nothing ever changes. At most, he gets a slap on the wrist. His comments would certainly never get him banned from tennis. The powers that be care too much about him bringing in fans and publicity and money. So, he'll continue to spew hate, and players like Liv and Gabe will continue to suffer for it. And Leo will continue to stay closeted.

"Can I have some wine, please?" Leo asked a flight attendant and then put on *Bridget Jones's Diary*.

With the first Slam of the year in the books (another victory for Russia's sweetheart, Sascha), a decent third-round appearance kicking off his season, Leo now has his sights set on the Delray Beach Open. Gabe mentioned to Leo that he'll be playing Delray, too, the event like a homecoming for both of them. He desperately needs Gabe to stop getting in his head as he tries to bump his ranking back up this season, and he knows that staying out of Gabe's head would be the right move, too. Gabe has far too much to deal with already—he doesn't need Leo getting on his case, too. Yeah. Queers supporting queers. Or something. It's complicated. Maybe he can at least try to be on his best behavior around the guy.

But first, he has to make it out of this interview with Paul, yet another guy who truly tests Leo's ability to be on his best behavior.

"The wife told me this shirt is 'giving AARP,'" Paul says with air quotes that could be seen from space. The shirt in question is a frumpy white polo with a stitched logo from Paul's favorite golf course in Boca. "Whatever that means. I told her, 'Honey, we booked that trip to Yosemite last year with AARP, so you must think I look pretty majestic!'"

Paul's wife is nearly half his age, if that wasn't already clear.

Best behavior. Best behavior. Best behavior. Leo is repeating this new mantra in his head as he sips his iced coffee, chuckling politely and waiting for Paul to stop blabbing so they can start recording and he can get back to training. His dad is sitting in the swivel chair beside him, inside a studio at the Tennis Network offices in Miami. Johnny hasn't quite been himself since Leo got home from Australia. And not just health-wise. Leo expected that Johnny would still be moving more slowly than usual, sometimes using the cane that stays in the hall closet unless he's experiencing an MS flare-up. There's something else going on here, though. There are no longer ten thousand miles between them, but his dad still feels distant.

"Now, Leo, how has it been on tour without your old man? Did the Australian swing feel different since it was the first time you were there with only Brian?" Paul asks a few minutes into the episode.

Leo's been waiting for this question, but, with his dad right next to him, it still sets his teeth on edge. He just has to stick to what he rehearsed, a diplomatic answer that both gives Brian credit for the incredible job he's been doing *and* assures his dad that it's not the same without him. No more, no less. Stick to the script.

"I said this in my Instagram post last fall, but my dad has been at all my matches since I first started playing tennis at five years old. So, of course it hasn't felt the same without him," Leo says, making sure to turn to his dad and give him a caring smile. Okay, sweet. This is going well. "But Brian is doing a great job, I have to say. He has that cool, tough exterior everyone knows him for, but can be a real goofball when you spend more time with him one-on-one. Overall, he really is stepping up. He's trying new things, letting me play with more freedom and risk."

Right. So, that was the verbal equivalent of making Brian a friendship bracelet directly in front of his dad. Great work.

"What kinds of new things?" Paul asks. "Practicing with Gabe Montoya? That was certainly something new for you, training with your rival. And, now, the first homosexual player in ATP history."

"Well, the first player to come out as gay in ATP history," Leo says. "But yeah, that was something Brian set up ahead of AO. He was just hoping to pair me with somebody who plays really opposite from how I do, study him outside of a match. Maybe even"—Leo practically gags on these next words—"learn a little from his variety to help round out my game this season."

"So, right, let's get into this season. You went to the third round at the Australian Open. Were you happy with that result?" He pulls off his glasses, fogs them up, and cleans them with his polo.

"You know, I was," Leo says. "Putting together a couple solid wins felt great after my hiatus. I told myself going into Australia that I would at least win a couple matches, and I did that."

"But we're hoping for more than a couple at the other Slams," Johnny chimes in, and Leo's brow furrows. "I'm planning to come back on tour with Leo and get things back on the right track."

"That is so wonderful to hear, Johnny," Paul says. "I know I speak for all my listeners when I say you're just so inspiring." *Whoomp, there it is.* "Even suffering from MS, and now from a stroke, you've managed to bounce back and plan to get out on the court again."

"He doesn't suffer, he just has it," Leo mutters.

"Say again?" Paul asks.

"I, uh, well, I just said that he doesn't *suffer* from MS, he just *has* MS."

Johnny shoots Leo a look that unsettles his nerves again.

"Ah, you millennials, always keeping us on our toes when it comes to language," Paul says backhandedly.

Leo can't resist a tête-à-tête when it comes to backhands, so he replies, "Uh oh, giving AARP again, Paul." He covers his sass with a laugh to keep things friendly. "But language really does matter. It shows people respect." He takes another sip of his iced coffee.

Paul pivots back to Johnny's plans to return to tour. "Leo, can you talk about what it was like for you when your dad had the stroke? Were you afraid he *wouldn't* bounce back?"

"I was just afraid, period," Leo says, fidgeting with his cup as the all too familiar anxiety from that day creeps back into his body without missing a beat. "Sorry, it's really weird talking about him when's right here," he continues with a nervous laugh, "but yeah, I was scared he wouldn't recover, wouldn't be himself again. Not just as a coach, but, you know, as my dad, too."

"I think, um," Johnny starts. "I, um, I was just going to say that, I, um—" He trails off, seemingly unable to find the words.

Leo takes off his headphones. "Dad, are you okay?" he says quietly, calmly.

"Yeah, sorry, guys, I just, uh, guess I'm having a senior moment," Johnny says with a forced smile. "I'm fine, I'm fine."

"Mind if we take a break, Paul?" Leo asks.

"Oh, of course, of course," Paul says, swiveling around to Jesse, who's always standing by in the booth. "Jesse, are there any bottles of water back there?"

Out in the parking lot after the rest of the recording, Leo and Johnny are standing by their cars. Leo's running out of emotional support iced coffee to sip.

"So, um, what was that all about?" he finally asks in a small voice. Looking at his dad in the glaring afternoon light, he can see how pronounced the bags under his eyes have become.

"What was what?"

"I don't know," Leo says at first. *Honor that*, he then remembers Tess saying about his relationship with his dad. With a steadying breath, he continues, "You just didn't seem happy with what I was saying, and then you seemed to sort of have trouble with your memory again."

There's a pregnant pause in which Leo genuinely thinks about jumping in his SUV and speeding off into the distance.

"Leo, I don't want you worrying about me. And I don't want you talking about my health in front of people like Paul. I'm fine. I'll be back to coaching soon."

"Dad, of course I worry about you," Leo says. "And sorry, but fuck Paul."

"Oh, come on, Leo."

"What? He lets so much shit slide on his show like it doesn't matter. Shit that he and people like Sascha say."

"This is what I mean, Leo. You've got to stop worrying about everyone else and worry about your game. I know you've had fun with Brian the past couple months, but it's time to get serious again."

"You're acting like I haven't still been working my ass off, like Brian and I have just been out pounding shots every night."

"Leo, you're out of line here," he says. "What is it? You don't want me there anymore? You want me to just retire now? You almost said as much in New York."

Leo shouldn't be, but he's surprised his dad would remember a passing moment like that, when Leo asked if he wanted to skip practice because of the heat. "Dad, I'm sorry, that's not what I meant. I was just afraid you weren't feeling well," he says. "Of course I want you to get back out on tour, but something has to change. I just want what's best for you."

"I appreciate that, but I'm the parent here."

"Then act like it!" Leo shouts.

From there, it isn't Leo who jumps in his SUV. "I'll see you at Delray," Johnny says, climbing into his car and shutting the door.

"What the fuck," Leo says, sighing, as he hears the engine start. He's not sure what just happened, but he's sure there wasn't any honor in it.

"Oh good, you're still here," Jesse calls out, jogging up with Leo's phone in his hand. "You forgot this in the studio."

"Shit, thank you so much," Leo says. "I wasn't thinking straight when I left."

"Yeah, that was—" Jesse starts to say, but finishes his sentence with a grimace. Below a mop of auburn curls, he has a diamond-shaped face with oversized features. Big eyes, big lips. Leo forgot how endearing he is. "Is your dad all right? Are *you* all right?"

"I . . . do not know the answer to any of those questions," Leo says. "But thank you. It'll be okay. I think."

"I'll just go ahead and cut some of that interview in post again."

"Thanks," Leo says, shutting his eyes. "I'm sorry I keep ruining your show."

"Oh, no, please, Paul has that covered on his own."

With a surprised laugh, Leo asks, "What does *that* mean?"

"Look, I think you know that Paul has some, shall we say, outdated takes. The show has its loyal listeners, obviously, but all these new players and new fans are coming in and they're nothing like what he's used to, so the show isn't exactly keeping up. He doesn't know what tennis fans want anymore. He doesn't know how to adapt or pivot. He also doesn't know how to talk to people with identities different from his. He still says *homosexual*," Jesse says, eyes widening, and Leo laughs. "Honestly, I don't know if the show will last. But all this stays between us, okay?"

"Yeah, of course," Leo says. "Can I, uh, ask you something?"

"No, I'm clearly unwilling to share," Jesse says.

Leo's laughing again. "So, why do you work with him, then?"

"Totally fair question. The totally honest answer is that I just fucking love this sport, and I don't want to let a job at the network go. I've been here for five years, and I'd be lying if I said I haven't learned a lot from Paul. I get to go to a ton of tournaments and Slams and edit interviews with players I used to just watch at home on my couch. Players like *you*."

Now Leo's blushing. Has Jesse always been this charming?

"What are you gonna do if the show gets canceled?" Leo asks.

"Hope they have another job for me, I guess. But I have some side hustles, too," Jesse says. "I don't know. I'm just crossing my fingers for now."

"Okay, well, consider mine crossed, too."

"Thanks, Leo. Anyway, I should get back, but it was good to see you, even if you did ruin the show," Jesse says, shrugging.

"Yeah, I'm gonna go ahead and post everything you just told me," Leo says.

"Good luck at Delray!" Jesse says, waving over his head as he walks away.

A couple days before round one of the Delray Beach Open, which is held at the same tennis center where Leo grew up practicing with his dad as a kid, the tournament committee is holding a Fans' Night—a smart move considering tennis is a religion in this city. There are merch giveaways, ace contests, a meet-and-greet with players, and a special bar outside center court run by two familiar bartenders: Leo Chambers and Gabe Montoya. Both of them being from the area, the committee thought it would be perfect to have their two hometown boys pouring regional wines and mixing a signature cocktail called the Orange Slice (it's really just an Aperol spritz).

Leo couldn't object to the request because the bar is also giving away reusable water bottles from an eco-friendly company that sponsors him, and they were intent on having him here. He finds that his brand obligations ahead of tournaments tend to be hit or miss—sometimes literally, like when he was the unlucky star of a dunk tank triggered by fans throwing tennis balls at a target. So, in comparison, this one could be worse, even if he does have to sling drinks next to Gabe for an entire evening. Though, part of him is actually happy they still asked Gabe to participate.

The first hour is awkwardly silent. Leo stares straight ahead at the dozens of fans lining up for their complimentary cocktail and an opportunity to ask for an autograph or photo. His line is growing longer than Gabe's, and while normally that would give him a petty sense of satisfaction, tonight he can't help but wonder if it's because some fans are avoiding Gabe, and that isn't satisfying in the least.

Finally, Gabe breaks the silence.

"You've really got it down to a science over there, huh?"

"What do you mean?" Leo asks, a towel over his shoulder, carefully and precisely measuring out each shot of Aperol, prosecco, and club soda as he dumps them into the wine glass.

"I just mean . . . it's one to one to one. You could just eyeball it. Your line might move faster. But if you want to be a real mixologist about it, don't let me stop you."

The next guy in Gabe's line has a US Open Pride shirt on and eagerly asks if he can get a selfie. "Thanks for everything," he says to Gabe before stepping out of line and showing the photo to a man who appears to be his boyfriend.

Leo turns to the next fan in his line before Gabe can catch him staring and smiling at the interaction.

"Oh, you are just as handsome as we always knew you'd be," one of Leo's childhood neighbors, Myrtle, says to him, reaching over the bar to give him a loving tap on the cheek. He could barely tell who she was at first, considering the size of her sunglasses and wide-brim hat. "Harry and I are so glad you're back for the tournament this year. We're counting on you to win it agai—oh, sweetie, do an old lady a favor and top mine off with a bit more prosecco. By the way, are your parents here tonight? I've been meaning to catch up with your mother for ages."

Leo, momentarily dropping his mixologist act, adds another splash of prosecco to Myrtle's drink. He isn't sure which of her comments to address, so he just goes for the last one. "They're around here somewhere!" he says, and hands over her Orange Slice. "It's good to see you, Myrtle. You and Harry better be front row next week."

"Oooh, that's the stuff," Myrtle says, taking the first sip of her extra bubbly drink. "Okay, see you soon, Leonardo!" Shimmying her shoulders as she continues sipping her drink, she strolls away from the bar and Leo is, truthfully, relieved that she didn't hang around longer, considering his line is now stretching back to the tennis center's entrance. Gabe's, not so much.

"Leonardo?" Gabe asks, uncorking another bottle of wine with an eyebrow raised. "I didn't know that was your full name."

"Oh, it's not," Leo says. He feels his ears turn as red as the Aperol he's currently pouring. "My mom called me that when I was little. Myrtle was one of our neighbors. She and her husband were over at our house a lot, so she kinda started saying it, too."

"Can I get an Orange Slice?" the next woman in line asks Leo, eyes shining. "And would you mind signing a couple tennis balls for us?"

"Of course!" Leo says, thrilled to move on from sharing tidbits of his childhood with Gabe. He scribbles his signature and poses for a selfie with the woman and her two kids.

"Hmm, that's a bummer," Gabe continues, now crouched down and looking for another wine bottle on one of the bar's lower shelves. "It's kind of a hot name."

Always the first to play it cool, Leo turns around after the selfie and knocks a nearly full, open bottle of Aperol onto the floor behind the bar.

"Shit, sorry, fuck," he says. "Did I get you?"

"No, Leonardo," Gabe says, deadpan. "Not a drop." Wearing a beachy white-and-blue striped button-down—short-sleeved, tight around his arms—he looks like he was shot.

"Oh my God," Leo says, seeing the bitter red liquid splattered across the shirt. He scrambles for a towel. "I'm so sorry. We can use some of the club soda. It'll come out."

"I don't think I'm gonna make it," Gabe says, touching Leo's arm and pretending to go all woozy. "No, it's fine, don't worry about it. I have a tank underneath. I'll just take this off."

As he takes the button-down off, Leo sees that he has a white, ribbed tank underneath, gripping his torso and riding up just high enough as he removes the button-down that it exposes the band of his underwear, which, of course, reads "Calvin Klein."

It's not like Leo has never seen Gabe's body before. They've been in the locker room together hundreds of times over the years. But he doesn't usually allow himself to look closely—not just at Gabe, but at any of the men, naked or nearly, entering and exiting the showers. He's always wanted to protect himself from suspicion, as if staring at the floor or into his locker with rigid focus isn't the most conspicuous move in the book. But more than that, he's always told himself that these men are off-limits. *Gabe* is off limits. He already distracts Leo enough with his curving slice and sloping topspin. He doesn't need to study Gabe's body in the locker room, too, with all its curves and slopes, with the kind of V muscles that Leo wants to trace down and down and down. *Ahem.* He's always been committed to keeping matters of the heart and dick out of his career. There's no room for distraction in tennis. There's no room for love, except on the scoreboard.

But just this once, behind the bar, up close, Leo allows himself to look—at Gabe's soft skin, the dark hair peeking out of his armpits, the scar on his shoulder from a surgery Leo now remembers him getting a few years back, the way his tank hugs the curve of his pecs, the way a trio of freckles below his collarbone resembles Orion's Belt, the way that fucking collarbone could get Leo to drop every grudge he's held ever against him. Ah, fuck. Leo doesn't think he's gonna make it, either.

With just a few guests approaching the bar from time to time—the kids across the grounds getting tuckered out and the adults getting sufficiently sloshed—Leo pours himself what he believes to be a much-deserved, nearly overflowing glass of prosecco for surviving both this bartender gig and that close encounter with Gabe's body.

"You want some?" he asks Gabe, who's glued to his phone during the lull in fans visiting the bar. Leo assumes he's texting a guy, which is totally cool and doesn't actually really affect him at all, as an objective, empathetic, non-publicly queer person. Haha.

"Thought you'd never ask," Gabe says, shoving his phone back in his pocket.

"Cheers," Leo says. He hands him a glass and clinks his own against it.

"Wait, wait," Gabe says, as Leo is about to take a sip. "You have to make eye contact while you clink or it's bad luck."

Sigh. Leo knows there isn't anyone more superstitious than a tennis player, who would rather die than tweak their rituals, just in case. "Okay, sure," he says. Breath caught—no, lodged, wedged, stuck—in his throat, he locks eyes with Gabe's, another place he doesn't allow himself to look if he can help it. Even at dusk, Gabe's brown eyes are bright, inviting, warm. His irises are tree trunks, holding history in each of their rings.

"Salud," Gabe says, staring into Leo's soul as if he has any right to do so.

"Yep, cheers," Leo says, and tosses back most of the prosecco.

It hasn't dawned on Leo that this bartending gig has kept them from eating anything in hours, which explains why they're now sitting on the floor of the bar, backs leaning against it, legs outstretched, a third glass of prosecco in their hands. At first, they only wanted to hide from serving more fans, but now they're comfortable and buzzed and chatty. It doesn't take much for Leo to get tipsy and, sure, Gabe is an asshole, but now that Leo's allowed himself to *look*, it feels impossible to tear himself away. He's trapped in Gabe's orbit at the moment and, like his head with all this prosecco, he's gently spinning.

"People started tipping after you took your shirt off, by the way," Leo says, failing to hide his smile. "Did you see? There's some money in a glass on the bar."

"Seriously? Who even put that there?" Gabe says. "That's fucking hilarious. You should take it. You're the reason I had to strip down, anyway."

"Oh, no, no, it's all yours," Leo says and, recalling his strategy to be on his best behavior for once, he avoids making some wisecrack about how Gabe could use the money since he's going to lose in the first round of the tournament. "That chest worked hard for the money."

"Really?" Gabe asks, puffing out his chest and looking back and forth at his pecs. "You think it was the girls?"

Leo snorts. "Ow," he says, grabbing his nose. "Bubbles."

Gabe's smiling now, too. "I think I'll actually just give it to the tournament committee," he says. "But this was an important lesson. When I retire from tennis someday, I think there might be a real future for me as a bartender in suburban Florida."

"I think you might be right," Leo says, chuckling. There's a long silence, in which he feels as if the bubbles and banter are making him levitate.

"I think *you* were right, by the way," Gabe says eventually.

"Thanks," Leo replies, then pauses. "Wait, about what?"

"About," he says, shifting uncomfortably and seemingly forcing the words out of his throat, "the whole, you know, tipped ball thing. I watched it back, and I think you were right."

Leo gasps dramatically and it turns into a hiccup and both of them are giggling again, their third glasses of prosecco polished off.

"Admit it—I was right about that ball being out in our juniors final, too!" Leo shouts.

"No comment," Gabe says, smirking.

"Hold please," Leo says, pulling out his phone and putting it up to his ear.

"Sorry, what's up?" Gabe asks.

"Just calling the ATP really quick," Leo says. "Reporting you for cheating."

"Oh, you are such a little teacher's pet!" Gabe says, laughing and lunging to grab Leo's phone. Gabe's body is reaching across

Leo's now and his familiar, fresh scent of cedar is there again, and Leo doesn't own an inhaler but, wow, maybe he should consider purchasing one.

"I'm not actually calling them," Leo says.

"I know, doofus," Gabe says, pushing Leo's shoulder as he sits back in his spot.

"You really think that, though, don't you?" Leo asks, liquid courage doing its job.

"What? That you're a doofus?" Gabe asks. "Yes. Absolutely."

"No, that I'm some, like, goody two-shoes daddy's boy who's horny for the rules."

Gabe raises an eyebrow. "You want to know if I think you're horny?"

Okay, yep, inhaler *stat*. He clears his throat. "Okay, seriously, I just want to know," Leo says, because if Gabe can address the elephant in the room, so can he. This confrontation is brought to you by Alcohol. "Is that what you think of me?"

Gabe heaves a sigh. "Leo," he says, tilting his head back against the bar. "Don't make me do this. What do you want me to say here?" He pauses. "Look, we've known each other for a long time. But have we? Really?"

Leo is entranced.

"You said it yourself on Instagram. We can't possibly know everything going on behind the scenes in a player's life. You were right about that, too."

Leo, still entranced.

"I've had my . . . opinions about you over the years, yeah, I won't lie to you. I'm sure you've had yours about me, too. But if I'm admitting things here tonight, and I can't believe you got all this out of me with some fucking prosecco, you asshole, I'm willing to admit that I probably don't know you as well as I think I do."

Leo, sweating.

"So, maybe we won't ever totally understand each other, but I hope we can put our claws away, at least," Gabe says. "Is that okay? Does that count as an answer?"

Leo is in the midst of the most adult conversation he's ever had with Gabe, on the floor of an outdoor bar stand, three glasses of prosecco deep, hiding from drunk Delray moms. He can't say that he had *this* on his bingo card for the year.

Buzzed or not, it's difficult for him to process everything he's just heard. But he knows how much it must have taken for Gabe to admit that. He knows he owes Gabe as much. He also knows he likes the sound of Gabe's voice even more when it's vulnerable.

So, yes. "That counts as an answer," he says.

They both offer each other a gentle smile. Their eye contact lingers.

"Truce?" Gabe asks, holding out his hand.

Leo stares at it for a moment.

He doesn't see a trap.

"Truce," he says, hoping that some water under the bridge might finally, actually do them both some good, might even help him loosen up while he plays. So, he grasps Gabe's hand and, unlike each of their handshakes after Leo's eleven losses to Gabe, this one reminds him of their first, all those years ago at BP.

Though Johnny was at Delray, he and Leo didn't talk about anything but tennis. Mentioning their little parking lot blowout? Not even close. They stuck to forehands, backhands, and second serves. Once Leo's run at the hometown tournament ended in the semifinals, Johnny simply told him, "I'm taking some more time off after this and will pick back up with you guys in Miami." And that was that. Well, actually, it was that *and* "I'll still be watching your matches."

Was that a threat?

The Miami Open, which Johnny was referencing, isn't until the end of March, so for about a month, Leo will continue to be fatherless on tour, which is pretty much the only reason he's out right now with Ollie in Mexico. They're both here for the Mexican Open, a midlevel men's tournament in Acapulco at the end of February that has a bit of a reputation as a place to party once the players have gotten knocked out of the tournament (or during the tournament, depending on your speed) and, again, want to get knocked out. Not that Leo has ever really participated before tonight, typically tucked into his hotel bed, his dad down the hall. He's trying not to read into it too much, but he's currently drinking an Aperol spritz, which he accidentally called an Orange Slice to the bartender. He's chalking up this order to feeling celebratory after he made it to the quarters. Another good run in the books this season calls for some more bubbles.

"You know you're supposed to make eye contact while you cheers," Leo says, still holding his drink out as Ollie brings the first sip of his margarita, on the rocks, with salt, to his lips. "It's bad luck otherwise. I heard that somewhere."

"Tabarnak. We're already out of the tournament. Drink your drink." Ollie takes a big gulp of his marg, leaving Leo hanging.

"Fine," he says, and takes a sip. "But at least hold out your glass so I can take a photo. Tess is always on me to share more on my stories. *People want to hear from you! Just be yourself!* I swear, she's worse than my agent."

On an expansive roof deck overlooking the Pacific, under a midnight-blue sky and zig-zagging strands of bistro lights, the two of them hold out their glasses for Leo's photo. Ollie's humming along to the Charli xcx song that's got the whole deck and its infinity pool, brimming with scantily clad vacationers, bumping along to the beat.

"Nice try," Leo says, reviewing the photo and seeing that Ollie, holding his glass from underneath, has his middle finger pressed to the front. Ollie gives him an angelic smile.

Once they've successfully captured a more kid-friendly photo, he posts it to his Instagram story with Ollie tagged and a quick caption: "But where's @tessa.soriano?"

Right now, Tess is back in Southern California, focusing on practice ahead of Indian Wells. Known as the honorary fifth Grand Slam, Indian Wells is the most highly attended tournament after the four actual Slams. It's a huge tournament with 128 men and 128 women, played on hard courts at the beginning of March in the desert, not far from Palm Springs. The Miami Open follows a week later and, together, the two tournaments make the Sunshine Double. Winning the Sunshine Double is something only a handful of players have achieved over the years, a tremendous feat given the events' quick succession. Like Tess, and with the Mexican Open out of the way, it's what Leo and Ollie have their sights set on now. But their own practice routines for Indian Wells don't start for another thirty-six hours, so before they fly up to California, they're allowing themselves to let loose a little tonight.

"Oh! This reminds me," Ollie says after taking another sip of his marg. "It's official. Pawsitive Futures is going to be one of the organizations for Miami Open Unites this year. They've seen our work so far and want to promote us."

"Yes!" Leo shouts, pumping his fist like he just hit a forehand winner. "Wait, what reminded you of that?"

"Ah, one of the new puppies we just rescued is named Tequila," Ollie says. "We think she's a corgi-chihuahua mix."

"And you're not pulling out your phone to show me a photo right now because?"

"Okay, tabarnak, give me a second," Ollie says. He pulls up the Instagram account for Pawsitive Futures, the Miami-based animal rescue organization he helped found last year. As Leo's just learned, it will be one of the five local organizations selected to participate in the upcoming Miami Open Unites—an annual day of service ahead of the Miami Open when a group of men's and women's players take a break from their routines to volunteer at various nonprofits around the city.

"Oh my God," Leo says, eyes in awe of the unbearably cute copper-and-white fluffball on the screen. "Look at her. Holy shit. An angel. I need her. Can I have her?"

"Hmm, let's see. We need to go over some qualifications. What's your work schedule like?" Ollie asks. "Do you travel often? Can you dedicate time to training her?"

"Yes, I'm a project manager who works from home and has years of experience in raising puppies into well-behaved dogs. I have no friends. Tequila would be my life."

"Well, the no friends part I can certainly vouch for," Ollie says, stroking his chin.

Leo stares at him blankly. "Look, I'll even prove how serious an applicant I am." He takes his phone out and pulls up Pawsitive Futures' post about Tequila, on which he comments:

"Can I have her?"

Almost instantly, there are dozens of likes on the comment.

While he's on Instagram, he pops back to his main feed and sees that he's just gotten a new reply to his story.

"Careful not to spill too much. I've seen people get thrown out of that place," the DM says, followed by a winking emoji. Guess the fuck who.

Okay. Okay. Okay! This is a moment to show he's taking their truce seriously. He could just send a laughing emoji? He could just like the message? His thumbs are circling the keyboard like he's about to start a thumb war. He decides to reply.

"Haven't slumped over behind the bar yet," he types. "So far, so good." Holding his breath, he hits send. Immediately, he sees Gabe start typing.

"Nice work, Leonardo," the message says.

For a second, Leo forgets where he is. It's not a big deal, though. Really. He looks up from his phone and briefly reenters the conversation Ollie has started with a few other players at the bar who overheard Leo basically squealing about Pawsitive Futures. They're all gathered around Ollie's phone now, making him scroll through all the adoptable dogs and demanding a spot in the group that visits his organization during Miami Open Unites.

"Everybody back off Tequila," Leo says. "She's mine."

"No, no, mate," Eddie, a British player, tells Leo. "That is the bloody cutest dog I've ever fuckin' seen. I'm adopting her. Corgis are a Brit thing anyway."

"And chihuahuas are our thing," Javier, a Mexican player who's here playing his home tournament, chimes in. "I think she should come with me."

"All right, all right, how about, whoever wins Indian Wells gets first dibs," Ollie says.

The group looks intrigued.

"That'll be me anyway," Ollie continues.

The group groans.

"Tabarnak, I'm only kidding," Ollie says. "Not about me winning—about letting any of you idiots have her!"

Leo groans again, but not at Ollie this time. Sascha is approaching them.

"Are we fighting over a girl or what?" he asks, gripping a Corona in one hand and putting the other on Eddie's shoulder.

"A dog," Eddie says.

"Ah, it's always some bitch, isn't it?" Sascha says, jabbing Eddie in the side, looking like he just told a joke that would get him an HBO standup special. Leo would like to walk straight off the roof deck and into the sea.

"Don't talk about Tequila like that," Ollie says sternly. "I should have never brought this up at all."

"Did I hear your rescue is part of the volunteer thing this year?" Sascha says. "I need to be there, man. I love doggos."

Cutting his hand across his neck, Leo attempts to signal to Ollie that there is no way in hell Sascha is joining them. It seems that Ollie gets the hint, because he says it's not confirmed yet before he pivots and asks if Javier is enjoying being the hometown hero, having made it to the semis at the Mexican Open for the first time.

Speaking of hometown heroes, for better or worse, Leo is reminded of his Delray bartending gig with Gabe every time he takes a sip of his Aperol spritz. After the latest one, he decides to check his phone again, just in case Gabe has sent another message. Not that he expects him to continue the conversation or anything. Gabe is at a different tournament in Santiago, Chile, this week, anyway. He's definitely too busy to be on his phone, chatting with Leo about total nonsen—

Nice work at Acapulco too. Out celebrating?

Breath. Caught. In. Throat.

Trying . . . someone who thinks
Peru is an island is here
And thank you!

Pull the fire alarm

You know I'm too big a teacher's pet for that

Mierda, not this again lol

Kidding, fire dept on its way
How'd you do in Santiago? Out celebrating?

Leo asks that question as if he doesn't know full well that Gabe lost in the first round, 6–3, 6–2. He *happened* to see it while checking scores online. But, for what it's worth, he's actually not asking to rub that scoreline in Gabe's face for once. He just wants to . . . continue the conversation? Ugh. Even though he also knows full well that Gabe is likely to be out partying, regardless of his first-round exit, always the first to be spotted at the hottest club in whatever city he's visiting for a tournament, his signature smirk lighting up the darkest of VIP corners. Leo is positive he's out in Santiago, probably in said darkest corner with some gorgeous guy. The one he was texting in Delray. Yeah. His new boyfriend. It must be. They'll be on magazine covers together soon. And it won't affect Leo. Not in the slightest.

Soothing my first-round loss with some smut

Leo would be positive, too, that this is a typo—surely Gabe meant "slut"—and that he is, as suspected, out at a club with a guy, if it weren't for the accompanying selfie that caused him to lock his phone with the speed of someone who's just accidentally scrolled by Twitter porn in public. Did he see that right? Was that really a photo of Gabe, lying in bed, reading glasses on, a romance novel resting on his bare chest? Did he seriously mean that he's getting over losing in Santiago with some *smut*?

"Speaking of bitches," Sascha says, jolting Leo back to the group, "somebody is sliding into Chambers's DMs over there. Look at his face. Who is getting you all hot and bothered, man?"

Hearing Sascha say "hot and bothered" in his Russian accent sort of makes Leo want to burst out laughing, but he's still speechless from the selfie he just witnessed and now he's searching, hopelessly, for the words to respond to Sascha's idiocy.

"Nobody," he comes up with, a smooth operator.

Beside him, Eddie says playfully, "Pretty sure I saw Montoya's name from over here."

"Oh ho ho, so it's not just any bitch, it's a boyfriend!" Sascha says, and pulls another swig of Corona, clearing his throat for whatever homophobia is about to spew out next. "Tell me, Chambers, who serves and who receives?"

"Dave Chappelle, ladies and gentlemen," Ollie says, and Leo has never been more grateful to call him a friend.

"Hey, I take that as a compliment," Sascha says, shrugging and starting to slur his words, perhaps on the verge of an actual slur. "I'm just saying what no one else will, like Chappelle! He gives you the facts, and so do I. And the fact is, I'm glad I wasn't the first one to lose to a fairy. Imagine this. Losing at the Australian Open to the only gay guy in tennis."

Walk into the sea? Nah. Leo wants to throw Sascha into its furthest depths. Rather than get arrested in Mexico, though, he finishes his drink and storms off.

"Sorry, gotta go put these drinks on Sascha's tab," Ollie says, and turns from the bar to follow Leo.

Over the bass, Leo hears Sascha shout after them, "Aw man, I hope I don't get canceled!"

Back in his hotel room, it's mostly the typical scene: tucked under the covers, AC blasting, *The Golden Girls* playing on his laptop. Only this time, Leo also has his DMs with Gabe open. In a rage blackout after his run-in with Sascha, he had nearly forgotten that he never responded to The Selfie. Curse his Nike sponsorship, because the only thing running through his head in this moment is: *Just do it.*

You want to practice again at Indian Wells?
I've got some questions about this "smut."

CHAPTER ELEVEN

Click.
"Yes, Leo."

Click.
"Love that."

Click.
"Good, more of that."

Nearly as intensive as Leo's practice schedule in the lead-up to Indian Wells is his sponsor schedule. Every day is a new obligation for the brands who fund him to wear their athleisure or drink their sports drink or eat their pasta. To be clear, it's a privilege to have such a solid roster of companies backing him, especially the pasta brand, but holy hell, there are only so many photo shoots and videos for TikTok and interviews for Instagram he can take when all he really wants to do is hit the court and stay in good form ahead of the tournament. He could never make it as an influencer. Today, he's thinking *Just do it*, yet again, as he poses in some new tennis gear for Nike ahead of their spring launch. Fortunately, Tess is here, too, having some solo shots taken and posing with Leo in others. Two perennial American favorites, they're the perfect duo to rep Nike's new line. Well, they're the perfect duo when Tess isn't off camera, teasing Leo like the little brother she never had.

"Yes!" she cries as he mimics his backhand for the next shot. "Make love to the camera!"

Leo fights his smile and his red ears as he tries to stay poised for the photographer.

"He's serving!" Tess continues. "It's giving '03 Roddick!"

The "R" word officially snaps his concentration, forcing an embarrassed grin and an apology to the photographer out of him.

"Totally fine, Leo," the photographer says. "This is good, actually. Let's keep up this playfulness in our next round of shots. Tess, you can step back in."

They have Leo and Tess sit on a bench by the practice court they've been shooting on this afternoon—Leo leaning forward, Tess leaning back. There are tennis balls scattered across the ground around them. They both stare into the lens with focused expressions.

"Perfect, keep it right there, you two," the photographer tells them. They turn to their lighting tech to direct the setup for their next shots, giving Tess an opening, unfortunately, to quiz Leo about his practice with Gabe tomorrow. Though, to be fair, it was his mistake for telling her in the first place.

"So, how are you feeling about *Practice with Your Nemesis: The Sequel*?" Tess asks, snapping out of her model-like expression and into a much sillier one. "Excited? Nervous? Full of dread? Who set this one up? Brian?"

"All right, stand down, Sporty Spice," he says.

"Um, Mel C wishes," Tess says, smoothing out her skirt as she turns to Leo. "So?"

"I'm feeling good about it? We're good now, I guess. It's all good," Leo says evenly, refusing to give away how giddy he is to practice with Gabe again.

"Riveting stuff, Leo." Behind her, the lighting tech is adjusting some reflectors, and the sun bounces off into Leo's face for a moment.

"Okay, well, I set it up," he says, relenting. "Is that more riveting?"

"Uh, yeah! Way more. What compelled this decision?" she says, eyes widening, leaning in closer.

"I don't know. I just figured I would keep following Brian's strategy. He's letting me be a little more creative with my approach, so yeah, playing with Gabe might help with that."

"Okay, cool, cool," Tess says. "And you're, like, friends now, or?"

"Maybe 'friends' is too strong a word, but definitely not enemies anymore. We talked things out at Delray. Well, sort of. We're putting our weapons down, at least."

"Wow, burying the lede!"

"It's not that big of a deal!"

"Yeah, well, your ears say otherwise."

He can feel them heating up, his face going all rosy. He's always betrayed by his blushing. In a blink, one of the makeup artists is already standing over Leo, getting ready to put a bit more foundation on his cheeks.

"I just think it's nice," Tess continues. "I know growth when I see it. Carrying around old grudges may feel good, but they're wasted space. Trust me, I'm a Virgo. I should know."

The makeup artist snaps his fingers in response and adds a final touch to Leo's face.

"Okay, let's get back to it," the photographer announces to everyone on set. "We don't want to lose the sun."

Leo always feels like he's woken up on a different planet during his time at Indian Wells. Opening the long white curtains that pool on the hardwood floor of his hotel room, his sightline is filled with the snow-capped Santa Rosa Mountains springing up in the distance and forming pockets of flat land decorated with palm trees. He feels as if he's slept inside a crater overnight.

Or maybe it's not another planet. Maybe it's the moon. Because when he steps out of his room to meet Brian in the lobby for practice, his body nearly defies gravity, almost floating off the ground when he sees Gabe walking by.

"Oh, hey," Leo says. Still only halfway in the hall and experiencing weightlessness, the heavy door closes automatically behind him, literally bumping him into Gabe, his hands breaking his fall on Gabe's arm. "Sorry."

"Well, good morning to you, too," Gabe says, and when he puts his hand on Leo's shoulder to help steady him, Leo's officially up in the stars somewhere. "Looks like we're neighbors. I'm right down the hall."

"Sweet," Leo says, beginning their walk to the elevators. *Sweet?* "I always try to get the same room every year. One of my own superstitions, I guess."

"How's it working out for you this year?"

Leo's not going to make a quip about how Gabe will find out when he goes further than him in the tournament. He's going to stay true to his side of the truce. He is. Really.

"So far, so good," he says, shrugging. "Practice has been going well. Just so much media and endorsement stuff to do this week."

"God, I know, like a million photo shoots."

"Yeah, you must be in heaven," Leo says. Shit. Okay, whatever, he's not perfect.

"Meaning?" Gabe asks, head cocked.

Welp, no turning back now.

"Oh, I don't know, I just mean, Mr. Cover Star must live for all this attention," Leo says. He then puts on his best Gabe smirk and voice. "*Remember: Always keep it neat.*"

"Did you just recite my whiskey commercial?" Gabe asks, a devilish smile curling.

Oops. A slight miscalculation. "Well, it used to be on TV, like, every other minute. It was kinda hard to miss." All right, decent save. "But, hey, if I'm allowed to be a bit of a teacher's pet, you're allowed to be a little full of yourself."

"Oh, is *that* what I am?" Gabe asks, eyes widening.

"Well, I, um . . ." Leo stumbles.

"No, no, don't get shy now," Gabe says.

"Okay, well," Leo says, realizing this is the chance he's been waiting for. The chance to call out the golden boy. "All I'm saying is that you seem to love the spotlight. Like, you must love scrolling through all the Instagram fan accounts dedicated to you. You must wake up in the morning and stare at your own reflection in the mirror. You must bask in your own glow. You must—"

Before Leo can dig himself in even further, Gabe asks, an eyebrow raised, "How do you know there are fan accounts dedicated to me?" And Leo nearly trips, suddenly a victim to gravity again.

"Gabe, thank God I caught you," a frazzled woman with winged eyeliner and a long black ponytail says, popping out of one of the hotel rooms on their floor like a prairie dog. "I know, I know, you're heading to practice, but I need you to sign off on one of these before this fucking company tars and feathers me. I also can't look at these things anymore. My night terrors are going to come back."

"Uh, yeah, sure," Gabe says. "Look at what exactly? And is it cool if Leo—"

"Yes, sure, hi, Leo," she says, speaking as quickly as Lorelai Gilmore and frantically motioning for them to step inside. "I'm Gabe's agent, Esme."

Leo would introduce himself, but as he enters the room, his mouth slowly opens at the singularly outrageous sight before him.

"Oh . . . my God," he says, stopping dead in his tracks.

Set up around Esme's room are at least a dozen life-size cardboard cutouts of Gabe modeling a new sport wristwatch in varying poses—arm across his chest, hand on his hip, arm resting atop his head. In all of them, his perfect smize would make Tyra herself root for him in the stands.

"I know, it's harrowing. The eyes . . . they follow you around the room," Esme says. "Why they want one of these greeting people at their launch is beyond me, but hey, glad to have a new brand coming on board right now."

Leo is simply standing there, gagged, gooped, gobsmacked at all these Gabes, whose suave expressions belong on the cover of one of Gabe's smutty novels. His mouth is still slightly agape, and he's forcing himself to squash the thundering cackle that's threatening to burst out of him. He glances over at Gabe with a wry smile.

"You are so pleased with yourself right now," Gabe says.

"I hate to say this—"

"No, you don't."

"—but *now* you must be in heaven," Leo says. Moving across the living room, he sidles up to one of the cardboard figures. "I think it's pretty clear you have to go with this one," he says, putting his hand on his hip as he stands beside the cutout of Gabe doing the same. He has to bite his lip to keep from smiling too hard.

"Oh, God, please not that one," Esme says, and looks down at her phone that's begun buzzing. "Ah, fuck, I have to take this. Okay, well, just put this Post-it on your favorite. If it were me, I'd pick the arm-across-chest. The rest of them look like you have a secret and we're done with that era, aren't we?"

With a knowing smile, Esme sticks the note on human Gabe's forehead and scurries into the bedroom, shutting the door behind her.

Leo has touched down on yet another planet, one on which he's standing in a forest of cardboard Gabes, each more handsome than the next. Through the forest, human Gabe walks toward him, and perhaps the conditions of this latest planet are overwhelming Leo, because as Gabe approaches, he can hear a small thought telling him that the Post-it is already stuck on his favorite. Must . . . get back . . . to Earth.

"All right, you win this round," Gabe says, stepping closer to Leo and leaning his head down. "You get to pick."

Carefully, Leo peels the Post-it from Gabe's forehead. He sticks it on the cardboard cutout of Gabe placing his arm across his chest.

"This one," he says. "I'm afraid of upsetting Esme."

With a chuckle, Gabe says, "Oh, she's all bark. But she's the best. She's really had my back through all the press and everything the past few months." He taps the cutout next to him. "She's right that it's good to get another endorsement right now, and she's been working hard to get them. We, uh, lost a couple after my announcement."

There it is again. That flash of vulnerability, which does bring Leo back to Earth and allows him to see Gabe—really see him—for a moment.

"Seriously? What fucking year is it?" Leo asks.

"Still 1953 for a lot of people, apparently."

They both sigh, and Leo has to break eye contact before he's beamed up again.

"Okay, yeah, Esme's right, this shit is creeping me out," Gabe says, his eyes darting around to each cutout. "We should get to practice, anyway."

"Hold on," Leo says, pulling out his phone, and he smiles for a selfie in the cardboard forest. "There's no way I'm getting out of here without documenting this."

Seated on a bench, side by side, on one of the dozen neatly aligned practice courts—a mountain range of fans in the bleachers, a desert mountain range on the horizon behind them—Leo and Gabe are catching their breath and drinking some electrolytes. Like last time (and, please, hold for applause), Leo edged out the win in their practice match. Unlike last time, it was much closer. Even with fans packed in and a few photographers on the sidelines, that nervous energy didn't seem to plague Gabe as much. There was less fidgeting with his backward hat, fewer slices into the net. Leo can't deny that they were in a groove today, a tight contest of sweeping backhands and smooth forehands, the two of them moving fluidly to one another's shots. There was a rhythm Leo hadn't felt with Gabe on the court before, like he was finally understanding Gabe's game better, like he could anticipate his next move faster. They felt like a synchronized pair.

"So," Leo says, toweling off his face.

"Here we go," Gabe says. He takes a sip from his water bottle. "Get it out. Get all the gloating out. Even though I will remind you, this was only another practice match."

"Actually," Leo says, "I was going to let you off the hook about that one."

"Wow, thank you," Gabe says, placing his hand over his heart.

"Please stop, you look like that cardboard cutout."

The two of them are giggling like schoolboys, and Leo knows the fans and photographers must be eating this up, but he tries to push past his anxiety.

"But I'm not letting you off the hook about your recently revealed affinity for—what was it again? Smut? Naughty, filthy smut? I hope you didn't think I forgot."

"I do hate you," Gabe says.

"Hey, truce, remember?"

"I take it back. I'm pulling out of the truce. I prefer war. Send in the troops."

With the truce in mind, Leo knows he still owes Gabe even a morsel of his own vulnerability. Gabe can't be the only one sharing if this little peace treaty will last. So, having told Tess and Ollie already, he might as well. He'll just spit it out. He'll disappear into the mountains if he needs to.

"Would you consider telling me about your obsession with erotica if—"

"It's not exactly erotica, but go on."

"—if I told you about my obsession with, um, *The Golden Girls*?"

"Shut the fuck up," Gabe says, turning toward Leo.

"Yeah, I know, it's embarrassing."

"No, no, my abuela fucking loved that show. It's even funnier in Spanish. But she watched it in English a lot, too. I think it helped her learn the language."

"Wait, seriously?" Leo asks, twirling his racket.

"Seriously. She lived in Lima most of her life, but then she came to live with me and my parents in Florida."

"That's amazing," Leo says. "I actually watched with my grandma, too. She lived with us when I was a kid. Do you still watch?"

"No, I haven't watched it in years. But it sounds like you still do, huh?"

"I, uh, yeah. It's kinda my thing on tour. It makes me feel more at home, living out of suitcases in hotels most of the year, you know?"

"Totally. It's not too far off from my thing for . . . naughty, filthy smut, was it?" he asks, cocking his head. "I'd call it my guilty pleasure, but I don't think you should feel guilty for something that brings you pleasure."

Leo swallows.

"They're just fun and campy and steamy. They're my escape on tour, like you're saying. Especially this season, when things have been a little, well—" Gabe trails off, instead pointing back to the photographers with his thumb.

Leo nods. "Yeah, I bet."

"I know you think I love the spotlight, but—" Gabe starts.

"I'll need you to confirm that those cutouts aren't made into a shrine in your closet, yes."

"*But,*" Gabe continues, shaking his head, "maybe that's not exactly true. Maybe that's just what I want people to think. I know that may come as a shock to you. But maybe I'd really rather just be up in my room with all my books. Maybe while you're busy watching *The Golden Girls,* I'm busy reading my smut."

"So what you're telling me is that you're *not like other girls,*" Leo says.

"Oh, yeah, I'm really just this adorkable bookworm who takes her glasses off and reveals she was beautiful the whole time."

Yet again, Leo can hear a small voice in his head that, in this instance, says, *I already knew the whole time.*

Disappearing into the mountains sounds awfully good right about now.

Leo looks over to Brian for some relief, to come up for air. Brian catches his glance and taps his wrist.

"Shit, right," Leo says. "I need to hit the gym with Brian. We're doing another session to warm up before Tie Break Tens tonight."

"Oh, I'll see you there!"

"You will?" Leo asks while packing up.

"Yeah, I got a call this morning that somebody had to withdraw, so they asked if I could swap in last minute." Gabe is using the bottom of his shirt to wipe some sweat off his neck, exposing his abs.

"Ah, sweet," Leo says, trying and failing to pull his eyes away from Gabe's torso. Gabe catches him staring, and Leo clears his throat to reset the moment, his eyes darting back down to his bag. "You're sure you can tear yourself away from your erotica? I could just bring one of the cardboard cutouts if you want. I doubt anybody would notice."

"I do hate you."

"Okay, fans! It's everyone's favorite night here in tennis paradise," the announcer says, looking around at the six thousand seats of center court, nearly all of which are filled. "It's time to play Tie Break Tens! The same rules apply—it's round robin-style and the first to ten points wins the round, whittling down to the final two. What's different this year is that we're playing mixed doubles! That's right: Some of your favorite men and women will be teaming up to fight for the grand prize of $250,000—donated to an organization of their choosing."

It's the night before Indian Wells begins and the temperature has plummeted in the pitch-black desert. Its bright lights polluting the starry sky, the steep stadium looks like a UFO touched down in California. The fans are bundled in sweatshirts, and the players are huddled beside the purple court, fuzzy white blankets wrapped around their shoulders. Some top-ranked and some fan-favorite, the sixteen players are goofing around like they're in gym class. The two mixed doubles teams who will go first in the competition are pedaling leisurely on stationary bikes, lined up next to the ump's chair, keeping their muscles warm before play begins. Leo feels lucky whenever he gets picked to compete in Tie Break Tens, a night when the fans get to kick back and see top players have some fun together for a good cause—especially this year, when he's hoping to claim his half of the prize money for the American Stroke Association. His partner tonight is Tess, of course, and they're hungry for the win after their unfinished run in mixed doubles this past US Open. This event is for fun and for fundraising, but it would be foolish to think that these two—and all the players—won't unleash their competitive sides, even when there aren't any ranking points at stake.

"You ready?" Tess asks.

"Oh, I'm ready," Leo says.

"Are *they* ready?" Tess asks, nodding to Ollie and his partner tonight, someone who's making her return at Indian Wells, the tournament that changed the trajectory of her career: Liv LaRochelle.

"It felt right to come back on tour here, where I won my first big title," she said in an interview ahead of the tournament, appearing cautiously confident. "I'll be playing Tie Break Tens for an organization in Canada that supports women recovering from mental health struggles. That felt right, too."

The four of them have their seats scooched in close, wrapped in fleece blankets, looking like they're ready to roast marshmallows.

"I don't think they're ready," Leo says, turning his head toward the pair of blond Canadians, who are glaring at him.

"You two are embarrassing," Ollie says.

"That may be true—" Tess starts.

"That's definitely true," Leo jumps in.

"—but we're still going to wipe the court with you tonight."

"You know this is for charity, right?" Ollie asks.

"And bragging rights," Tess says, shrugging and putting a hand in Ollie's face. She then leans forward so she can see around Ollie. "It's good to see you back, Liv."

Liv offers a small smile. "It's good to be back. I wasn't sure I'd come tonight, but this one encouraged me," she says, bumping her shoulder into Ollie's.

As the four of them chat away in low voices, the competition is heating up, each of the tiebreaks nail-bitingly close. The fans are on their feet during the longest rallies, screaming for the players as they show off a little more than usual for some extra entertainment, diving for balls at the net and hitting tweeners whenever possible. The blanketed bunch is getting in on the rowdiness, too, hollering for their favorite shots to keep the competition spicy. In between tiebreaks, Leo is talking with Ollie when he feels a new weight on his chair. He turns and finds

Gabe sitting on the chair's arm, also with a blanket wrapped around him, smiling.

"This seat taken?" he asks.

"Uh, no, no, go for it," Leo says, gripping his blanket tighter now.

"What's up, Ollie?" Gabe says, reaching across Leo's body for Ollie's hand. *Cedar.*

Over the next ten minutes or so, the group, including Gabe, joke around like kids, putting their blankets over their heads, Ollie wearing his like a cape at one point, Gabe pointing out that Tess is giving Marie Antoinette when she turns hers into a wig. It's only silly things like that, but Leo's unfamiliar with the feeling that begins to warm his body even more than the blanket.

When it finally comes time for Leo and Tess to prepare for their turn on court, they hop on the stationary bikes, and so do Gabe and his partner, Camila Díaz, a young Peruvian player—the opposing team they'll face in the first round. For once, and the quick pace at which he's pedaling might give this away, Leo actually isn't dreading an early-round clash with Gabe.

He's kind of, maybe, well, hyped for it.

"It's a good thing you have some time on the bike," Leo says, staring straight ahead.

"Oh yeah?" Gabe says, and Leo can feel his deep-brown eyes on him. "Why's that?"

"Well, it's important to stay loose. With so much money on the line, you don't want to get stiff out there like, say, cardboard, do you?"

"Leo Chambers telling *me* to stay loose," Gabe says. "Now I've heard it all. But don't worry, I never get stiff on court."

"Oh, grow up," Leo says.

He then turns and offers a playful look, one that's returned by Gabe, and their flirting—yes, Leo might even admit that this is flirting—spills onto the court during their tiebreak.

Whenever the two of them are up at the net, waiting opposite each other for the next serve—crouched down low, asses out, thighs bulging—Leo steals a glance at Gabe through the criss-crossing mesh. He's brave enough to look, but his eyes still dart away when Gabe meets them, biting his lip to contain his emotion. There's a wink from Gabe after he hits a winner down the line, a raised eyebrow from Leo after he hits a near-perfect volley. They squint at each other to show their focus. Observing your opponent's body language is key in any tennis match, but this is a different language altogether. For Leo, at least, the signals he's sending are loaded with something much more intense, much more sensual than typical competition. Point after point, Leo is determined to show Gabe what he's capable of, moving side to side on the court with the kind of agility that fans know he can bring. They're mirroring the energy displayed on court, too, growing louder and louder as the tiebreak barrels toward 9–7, Chambers/Soriano.

This next point could put them into the second round. After a high, sloping kick serve from Tess and a few fierce crosscourt forehands between her and Camila, Leo finds himself locked into a volleying duel with Gabe at the net, both of them punching the ball back and forth and back and forth and back and forth as the crowd's cheering reaches a climax.

The fans are roaring, ignoring the number one rule in tennis that the crowd stay quiet during a point, and Leo harnesses their energy as he steps in and smashes the next shot at Gabe's feet, the ball bouncing straight through Gabe's legs and off the court. Leo whips around and runs at Tess for a hug as the fans rise out of the navy-blue seats.

"It's a win for Chambers and Soriano!" the announcer declares.

They shake hands with Gabe and Camila at the net, and Gabe, glistening with sweat as he removes his backward cap, tells him, "Nice move. I'll have to borrow that some time." Leo's body already pumping with adrenaline from that final point, he could probably lift the entire stadium into the black sky after hearing that comment.

Leo and Tess carry the electricity of that first tiebreak all the way into the last round, where they face Ollie and Liv. It's all fun and games, even though the stands are rocking like it's a Grand Slam final, but Leo wants this win pretty badly. He wants the bragging rights to hold over Ollie for the foreseeable future, obviously, and he wants the donation even more now that he's this close to the quarter-of-a-million check. After everything he's been through with his parents the past several months, earning this prize money for the ASA would almost—almost—feel like closure for him.

That's what fuels him during the final tiebreak. He and Tess continue to work beautifully together, communicating with ease, covering each other as they shift their positions around the court. This is them at their best. With both of them locked in, it's not even a contest. Sending an ace down the T, Leo closes it out 10–3, and leaps for joy with Tess as the stadium roars in celebration, and then bursts into laughter as Ollie pretends to snub them at the net.

When the announcer asks Leo what it means to win this event tonight, he says, "Oh, it means the world. I got to win Tie Break Tens with this legend next to me. But I also have to say, it hasn't always been easy for my dad, or for my mom and me, while he's been recovering from his stroke last fall. So many families go through this every year, so to be able to earn this donation and support the American Stroke Association really means a lot to—"

He's cut off by a long round of applause and whistling from the bundled crowd.

"And thank you to all of you for coming out tonight even though it's so chilly out. The atmosphere really heated things up. I hope to see you at some of my matches!"

There is no shortage of fans at Leo's matches. He's felt them during every point, throwing their full support behind him, even if he isn't the top American right now. Galvanized by their support, his continued groove with Brian, and, okay, his budding—friendship? Would he call it a friendship? Whatever it is, he can, begrudgingly, tell that the truce is loosening him up, too.

Was Gabe really having that much of an impact on his mindset? He'd prefer not to answer that question. He'll sweep that aside for now, backhand it out of sight and out of mind.

His rhythm during Tie Break Tens extends into his run at Indian Wells, where, in the dry heat, he smacks and strikes and slices his way into the quarterfinals—four match wins in a row—no small accomplishment at a massive tournament of this magnitude.

"Cheers, y'all," Brian says, holding up a pint glass at the sleek hotel bar. "To LC for a breakthrough run—"

"I wouldn't call it a breakthrough," Leo interjects.

"Well, I would. You've found new ways to get the win even when you're not at your best. You've trained damn hard to get back here after a tough stretch. The final eight at Indian Wells? We're drinking to that. I'm proud of you, LC."

"Brian, you big softy," Leo says. "Don't think I'll let you win at Uno just because of this toast."

With his eyebrows raised, Brian simply stares at Leo with his glass still raised, like an unimpressed uncle.

"Okay, okay," Leo says. "In all seriousness, making the quarters at Indian Wells feels really good. I didn't know how this season would go, but here we are, heading into Miami with some real momentum. Cheers to that."

The team clinks their glasses to a successful tournament, and with nearly the same intensity he brought to said tournament, Leo crushes them, round after round, at Uno.

Later, sitting up in his hotel room, his things neatly packed for his flight to Miami the next morning, where he'll immediately begin prepping for the Miami Open, he's watching his favorite show when his phone buzzes.

"Nice work at IW," it reads. "See you soon."

It's the most he's heard from his dad over the past few weeks. Leo is sure he's been watching every match, as promised, but it's still been quiet between them. He was hoping for more from his dad, especially after Tie Break Tens and the ASA donation, which was partially Leo's olive branch, but he'll take it—a break in the silence before they see each other in Miami. Leo has been feeling sheepish after their post-*What a Racket* tiff, so he's relieved he didn't have to be the breaker. Still, his thumbs hang hesitantly over the keyboard as he struggles to come up with a reply.

He keeps it simple: "Thanks, Dad. See you soon."

As "delivered" appears below his text, there's a knock at the door that makes him jump, as if somehow it's his dad, who meant "see you soon" a bit more literally.

Swinging the door open, Leo finds Gabe standing there, dressed in a white crewneck that has PALM SPRINGS across the front in mint letters and—good Lord—a pair of gray sweatpants. It's fine, though. Really. What even are heart palpitations?

"Hey," Gabe says. "I'm not interrupting anything, am I?"

Just my sanity. "Uh, no, not at all," Leo says, now realizing he's standing there in his boxers and a T-shirt. Thrown by his dad's text and the knock at the door, he not only forgot to put pants on, but also left *The Golden Girls* playing on his laptop.

"I knew you were in this room from the other day," Gabe says. "Your birthday, right?"

Gray sweatpants. "Huh?"

"Your room number—719. July 19. That's your birthday, right?"

"Oh! Oh, yeah, that's part of my whole superstition about getting this room every year," Leo says, playing with the doorknob. "What do you, like, keep a log of people's birthdays?"

"Leo, we grew up together. And, you know, it's on your ATP profile," Gabe says, running a hand through his thick, Head and Shoulders-sponsored hair. Wait. Is he *nervous*?

"Mmm, right," Leo says, nodding his head suspiciously.

"Do I hear Blanche?" Gabe says, poking his head into Leo's room.

"Ah, yeah, you caught me. I'm in the middle of an episode. And I'm . . . not wearing pants. Please excuse me," he says, bowing his head formally.

He walks hurriedly over to the black shorts on the floor by his bed and pulls them on before turning to find that Gabe has now fully entered the room.

"What episode is this?" he asks.

"Um," Leo says, and then chuckles, realizing what he's about to say. "It's actually the one where Dorothy's old high school rival is visiting. They used to play these super-intense pranks on each other back then, and now the friend fakes a heart attack while they're playing tennis."

"Stop," Gabe says. "That's amazing." Gabe just stands there, facing the laptop on the bed, watching the episode.

Leo's eyes shift from side to side like one of those Kit-Cat clocks, wondering, well, what the hell Gabe wants.

"What do you want?" Leo asks, and it comes out a bit more forceful than he intended.

"Sheesh, this isn't a stickup," Gabe says. "Can't I just stop by and say hello?"

"I mean, you can, but you don't? We don't—" he says, gesturing between them, "do this. Say hello. Do we?"

"Maybe we do now," Gabe says. "Can I sit?"

"Uh, sure," Leo says, sitting down now, too, but slowly, like the bed might be lava.

"Ever since Tie Break Tens, I, well, I just wanted to say I'm sorry about what happened at the US Open," Gabe says, staring at the spot on the white duvet he's been picking at, instead of making his usual cocky eye contact.

"Gabe, thank you, but didn't we already do this? At Delray? You told me I was right about the tipped ball, and it's fueled me ever since?" Leo says, attempting to cut the tension.

"I apologized for getting the tipped ball thing wrong. But I didn't apologize for what I said to you after . . . at the net. The thing about you crying to your dad about it."

Leo is sitting there, stunned, like Dorothy on his laptop screen as she reacts to her friend fake-dying on the tennis court.

"That was shitty of me. I know you've gone through a lot with your dad," Gabe says, making eye contact now.

"Thanks," Leo says. He looks down and, as he begins to brush over his blister scars with his thumb, he huffs out a small laugh.

"What?" Gabe asks.

"No, nothing."

"Okay, now you have to tell me."

"I just," Leo begins, "can't believe this is happening? You're always taking jabs at me on Instagram, in interviews. And now you're apologizing. It's just . . . surprising."

"Oh, Leo, come on. That shit is so fake. It's part of the game we're both playing here. It's all about optics. You know that."

"Fake? Really? You seem to take it pretty seriously. You always make it sound like you hate me."

"You want to be the pot or the kettle?" Gabe asks, his eyebrow raising, nostrils flaring.

"You know everybody's always pitted us against each other since juniors, and you've never exactly made it any easier," Leo says, raising his voice.

"I'm here apologizing to you, and this is what you want to talk about, how I tease you in interviews?" Gabe asks impatiently, his posture stiffening.

"That's not what I want to talk about!" Leo shouts. "What I want to talk about is that you've been a dick to me long before what you said to me at the Open."

"Please, enlighten me," Gabe says, his eyes cutting into Leo.

"I'm talking about this one time back at BP. My dad was doing bad in the heat. His MS gets worse when it's hot out. And he fell while we were practicing. So, when he went to get cleaned up, Patrick stepped in to practice with me. I overheard you say something about how I only got to play with Patrick because of my dad and I, like, get whatever I want."

The cutting look disappears from Gabe's eyes now. It's replaced by a look of concern that Leo hasn't seen from him before.

Gabe sits quiet for a few moments, even looks sheepish. "I guess I forgot about that," he finally says, conceding. "That . . . was a dick move. I didn't realize that your dad was, you know, having trouble. Ah fuck, so when I said that thing at the Open, that must have really—"

It wrecked me for weeks. "It . . . stung a little," Leo says.

"Shit, I'm sorry," Gabe says, shaking his head.

"Thanks," Leo says, and the tension in the room is too much for him to handle. He can't help but walk it back. "Now that I'm saying it out loud, it doesn't really seem like that big of a deal. You didn't know what was up with my dad. We didn't exactly talk much."

"No, don't do that. It was shitty of me," Gabe says. "But I . . . do remember feeling like you wouldn't even give me the time of day back then. When you sorta dropped me, I just assumed you thought you were better than me. I thought you didn't want . . . me. To be my friend, I mean."

"I did want to be your friend!" Leo jumps in. "And it was *you* who was better than *me*. At tennis. I came to BP ready to be the next big thing, to take over my dad's career. And then it was like I couldn't even find my way around a court when you and I practiced together. It really threw me off, so I just avoided you." *Also, I didn't know how to be around you.*

"You couldn't be my friend because I was . . . better at tennis than you?" Gabe asks, his chin titled down, his eyes looking up at Leo as if to say, *Seriously?*

"Yeah, I know, it's stupid," Leo says, studying the white duvet cover for a few seconds, its herringbone design, lines interconnecting. "But I didn't just hate that you were better than me. I'm not *that* petty."

"Mmhmm," Gabe says.

"Yeah, yeah. I just mean, playing you felt like this speed bump in my path. And that path was everything to me." Leo pulls a pillow onto his lap, tugging at one of the corners of the white sham. "Since I was a kid, I've felt like I've had to finish what my dad started."

He can't believe he's saying this, but he's almost relieved, too. He reminds himself to breathe, and keeps going.

"And it's like I can feel time running out on that dream. That's such a familiar feeling for me, too, watching his health get worse and worse over the years. It's like I've watched time running out for him. And the stroke only made it worse. So, I have this part of me insisting that I better make the most of it, I better reach this goal of winning the Open, because there isn't much time left. When you came along at BP and basically dismantled my game, I ran away from you, even if I wanted to be your friend. I ran because I couldn't have anything throwing me off my path."

In the midst of what feels like a lifelong pause, Leo manages to lift his eyes from the duvet and meet Gabe's, which seem to be connecting every freckle sprinkled across Leo's face.

"Well, now that I've trauma dumped all over the bed, feel free to—"

"I had no idea," Gabe says. "You're a strong person, Leo. I don't know if anyone's ever told you that, but something tells me they haven't. So, I guess I want you to hear it from me."

"Thanks," Leo says, his eyes darting down to the duvet cover, and then back to Gabe. "I just wanted you to know. There was so much more there. I didn't think I was better than you, and I didn't just resent that you always beat me."

"Well, thanks for telling me," Gabe says.

They linger on a shared, soft smile.

"Oh my God, here I am, droning on and on about my problems, but you also had so much to deal with," Leo says. "I know what you were going through back then, too."

"You do?" Gabe asks, his posture perking up a bit.

"I mean, you know, like, now that you went public and shared your story in interviews and stuff," Leo says, feeling wobbly, on the edge of telling Gabe they're more alike than he knows. But he's shared enough tonight. Holy hell, he's shared way more than enough.

"Right," Gabe says, shoulders lowering a little. "Yeah, shit, it was a lot. I was realizing that I was gay, and on top of that, it's not easy for a Brown kid in tennis, either. It was practically all white kids at BP. My parents went out on a limb for me, they put so much money into my training, money my dad worked so hard to earn. He climbed the fucking corporate ladder, as an immigrant from Peru, and then his son is like, *I want to be a tennis pro*. Christ."

The *Golden Girls* credits music starts playing, and it's not exactly the right backing track for this moment, so Leo slowly closes his laptop, maintaining his gaze on Gabe so he knows Leo is here. Right here.

"But I knew I was good, and they agreed to let me train at BP. I had to work twice as hard. I wanted to prove to everybody that I was worth their time. And when you made it seem like I wasn't, and you were Johnny Chambers's son . . . it messed with me. So, I got in this habit of acting like none of it affected me. I put on this cheeky grin, acted like a goddamn star in the ads or the club just to seem untouchable."

"Fuck." That's all Leo can manage at first. He's too stunned by Gabe's honesty, by how wrong he's been about him. His perspective on Gabe is being reframed in real time, and he has to steady himself. He swallows. "I should've known better. I shouldn't have ignored you like I did. I'm really sorry. Seriously."

"Thanks," Gabe says. "It sounds like we were both growing up way too fast."

"Yeah, you could say that," Leo says with an awkward chuckle. He scratches the back of his head. "Have things gotten any easier since you came out?"

He wants to know that Gabe is okay, and he also, cautiously, wants to know the answer for himself, as if Gabe has been on some gay reconnaissance mission.

"Maybe 'easier' isn't the right word. It's hard in a new way, knowing people are watching me more closely. I guess it's . . . lighter. I felt like I was going to explode for a while there."

Leo nods, still in awe that this conversation is happening.

"The thing is, right after, it was all this glowing press. All the I-can-finally-be-myself stuff. Inspiration porn for straight people," Gabe says. "But I was still proud of it. I was actually being open with everyone and it felt amazing. But since all that's died down, I watch my matches back to take notes, and I hear the commentators talking about whether or not my being out is a distraction. There are guys on tour who have been accused of domestic abuse, and they're still allowed to play and the commentators will still praise them every fucking match. But a gay player? That's too much."

Gabe shakes his head and exhales slowly.

"I try to put it out of my mind because it's all bullshit, but of course that's all the press wants to talk about now. They give so much attention to the commentators, the hecklers. The only place I always see positive stuff is on that one account, Serving Looks."

"Oh, yeah, I think I've seen that," Leo says, as if it's not the top account in his algorithm.

"I do feel this huge weight off my chest," Gabe says. "But it's hard to not let the negative shit get in the way when the headlines won't stop reminding me about it. That's been messing with me, for sure."

With a laugh, Gabe begins rubbing his temples. "It's so funny to hear you talk about me like I'm unbeatable because I can barely win a fucking match this season. I come out of the closet and I'm supposed to be this gay role model, and I'm bombing out there."

"Hey, you did look good the other day," Leo says. "You seemed locked in, much more than our first practice. And you *have* won matches. I mean, you won a match at AO and you made it to the third round here, right?"

"Not exactly my best, but yeah, I did," Gabe says, his face brightening. "Wow, was that a little pep talk from Leo Chambers?"

It dawns on Leo that the two tournaments where Gabe actually has won matches this season are the two where they practiced together beforehand.

Leo is just as shocked as anyone when he adds, "If that little pep talk wowed you, you're gonna fall off the bed when I say that there may be a world, possibly, potentially, where we . . . make each other better? Practicing together *maybe* hasn't been the worst thing in the world."

"Huh, who would've thought?" Gabe asks, tilting his head, which only accentuates his puppy eyes. "So, I guess you admit it. If you had just been my friend and practiced with me, you might've won a Slam by now."

Leo hits him with the pillow. "Hmm yeah, and you might've won more than one title by now," he says, unable to leave a swipe unmatched.

As Gabe flips him off, Leo leans back on the oak headboard. "All right, I can't believe I'm saying this, but I have an idea."

"Which is?"

Leo groans. "We could . . . try playing doubles together in Miami? Brian's been encouraging me to play more doubles to round out my game this season, and you and I are both trying to get back in form, and, if you aren't already signed up with someone else, it might—"

"I'm in," Gabe says.

CHAPTER TWELVE

Leo has been looking into a lot of puppy eyes lately. Currently, there are two sets gleaming at him inside Pawsitive Futures, where he and Gabe are washing a fifty-pound husky-lab mix that has one amber eye and one icy-blue eye.

"I hope you didn't think you were just coming here to pose with the dogs," Ollie made sure to tell the group of players that's here volunteering. Despite their attempts to argue their way in, Ollie didn't end up inviting any of the guys from the group in Acapulco to his rescue agency's facilities for Miami Open Unites. "You're all here to help get these perfect babies ready for the Pawsitive Futures adoption event this weekend. That means chipping in with baths and cleaning up the play area where they'll meet their potential owners."

The rescue that Leo and Gabe are washing—er, trying to wash—is named Achilles, and Achilles would prefer to put his paws on Gabe's shoulders and lick Gabe's face than take a bath. Leo, as is becoming harder and harder for him to deny, can relate. Dozens of bubbles floating up from the stainless-steel groomer's tub, Gabe has managed to get Achilles's thick coat sufficiently sudsy, but Leo is failing to rinse him down with the sprayer. Achilles refuses to stand still, jumping up on Gabe's shoulders and dodging Leo's every move as both his tail and his long, pink tongue wag excitedly. Engulfed in an iridescent glow, Leo gazes at Gabe as he tilts his head back to avoid another French kiss from Achilles. Gabe's booming laugh filling the room, his wide smile that creases his cheeks, his ears that wiggle a little when he talks enthusiastically—it's all so infectious when he's unguarded. Not that Leo has noticed or anythi—

Ah, fuck it.

Leo's noticed.

He can't *stop* noticing.

"You're spraying me more than you're spraying him, just FYI!" Gabe shouts over the noise of the sprayer and Achilles's aggressive panting. He spits out some water. "Between this and the Aperol spill, you really love to get me wet, huh?"

Leo blinks at him. He then rolls up the sleeves of his teal Miami Open Unites T-shirt, farmer's tan on display, ready to get the job done. The hair on his forearms, usually light and wispy, is brown and matted from the bath.

"Try to hold him still!" Leo says, pressing more firmly on Achilles's back. "Let me adjust the nozzle and see if that helps."

Gabe grips Achilles's front legs. "Okay, go!"

Leo pulls the trigger and a firehose-stream of water sprays across the tub, bouncing off its metal walls and back at them. Achilles barks and shakes off his coat as the blast continues streaming out like Niagara Falls.

"Why is this even a setting?" Leo yells, fumbling to readjust the nozzle.

Finally, the sprayer shuts off.

The three of them, drenched and dripping, are all panting from the commotion.

"Well, he's rinsed," Gabe says. He brings the crook of his arm up to his face to wipe it down, as if that's going to help, wet skin on wet skin. "And so am I."

"Yeah, I'm a little . . . damp," Leo says, thick streaks of water streaming down his face.

They look at each other and start laughing, while Achilles starts licking Leo's cheeks.

Click. Click. Click.

"I'm sorry but this, as they say, is a Kodak moment," the photographer hired for the day says, appearing behind them suddenly. "Can I get a posed one now? Big smile. You too, pup."

Gabe puts his arm around Leo and, without needing any direction, Achilles, a natural model evidently, stands up with his front paws on Gabe's shoulders.

Click. Click. Click.

"Amazing, thank you, guys," the photographer says. "When you're done, uh, drying off, come meet everybody in the lobby for a group photo."

Leo has seen Gabe towel off in the locker room more times than he can count, but this, here, covered in dog hair, smile creases, and soaked tees, he likes this better.

"What happened to you two?" Ollie says when they enter the lobby, their T-shirts a darker shade of teal than when they left to bathe Achilles.

"He wouldn't stay still," Leo says.

"The dog or Gabe?" Tess says, chuckling.

"You know there's a harness in there you can clip the dog to, right?" Ollie says. "To hold him steady? Tabarnak. Well, thank you guys anyway."

Leo is now picturing Gabe in a harness and almost starts panting like Achilles.

While the photographer sets up, the group gathers for the shot, each of them holding a small puppy or the leash of a bigger dog. Gripping Achilles's leash, Leo turns to Tess and catches her smiling mischievously at him.

"What?"

She leans a little farther to see Gabe, who's standing next to him. "Pssst, Gabe," she whispers. "You coming to Leo's game night after the tournament?"

"I don't know, I wasn't invited," Gabe whispers back. A pit bull-mix puppy with a brindle and white coat is squirming in his arms.

"Well, you are now," she says. "Leo will text you the details. Bring a game, drink, whatever. It's the best."

"Cool, thanks," Gabe says, eyes bright. "Can I bring my friend Billie?"

From beside Tess, Ollie leans forward. "Billie Jean King?" he whisper-yells.

They all turn to look at Ollie.

"No," Gabe whispers back, brow furrowed. "I'm not just, like, friends with Billie Jean King now because we're both gay. I mean, I did meet with her back in January, but—"

"Are we, um, good to go?" the photographer says, camera directed toward the group.

"Yes, we are," Leo says, facing forward, ears reddening.

Gabe elbows him gently in the ribs.

"I feel like I still smell like that dog shampoo," Gabe says, loading up his bag in the locker room. He sniffs his arm. "Oatmeal. Or coconut. I don't know."

"Let's just pray we're better doubles players than we are dog groomers," Leo says.

He's been joking around with Gabe as they get ready for their first match together, but truthfully, he's extremely nervous. This was *his* idea, and now it's haunting him. Things were going just fine with Gabe. The truce was working out well. With their feud seemingly at an end, he had one fewer problem on his plate. Did he really have to push it by suggesting doubles?

It's too much too soon.

What if they crash and burn? What if they embarrass themselves all the way onto the Tennis Network highlight reel? What if this reignites the hatred between them? Wait, when exactly did he stop hating Gabe again? These questions—and more!—kept him up last night.

Leo's not one to renege on a promise, though, so he's here now, and he's channeling his anxious energy into his racket, slowly rotating it as he changes the overgrip. He likes it extra tacky, and he's going to need it more than ever today if he doesn't want the racket to fly out of his clammy hand in the middle of a point.

"Go get 'em, boys," Ollie says as he walks up with his gear, fresh off a press conference after his second-round match. "I tried to wear him out for you."

That's one thing they have going for them, at least. Earlier this afternoon, Ollie beat Juan Carlos Puentes, one of the Spanish players they'll be taking on in doubles. The players are given "suitable rest" between singles and doubles matches, but Leo can hope that Ollie's victory will still be weighing on Puentes's mind and body.

"That serve out wide," Ollie adds, eyes bulging. "Tabarnak. Stay ready for that."

"Thanks, Ol," Leo says.

"Yeah, thank you," Gabe says.

Ollie leans over to Gabe conspiratorially, and in a voice that isn't as quiet as he seems to think it is, says, "Take the overheads when you can. Leo sucks at those when he's nervous."

"You're really bad at whispering, you know that?" Leo says, and he throws one of his wristbands at Ollie.

"And you are really bad at overheads when you get nervous," Ollie says with a shrug, then walks away, bumping fists with a fellow Canadian player as he heads for the exit.

"I'm not actually that bad at overheads," Leo says to Gabe. "Really. If I miss, it's usually just because of the sun. Blue eyes are especially sensitive to the sun. That's all."

"Uh huh," Gabe says, failing to conceal a smile as he shuts his locker. "All right. So. Ready for this?"

"Yeah," Leo says, putting his freshly wrapped racket in his bag. He stands and meets Gabe's eyes. "Ready."

Leo is, in fact, not ready for this.

He's about to serve the opening point of their match against the Puentes brothers and Gabe is up at the net, signaling which serve Leo should go for first. Why didn't he realize he would be spending a large portion of this afternoon staring at Gabe's ass? The man is crouched down at the net. Bent over. Butt out. In tight black shorts. Flashing a middle finger quite literally between his cheeks. Yes, it's a signal to serve into the opponent's body, but my God. Leo was so concerned about the potential emotional ramifications of playing doubles with Gabe and not nearly concerned enough about the ass of it all. Hoo boy. They're playing on a side court in the shadow of Hard Rock Stadium. Hard. Rock. Rock. Hard. Okay, he needs to stay focused. Deep breath.

Leo follows Gabe's orders—why is *that* horning him up even more?—and hits a body serve. Juan Carlos returns it back to Leo, who hits it back crosscourt with even more pace on it. When Juan Carlos hits it back crosscourt again, Gabe is already shifting over to the middle of the net, where he intercepts the shot, smacking it hard. It bounces in and flies off the court and into the crowd.

"15–love," the ump announces.

Leo jogs up to Gabe, uncontrollably beaming. They give each other a low five.

"Nice!" Leo says.

They walk back to the baseline of the blue-and-teal court as a ball kid tosses Leo two new balls for his next serve. His face mere inches from Gabe's now, both of them with a hand covering their mouth, they whisper about their next move.

"Let's run it back, see what they do this time," Gabe whispers.

"Same play? Really?" Leo asks.

"Yeah, show them we have this down."

"Okay, cool. I like it."

Leo likes the play, but he mostly likes telling secrets with Gabe.

They bump fists before Gabe runs back up to the net and, for better or worse, reassumes his crouched position.

Again, Leo rockets a serve at his opponent. It's the mirror image of the previous point. Juan Carlos's brother, Roberto, sends a forehand crosscourt to Leo's backhand. Leo runs for it and hits a screaming one-hander back to him. Gabe is up at the net, in constant motion, waiting for his moment to pounce. After a few shots back and forth, Gabe finds his opening and volleys the ball at a hard angle, sending it sliding off the court.

"30–love," the ump says.

Leo and Gabe meet in the middle and low five each other again.

"Let's go," Gabe says.

With an ace from Leo in the next point, followed by an error from Roberto, they go on to secure their first game as an official doubles team.

As the match continues, Leo no longer cares whether Juan Carlos is tired from his match with Ollie. It doesn't even matter. Leo and Gabe are crushing them, anticipating nearly every shot, moving fluidly across their shared side. Something about the way Gabe says "Mine!" when he claims a shot for himself gets Leo's stomach twirling like his racket.

As they get in a groove, the match ends up lasting about a tenth of the time Leo spent worrying about it. After Gabe hits yet another smash for a winner, the two of them turn and look at each other, and for whatever reason, they both start laughing, when that smash officially clinches it: 6–2, 6–3, Chambers/Montoya. They run up to each other and instead of a low five, they move in closer and, suddenly unsure of what comes next, they morph into some kind of half-hug, half-chest bump? Sure.

"We did it," Leo says, almost shocked.

"We did it," Gabe says, grinning.

Afterward, during the on-court interview, the announcer asks them, "What made you two want to team up?"

"Well," Leo begins, "we've been trying to move past the, uh, incident at the US Open. And I think we realized how when we put our styles of play together, you get a pretty well-rounded game."

"Looks like we were right," Gabe adds.

The crowd starts to applaud again, and an oddly familiar whistle echoes in Leo's ear. He jerks his head to the right and spots Patrick in the stands, clapping and giving him an I-told-you-so grin. *"I thought you'd click, that's all."*

Leo shakes his head and smiles.

Over the course of the next week, Leo not only makes it to the quarterfinals again—his home crowd loving every minute of his newly energized game, free-flowing and assured—but he and Gabe also go on to win a couple more matches in doubles.

The way they complement each other on the court is undeniable, or, as Serving Looks has put it:

servinglooks My new favorite doubles team, Chambers/Montoya, absolutely ATE in their latest match. Color me obsessed with these two.

But what really gets Leo's heart pumping during the tournament is their conversation during changeovers. Like some kind of tennis speed-dating, sitting side by side during the ninety-second changeovers that take place after games 1, 3, and 5, they get into the habit of quizzing each other on their favorites and firsts.

"Favorite movie," Gabe says while retying one of his sneakers.

"Oh, *Casablanca*. Something else I watched with my grandma a lot. She always called me an 'old soul.'"

Leo now knows full well that the Venn diagram of adults who were considered old souls and adults who are gay is a circle. He looks down and can see Gabe smiling as he loops his laces.

"Favorite food," Leo says.

"Ají de gallina," Gabe says. "Especially my mom's. It's my comfort food. It's like this creamy chicken stew. All right, um, favorite walk-on song?"

"'Don't Stop Me Now' by Queen. Favorite book?"

"You know I love my romance novels, but my favorite book is this queer YA story, *Aristotle and Dante Discover the Secrets of the Universe*."

Leo finishes sipping his electrolytes. "Sounds really cool. I'll have to pick it up."

"Okay. First kiss," Gabe says slyly.

"Oh, God. This girl at my middle school, Abby Jennings. It sucked. We both had braces. All I tasted was metal."

Gabe puts a hand over his mouth so he doesn't spit out his water. "Hot," he says after successfully swallowing.

"Okay, well, what about yours?" Leo asks, fiddling with the strings on his racket.

"Wes Altman. When we were sixteen."

"Shut the fuck up," Leo says, whipping his head around. "At BP?"

"Yup, for, like, two seconds in the locker room," Gabe says. "Since he didn't end up going pro, I don't mind telling you.

What you might *not* know is that he now runs this little gay boutique hotel in Key West. Go figure."

"I had no idea," Leo says. "Makes you wonder how many other gay players there are."

"It does," Gabe says, and takes another swig of water.

"Time," the ump calls.

Inside the players' dining hall, following Leo's workout, post-match press conference, cool-down—the works—after his tight loss in the quarters, he sits down to have dinner with his dad. The conversation starts hesitantly, mostly about how there's a new chef at the tournament this year and the cooking has gone up a notch, but then it changes.

"I wanted to say thank you, by the way," Johnny says. "Dedicating your Tie Break Tens win to the ASA. That was really special, Leo. I should've said something sooner. Thank you."

But Leo's not surprised his dad waited until after the tournament to say something. It was all business the past week. No place for emotion in the midst of a deep run. Johnny simply acted like the gap in his time on tour never happened, slipped right back into his place as the uncompromising head coach. That's his way.

"It was nothing," Leo says. "I was happy to do it. Listen, Dad, what I said after the podcast recording, I—"

Johnny waves him off. "You don't have to apologize. We both said some stuff. Let's just move on from it, okay?"

Just then, Brian walks up and joins them at the table.

"Ah, the gang's all here," Johnny says, reaching to put a hand on both Leo's and Brian's arms, shaking them. "This was a solid way to kick off spring. Back-to-back quarterfinals. Some great momentum."

"Hell yeah," Brian says. "You're killin' it out there, LC."

Leo's lips curl into a bashful smile.

"You have been," Johnny says. "Your double faults are way down. You're looking good. And you've been *killing it* too, Brian."

"Dad, please don't say 'killing it,' you're making Brian uncomfortable."

"Well, he is! Murdering it!" Johnny says. "I know I've texted you over and over, Brian, but I can't thank you enough for taking the lead these past few months. You've made things easy for me to come back for the rest of the season."

"You're coming back?" Leo asks, eyes widening. He isn't sure if he's excited or nervous or both.

Johnny gives a drumroll on the table with his fingers, then stops when he announces, "I am! My docs have given the all-clear. I'll pull back if I need to, but I'm confident. Madrid, here we come!"

"Gotta give a hell yeah to that, too!" Brian says. "That's awesome. It'll be great to have you back on the team, Johnny."

"Yeah," Leo says, sounding more conflicted than he would've liked. He glances at Brian, who's looking at him curiously. Leo shifts his attention back. "That's amazing, Dad."

"Now, I don't want to get ahead of ourselves, but the US Open is just five months away," Johnny says, getting ahead of himself. "Let's keep our heads down and focus as we move into the clay swing. Keep that rank climbing. No distractions. I know you like playing mixed with Tess here and there. And I'm really glad you're on better terms with Gabe now. But we've got to stick to singles from here on out if this is going to be your year in New York."

Nibbling at the inside of his cheek, Leo tries to digest his dad's plan.

"No distractions, okay?" Johnny says.

Leo sees a familiar fire in his dad's eyes. He's glad it's returned, that he still has a chance to win the US Open before his dad retires. It'll just take some readjusting with his dad back on the team. But he can keep everybody happy. He can.

"Right," Leo says hesitantly. "Okay."

CHAPTER THIRTEEN

"It's wild to see it from behind," Leo says. He's not talking about Gabe's ass, but the image certainly does cross his mind. "His drop shot, it's—it's like poetry or something."

"His drop shot," Tess deadpans, and then pauses, finding her way through this sentence, "is like poetry."

"Whatever, you know what I mean," Leo says. "His hands are so soft. At the net, I mean. It really is incredible when you see it from a new perspective, that's all. Playing doubles with him, watching him up at the net, it—I don't know. It made me appreciate his game more."

They are pulling down dishes from Leo's kitchen cabinets to put out snacks. It's here. Game night. Usually it's just for him, Tess, and Ollie—maybe one other friend or the current sexual partner of the latter two will tag along—but tonight, Liv is joining and Gabe is coming with his friend Billie. Gabe. In Leo's condo. The matrix is surely broken. Regardless, Leo did spend most of the day scrubbing every inch of the place from baseboard to curtain rod.

When he finished cleaning, he baked chocolate chip banana bread. Then, he cleaned himself up. He chose a rust and white-striped bowling-style shirt, kept unbuttoned to show his white tank underneath, while Tess is wearing a denim shirt-dress.

"I know what you mean," she says. "The man is spectacular at the net. I'm just shocked to finally hear it from you. For the past decade, all you've done is talk about how overrated he is, how conceited he is, how arrogant he is, how—"

"Okay, okay. Yeah. I know. Well. I've gotten to know him a little better."

"I'm not saying I told you so," Tess says, reaching for another plate.

"Told me what, exactly?"

"That you two were destined to become besties."

"I wouldn't go *that* far."

"Leo, he's coming to game night. Your most precious evening of the year."

"*You* invited him!"

"And *you* set up a spritz bar!" Tess shouts, extending her arm toward the kitchen island, where he has, indeed, set up a spritz bar. Wine glasses in two neat rows of three, orange slices fanned out on a small wooden cutting board, a couple bottles of Aperol, and prosecco on ice.

"So?"

"So, you've never done this for me and Ol," Tess says. "We have snacks, sure. Wine, absolutely. But this? I'm just saying, you clearly want to impress him. Your new bestie. Gabe Montoya."

"I'm just mixing it up, okay? We have a few extra people coming tonight," Leo says. "That opens up the variety of games we can play, too. And that's also why I made tonight a potluck. I'm dying to get into the lumpia."

Leo nods over to the plate Tess brought, piled high with crispy Filipino egg rolls and small bowls of sweet and sour sauce.

"Nice. Nice transition," Tess says as Leo smiles innocently.

"Hey, you," Gabe says as Leo opens the door. "This is my friend Billie."

At least, that's what Leo assumes he said. Considering Gabe is wearing a sage-green knit polo buttoned low enough to show off his gold chain resting at the edges of his pecs, he could've told Leo they were there to kill him and he wouldn't have registered it.

Meanwhile, Billie herself is striking. A Black woman just a bit shorter than Leo, her braided hair is pulled back in a thick ponytail. She's in a butter-yellow dress with an empire waist and ruffled shoulders.

"It's so great to finally meet you," Billie says brightly. She gives his hand a firm shake. "I've been hearing about you for years now."

"Really? And you still came?" Leo asks, only half kidding.

"Gabe told me you were funny," she says, a sly twinkle in her eye.

As the two of them enter Leo's condo, she turns to Gabe, then back to Leo. "And *I* told Gabe that I was definitely overdressed."

"No, no, you're gorgeous," Tess says from behind Leo, whose ears have rosied. "I mean, you look gorgeous. I love that dress. Hi, I'm Tess. Sorry, that rhymed."

"Nice to meet you," Billie says with a chuckle, then says hello to Ollie and his plus-one, Liv. "Thanks for having me. All Gabe told me was that tonight was special, so here I am, dressed for the Oscars."

"Billie and I grew up together," Gabe tells them. "We hang out whenever I make it back to Miami."

"Yes, I just sit by the phone, waiting for his call," Billie says, gazing out the floor-to-ceiling windows to her left, speaking in a transatlantic accent. "When will my husband return from war?"

She already has the group laughing.

"But yeah, I've known Gabe forever," she continues. "Way before his glow-up."

"Okay, I hope that means photos are imminent," Liv says.

"Oh, you know I came prepared," Billie says. "Let me just set this food down somewhere first."

"Thank you so much," Leo says, grabbing the dish from her. "What'd you bring? Besides prepubescent photos for blackmail."

"Some of my favorite food from this takeout spot in Little Haiti," Billie says. "Best in the city. I had to treat y'all."

Leo's mouth begins to water. For the food. Not Gabe. Just to be clear.

"Here's us at a school dance, and here's us in Gabe's bedroom taking magazine quizzes, and here's us at the Pizza Hut where Gabe came out to me," Billie says, scrolling through a parade of awkward middle school photos on her Facebook for the group to see, Gabe's face broken out and his hair unkempt. "And I shouldn't have been surprised when he told me, considering the fact that, if you look closer at that photo of us in his room, he has a life-size cutout of Legolas. That was sus. Look how big it is, right next to his bed."

"I loved *Lord of the Rings*! Sue me!" Gabe yells.

During a game of Rummikub, the night's finale after several rounds of Uno, Codenames, and Monopoly—not to mention several rounds of embarrassing old Facebook photos—the group is chatting playfully, Billie and Liv next to each other, giggling about something. Leo listens in and hears Billie, seemingly caught up in the moment, say to Liv, "I have to ask. What made you want to be with Sascha?"

"Billie," Gabe says. He clearly caught the question, too, and gives Billie a look like, *What the fuck?*

"That is . . . a fair question," Liv says, fidgeting with the tiles in front of her on the table. "I've thought about it a lot over the past couple years. I was avoiding a lot of pain in my life back then. And I saw that in him, too. I think, in a way, we both wanted to disappear into each other. I ignored so much of the bad about him because he was the distraction I needed at the time."

Billie offers her a sympathetic smile. "Sorry, I shouldn't have pried."

"No, it's okay," Liv says, then gives her a coy look. "We've all got that one ex, right?"

"Cheers to that," Tess says, exasperated, shaking her head while raising her glass.

"And Gabe," Liv says, her eyes more serious now. "The things that he's been saying, you know, about you. There's no excuse for that."

Gabe gives her a little nod. "Thanks," he says.

The group gets back to playing, and after another round of Rummikub, Gabe excuses himself to the bathroom. When he doesn't return after nearly ten minutes, Leo decides to check on him. As he walks down the hallway, passing by his bedroom, he glimpses Gabe out of the corner of his eye, holding one of the framed photos he keeps out on his dresser. He steps backward and moves into the doorway, waiting a moment before speaking.

"That was one of our first practices together," Leo tells him. He can see which frame Gabe has picked up and knows it's the photo he posted last fall, the one of him and his dad posing together on a court, little Leo's tongue out.

"Shit, sorry," Gabe says. "I went to the bathroom and then wandered in here. I guess I just had to see where the magic happens."

"Ha, ha," Leo says.

"I love this picture," Gabe says, looking back at the photo. "You looked so much like your dad, even as a kid."

"And everybody made sure to tell me," Leo says, making his way over to the dresser.

Gabe is still looking at the photo intently. He puts it down and picks up a wrinkled piece of looseleaf paper next to the frame that says "Hold your own" in black Sharpie. "What's this?"

"Oh, I used to keep that in my bag. My dad always said that to me when I wasn't feeling good about my game or just wasn't believing in myself."

Gabe smiles, then returns his gaze to the paper. "I don't think I've ever known anybody with MS," he says. "Christ, sorry. Ignore me."

"No, no, it's cool," Leo says, leaning back on the acorn-colored dresser. "I never did either growing up, besides my dad, obviously."

"That must've been hard," Gabe says.

"Yeah, it could be lonely," Leo says. "I would sometimes wish I had a dad like the other kids did. I would wish for him to get better, for him to change. So things could be easier. But as I got older, I guess I just started to think, fuck it, the world should change for him, not the other way around."

When Leo works up the nerve to look at Gabe, he finds tender eyes.

"You know, what you wrote, when you posted this photo," Gabe says, "about how people need to be more patient with players, because they don't always know everything that's going on behind the scenes—it really hit home for me. I already couldn't stop thinking about coming out back then, and seeing your post, it, well, definitely gave me a boost. Thought you should know."

Leo smiles at him, remembering the heart emoji.

Gabe inhales sharply. "All right, well, I don't know about you, but I need a new drink."

They head into the kitchen, and as Gabe begins to loosen the cork in a new bottle of prosecco, he nods to the spritz bar. "Nice touch, by the way."

As Leo walks up to him, champagne flutes in hand and face flushing, the cork pops and an abrupt rush of prosecco sprays onto his shirt.

"What was that about *me* loving to get *you* wet, again?" Leo asks, cocking his head and licking the bubbles off his lips. He sets down the flutes.

"Oh my God," Gabe says, rushing to grab the blue-and-white dishtowel from the oven handle. "Let me help."

He steps up to Leo and begins dabbing his shirt. Leo is looking down at Gabe's hand patting his chest, and he can only hope that Gabe doesn't feel how hard his heart is pounding. When Leo lifts his head, he finds Gabe staring directly at him.

"We have to stop meeting like this," Leo says, trying, as always, to cut the tension.

Gabe isn't dabbing Leo's shirt anymore. They're both just standing still, Leo blinking quickly, Gabe breathing slowly.

"I don't want to stop," Gabe says.

Cautiously, Gabe starts to lean in.

Unable to fight Gabe's magnetic pull, Leo leans in, too.

Gabe leans in farther.

Like the final moment before a match begins, the whole world seems to fall away.

No grudges, no misconceptions, no animosity, no space between them now.

Only fondness.

They kiss.

Gabe cups Leo's head in his hands, pulling him deeper into the kiss, like he wants to make sure he gets this right. Their mouths move faster and faster, as if they can't absorb each other quickly enough. Leo loses himself in the moment, lets it swallow him whole. Gabe's mouth is warm and his tongue tastes like orange, pear, and rhubarb. Leo didn't even know he could pinpoint the taste of rhubarb. As he feels Gabe softly suck on his lower lip, Leo opens his eyes, just briefly, to reassure himself that this is really happening.

And it is.

He really is in the midst of an effervescent first kiss with Gabe. That magnetic pull may have been there the entire time, he realizes. It feels like coming home—something he doesn't feel often throughout the year, something he didn't even know he could feel with Gabe, having spent so many years in the grip of his intense grudge against him. For the first time, he lets the thought linger.

There's a crash in the living room, and they pull apart.

"Tabarnak!"

Leo, pretending his eyes had only opened just then, at the sound of the crash, looks at Gabe, and before either of them has a moment to process, they scurry into the other room.

"I am so sorry, Leo," Ollie says, slurring his words a little and blotting the Rack-O cards on the table, which are sticky with prosecco from the glass he just knocked across the table. "I got a little excited when I found the card I needed."

"That's—that's okay," Leo says, his head buzzing.

"We moved on to Rack-O since y'all were gone so long," Billie says, and the sly twinkle has returned to her eye.

As Leo gathers the cards, brushes the small shards of glass into a trash can, carries dishes into the kitchen, he glances at Gabe and it sends a jolt of anxiety coursing through his limbs. He thinks about the kiss and his heart starts to race. Except, it's not racing in passion now but in panic. An endless parade of thoughts marches through his mind.

What happens now?

What does this mean for them?

Will he have to tell everyone? Tell his dad?

Could he even win a match, let alone the US Open, if he had to come out?

Can he handle this and his dad's return to tour all at once?

The only voice he can hear in his head is reminding him, over and over: *No distractions.*

It sounds an awful lot like this dad. He can't seem to silence it.

Once the table's tidied, Tess pats Ollie's arm and says, "Well, that might be our cue. Our sweet prince could probably use some beauty sleep. Are you cool if we head out, Leo?"

Ollie makes a groaning sound in response.

"Yeah," Leo says, blinking furiously to focus himself. "It's getting late, anyway. But this was so great. Thank you all for everything."

When he pulls out of his hug with Tess, Leo hears Gabe ask, "Do you want me to stay behind? Help you clean up some more?"

No distractions.

No distractions.

No distractions.

Leo knows what he's asking, but he can only muster a response that, somewhere deep inside his alcohol-soaked brain, he knows is sabotage, but he says it anyway.

"No, no, you should go, too. But it was good to see you."

A line forms between Gabe's eyebrows as his expression grows confused. Then, it goes slack again. "Got it," he says flatly. "It was good to see you, too."

Leo tells Billie again how nice it was to meet her, and though she says the same, the twinkle is gone now.

Once his guests have filed out, Leo meanders around his condo, switching off each of the lamps. He walks into the kitchen, sees the remaining mess—dishes in the sink, glasses on the island, empty chip bags crumpled. He turns, makes his way down the hall, and crawls into bed.

Grand Slam: Roland-Garros
Surface: Clay
Where: Paris, France
When: May 26–June 10, 2024

CHAPTER FOURTEEN

The next two months on tour are not kind to Leo. Madrid, Monte Carlo, Rome—they're all an absolute bust. A series of losses that do absolutely nothing for his ranking. And a series of European pigeons that all seem to want to use his head for target practice. Let it be known that getting shit on by a bird is, evidently, not good luck.

It's not lost on Leo that he rejected Gabe in order to heed his dad's advice and avoid distraction—and now that very rejection is keeping him deeply distracted the entirety of the clay swing. It's leaving both him and his dad disappointed, to say the least. More often than not, Leo's awkward movement on the clay resembles a baby giraffe attempting its first steps. He slides to the left, slides to the right, crisscrosses (everybody, clap your hands!), and then finds himself tripping over his own feet or sending his shots sailing far too long. With each motion, he tries to zero in on the ball, but as it comes flying toward him, his mind flashes the image of Gabe leaning in to kiss him. That glorious first kiss blurs his field of vision at every tournament. Still playing a limited season, Gabe doesn't enter most of these events, and when he does, he maintains a strict distance from Leo, avoiding his glances or half waves in the locker room. Exiting tournaments in the early rounds, Leo is never in any location for a long stretch of time either, forced to fly to his next destination to immediately continue training.

Even though Gabe is mostly out of sight, he is most definitely *not* out of mind. Leo thinks about him all day, every day. He thinks about their kiss and what he would give to slip back into that moment. But more than that, he thinks about Indian Wells and what Gabe said in his hotel room about their time at BP: "I thought you didn't want . . . me." To make Gabe feel unwanted again is what makes Leo ache the most. He's opened that old wound for Gabe, a payback he never intended.

Even if he can't pick up where they left off in his kitchen, even if he's lost his chance with Gabe, he knows he still needs to repair the damage as best he can. After everything they've shared with each other, he owes Gabe that much.

Fortunately, the ranking points Leo earned earlier this season, especially from those quarterfinals in Indian Wells and Miami, are keeping him at a healthy 27, which allows him to be seeded at Roland-Garros.

Playing at a Slam certainly pushes him to bring his best, but he isn't quite sure how he manages to find his way into the third round of this one after that extremely mediocre clay season. Maybe he feels comfortable with his section of the draw. Maybe he's fed up with all his lousy results as of late. Maybe—and, okay, most likely—it's that Gabe is still alive in the draw, too, and Leo doesn't want to part ways with him yet. He's well aware that they might not have much more time during this Slam. Either one of them could easily be knocked out in the next round, and then it's *au revoir, Paris*. The grass swing comes next, and Leo has no idea which tournaments Gabe will be playing. He knows he has to seize this opportunity while they're both still here.

"To be frank, I imagine this year's clay swing didn't go the way you hoped, did it?" one of the reporters at the press conference after Leo's third-round win asks.

"No, it definitely didn't," Leo says, his shoulders rounded as he leans toward the mic on the table in front of him. He wears an oversized heather-gray Nike crewneck and his hair is still a bit damp from his shower, a single light-brown lock falling onto his forehead. "I'm certainly not a clay specialist, but I wasn't happy with my string of losses. I had some double faults creeping back in, too."

"You had a lot of momentum heading into the clay swing," another reporter adds. "Back-to-back quarterfinals. But then you went on a losing streak. Was there something other than the change in surface that affected your game?"

"No, not really," Leo says, his leg bouncing under the table. "It was an adjustment bringing my dad back onto the team, but we're all really glad to have him with us again."

"Well, you seem to be back on track now," the reporter continues. "You're into the round of sixteen here at Roland-Garros. What's been different for you here?"

"I guess I don't want to leave Paris yet," Leo says with a slight smile, his posture straightening. "But really, I always love playing the French Open. The city, the fans, the organizers. It's just a blast. It always makes me want to rise to the occasion, so I'm glad I've finally been able to do that after the past couple months."

"How is your dad doing now that he's back as head coach, Leo?" a reporter interjects.

"He's doing fine, just fine, thanks. We're so lucky that he's had such a successful recovery. He's really gotten back into the rhythm of things."

Of course, by that he means Johnny has gotten back into coaching Leo to play the same, one-dimensional game on court and the same, one-dimensional schedule off court. Johnny likes to stick with what he knows, what's brought Leo success in the past, even if it's clearer than ever that this strategy is weakening and Leo is desperate to evolve.

"You were practicing with Gabe Montoya earlier this year and even won some doubles matches together in Miami. But from what I can tell, you haven't been teaming up much since. Can you tell us what happened there?"

"There isn't much to tell," Leo says, squirming in his seat. "We enjoyed playing together. Our games meshed well. Our schedules just haven't, um, aligned this spring."

Though many of the reporters at this press conference are French, the one asking about Gabe is American. The thirty-something man is white with a fade haircut and wears charcoal chinos and a white button-down with a navy-blue vest over it. Leo knows they're in Paris right now, but looking at this man's outfit, he could swear he's back in New York, in the Financial District. And, now that he's looking closer, he actually recognizes this guy.

"Wait, aren't you from that blog, *The Sportsman*?" Leo asks, leaning in, his elbows on the table now. As the reporter nods, Leo continues, "Didn't *Sportsman* publish something last month about how coming out might not have been the right move for Gabe because his game has suffered ever since? That was you, wasn't it?"

The reporter is squirming in his own seat now. "Uh, yeah, that was me."

"Maybe it's not my place, but—" Leo begins. "Actually, whatever. The article basically implied that coming out wasn't good for his game and so maybe he shouldn't have. As if his game could ever possibly be more important than his mental health or just his life in general. Don't you think it's natural that he'd be feeling more pressure now? And that would affect his game for a little while? And why not focus on the fact that even if his own game isn't where it was before, his coming out is still amazing for him and for tennis overall?"

"Well, uh," the reporter starts, "I just think that—"

"I guess that wasn't really a question. I just wanted to point that out, so you have that context for next time," Leo says, his leg bouncing again. "Okay, thank you all for your time. I'll see you again in a couple days."

He gets up from the table and exits the conference room, exhaling slowly and shakily.

When Leo sees the reporters again a couple days later, it's after a loss. He took his fourth-round match to four sets, but he couldn't quite pull it out in the end. He was already distracted by the Gabe of it all, and then he found himself playing in front of Jonathan Bailey and Andrew Scott, both of whom watched from behind massive sunglasses in the front row. Serving Looks posted an extensive carousel of photos.

> **servinglooks** Leo, Andrew, AND Jonathan all in the building? A ménage à trois of the highest order. Pardon my literal French, but OUI OUI. Jonathan bringing the eleganza, per usual, in Loewe. Would love to see Leo collab with them next.

If Loewe could send Leo some clothes from their spring line, along with a detailed plan on how to win Gabe back before it's too late, that would be excellent.

With his run at the French Open behind him, Leo finds himself free to peruse an art gallery tonight. He can't say he *understands* the Mark Rothko painting hung before him, but it does remind him of the sweeps and swirls his sneakers have made on the red clay courts this past week in Paris. He's sitting on a white metal bench, feeling pulled into Rothko's *No. 9 / No. 5 / No. 18*—a blood-red block of color at the top, a muted-yellow stripe through the center, and a maroon block of color at the bottom. The rectangular piece, one of the abstract artist's famed color-field paintings of the 1950s, displays his signature broad, cloudy strokes across the canvas. Its title also reminds Leo of the fluctuation of his ranking over the years.

He's traded his tennis kit for a tuxedo this evening, as he's attending the closing of a Rothko retrospective hosted by the Fondation Louis Vuitton, a contemporary art museum that looks like a glass Sydney Opera House. A former brand ambassador for the French luxury giant, Leo happily accepted the foundation's invitation. He wanted to snap out of his tennis mindset even for a couple hours, but now, staring at this painting, he feels as if he's staring down at the baseline of a clay court before he serves. The court's red dirt shows his own broad strokes throughout the match, mapping each point with the marks of where he had to slide and glide to reach the ball in time. After each set, the messy court is smoothed over with a gentle raking and hosed down to add moisture. The lines are then carefully restored, creating a fresh slate for play to begin again, a process that never ceases to soothe him. A clay court is an art form all its own.

He's far from soothed, though, sitting on this bench, overthinking how to approach Gabe after weeks of suffering in silence. With Gabe having lost his round of sixteen match, too, Leo can safely assume he'll be leaving in Paris in a couple days. He's running out of time. What would he say to him? What would he expect Gabe to say back? What would it mean if they were together? What would that even look like? Is he prepared for that? Did he tie his bowtie correctly tonight?

While he would love to be pondering this whole situation in grander terms right now—given the sublime painting in front of him, the sophisticated setting of the exhibition he's attending—he simply cannot. So, here he is, in a gallery surrounded by a who's who of Paris, thinking, *This sucks balls*.

Among the who's who is Louis Vuitton's newest brand ambassador, Leo's successor: a hunky nineteen-year-old Greek tennis player who seems to have been crafted by the gods themselves in the image of Adonis. He's being shuffled around the event, shown off to every guest by the foundation's director. As if it weren't already abundantly clear that Leo has been replaced by an actual child, the small patches of acne on both of this kid's cheeks only serve to prove the point further. He's still a teenager! With zits! He probably uses Neutrogena acne wash!

Suddenly, Leo feels like he's giving AARP, too. Thank God there's champagne here.

"Got you another glass," Sheryl says, returning from the restroom and taking a seat beside Leo on the bench. His date for the evening, she's in a midnight-blue mesh gown.

"I probably shouldn't," Leo says.

"Oh, go for it," she says, handing him the flute. "You had a great week. And Julianne Moore just complimented my dress in the restroom. I need to toast to that."

"Okay, I'll toast to that," Leo says. "You do look beautiful, Mom."

"Thanks for bringing me tonight, Leonardo."

"Of course. Thanks for coming to watch me play."

When Leo turns back toward the painting, still feeling sulky, he can feel his mom's eyes lingering on him. They sit quietly for a moment.

"Your art looked like this as a kid," she says, studying the piece now.

"My art looked like Rothko?" he asks, mockingly.

"They're just big messes of color," she says.

"Mom, they will throw you out of here if you don't lower your voice," Leo says, laughing a little.

"Okay, well you know what I mean, honey. You colored all over the page back then, kind of like these. You didn't care if you colored outside the lines. You'd hand me your big mess of color, smiling ear to ear, so proud of yourself."

Leo looks at her warmly, and she considers the painting again.

"I haven't seen you smile like that in a long time," she says. "I haven't seen you that proud of yourself in a long time."

He looks at her inquisitively.

"But there it was, that smile. Earlier this year. You looked like a kid again, at least from what I could see in photos on Instagram or watching your matches. Your dad would be coaching from the couch, shouting his advice at the screen. But I was so focused on that smile. And seeing it in person in Miami? Especially in your doubles matches? That was him. That was my Leo."

"Mom, what do you—"

"I haven't seen you like that much this spring, or here in Paris," she continues. "And I don't know everything that goes on in that head of yours anymore. I know that. But I haven't seen you practicing or playing with Gabe anymore. You haven't mentioned him when you call me anymore, either."

Leo is staring at her intently now.

"I was so happy that you two were getting along after what happened at your last match against each other. I'm sure he's appreciated having you close this year, too. It made me so proud to know you were stepping up and being there for him when I bet a lot of people have kept their distance," she says, leaning in closer. "I could be way off the mark here, but if I'm not, I hope you don't lose touch with him. I can tell he's special to you. Am I way off the mark?"

He shakes his head no, and she gives him a knowing smile. He's kept this part of himself locked away so tight for so long, and as his mom allows him to finally open it, the overwhelming relief fills his eyes with tears.

"You don't have to stay inside the lines all the time, honey," she says, putting a hand on his knee. "I know that's your job in this sport. But if he makes you happy, if he brings out that version of you I remember from when you were younger, you should keep him close."

It's surreal for Leo, having this conversation with his mom, realizing that maybe she's known for longer than he thought. But he doesn't let his surprise keep him from seizing the moment, an opportunity to let her in further, to seek her advice. "Mom, I think I really hurt him."

"Well," she says calmly, "if he's hurting, it's because he cares about you, too. And if he cares about you, I think he'll hear what you have to say. You'll do the right thing. I know you will."

Leo bites the inside of his lower lip. "You don't," he starts, finding the words, "care that he makes me happy?"

"Leo, that's all I've ever wanted for you. I should have told you that. I should have made sure you knew that," she says, her eyes filling up, too. She grabs his hand, squeezing it tight. "I think you've probably heard enough motherly wisdom now, but let me just say one more thing before we get back to the party."

She takes a sip of her champagne.

"Your dad and I were just engaged when he was diagnosed. A lot of people, my own mother included, weren't sure I should go through with marrying him. They weren't afraid to tell me that, either. I know they thought they were looking out for me. They didn't want me to struggle, caring for him, watching him get worse. But a lot of people can be wrong, Leonardo. Whatever happens with you two, or with someone else down the line, don't give up on a person just because your relationship isn't what other people think it should be," she says, then gives him a conspiratorial look. "Fuck 'em."

Leo's staring at her, expressionless, in awe. He throws his arms around her.

After a moment, she pulls away, saying, "Now, let's take a walk around the room and see if any other celebrities compliment my dress."

She links his arm, pulling him up off the bench.

CHAPTER FIFTEEN

As Leo walks through the lobby of the posh hotel he's staying at in Paris, lost in thought on his way to the elevator bank, he stops in his tracks when he sees the woman coming toward him.

"Billie?"

"Oh, hi, Leo," she says coolly, looking up from her phone.

"I didn't expect to run into you," Leo says. "Are you here for the French Open?"

She grins. "You don't think twice when Gabe extends an invite to Paris."

Leo's heart leaps. "Wait, is he staying *here*?"

"I'm . . . not sure if I should say. And I'm just on my way out. But it was nice bumping into you, Leo," she says.

After they part, Leo slinks away, feeling defeated, but then he notices that her heels have suddenly stopped clacking on the marble floor. He turns around and sees her looking at him.

"Room 331," she says, sighing. As she turns for the exit, she looks him up and down and adds, "You never saw me."

Standing outside Gabe's room, Leo simply stares at the room number, waiting for his hand to raise and knock on the door. *Am I doing it?* he thinks.

He is not.

He maybe should have gone back to his room and prepared for how this confrontation would go, but instead he immediately got on the elevator after his run-in with Billie, pressed the button for the third floor, and found himself here. He was ecstatic that the universe handed him this opportunity. He couldn't wait another moment. They're staying at the same hotel? How did he not know that Gabe was right under his nose this whole time?

When Leo finally moves to knock, Gabe opens the door first.

"Mierda," Gabe shouts, stepping back in surprise. "Leo, what the hell?"

"Sorry, sorry," Leo says, cringing. "I've only been standing here for a few minutes."

"That's not a short time to be standing outside someone's door," Gabe says, deadpan.

"Yeah, I just heard how that sounded," Leo says and laughs a little, hoping to cut the tension. It doesn't work.

"Can I help you with something?" Gabe asks flatly. "I need to catch up with Billie."

"Billie's here?" Leo asks, his voice going up one octave too many, a terrible actor.

Gabe looks at him, unimpressed. "I think you know that."

"No, no, I, um, got your room number from the front desk," he says, doubling down.

"Uh huh." Gabe crosses his arms.

"Can we talk?" Leo asks cautiously.

Gabe sighs and looks down at the floor. "Leo, I don't know, I—"

"Please," Leo adds, his eyes pleading.

After an excruciating few seconds, Gabe gestures for him to come in.

"Wow," Leo says as he steps inside. "Your view is way better than mine."

Through the French doors, which lead out to a small balcony glistening in the gentle afternoon light, he can see the Arc de Triomphe in the distance, Paris stretching out in every direction around it. When he glances toward the bed, he notices what looks like a romance novel on Gabe's nightstand, alongside a pair of glasses and an empty mug with the string of a tea bag hanging over the side.

"Congrats on the round of sixteen," Leo says. "That must've felt great, to get those match wins. I knew you'd be back at it soon."

"Thanks," Gabe says. "Did you just want to talk tennis or—"

"I miss you," Leo says abruptly.

Gabe, who has the audacity to be wearing a black T-shirt with the sleeves cuffed, looks immediately disarmed.

"I know I hurt you, and I know I should've apologized sooner," Leo continues. "But I'm really sorry. I'm sorry that I asked you to leave that night at my place. That was a mistake. I freaked out because, well, I don't know about you, but I did not see this coming. You know, with us. After all this time. My dad had also just told me he was coming back on tour and he seemed so happy, and he told me that if I want to have a shot at the US Open, I can't have any distractions. It got in my head, and I panicked."

"Leo—"

"Wait, just let me finish. I've had a lot of time to think over the past couple months. You're not a distraction, Gabe. Not to me. Not to any player. Not to tennis. It was wrong of me to push you away. Getting closer to you has been the best part of my year. You've made me feel happier and more at home on the court and with myself than I have in a while. Maybe you're back to hating me again, but I needed to make sure I told you that."

Leo might not have taken a breath during his entire monologue. He inhales deeply, and then lets it go. He can't read Gabe's face. He's just standing there, arms crossed, staring at Leo.

"I don't hate you," Gabe finally says. "You suck, Leo, but I don't hate you. I was hurt after that night. I figured you were caught off guard. I was too. I never expected to be making out with Leo Chambers, in his kitchen, at a fucking game night. But after all those talks we had . . . I don't know. I just thought, *Well, he must've satisfied some curiosity, and then realized he wasn't interested anymore.* I felt rejected. And stupid. Familiar feelings, you know?"

"I know," Leo says. "I hate that I made you feel that way. I'm really sorry."

"I appreciate it," Gabe says, uncrossing his arms and putting his hands in his pockets.

"For what it's worth," Leo says, "you weren't just some curiosity. I understand if maybe the moment's passed now. But if you're willing to give me a chance, I hope we can at least . . . reinstate the truce?"

Gabe studies him for a moment. "That could be arranged."

Leo smiles, still feeling cautious. "Okay, well, I don't want to make you any later for Billie. And I should get going, too. But thank you for hearing me out."

"I'm glad you came by," Gabe says.

As Leo approaches the door, he feels compelled to ask. "Did you know? About me?"

"What?" Gabe asks, smiling slightly. "That you're into guys?"

"Yeah, that I'm gay," Leo says, and as these words spill out, he realizes it's the first time he's allowed someone in his life to hear them. He also realizes that it never even crossed his mind until now that Gabe could have easily told people about their kiss, that he could have easily outed Leo at some point over the last two months. But he doesn't need to ask whether Gabe has told anyone, other than Billie, of course. He already knows the answer.

"Yeah, I had been wondering," Gabe says, shrugging. Then he raises an eyebrow. "But the moment you told me you were into *The Golden Girls*? I stopped."

"Hm, yeah, that wasn't . . . *not* code," Leo says. He opens the door and as he steps out, he turns. "Hey, I know we, like, just reinstated the truce two seconds ago, but if you and Billie are free tonight, Tess has some big thing planned since it's our last night in Paris. She's calling me, her, and Ollie the 'Unsweet 16' since we all lost in the fourth round. But you're in that club, too, so if you feel like joining, you're more than welcome."

"I'll think about it, see how Billie's feeling," Gabe says, nodding. "Thanks, Leo."

On his way to the elevators, Leo has yet another run-in.

"Jesse?"

"Leo!"

"What, is *everyone* staying here this year?" Leo says.

"Who else is staying here?" Jesse asks.

"Oh, um," Leo stumbles, unsure if he should mention that he's coming from Gabe's room. "I'm just heading to see my friend Tess right now. She's a few floors up."

"Ah, nice," Jesse says. "She's having quite the season."

"Yeah, she's been smashing it all year," Leo says. "You should really have her on the podcast sometime."

"Good idea," Jesse says with a smile. "I was at your fourth-round match, by the way. I know that was probably a tough loss, but damn, the fans were getting their life."

"I'm glad," Leo says with a laugh, "because I was fighting for mine by the end."

"Well, it was fun to watch," Jesse says, big brown eyes sparkling. "Speaking of fun to watch, no doubles for you anymore? You and Gabe really had the crowd going back in Miami, just saying."

"Yeah, I, um, just want to focus on singles for now. Trying to build up some momentum heading into the summer," Leo says.

"Mmm, yeah. Makes sense."

Though, something tells Leo it doesn't. The conversation stalls.

"Well, I gotta go talk to Tess, but it was great bumping into you," Leo says, stretching for a tone of normalcy again. "And thanks for watching my match."

"Anytime," Jesse says, a lilt in his voice. "It was good to see you, Leo."

Visiting what feels like every guest at the hotel, Leo journeys on, feeling uplifted by his conversation with Gabe, and finds himself outside Tess's door next. He knocks, and before she can even utter a word to greet him, he spits out, "I have feelings for Gabe."

She slams the door in his face.

Leo is briefly horrified—until he hears her scream on the other side at an octave he's never heard from her before.

She reopens the door. "Sorry, I didn't want security called on us. Oh my God. Get in here."

Her hair wrapped up in a towel, her white plush robe flowing behind her, Tess whisks Leo over to the edge of the bed and sits down with him.

"My angel, first of all, I just want to say, I'm here for you, I'm here for this, and I'm really grateful you want to share this with me."

"How are you so perfect?" Leo says through a laugh.

"Back atcha. Now, dish."

"Okay, well, the Spark Notes version? We've gotten much closer this year, practicing together and playing doubles and messaging each other, and then at my game night, we sort of, like, made out in my kitchen."

Afraid of the banshee cry that's likely going to pour out of her, Leo puts his hand up and quickly adds, "But I fucked up and pushed him away, and we didn't talk for the last two months."

Tess winces.

"But I actually just came here from his room."

"M. Night Shyamalan would be proud of the twists in this story," she says.

"I think I made things right. And I told him how much it's meant to me, getting to know him and all. And I invited him and Billie to come out with us tonight."

"Wait, Billie's here, too?" she asks.

"Yeah, I ran into her in the lobby and she gave me his room number. That's how I knew where to find him."

"Wow. All right. So," Tess says, leaning back on her elbows with an extended exhale. She's staring at the dresser in front of them, seemingly collecting her thoughts. "Where to start."

"Yeah."

She sits up and takes Leo's hands in hers, looking at him with a focus that tells him she's fully here, seeing him.

"Well, let me start with this: Thank you, thank you, thank you for telling me, Leo. You mean the world to me. And knowing this about you only makes me love you more."

Leo forgoes finding the right words and pulls her into a hug, his eyes shutting as he tries to imprint this memory on the backs of them.

"Is Gabe the first guy you've liked?"

"He's the first guy I've had these feelings for, yeah. But he didn't make me realize that I'm into guys, if that's what you mean. I've actually known I'm gay for a long time. There have been, uh, a lot of one-night stands along the way. But I decided from the beginning to keep that separate from tennis."

"Oh, my angel. I hope I haven't given you the impression that you couldn't talk to me about all this. If I've ever said anything that did, I'm so sorry."

"No, trust me, you've been the best. I always thought if I was going to tell someone, you would be the first," Leo says. "And I would've told you sooner, but I just felt like I wanted to keep this one thing for myself. I wanted to keep it safe. Does that make sense?"

"It does," Tess says, nodding. "Does anyone else know?"

"Gabe. Well, I guess that's obvious. My mom. I just told her the other night. I haven't figured out what to do about my dad or the rest of my team. I don't think I want to go public. Not yet, anyway. I do want to tell Ollie, though."

"So, what changed?" Tess asks. "Why now?"

"Same answer," he says, his eyes shifting down, feeling hesitant but exhilarated, laying it all out for Tess like this, a conversation years in the making. "Gabe."

"I'm really proud of you," Tess says, smiling. Her expression turns urgent. "Not that you need my approval or validation or anything. You shouldn't even have to come out. You don't even really need me to—"

"Tess," Leo interjects, laughing. "Don't blow a fuse. I know what you mean. But I wanted to tell you. Honestly, I could use your help. I really want Gabe to come tonight, and we did leave things in a good place just now, but I don't know, I'm worried the moment's passed and he's totally turned off now. What if he doesn't show? What if it's too late?"

"Hold on," she says, pulling her phone out of a big pocket in her robe.

"What are you doing?"

"Messaging him."

"Oh, you don't have to—"

"No, no, I do. Once I tell him where we're going, he won't be able to resist. I also think he can't resist *you*. I've seen the way he looks at you. That doesn't just go away."

"Yeah, yeah," Leo mutters. He feels his face flush at the thought of Tess noticing all his little moments with Gabe this season, at the thought of Gabe finding him *irresistible.*

"Can I ask," Tess says, "if you've always had a thing for him? Is that why he's bothered you so much? I had a hunch, but I hoped you'd get there on your own if that was the case. And I'm glad you did. You seemed so much happier when you were spending time with him."

"My mom said that, too," Leo says, the corner of his mouth curling up. "I haven't quite figured out the answer to that question. And I've been asking myself that a lot lately. But, to be honest, I guess I'm afraid the answer will mean I wasted way too much time getting here."

"You know," she says, "it's okay if things take a little longer than you thought."

Leo nods a few times at this and, before he can get lost in his mind again, a different question hits him. "Wait, where *are* we going tonight?"

CHAPTER SIXTEEN

Standing in a row, bored and impatient, outside a small corner pharmacy in the 11th arrondissement, Leo, Tess, Ollie, and Liv are in formal black outfits and multicolored masquerade masks that Tess ordered for them. They got ready in Liv's room together for some mystery party that Tess promised would be worth the effort—and, hopefully, the embarrassment. Stylish Parisian after stylish Parisian walks by them, stepping out into the night wearing leather jackets, short plaid skirts, wide-legged pants, corset tops, little black dresses.

"We look like a knockoff Blue Man Group," Ollie says. "Tabarnak."

"Yeah, Tess, I don't think they're coming," Leo says, watching the headlights of taxis and motorbikes streak past them. "We can go. It's fine. Really."

"No, I told Gabe to meet us here," she says. "He said they were down. They'll come."

"I do sort of have to pee," Liv says, grimacing.

"Did he tell you they were on their way?" Leo asks.

"Well, no," Tess says. "Not yet."

"We should get to the party," Leo says. "It's already getting late."

"Are you sure?" Tess asks him quietly.

"Yeah," he says, the disappointment settling in his gut. "I haven't heard from him, either."

"He could still show. I'll keep an eye on my phone," she says, putting a hand on his arm before addressing the group. "Okay, friends. Let's go have a ball."

Tess turns around and steps up confidently to the nondescript pharmacy, which is dark inside given that it's nearly midnight, and it's as if she's been here a million times to pick up a prescription. Beside the door, she flips open the lid of a keypad and punches in a series of numbers. Leo hears the door click. She pulls it open and turns back to the group.

"All right, are we ready to go?" she asks.

"I beg your actual pardon?" Ollie says. "Where are we going? To get some Robitussin?"

"Did you just break into a pharmacy?" Leo asks.

"Come on," she says, gesturing for them to enter. "You'll see."

One by one, they walk into the pharmacy, and as Leo walks down one of the aisles, he stops to lean closer to the items on the shelves and picks up a tube of toothpaste.

"They're not real," he says to himself, excitedly.

"Look at these!" Liv exclaims, holding up a box of tampons from the next aisle. She pulls out a couple that were poking through the top of the box. "They're just felt!"

"It's all fake," Tess says slyly, an eyebrow raised. "Follow me."

Leo walks to the back of the store, admiring the adorable felt toothbrushes and pill bottles and condoms on the way. Tess leads him and the group into what appears to be a stockroom, where a man who looks like the Babadook greets them.

"Bonsoir," he says. There's white paint brushed along his cheekbones, a tiny slit of a black mask across his eyes, and a top hat resting on his shoulder-length black hair. "Quatre?"

"Oui," Tess says, and the Babadook clicks his tally counter four times.

"Parfait, par ici, s'il vous plaît," he says, and opens the door for them.

The group steps through, walks up a short staircase, and opens yet another door. They then enter an abandoned four-story townhome with grand cobwebbed chandeliers, patches of burgundy and gold wallpaper peeling, and graffiti sprayed everywhere, the legible bits telling them things like, "TOUT EST POSSIBLE" and "PARIS EST A NOUS." On one side of the ground floor is a DJ in a scarlet Venetian masquerade gown, a white mask covering her entire face, and a scarlet feather sticking out of her up-do. On the other side is a bar flanked by monstrous brass candelabras and tended by three shirtless men in black pants and black masks. The place is dim, aglow only with candles, the tall arched windows covered with sheets, like ghosts overseeing the soiree. Stepping into the center of the room, Leo looks straight up and, along with a few pigeons perched on a skylight at the very top, he sees that on each floor, masked guests are dancing to the thumping house music, some with sparklers in their hands.

"So?" Tess yells to them over the music. "What do we think?"

"Tess," Ollie says, "I don't know how else to ask this, so I just will: Is this a sex party? Like, is this an orgy? Are we in an *Eyes Wide Shut* situation right now?"

"Great reference, but no, not a sex party," Tess says. "Though, I think there are some rooms for that on the top floor if you're interested. All I'll say is that I made it on a list for this group that throws secret parties all over Paris. Good thing we're all out of Roland-Garros already, or we wouldn't have been able to come."

"This woman is a legend," Liv says, lifting her hands in praise, the sleeves of her oversized tuxedo blazer slipping down her arms. Her blond hair is slicked back.

"Hear hear," Leo says, looking around the place in amazement.

Tess curtsies in her black tulle dress.

"First round's on me!" Ollie shouts, heading for the bar. "Tess drinks free tonight!"

Like Ollie, Leo is wearing a tailored black suit, but opted to wear a white T-shirt underneath instead of a button-down. He checks that it's still neatly tucked in and makes his way over to the bar, quickly realizing that scanning the room for Gabe is a futile endeavor thanks to all the masks. His cerulean eyes pop beneath his own mask of royal blue and gold.

With a French 75 in his hand, Leo wanders around the party with the group, getting the lay of this lustful land. There's something decidedly spooky about it, too, as if the attendees are specters, still here, dancing years after the final party at this home ended, before it sank into disarray, left to decay. It doesn't help that as the party grows more crowded, Leo loses his group on the second floor, left alone to move among the masks, the limbs of their owners swinging languidly. A man with a white mask covering half his face like the Phantom of the Opera, tugs at Leo's jacket sleeve, interested.

"Sorry, I'm looking for someone," Leo says bashfully.

As he continues his search through each level of the party, he leans on the railing of the third floor to get a bird's-eye view, peering over. The spooky feeling of the place only increases when he hears a whisper from behind him.

"Leonardo," the voice says quietly and eerily.

He whips around to his left, but no one's there. When he turns back, he looks to his right and discovers that it's not a ghost. Although, isn't it?

"Hey," Gabe says.

He's standing there, leaning on the railing, in a red and gold mask, a buttoned black suit vest—no shirt or jacket—and baggy black pants. Must this man continue to torture Leo with his arms? With his chest?

Leo swallows. "You made it," he says.

"You think I'd miss this?" Gabe says, looking around at the party.

"Yeah, Tess had a feeling you wouldn't be able to resist."

"I tried to message you both, but the service in here sucks, sorry."

"Oh, have you been here a while?" Leo asks.

"For a bit, yeah," Gabe says. "Billie's around here somewhere. We wanted to wait for y'all, but we were way too curious."

"What, um, have you been up to so far?" Leo asks.

"I actually just came from the fourth floor," Gabe says, pointing up with his thumb, "railing some twink in one of the sex rooms."

Leo nearly spits out his drink.

"Relax," he says, laughing. "It was really more of an Eiffel Tower. Felt more appropriate for the setting."

"Ha, ha," Leo says.

"No, we've just been dancing a little, checking things out. I love how haunted this place feels, right?"

"Yeah, it's incredible," Leo says, glancing down below. "I don't know how Tess does it."

"What?"

"She always knows the cool places to eat, the cool stuff everybody's up to on tour, the cool parties to go to. Everywhere we go."

Gabe smiles. "She seems like a great friend to have."

"I, um, told her about us today," Leo says. "I hope that's okay."

"About us?"

"Not that there's an 'us,'" Leo says, suddenly panicking. "Just that, you know, we, well, kissed, and that we've gotten to know each other better. That's all, really. She didn't know I'm gay and, I don't know, it felt like the right time to tell her, and—"

Gabe puts his hand on Leo's shoulder. "Take a breath," he says. "That's amazing that you got to talk to her about it."

Leo smiles and nods. Best not to open his mouth again.

Gabe takes a sip of his drink. "Do you . . . want there to be an 'us'?"

Leo looks at this man standing in front of him. His curls, his soft skin, his eyes made even more golden-brown by the sheen of his mask. This beautiful man with his beautiful heart. Leo's wasted so much time already. There's no way he's running again.

"More than you know," Leo says in a low voice.

Gabe moves closer. "Are you sure?"

"Can I kiss you?" Leo asks.

Gabe nods.

There's no hesitancy this time. No gradual meeting in the middle. The past two months of agony keeping himself away from this man rush forward into a deep, fervent kiss, his right hand on Gabe's cheek as he shows him just how sure he is that he wants—needs—them to be together now. As other guests lift their sparklers into the air and the taste of prosecco lingers on his tongue, Leo feels hot, fizzy, bubbling over. Their lips move in sync, their hands study the curves of the other's body. Before the kiss turns frantic, Leo pulls away to catch his breath.

They stare at each other for a moment.

"That was a yes, by the way," Leo says. "I'm sure."

"Yeah, I got that," Gabe says as he thumbs the corner of his mouth, still wet from Leo's.

Leo turns away, biting his lip to keep from smiling wildly. When he looks down to the second floor, he sees Tess and Billie leaning on the railing, Billie in a black, strapless jumpsuit. A cheeky grin on both of them, they each give a nod of approval and then clink their glasses. A job well done.

"Do you want to go dance with our friends for a bit?" Leo asks.

"Yes," Gabe says, leaning in closer. "And then I want to bring you back to my room and do what I've been imagining ever since we kissed in Miami."

"Okay, yeah, maybe only one dance," Leo says breathlessly, grabbing Gabe's hand and pulling him along to find Tess and Billie as quickly as possible.

Leo's glad to see that Tess has Billie to hang out with tonight, considering he found Ollie and Liv also making out in a corner.

"Gee, who could've seen that coming?" Tess asks Leo, smiling.

As they all come together on the ground floor, where a central dancing area has formed, they look blissed out, bobbing and swaying and spinning to the music. The bass thumps harder. Candles flicker. Leo can't help but scan each face in his group, seeing the joy in them, feeling the same warmth he felt the night of Tie Break Tens, the kind of warmth, he's realizing, can only come from finding a group like this. He lets himself slip into its tenderness, its safety.

"We're getting another round for everyone!" Liv shouts, and Ollie follows behind her, whispering something in her ear that makes her laugh.

"Ugh, this is my song!" Billie says sarcastically as the DJ transitions to the next house track, nearly indistinguishable from the previous one.

Leo squawks and moves closer to Gabe. "I love her."

Gabe laughs, grabs Leo's waist, and pulls him in. They let their limbs intertwine as they dance, familiarizing themselves with each other's movements, anticipating what the night holds. Leo pulls his gaze away from Gabe's chest and makes eye contact with Ollie as he's walking back to the group with Liv, balancing drinks in their hands. He feels himself tense, but the sensation is gone in an instant as Ollie offers him a knowing smile, then clenches his fist like he just won a point in a match. Leo huffs out a laugh.

"Love you, dude," Ollie says as he hands Leo a new French 75.

"You too," Leo says.

He leans his head back to look up at the skylight at the top of the house, and he can't remember the last time he felt this free.

"You have a nice place here," Leo says as he hovers near Gabe's hotel bed, a little buzzed, making an inside joke with himself.

The lights low, he watches as Gabe puts his phone down on top of his romance novel on the nightstand, and he hears the modern disco sounds of Jessie Ware's album *That! Feels Good!* begin to play, the unofficial soundtrack of gay sex everywhere.

"So," Gabe says, stepping up to Leo, putting his hands on his waist.

"So," Leo says, his breath caught in his throat, his heart beginning to race, almost in sync with the song's drums.

"I feel like I should just ask," Gabe says.

"Ask what?"

"Have you, you know, gone all the way before?" Gabe asks. "With another guy? Because I can take the lead here. I'm happy to, actually." He smirks.

Leo looks at him for a second, then bursts out laughing.

"What?" Gabe asks, slightly horrified.

"No. I'm sorry. I'm not laughing at you. You're the sweetest for checking," Leo says, and he kisses his cheek. "But this isn't my first time. Far from it. But, duh, how would you know that? I'm glad you asked."

"Oh," Gabe says, surprised.

"I just started telling people in my life that I'm gay, like, this week . . . and I'm only telling those people for now," Leo says, and Gabe nods assuringly. "But I've been, um, let's say, sexually active for a long time now."

"Let's not say 'sexually active,'" Gabe says, nose turned up, like he just sniffed sour milk.

Leo cringes. "Yeah, I just heard how that sounded."

Gabe laughs.

"So, yeah," Leo says. "I, um, came prepared for tonight. Literally and figuratively, if you know what I mean. Just in case."

"Wow, a little presumptuous, don't you think?" Gabe teases. "But I guess that answers my next question."

"Something tells me you're cool with the answer," Leo says.

"Yes," Gabe says. "Very cool."

"I suppose we should take these off," Leo says, removing the masquerade mask from his face, then doing the same for Gabe, unsure why they were even still wearing them.

They kiss their way onto the bed, and as Leo and Gabe furiously take off each other's clothes, piece by piece, Leo is almost quivering as he feels the heat radiating from Gabe's skin. Looking up at Gabe as he lies underneath him, Leo can tell Gabe is studying his body, first admiring his tousled brown hair, which is gaining a blond tint from the spring sun, then staring into his eyes, and finally following the trail of hair down from his chest to where it disappears into the waist of his pants.

"You're beautiful," Gabe says.

Leo wants to disappear into this man. He settles, instead, for another long, feverish kiss.

Gabe lays Leo back onto the bed, takes his arms, and moves them above Leo's head. He kisses Leo down his neck and then buries his face into the hair of his armpits, licking. Leo lets out a moan and, at first, feels the heat of embarrassment rush over him, but forgets all about it when Gabe continues kissing down his torso.

Gabe sits up and, except for his chest rising and falling, remains perfectly still for a few seconds. It's as if he's savoring this final moment, a farewell to a time when they never would have laid bare their bodies and their feelings like this.

"I need you," Leo says, breaking the silence.

Gabe smiles, a hunger in his eyes. He takes Leo in his mouth and another moan emerges from Leo, without embarrassment this time. Leo's hands grip the white sheets as he writhes, Gabe taking the whole of him over and over. After some time, the length of which Leo can't be sure, lost in the pleasure of it, Gabe lifts Leo's legs. Leo bends them back and, again, can't control the sounds coming out of his mouth as Gabe kisses and licks, his eyes opening and meeting Leo's from time to time with a mischievous glint.

When Leo puts his legs back down, he gets on his knees and gets to work. In the back of his mind, he feels how surreal this is, being with Gabe after all these years, but he's too distracted by the gorgeous man in the back of his throat right now to be too wrapped up in all that. Gabe's moans are the only sounds in the world right now. Eventually, Leo lies back on the bed and Gabe lifts Leo's legs again.

"Are you ready?" Gabe asks softly.

"Yes," Leo says, and he watches closely as Gabe covers his dick in lube, Leo's excitement building and building and building as Gabe continues stroking, preparing himself.

Gabe kisses him, and Leo takes a deep breath and exhales with a faint groan as he feels Gabe push inside of him. He places his hands on Gabe's back and feels his way down, gripping his ass as he thrusts. They're perfectly in sync.

Leo's used to sex being transactional, but tonight it's tender. Gabe isn't in any kind of a hurry. He's steady, sensual. Leo leans up and kisses him, then pulls back, looking at him in a way he's never looked at a lover before.

"I'm yours," Leo whispers, in case his eyes hadn't already made that clear.

Gabe kisses him again, and only then does he begin to pump faster, unable to hold back, bringing both of them to the edge. Leo finishes on his own stomach, and Gabe quickly follows.

For a while, they lie beside each other in contented silence. At one point, Gabe begins to laugh, seemingly out of nowhere, and Leo can't help but join him. Gabe turns off the music and then invites Leo to rest his head on his chest, putting an arm around him.

"Stay with me," Gabe says quietly, an invitation that Leo never receives from the men he sleeps with or, at least, an invitation he never accepts.

But he settles in, listening to Gabe's heartbeat.

Leo drifts in and out of sleep, waking in both disbelief and euphoria at the sight of Gabe lying on his stomach, dozing next to him, his dark hair wavy and wild. He's unable to fall back to sleep as the sun begins to rise, peeking through a narrow opening between the curtains. He sees a distant sliver of the Arc de Triomphe and hears a few motorbikes buzzing by as Paris yawns and stretches, waking up slowly, as it always does. A strong ray of warm morning light pools in the valley between Gabe's shoulder blades, and the sheer beauty of it is so new to Leo that he could swear the color orange was born right there, on Gabe's back. As his eyes linger on the body before him, there's a longing in his chest that definitely doesn't feel new. It's lived there, at his core, for a long time. He knows that now.

"Good morning, Leonardo," Gabe says as Leo stirs.

Leo must have fallen back to sleep. With the curtains drawn now, the room is bright and the streets below sound busy. Gabe's eyes are shining and he's lying there, on his side, still naked, like some kind of god. His hair is back in place and Leo detects a whisper of peppermint.

"What, did you have hair and makeup come in while I was sleeping?" Leo asks.

Gabe's head flies back with laughter.

"This is so unfair," Leo says, rubbing his eyes. "I'm crusty and have dick breath."

"Does it look like I care?" Gabe asks.

Leo scans down and sees that Gabe is getting hard.

So, yes, they go at it again, without hesitation.

Once they've finished, Leo, crusty in more ways than one now, puts on his T-shirt and pants and stands by the bed, holding his suit jacket.

"So, um, when will I see you again?" he asks shyly. "I'm flying to Stuttgart later today. Will you be there?"

"Ah, no, I'm skipping the beginning of the grass swing," Gabe says, standing there in just his briefs, the tease. "I'm actually heading to New York for some Pride Month events. You can tell Ollie I'm going to be on a panel with Billie Jean King."

Leo chuckles. "That's amazing. I wish I could be there."

"Me too," Gabe says with a gentle smile.

"Well, I'll be in London, then Eastbourne, and then Wimbledon, obviously," Leo says. "You'll be at those, right?"

Gabe grimaces. "I'm, uh, playing Halle and then Mallorca," he says. "But I will be at Wimbledon. Wouldn't miss it."

"Okay, good," Leo says, stepping closer to him. "Hey, I'm sorry we can't be together in public yet. I mean, without masquerade masks. I'm just not ready to tell the world yet. If you feel like I'm holding you back, you—"

"I feel the opposite of held back right now," Gabe says, and then kisses him.

"Okay," Leo says, shoulders relaxing. "Thanks."

Leo opens the door to leave, and as he steps into the hall, Gabe follows behind him, turns him around, and gives him another long kiss. "You better write, Leonardo."

Grand Slam: Wimbledon
Surface: Grass
Where: London, England
When: July 1–14, 2024

CHAPTER SEVENTEEN

It's impossible to overestimate how many matches Leo has watched in his twenty-nine years on this earth. Tens of thousands, easily. Not much can shift his view of tennis and the way it's played at this point. But now, having had Gabe quite literally inside of him, the sport has been turned on its axis. In the lead-up to Wimbledon, his body goes berserk every time he watches one of Gabe's matches in the gym, in his hotel room, wherever.

For instance, it goes without saying that Leo knows what brand of racket Gabe uses. After all these years, how could he not? And yet, when he sees the word "HEAD" in giant white letters on the bag beside Gabe's chair, he starts sweating on his bed.

"NEW BALLS, PLEASE," the ump's voice booms when it's time to swap in a batch of fresh tennis balls, and Leo starts to tip to the right on an exercise bike, prompting the German player riding next to him to ask, "You okay, Chambers?"

"I like that play from Montoya. I'd like to see him go hard and deep down the middle more," the commentator says after

Gabe rockets a forehand through the court, and Leo feels his face flush in the cafeteria.

As Gabe starts hitting winner after winner: "The points are coming thick and fast now."

"How do you respond to balls so hard and deep?" the commentator continues.

When Gabe hits a feather-soft drop shot: "Such good hands, Montoya. His touch. His feel. It's sumptuous."

"That was a gut-buster of a point."

Will someone fetch Leo a fainting couch, please?

Fortunately, this newfound horniness hasn't deterred his success. If anything, it has energized him in a new way, leading him to move with more fluidity and attack his shots with less hesitation. His grass season has been stellar so far, especially his run to the semifinals at the Queen's Club Championships last week, a midlevel men's tournament. Founded in 1890, it's one of the most historic and—given the stately brick architecture and pristine grass courts—poshest tournaments of the season. More important than its beautiful grounds, though, is its reputation to predict who will make a deep run at Wimbledon, a real boost to Leo's confidence as he heads into the third Slam of the year.

"Making the final here would've been amazing, but I'm still so excited to have given this performance right before Wimbledon," Leo said during his press conference after his loss in the semis. "I felt like I was more aggressive and showed more of an all-court presence, which I've been lacking for a while now."

"What brought about this new spark?" one of the reporters asked.

"Um," Leo began, a smile sneaking out at the thought of the often-cute and sometimes-racy texts he and Gabe had exchanged throughout the month. "I definitely feel more comfortable on grass than clay, for one thing, and adding Brian Wilkins to my team has been huge. But yeah, I guess something just, well, finally clicked for me."

"I'm stoked for you, and so proud of you, LC," Brian said afterward, "but I'm not mad your run here is over. This club has always given me the creeps, if I'm honest. It's like the Sunken Place, you know? I gotta get outta here before another white person offers me tea."

Even though Leo and Brian have celebrated his grass victories at the past few tournaments, Johnny has still had a somewhat sour attitude. Yes, he's applauded after Leo's excellent points or match wins, but that familiar distance—the lack of communication in Australia, the argument after the podcast recording, the disappointment in his clay losses—hasn't closed just yet. He's been quieter than usual and, when he has spoken up, he's been overly critical of Leo's choices. Though Leo has built his career on being a baseliner, taking the racket out of his opponents' hands by vaporizing his forehands and backhands, lately he's felt the urge to approach his matches more creatively. Instead of remaining glued to the baseline, his body has glided him around the court, bringing him into the net for a skillful volley or inside the baseline to find new angles he never studied in geometry class. It's certainly led to some mistakes, but he's getting the wins and, what's more, he's having fun—something he hasn't felt on a court in months. Seeing this new approach, his dad has been shouting from his box to stick to his repertoire, to pull back on the drop shots, to minimize his risk. Leo has simply brushed him off, turning to his box for advice less and less and stepping up to the line with nothing but his own instinct.

"You're playing carelessly," his dad told him after the quarters at the Queens Club.

"I'm winning," Leo said, his face turning impatient.

"Leo, it's getting messy," Johnny said. "Way too many errors. You need to stick to plan A, your A game, what's gotten you to this stage in your career. Stick to what you know, and you'll get there."

"A messy win is still a win," Leo said. "I can't always find my A game when I'm out there, and when I try to force it, I play even worse. That's why my ranking was slipping. I need to have other ways to get the win. I'm expressing myself, too. I'm actually having fun. Why can't you just let me find what works for me?"

"We know what works for you. It's gotten you fifteen titles."

"Well, it's not working for me anymore. Brian sees it. I see it. I don't know why you can't." Leo walked away then, and they haven't returned to the conversation since.

He and his dad may be at odds more than ever, but the odds of him going far at Wimbledon have only increased. His recent results have bumped him back into the top twenty, securing his spot as the number fifteen seed at Wimbledon. It should set him up with an easier draw—in the opening rounds, at least.

In tennis, over the course of one season, one tournament, one match, even one point, a player can have a breakthrough. Maybe they beat a certain opponent they've never been able to beat before, or they finally nail a certain shot that's always given them trouble. Whatever hurdle they're clearing, it unlocks a fresh belief in their brain, a new level they didn't even know they could reach in their game, and they'll begin to climb the rankings. These breakthroughs happen every season, and each time, it's a marvel to witness a player fulfill their potential for greatness.

For Leo, he never imagined that he would have another breakthrough this far into his career—the first being his maiden title at the Delray Beach Open when he was nineteen—and he certainly never imagined Gabe would help unlock it. At last year's Wimbledon, he was furious to see Gabe blocking his path to the trophy and, like a self-fulfilling prophecy, he fell to him in the third round. He could barely stand to hear Paul mention that match last summer at the podcast studio. Now, one year later, he's falling *for* Gabe at Wimbledon, in the wake of his best grass swing ever. He's ecstatic to see him later tonight, a couple days before the Slam begins, for the first time since their rendezvous in Paris.

Before he can reunite with Gabe, though, he has a full afternoon of practice, and while Johnny may find Leo's new playing style messy, the backdrop for it is now quite the opposite. Held at the All England Club Lawn Tennis Club, Wimbledon is the most immaculate of the Grand Slams, a neat and tidy grid of grass courts, each one like a traditional English garden trimmed and pruned to perfection. The iconic, towering Centre Court has ivy climbing up its sides, and the grounds' paths are lined with bushes, trees, and white-and-purple flowers. The players must wear tennis whites at their matches, a rule enforced since the tournament's founding in 1877, and while the fans don't have a dress code, they still don their British best for the event of the summer: smart double-breasted suits, pastel dresses, brimmed hats, designer sunglasses. They dip into boxes of strawberries and cream while sipping on Pimm's cup.

The Grand Slam schedule is meant to chase the sun—hence the Australian summer kickoff—but it's always a roll of the dice when it comes to Wimbledon in July, beholden to London's unpredictable forecast. But today, the sun has decided to cooperate, which Leo is grateful for as his feet crunch on the scrupulously mown grass of this practice court, given that his team has had a dark cloud hovering over it as of late. Each of the practice courts in the row is being used, all the players prepping for this tournament that has come to define tennis throughout history. He can see Tess a few courts over, and he can *hear* Sascha at the court beyond hers. "Stop being so soft, man!" he's yelling at his hitting partner.

"Same drills today?" Leo asks his dad with a touch of strain, expecting the typical rounds of forehands, backhands, and second serves.

"Uh, actually no, I thought you could do a couple last practice sets this afternoon before the first round," Johnny says.

"Oh, I thought Ollie wasn't free today."

"He's not."

"So, who am I—"

"Gabriel! It's been so long," Johnny says cheerily, slowly approaching him and then shaking his hand. "Or, no, you prefer Gabe, right?"

Leo rubs his eyes like a cartoon character, dumbfounded at this interaction. Did he miss something? How is this happening right now?

"Yeah, Gabe is great," he says, smiling reverently. "My parents call me Gabriel, but everybody else calls me Gabe. Thank you so much for setting this up, Mr. Chambers."

"Please, call me Johnny. Mr. Chambers is my son," he says, nodding over to Leo, who would roll his eyes at this dad joke if they weren't glued to the sight of Gabe in his all-white practice clothes, shining like a freshly carved marble statue in the hot summer sun.

Leo hasn't had to worry about randomly popping a boner on court since he was a teenager, but Jesus Christ, this man. He wants to drag him down onto the grass and ravish him. He wants to get grass stains on his knees. He—

He is at Wimbledon. Ahem. Right. Manners and decorum and whatnot.

"Hey," Leo says, smiling stupidly as he walks up to him. "What are you doing here? I thought you were practicing in Mallorca till tomorrow."

"I wanted to get used to the conditions here sooner. Plus, your dad reached out to Diego about getting a match in with you, so here I am."

"Here you are," Leo says, stifling the urge to kiss him. To cut the tension, he says hello and shakes hands with Diego and the rest of Gabe's team.

"You know, Mr. Ch—Johnny, you have a couple fans in my parents," Gabe says as they all make their way to the benches to drop off their gear. "I told them I'd be seeing you today, and my dad said they'll never forget watching you in that US Open final."

"No! Really?" Johnny says, eyes widening. "That's too kind. Tell them I say hello. Give them my best, will you? They're not here, are they?"

"No, not this year. But I'll tell them," Gabe says.

"Good, good. That's so kind of them. So kind," Johnny says. "How were they? You know, with your coming out and all."

"Dad—" Leo interrupts.

"No, no, Leo, it's fine," Gabe says, setting his Head bag down. "It honestly went better than I thought it would. I told them before I made the official announcement. My mom definitely needed a second, but she gave me a big hug. My dad looked me in the eye and said, 'If anybody gives you shit, they answer to me.' And you know what, I think about that every day now," Gabe says, chuckling. "Mostly because my dad is, like, five and a half feet tall, so it makes me laugh. But, hey, he's in my corner. And not everybody is."

Leo can barely keep himself from throwing his arms around Gabe. He loves hearing how supportive his parents are, but the thought of anyone hurting him? He just wants to hold Gabe close, protect him from the world.

"Well, I think what you did took guts," Johnny says.

"Thank you. It means a lot to hear that from you," Gabe says with a tone of deference.

"It's good to see you winning again, too," Johnny says. "I saw you had some nice results in Halle and Mallorca."

"Yeah, thank you," Gabe says, still smiling humbly.

"All right, well, let's keep it going," Johnny says, and he claps a few times as Leo and Gabe jog onto the grass, their hands brushing before they part ways.

Leo jogs back to his dad briefly. Johnny must have finally heard him during their argument at the Queens tournament. "Dad. Thanks for setting this up. I know that . . . Well, I know that we . . . I—"

"Have a good time," Johnny says, nodding for him to take the court.

"Thanks," Leo says, offering a conciliatory smile.

Encouraged by this sudden reprieve in their feud, Leo does enjoy practicing for the first time in a while, flirty looks flying back and forth between him and Gabe as frequently as their forehands and backhands. It's easy to slip when playing on grass, but Leo's legs feel even wobblier today, turning to jelly whenever Gabe lifts his shirt to wipe his face. But the thrill of it, the secret between them, keeps him on his toes.

"Yes, LC!" Brian says from the back of the court after Leo runs along the baseline and slides into a forehand, smacking it for a crosscourt winner. "The ball's making some weird-ass bounces in this heat. Keep your eye on that, okay? Take those extra little steps as you set up. They'll make all the difference."

"My thoughts exactly," Johnny adds.

While Johnny and Brian typically work in tandem during practices, Brian seems to take the reins in coaching Leo throughout this one, Johnny remaining in his shadow more than usual. It's the only shadow to be found on court, the sun at its highest point becoming more and more oppressive. Out of the corner of his eye, one of the many reflexes he's developed while playing, Leo starts to notice his dad feeling sluggish in the heat, his walking unstable as he moves around Leo's side of the court. Leo's eyes dart between his dad's movements and Gabe's, his focus split, and it begins to show. He's sending routine forehands long and flinging his favorite shot, his backhand down the line, into the net a little more often. He pauses between points, takes deep breaths. *Just play tennis.*

After their first practice set, as Johnny comes to meet Leo on the court and share some notes, Leo sees his right knee buckle. Before his body drops to the grass, Leo lunges forward and grabs him, keeping him on his feet and helping him find his balance again.

"Dad, are you all right?" His eyes then glance over at Gabe and his team.

"Yeah, yeah, all good," Johnny says, attempting to laugh it off. "Don't worry. This damn grass can be so slippery."

"It's really hot right now. Do you want to head back to the gym? Get some AC? We'll also be done soon if you just want to hang at the house." Leo can hear it this time. How it sounds like he's trying to get rid of him. But he knows if he doesn't push, encourage, hint, his dad will be too stubborn. He will always stay on court, even at his own risk.

"No, no, really, I'm good. I'll just take a break in the shade for the next set."

"Okay. If you're sure."

As Leo helps his dad over to take a seat, he glances at Gabe again and sees him looking on with concern. For a moment, Leo expects to feel the dread sink in his gut, the dread that always comes whenever he can feel eyes on him and his dad. But instead, he feels comfort.

"Gotcha this time," Gabe says, teasing Leo over his first-set victory as he approaches him by the benches. But when he steps closer, his eyes turn concerned again, his voice drops lower. "Is everything okay? Can I do anything?"

"Yeah, it's just the heat," Leo says, fighting the urge to embrace him. "I think he'll stay in the shade for a bit, cool off. Thanks for checking."

"We can skip the next set if you need to."

"No, no, let's do it. I need to get my revenge," Leo says halfheartedly.

"Okay," Gabe says, giving him an encouraging look before returning to his side.

With Johnny resting in the shade, Leo's anxiety recedes slightly, and this is enough to allow him to refocus and clinch a tight second set against Gabe. It's still such a new feat for him that it never ceases to brighten his mood.

"Revenge complete," he says as they meet at the net afterward, shaking hands and letting them linger.

"Yeah, yeah," Gabe says, and he shoves Leo's shoulder gently. Even having slept with Gabe, little gestures of affection like this still, apparently, send his head spinning. They pack up their things and begin their walk to the locker rooms, waving to Wimbledon social media managers who are pointing their phones at them, trying to capture the players about the grounds.

"Your serve really was firing today," Gabe says, adjusting the bag slung over his shoulder. "Puta. It comes out of nowhere sometimes. I've always wondered how you get so much power behind it."

"Hold on," Leo says, wiping the sweat from his forehead and turning his gaze to his . . . boyfriend? Lover? Fuck buddy? He'll figure out that game plan later. "Gabe Montoya is asking *me* about *my* game? He doesn't have *all* the secrets on how to dismantle me?"

"Well, I wouldn't go that far," Gabe says, smirking. Leo's head is about to fly off now. "Really, though, your serve is wild."

"I got some tips from Andy, actually," Leo says. "Way back when. He helped me shorten my motion to make it more consistent. Other than that, it's all in the wrist."

"I know that's right," Gabe says.

"Please stop," Leo says, shooting him a wry look. Then, voice quieter, he adds, "This limp wrist has won me a lot of points."

Gabe rolls his eyes, smiling. "Wait, but back up. Andy? Andy Roddick?"

Leo nods. "Yeah, he wanted to help me a little when I first went pro."

"Okay, damn. I guess they don't call you Baby Rod for nothing."

"Now I *insist* you stop," Leo says, and he realizes that he's reached his destination. "Oh, actually, good timing. This is where I leave you."

They've arrived not just at the locker room but at the "Gentlemen Members' Dressing Room," the changing room and adjoining physiotherapy room reserved during the fortnight, as it were, for the top sixteen seeds and former Wimbledon champions. Other than its hallowed reputation, Leo has never found it to be an especially remarkable space, just a collection of pine lockers and golden hooks.

"Ah, right, back on top," Gabe says. "Well, you know, in tennis anyway."

"You're out of control," Leo says, grinning.

"Guess I'll see you later, then. I'm off to clean up with the other peasants, m'lord. 'Twas a hard day's work," Gabe says in a horrendous British accent, releasing an unexpected yelp of laughter from Leo.

With the tournament just beginning, players and coaches and members of the All England Club shuffle by in masses, not to mention security guards posted outside the Gentlemen Members' Dressing Room, so in lieu of a kiss, Gabe merely brushes his fingertips against Leo's before walking off to the main locker room upstairs. Leo can feel his ears burning as Gabe turns back briefly with a devilish flicker in his eye, feeling as if they're in one of Gabe's Regency Era forbidden romances.

Up in his room in the chic Georgian townhouse he's renting near Wimbledon for the next couple weeks, Leo isn't exactly hiding from his parents, but considering they're downstairs marathoning *This Is Us* episodes for the eight thousandth time, he's happy to be holed up by himself—with his own comfort show.

"You can't come in here. This house has been quarantined," Blanche yells, back against the front door, dead set on avoiding the man who's knocking. "We all have, uh . . . quick, Rose, give me a deadly disease."

"Oh, I'm sorry, Blanche. I don't have a deadly disease," Rose says, always confused, from across the room.

Blanche glares at her. "Well, get one."

Leo snorts as he scrolls on Instagram, full from dinner. A few posts down, he comes across Serving Looks' latest entry, photos of players practicing and palling around ahead of Wimbledon, pulled from wires and other social accounts. All clad in white, there's Tess throwing up a peace sign to the camera, Ollie and Liv chatting as they sit beside each other on the grass, and the final photo: Leo and Gabe grinning at each other as they walk by the ivy-covered walls of Centre Court.

> **servinglooks** It's giving University of Oxford brochure and I'm living for it—especially for my fave breakout duo of the season, Leo and Gabe. Doesn't look like they're in the doubles draw (rude), but I'm so excited to see them back to their bestie ways at practice. Seeing everyone at Wimby always does my lil' heart good. I want to hear your predictions for this year—who ya got?

Leo does see it now, staring at the photo of him and Gabe. The happiness on his face that everyone's been telling him has been missing for a while? It's there. You can't miss it. At once, he feels an overwhelming rush of gratitude for the joy Gabe has freed in him this year and a knot in his chest from the guilt that he still hasn't told his dad. He trusts that his mom hasn't said anything. She must know he would want that moment for himself, how important it would be to their relationship. But is tonight really the night to come out to him? Leo doesn't think so. His round one match is scheduled for tomorrow at one PM, so tonight is just about kicking back, staying centered, and, like he does the night before any match, eating lots of sushi. Check, check, and check. This brick townhouse—three stories, high ceilings, big windows, orb chandeliers—is part of his routine during Wimbledon, too. His team rents this place every year, not far from the All England Club, as a reprieve from the endless, often-soulless hotel stays throughout the year. Ruining the stability of this familiar place by dropping the gay bomb—when his dad is already emotional over Mandy Moore's performance in his favorite network TV drama—doesn't seem like the best idea. Besides, Leo has something else planned for tonight that he's much more excited to see through.

Can you meet me at the GMDR at 9?

After waiting eons for a response (two minutes), wiggling his toes nervously under the covers, Gabe finally messages him back.

The hell is the GMDR?

Gentlemen Members' Dressing Room

Ah sorry, your highness. But yes—what for?

It's a secret

You gonna get me in trouble, Leonardo?

I make no promises

The air cooler tonight, Leo pulls on a pair of light jeans and the white cable-knit sweater Wilson gifted him for Wimbledon this year. It looks old-school, a little saggy with two green stripes outlining the V-neck, like the one he's seen his dad wearing in pictures from his own Wimbledon days back in the '80s. He smooths out his hair as he jogs downstairs and, before he can even get a word out to his parents, his dad asks, "Where are you off to?"

"I just forgot something in the GMDR. I'll be back in a bit."

"You can't grab it tomorrow?" his dad asks, sitting with his arm around Sheryl on the curved ivory sofa. Milo Ventimiglia is delivering a line in a tight white T-shirt on the flatscreen mounted opposite them (maybe Leo *should* get into this show?) above the marble fireplace.

"No, it's, um, a good luck thing. A pre-match superstition, that's all," Leo says with a grin, knowing his dad of all people will understand.

"Okay, but don't be out too late. There and back. You need your rest. Great practice today, bud. He looked great," Johnny says, turning to Sheryl now. "Even in that heat, with the ball jumping up real high, he looked great."

"Thanks, Dad," Leo says quickly, antsy to get going. "Anyway, I'll be right back."

Before his parents can keep him any longer, he slips out the door.

"Okay, I knew you had a surprise for me, but I didn't think it would be a third," Gabe says, approaching Leo outside Centre Court.

"Too soon?" Leo says, walking up to him and using every muscle in his body to keep himself from pulling Gabe into a kiss.

There aren't many people around the grounds at nine PM, but Leo does have another guy with him: a short and stout Englishman with wispy white hair, a thick white beard, and a belly that's apparently kept score of how many pints he's had down at the pub.

"Gabe, this is Arthur. He keeps the whole club afloat, pretty much. He's been working here since my dad was playing Wimbledon."

"Nice to meetcha, mate," Arthur says in a heavy accent, gruffer than the usual posh ones you hear at the All England

Club. His eyes are green and friendly. "Call me Archie. I'm the facilities manager here, and a big fan of this kid." He shakes Leo with his rough hands.

"Nice to meet you, too," Gabe says. "You're a friend of Mr. Chambers, er, Johnny?"

"Johnny boy, yeah. My dad worked in facilities at this club way back when. He used to bring me 'round, hoping I'd get into tennis. I did fall in love with it, but I don't know if you noticed, I'm a bit height-challenged. So, it wasn't meant to be," Archie says with a chuckle. "Dad eventually got me a job on the grounds instead. I was starting out when Johnny was starting out, playing his first Wimbledon. We got to talking one day in the locker room. Johnny's dad was a plumber, too. We both came from nothing, but Johnny had the height and the talent for this game. So, he got scouted, and I got stuck with a plunger," Archie says, and laughs, raspy and guttural.

Leo and Gabe both laugh. The summertime bugs are laughing into the night, too, chirping and buzzing in the hundreds of bushes and trees across the club's forty-two acres.

"But I love this place. Know it like the back of these calloused hands," he says, looking down at them. "And I'm glad I do. I was able to help out when Leo came asking questions about his locker."

"Yeah, Leo, what's up?" Gabe asks, confused. "What are we doing?"

"You'll see," Leo says, bursting with excitement. "I want to show you something."

"I've never had this locker before," Leo says, unlocking it. "But when I was reaching for a wristband that got shoved to the back earlier today, I saw something small carved into the wood."

He lifts up the door to the locker and moves his stuff aside, exposing the back left corner.

"I couldn't be sure, but I had a hunch, so I found Archie and asked him."

"What am I looking at?" Gabe asks. "Besides your sweaty gear."

"It's not sweaty! Whatever. Get closer," Leo says, moving so Gabe can step up to the locker. "Put your head in if you have to. Look in the corner."

After a few seconds, Gabe pulls his head out, almost smacking it on the locker door, and gazes at Leo, eyes like a child's on Christmas morning, beholding the gifts under the tree.

"AOR," Gabe says, repeating the initials carved into the back of the locker. "AOR. Do not tell me that's who I think it is."

"Archie, tell him," Leo says, grinning.

"Alex Olmedo Rodríguez," Archie states proudly. "Wimbledon champion, 1959. My dad was working here then, used to show me all the ways former champs would leave their mark at the club, sometimes literally, like this. Wouldn't forget it. He had this locker during that run."

"No fucking way," Gabe says, astounded.

"Better fuckin' believe it," Archie says with a cheeky smile. "Leo told me his mate idolizes Olmedo. Glad I could help out. You've been making your own mark on the tour this season, from what I can tell. Good on ya."

"Thank you," Gabe says, and he shakes Archie's hand, looking speechless. "Thank you so much for this."

"Seriously, thank you, Archie," Leo adds. "I think you just made this guy's life."

"Anytime, buddy," Archie says, patting Leo on the shoulder. "Tell Johnny boy he better get his arse over to my office to say hello."

"Don't worry, I will."

"This facility is closing soon, so don't hang 'round too long," Archie says. "I gotta get back. Final prep before everything starts tomorrow, y'know? Showtime. Good seein' you boys. Go get 'em this week."

"Thanks, Archie," they say in unison.

Once Archie is gone, Gabe turns to Leo. "And you're positive that wasn't Santa Claus?"

Leo knocks his head back with a laugh.

"Or, like, the ghost of Wimbledon past?" Gabe asks.

"Actually, yes. That man has been dead for twenty years," Leo says.

Gabe moves him against the lockers without a word and kisses him slowly and softly.

"So, you liked your surprise, then?" Leo asks.

"I can't believe you," Gabe says, staring at him in disbelief.

"As soon as I saw it, I had a feeling it was Olmedo," Leo says, speaking excitedly. "AOR. I mean, I went through a list of players who would've been top-seeded at Wimbledon over the years in my head, and then I went through an actual list on Wikipedia, and he was the only real option that would've had access to this locker room with those exact initials—"

"No, trust me, I can believe you did your research," Gabe teases. "But I can't believe you remembered how much I love Olmedo. I told you that, what, when were, like, fifteen?"

"The first time we met," Leo says, nodding. "At BP. You told me how much he meant to you because he was Peruvian and he played for the US and he was so successful."

Gabe still looks like he can't compute, mouth parted slightly, eyes narrowed.

"I know you haven't had the season you wanted since you came out," Leo says, taking advantage of Gabe's current inability to speak. "Maybe you haven't won as much as you had hoped. But you still mean so much to people, just being on court, as you."

Part of Leo wants to bolt for the door, the part that's still getting accustomed to being this unguarded in front of Gabe.

But he stays put, following the path of each dark wave on Gabe's head to distract himself from how exposed he feels. How does this man still look this good under fluorescent lighting?

"You—" Gabe appears to be searching for the words.

"Should stop talking now? Yes, I agree."

"—are not what I expected, Leonardo."

They kiss some more. And some more. And some more.

"What if I, you know," Gabe trails off, his eyes trailing down.

"Here?" Leo asks, eyes widening, a bit scandalized.

"Here," Gabe says, leaning in closer as two of his fingers latch onto the belt loops on Leo's jeans. "No one's here this late. And you heard Archie. It's closing soon anyway. We can be quick. If you're up for it."

Leo looks at the door, biting his lip, tapping his foot. "Okay, when I think about how all the stuffy straight British people would collapse if they knew what was going on in their Gentlemen Members' Dressing Room," Leo says, turning a pinkie up, "that's too good."

"I doubt we're the first," Gabe says. "I'm sure Archie knows all the tea."

"Do you think so?" Leo says. His eyes scan the room as he ponders this room's past. "Wow, yeah, I mean, that would make sense, because historically, if you think back to—"

"We don't have time," Gabe spits out, putting a hand up.

"Right, sorry," Leo says, snapping himself out of it. His mouth contorts into a mischievous half-smile. "Okay, yes, I'm in. This is probably the hottest and baddest thing I've ever done."

"I . . . believe that," Gabe says, smirking. He kneels down, and unzips Leo's jeans.

A small yelp pops out of Leo as Gabe wraps his mouth around him.

Walking down a winding street lined with brick townhouses, Leo is pulling the sleeves of his sweater over his hands. There's this moment when he looks at Gabe before he's about to tell him something that still sends a bolt of electricity down his spine. He sees Gabe's face and his brain can't cope with the fact that this is the face of someone Leo can now laugh with, gaze at, confide in. The moment remains such a thrill that he grips at the wool of his sweater to steady himself.

"I hope tonight makes up for me missing your birthday, even a little," Leo says, eyes fixed on Gabe as he passes under a streetlamp. Gabe's birthday was April 10, the early days of their post-kiss silence.

"Eh, it was all right," Gabe teases, staring down the street. There's a pub a bit farther down. Some folks are clinking pints at picnic tables on the sidewalk, under the lit-up sign that reads: THE EARL SPENCER. All the local spots will be packed with Wimby lovers over the fortnight. "My mom got me a gold Saint Michael pendant to wear during my matches. So, you know, tough to top that."

"I take it you're not at church every Sunday, then?" Leo asks. "Also, insert joke here about me not being tough to top."

"Gonna go ahead and move right along to your question," Gabe says, nudging Leo's shoulder with his own. "I did go to church a lot growing up. My parents still do. My mom knows I don't anymore, but I think she feels like it's her duty to at least try and keep me close to God. She means well. Like, she prays that I'm safe while I travel and that I stay true to who I am. And I know plenty of people who are praying that I *don't* stay true to who I am, so."

Leo wants to grab his hand but hesitates.

"Wait so, your dad's dad was a plumber?" Gabe asks. "That's what Archie said, right?"

"Yeah, he was. My grandma stayed home with my dad and the other kids. There were five of them. They didn't have much money at all. But my grandpa was a huge tennis fan and would take my dad, the oldest of the kids, to the public courts nearby. He practiced every day, played in some local tournaments, and he caught the eye of a coach who thought he could be a big talent, and he offered to fund him. The rest is, well, you know."

"Damn. That's wild," Gabe says. "Your grandpa must've been so proud of him."

"Oh, yeah. He died before I was born, but he did get to see my dad play in the US Open final. He was, to quote my grandma, 'weeping like a willow.' He was so proud of him."

Leo glances over and Gabe's just there, walking beside him, looking on in wonder. The little bolt of electricity strikes again.

"She moved in with my parents and me. I don't think she liked living alone, and she wanted to help out how she could. They were paying for all these new medications and taking my dad to get all these new treatments, and my mom was still working. She was a journalist, but then she quit and became a realtor so she could be closer to home and see me more. My grandma knew it would be a lot with my dad adjusting and my mom busy, so she moved in with us."

"Is he doing okay, by the way, your dad?"

"Yeah, he's okay, thanks," Leo says.

And, for once, he doesn't feel he needs to stop there.

"Usually, I'm not *hoping* for rain at Wimbledon, but I actually am this time, just so things cool down," he says. "It's tougher for him during the summer tournaments now that it's getting hotter and hotter every year. He should really use his cane, but I know he's embarrassed. Which I get. And I hate that he has to feel that way. But I just want him to take care of himself."

"Yeah," Gabe says. "Of course."

"He's been trying to let me do my thing on court this week, at least. And he set up that practice with you. So, I'll take the wins I can get."

"I mean, with *that* second serve, you should."

Leo stops walking and blinks at him, a smile slowly emerging.

"Kidding," Gabe says, stepping closer. "You've barely been double faulting lately."

"You've been watching my matches, Montoya?" Leo asks, cocking his head.

Behind Gabe, he sees a black taxi trudge down the street, followed by a double-decker bus. He knows it makes him a typical American tourist, but he's always loved how picturesque the transportation is in London, like souvenir fridge magnets come to life.

"I guess I *should* thank you, though," Leo says.

"What for?" Gabe asks, brushing his fingertips against Leo's.

"You—I don't know," Leo says. "You help get me out of my head."

Gabe looks at him for a moment, then says, "Just know that I would kiss the shit out of you right now if the paparazzi weren't such dickheads here. They're swarming outside my hotel with the amount of players staying there. And I'm guessing a photo of the first out gay guy playing Wimbledon pays a pretty penny . . . shilling? Pound? Quid? I can never keep track."

Leo recalls a paparazzi photo he saw of Gabe during Wimbledon last year—a heavy flash spotlighting him as he left a London nightclub with Cara Delevingne on the Friday night before the tournament. Meanwhile, the only tabloid images one can find of Leo during Wimby are those of him riding a green fixed-gear bike from his townhouse to the All England Club ("BABY ROD'S HOT ROD," one of the headlines read).

"I'm sorry again that we can't be public about, well, this," Leo says, gesturing in the slim space between them. "I'm just, you know. I'm still not ready for that. It would be a media circus if I came out, let alone if they knew we were together. I don't want that mess for you, either, after everything you've been through already. Not to mention, I still haven't told my dad yet."

"Leo, it's fine. Seriously. Trust me, I know better than anyone that you can't rush these things. Esme had an entire play-by-play guide in the works for *months* before I told everyone, just to make sure it all panned out how we wanted it to. She should maybe just be my coach?"

"She should really sit in your box more often. It would intimidate people," Leo says. "Ooh, and she could prop up one of the cardboard cutouts next to her, too."

Gabe narrows his eyes while feigning a laugh, then pulls Leo into the dim alleyway to their right. He leans Leo's back against the brick wall.

"But really, Leonardo. Being with you, even in secret, is more than enough for me," Gabe says. "Way more."

He gives Leo one long, lingering kiss.

CHAPTER EIGHTEEN

Leo expected his first-round match to be a bit more challenging, considering his opponent, an eighteen-year-old Dutchman, has been making a splash this season: Johan de Vries, the youngest player to crack the top one hundred, behind Chris Robinson, of course, the American teen Leo met back at BP in September. But the crowd at the side court he's playing on this afternoon—an intimate gathering of fans applauding politely in their sun hats—haven't been treated to a long tussle. After just an hour and forty-five minutes, during which Johan has been nervously flinging most of his shots long, Leo has reached match point.

He pulls at the shoulder of his white polo, readjusting the sleeve so his arm feels looser. He glances at his box for encouragement, where both Brian and Johnny have looked more than pleased with his performance today, as has his mom, who hasn't needed to bite her nails or cover her eyes at all. In the back of his mind, he's also glad this match has been short so his dad doesn't have to sit in the sun for too long. He steps up to the painted white line and bounces the ball. He blocks out the sounds of the action on the adjacent courts. He tosses it up.

Leo serves big at 136 mph.

Johan manages a weak return.

Leo sends a forehand screaming into the corner.

Johan lunges over and whacks his own forehand back.

Johan has barely returned to ready position after his last shot when Leo finds an even sharper angle for his next forehand, the ball leaving small blades of grass in its wake as it zips off the court for a winner.

"Game, set, and match: Chambers," the ump calls. "6–4, 6–3, 6–1."

The crowd rise to their feet, applauding more loudly now with some whistles mixed in, and Leo clenches a fist with a smile as he looks to his box, where he's met with even bigger smiles. When he turns back to meet Johan at the net, though, there's no smile to be found. Leo can see the utter dejection in his eyes. This was Johan's first main draw match at Wimbledon, a moment that would overwhelm anyone. With the success he's been having this season over some of the top players, he likely hoped to come out here and continue to wow the fans, taking out a seeded player like Leo, or at least making him work hard for the win. But instead, he couldn't meet the moment, and Leo trampled him in under two hours. Any seasoned player remembers that feeling well, when you're an up-and-comer and you believe you're invincible, and then you get your ass handed to you while the world watches. It's humiliating.

Before Johan can sink too deeply into his own head, Leo clasps his hand over the net and leans in and says in a low voice, "You're an amazing player. Wimbledon hasn't seen the last of you. You have so much time."

"Thank you," Johan whispers back, and pats Leo on the chest. "Thank you."

They each shake the ump's hand, and Leo walks back onto the court, applauding with his racket and waving to the spectators in thanks. One down.

The stars over Britain seem to have aligned for Leo, because over the next several days, he's able to continue his dominant performance. Not only is he managing to strike a balance between creativity and reliability on the court that keeps both Brian and Johnny happy—his dad is always a bit happier when Sheryl is there, too—he's also playing matches later in the afternoon, as the sun descends from its peak, so his dad is able to enjoy some relief from the July heat. He cruises through his second- and third-round matches, wrapping up the former in three sets and the latter in four. He's on an opposite schedule from Gabe, Tess, and Ollie, so on his off-days throughout the week, he's able to watch their matches from the gym and his townhouse. They, too, are finding their rhythm, confidently securing their spots in the round of sixteen. Leo expected as much from Tess and Ollie, but making the fourth round at Wimbledon is a first for Gabe, and when he wins his third-round match, Leo is glued to the TV, watching as Gabe drops his racket and thrusts his fists in the air, staring up into the heavens.

Leo wants to immediately unstrap his feet from the rowing machine he's using in the gym and race over to Court 2, shove his way past security, and pull Gabe into the biggest, wettest, gayest kiss in UK history since King James and George Villiers. But, instead, he settles for increasing his stroke rate on the rowing machine from twenty-four to twenty-five.

When Gabe approaches the camera after his win—his big brown eyes a bit watery, a few sweaty curls matted to his forehead—he takes the Sharpie from the cameraman, and on the screen he writes "For Olmedo" and a heart.

Leo's rate on the machine jumps from twenty-five to twenty-six.

Experience, more than anything, is often what determines how a player performs during the second week of a Slam, including Wimbledon. In those stages of such a high-profile event, when the player field grows smaller, the stakes, the arenas, and the audiences grow much larger. A player who has made it to the final rounds of Wimbledon knows that added weight well, and it can become like muscle memory. They know what's ahead of them: how to manage the volume of the crowd, how to play every point like it's their last, how to control their breath when it washes over them that they're among the last players standing at the most prestigious tournament in tennis. Their body remembers how to perform under such pressurized conditions. It has never felt particularly natural to Leo, but it does feel familiar, having been to the quarterfinals of Wimbledon before. And it's this experience that carries him there again, lifting him to victory in his fourth-round match on Court 1: 7–6, 6–7, 6–2, 6–4.

"You looked so good at your match today," Gabe says before kissing Leo on the cheek. Leo has just arrived at Gabe's hotel room a little after ten PM after sneaking by his parents, who were both asleep on the couch while, again, marathoning *This Is Us*. He then snuck past the paparazzi buzzing outside the hotel. Unlike with the men he's met with in the past, he didn't need to rely on any Grindr ambiguity or a question about an affinity for sports in order to make this hookup happen—just a good ol' fashioned disguise comprised of a baggy sweatshirt, a baseball cap, sunglasses, and a KN95 mask.

"Thanks," Leo says, blushing, and kisses him back. He removes his sunglasses.

"You know those probably made you look *more* suspicious, right?"

"That's what you think. The paps would recognize these blue eyes anywhere," he teases.

"Uh huh," Gabe says, kissing him again. "Well, I'm glad your *sensitive* blue eyes weren't too affected by the sun out there today. Quarterfinals. That's huge, Leo." Gabe's beaming.

"We don't have to talk about it," Leo says, cozying up against the mahogany headboard of Gabe's bed.

"Why?"

Leo shrugs, gesturing vaguely toward Gabe, knowing he can infer the answer.

"I'm not upset I didn't make it to the quarters, if that's what you're worried about. I didn't even expect to make it to the third round with the draw I had, let alone the last sixteen. I was playing with house money as it was. I'm still riding that high. Promise."

"I'm really glad to hear that," Leo says. "You should be so proud. I know I am. I still can't get over your camera message."

"I know. You texted me about it, like, every hour on the hour that day. Esme thought my number was leaked on Reddit or something," Gabe says, laughing as he leans back on the headboard. "After seeing those initials, though, I do think keeping Olmedo in mind helped me. Thank you for that. Again."

Leo kisses him. "You're welcome. Again."

"Okay, so, how are you feeling about your next match?" Gabe repositions, lying on his side, propping his head up with his left hand.

He knows it's corny, but he loves seeing Gabe like this, totally at ease, including his hair, which isn't perfectly coiffed for once.

"Well, I'm sure you know, but I'm playing Sascha."

"Fuck that guy," Gabe says.

"Again, pass," Leo says, giving him a cheeky smile.

"No, seriously," Gabe says, nudging Leo's leg with his foot. "Everybody acts like he's superhuman because he's won a ton of

Slams, but he's not. He's . . . regular-human. Liv said as much, about how she saw pain in him, too. Try to remember he's just another guy on the other side of the net."

"I know you're right," Leo says, leaning his head on the headboard. "But that's way easier said than done."

"I know," Gabe says. "And I know you lost to him in Australia, but you've been playing so well on grass this season. You can take him."

Leo squirms as he tries to digest Gabe's compliment. "Who knew you were so sweet?"

"And a little spicy," Gabe says as he stretches over to his nightstand, picking up the worn romance novel laid there, spine up, pages flayed out. "Reading these bookshelps distract me from my nerves the night before a match. They're so fucking good—and steamy."

Leo grabs the paperback in Gabe's hand, *Love in Bloom*. The title is written in elegant, swirling script, adorned with delicate floral accents. Below it, two muscular men gaze into each other's eyes, surrounded by a ring of rose petals. Behind them is a picturesque little town nestled in the English countryside.

"Ahem," Leo says, and begins to read aloud from the back cover. "In the quaint town of Meadowbrook, where gossip blooms faster than spring flowers, Colin, a reserved botanist, finds solace in his greenhouse amid the chaos of his family's bustling floral shop. But when his childhood crush, Dexter, returns to town, Colin's carefully cultivated peace is uprooted."

Leo looks up from the book. "Colin and Dexter? I'm obsessed."

"The whitest names ever," Gabe says. "Keep going, and in a British accent, please."

"Fine," Leo says, and sits upright before resuming his narration. "Dexter, now a successful landscape architect, has always carried a torch for Colin, but never had the courage to reveal his true feelings. Returning to Meadowbrook to care for his ailing grandmother, Dexter wants to finally seize the opportunity he missed years ago. As the two reconnect, their friendship blossoms into something more. But their budding romance faces opposition from Colin's overbearing mother and the judgmental townsfolk. Colin and Dexter must find the strength to let their love bloom, even if it means weathering the storm of small-town prejudice."

"The sex scene on page 152? You're not ready," Gabe says.

"Um, yes the hell I am," Leo says, handing Gabe the book. "Please, please, please read it. But not in a British accent. Yours is horrifying."

"Asks me to read him smut and then insults my accent work." Gabe shakes his head. "Wow."

"Oh, just read," Leo says, smiling.

Gabe stands on the bed and clears his throat, holding the novel out like he's about to perform Shakespeare. "The sun was setting over the sprawling garden, their hands covered in soil and sweat glistening on their skin. The air was thick with the scent of blooming flowers. Colin wiped his brow, casting a glance toward Dexter, who was kneeling nearby, his muscles flexing as he tended to a bed of roses. A rush of heat flooded Colin's cheeks as he felt Dexter's eyes roam over him, igniting a fire deep within. Wordlessly, Dexter rose to his feet and closed the distance between them, his movements smooth and confident. Dexter pulled Colin into a deep, passionate kiss, and Colin, like the roses below, was ready to bloom for him."

"Did Troye Sivan write this?" Leo interrupts.

"*Anyway*," Gabe says, and returns to narrating. "Moaning wildly, Colin's hands dug into the earth, grabbing fistfuls of dirt as Dexter's wood dug into—"

"Oh my God," Leo says.

"AS DEXTER'S WOOD," Gabe continues loudly, impatient with Leo's interruptions, "dug into Colin's own secret garden."

“I changed my mind,” Leo says, laughing uncontrollably. “I can’t do this. I’m such a child, but I can’t do this.” He pulls Gabe down onto the bed. “But I love that you love this. And . . . let me just say . . . I wouldn’t hate if you, well, dug your wood into my secret gar—”

Gabe wrestles Leo on top of him, laughing. “I do hate you.”

Leo grins stupidly. “For real, though.”

“You really want to *bloom* for me the night before your quarterfinal?” Gabe asks.

“I mean, I need to be able to walk tomorrow,” Leo says, running a hand through his hair. “But yeah, I think I can manage, even without grabbing . . . what was it . . . fistfuls of dirt?”

Another fit of laughter takes over him as Gabe yanks him down for a kiss.

A few minutes after Gabe has finished planting his seed in Leo’s secret garden, their afterglow is interrupted by a rapping on the door.

“Mierda,” Gabe says, jumping. “Uh, just put your clothes on and hide in—”

“Gaaaaabe,” the woman at the door whines.

“Oh, it’s Esme,” Gabe says. “Still, put your clothes on.”

“Obviously,” Leo says, tugging his jeans on. “Should I put the sunglasses back on, or?”

“You’re so funny,” Gabe teases.

Another rapping on the door.

“Okay, okay,” Gabe says as he pulls on a gray T-shirt. He checks that Leo is fully clothed and then opens the door, though not all the way. “Es, hey, what’s up? It’s . . . eleven o’clock.”

Esme’s thin frame slinks past Gabe into the room. “I know, I know, but you know I don’t sleep and I was looking over you summer schedule and I wanted to go over few things before I fly out tomorrow mor—”

As she's tucking her hair behind her ears, she clocks Leo standing uncomfortably by the bathroom. "Hi again, Esme," he says bashfully. "We met back at Indian Wells. I'm—"

"You're fucking," she says, turning back to Gabe. "I knew it."

"What makes you say that?" Leo asks innocently.

"My love, your shirt is on both backward *and* inside out," she says to him.

Gabe palms his own face.

"Listen, I'm happy for you both, don't get me wrong," she says, standing there, a hand on her hip, wearing a lavender sweatsuit. "I love a sporty power couple. I can't think of any off the top of my head, but I love them. I just want you to be careful, okay? Dating another guy on tour, if that *is* what's going on here, would be big, big news. Not to mention Leo being queer, too. Mazel, by the way," she says, nodding to Leo before speaking to Gabe again. "This season has been rocky enough with sponsors and hate mail and—"

"I know, I know," Gabe says, frustrated.

Esme sighs, looking at Gabe like a little brother. "I love you, kid. You know that. I just think it would be wise to keep this on the DL. For your own sanity. For Leo's, too."

Gabe smiles halfheartedly. "Yeah."

"Andre Agassi and Steffi Graf! There's one," she says with a snap of her fingers. "They're still together, right? Okay, well, I'll let you two do your thing, and I'll send you my thoughts on your schedule in an email instead," she says, walking to the door. "Night, boys."

And with that, the tornado that is Esme sweeps out of the room. The door clicks shut.

"I'm sorry about that," Gabe says, shaking his head. "Esme is, uh, hashtag no filter."

They're both frozen where they're standing.

"It's okay," Leo says quietly, crossing his arms, shoulders hunched. "I mean, she's right. There *would* be a ton of press, even if I *were* out already. I still just don't know if I can't handle that right now, coming out, going public. I—I guess we should be more careful, until we have this figured out. And I'm the one who should be sorry. You shouldn't have to hide again, because of me. That's not fair. You should be off finding somebody who already has their shit together."

"I like your shit," Gabe says, and then winces. "Sorry. You know what I mean. I told you, Leo, I want to be with you, even if it's in secret."

Leo studies his face. He wants to believe him, and mostly he does, but he can't shake the sinking feeling that he's keeping Gabe from something better, from a truly open life. But he doesn't want to push the subject, especially when Gabe seems like he might be getting tired of Leo's apologies.

"Okay," Leo says. "I do think you coming to my matches isn't the best idea. Esme might be right. But would you stick around a few more days? In London, I mean? We have our house through the weekend. We stay the whole two weeks every year, even if I don't make it far in the tournament. My parents have a little birthday thing for me in the backyard before we head back to Florida for the summer. You can ask Esme, but I don't think that would exactly be high-risk, do you? If you're free. And if you want. I missed your birthday, so it's not like you—"

"I wouldn't miss it, Leonardo. Text me the details and I'll be there. But for now," Gabe says, his face turning stern, "go take down Sascha."

Leo doesn't speak Russian. But as he's preparing for his quarter-final match inside the Gentlemen Members' Dressing Room, tying and retying his sneakers, he can tell that Sascha and his team are talking about him, their sneering and snickering aimed in his direction. It could just be Esme's frantic speech from the night before causing him to project, but he's paranoid that somehow Sascha knows. About him. About him and Gabe. The thought of a secret like that in the hands of a man like this? It sends a shiver down Leo's spine. As the Russian team leaves the room, he hears Sascha mutter something under his breath. Leo tries to remember what he heard, thinking he could try his best to type it into Google Translate, but then Brian appears.

"Hey, LC, how are you feeling?" Brian asks, giving him a pat on the arm. "I wanted to tell you this now before you get out there and see for yourself, but your dad won't be in the box today. We were heading over here and he was having too much trouble in the heat. Sheryl and I had to do some convincing, but we got him to stay behind. She staying with him and watching from the house. I'm sorry, LC. I know it's not ideal when you were expecting him. But I'll be out there, the rest of the team will be out there. We played a lot of this season just you and me. We got this. You got this."

"He's okay, right? Did he fall? What happened?" Leo asks, rising from the bench.

"No, no, nothing like that. He was just having a hard time walking, even with his cane. The goddamn weather here is so humid. We didn't think he could do the stadium stairs. He didn't seem to think he could, either."

"Fuck. Okay. Well. Um." Leo's eyes search the locker room for an answer. To what, he isn't sure.

"I'll be in your box whenever you need me. Same game plan," Brian says, maintaining clear, steady eye contact. Leo is aware of it, even as his own eyes are scanning the room anxiously. "Play without fear."

The room leading to Centre Court is a blend of grandeur and tradition, just like the esteemed tournament it serves. The walls are adorned with photographs and memorabilia from Wimbledon's storied history, capturing iconic moments and players frozen in time. Grand wooden staircases and parquet floors lend an air of sophistication to the space. Ahead of Leo and Sascha are the imposing doors leading to Centre Court, their polished surface reflecting the soft glow of the overhead lights. Tall and majestic, they serve as a gateway to tennis greatness. Ornate brass handles adorn each door, gleaming in the ambient light. Though he's been here before, as Leo approaches, he can't help but feel a surge of anticipation building in his gut. These doors symbolize the culmination of years of hard work—his own and that of his predecessors. Above the doors is an inscription, a line from Rudyard Kipling's poem "If—": "If you can meet with triumph and disaster / And treat those two impostors just the same."

Before he can fully center himself, he's on the legendary Centre Court, fifteen thousand spectators in the sweeping yet intimate arena, the relentless sun blazing overhead as he faces off against the Russian. Not a blade of grass is out of place, the path of the lawn mower's meticulous work shown in perfect, wide stripes.

It's a high-speed match from the beginning, but while Leo's body is thrashing about the court, his mind is preoccupied with his dad. It gnaws at him, distracting him from the match. He wants to look to Brian in his box for encouragement or words of advice, but looking there is just a reminder of his dad. He should be there with him, at the house. Brian's right that they've done this just the two of them for most of this season, but Johnny's sudden absence feels different today. They seemed to be getting back in a groove, seemed to be finding their way, and now his seat is there, empty. And it's one of the only seats that is. The stadium is packed, including those in the royal box—a slew of celebrities like Ariana Grande, Cynthia Erivo, Andrew Garfield, David and Victoria Beckham, Emma Watson. The list goes on, and on goes Leo's anxiety.

As the match progresses, he tries to focus, tries to think of Gabe, tries to remember that Sascha is just some guy on the other side of the net. But Sascha's impossibly precise play leaves him struggling to keep up. Each serve, each volley, feels like a test of his resolve. The tension builds with every point, but he can't shake the feeling of unease. Fatigue sets in, weighing down his limbs and clouding his mind. He fights with everything he has, conjuring his past experience at this stage of Wimbledon, but Sascha's relentless assault leaves him on the defensive. Frustration bubbles up inside him with every missed shot, every lost point—each one punctuated by an obnoxious roar from Sascha to the crowd, his index finger tapping his ear, urging the fans to get even louder for him.

Though he manages to hold his own in the third set, at five–all, the Russian goes up a break, and victory seems to slip further and further from his grasp. Sascha's dominance is unwavering, his triumph seemingly inevitable. And then, in an instant, it's over. With his twenty-third ace of the match, Sascha takes Leo down, the stadium up on its feet. With his opponent's muttering in the locker room still worming around his brain, Leo can only muster a weak handshake at the net, Sascha smiling smugly.

As he walks off the court, waving farewell to the stadium (mostly to Ariana Grande), the defeat is heavy on his shoulders. But he stops for the fans, especially the kids, reaching out to get his autograph on hats and balls and printed-out pictures. He makes his way down the line, picking up each item and signing, but as his hand moves to the latest photo, he realizes it's not a photo of him. It's his dad. At Wimbledon in the '80s. Leo can tell by the white retro sweatband he's wearing in the photo. He looks up at the fortysomething man who handed it to him.

"I'm a big fan of your dad's, too," he says, grinning widely.

Leo wants to reach out and hug the strawberries and cream out of this guy. But he just smiles and says, "That means so much." He signs the photo and returns it to him.

If Leo is hoping to downplay that he's turning thirty, his friends and family have other ideas. When he walks outside to the lush backyard garden of his London rental, he sees his least favorite number spelled out with two huge, shiny, golden balloons floating above his most favorite people.

"There he is!" Tess yells, and the group—his mom, dad, Brian, Ollie, Liv, and Gabe—all turn toward him, clapping and cheering. She jogs up to him and wraps him in a black sash that says "Thirty, flirty, and thriving" in sparkly gold letters. "The birthday boy! Welcome to the thirties club, dude!"

Yeah, downplaying this dreaded milestone is not in the cards.

Leo agreed to stay upstairs while everyone finished decorating the backyard with balloons, streamers, confetti, and a spread with his favorites: sushi, tacos, and an assortment of chips and dips. The sight of Gabe there with everyone—his guy, a part of his circle—settles warmly in his belly, a new sensation he wishes he could bottle. If only he could find it in himself to tell Brian and his dad the whole truth. He'll still need to keep up appearances today.

He hopes being surrounded by his people will help ease the sting of reaching *the* age. The age that for him, and for so many other players, signals the beginning of the end of his career. The age when Andy Roddick announced his retirement—

"On his thirtieth birthday," Gabe says in unison with Leo. "Yes, you've told me."

"Hey! I'm sensitive about it, okay?" Leo says, snatching a chip out of Gabe's hand. "I've had that in the back of my mind for a long time now."

"I know, I'm sorry," Gabe says, brushing his fingertips against Leo's, a habit of his now. "I just think, look at Tess. She made the top ten and the finals of Wimbledon at thirty. Being in your thirties isn't a dealbreaker anymore. Maybe the best is yet to come for you, too."

That's what's kept Leo busy and distracted in the couple days following his quarters loss: Tess's incredible run to the finals. He went to each of her last three matches, holding his breath during every point, holding her mom's hand, holding back tears as Tess made her runner-up speech after losing a nail-biter of a final—6–4, 7–6.

"I might not totally feel it in this moment, but I'm really proud to be a final girl," she said tearfully to a packed Centre Court, referencing a classic horror movie trope: the last girl left alive, the one to confront the killer, the survivor. "I hope every girl watching knows they have it inside them to be anything they want. Look at the two women competing today. Both women of color, both competing at the highest level of the game. This is what tennis looks like. I want us to keep uplifting each other. I also want to say that I couldn't do any of this without my amazing friends and family. I love you, Mom and Dad. So much. And Dad, maybe now you can finally stop telling me I could always come work at your law firm."

Leo and the entire stadium, including Tess's mom, laughed along with her, grateful for the comic relief—though they were quickly moved to tears again when Kate Middleton presented Tess with her trophy. Gabe's mention of her run to the finals reminds Leo that he has something else to present her with now.

"It did take until twenty-nine for us to finally"—for a moment, Leo wants to say to Gabe, "start loving each other," but he balks, and pivots—"stop hating each other, so, yeah, maybe you're right. Maybe the best is still yet to come." He blushes at the sound of his own corny words, though he's not sure he totally believes them. "I'll be right back. Ollie and I have something to give Tess."

From inside the house, they carry out a round white cake with thin, black birthday candles circling the edges and "CONGRATS, FINAL GIRL" written in blood-red icing, which is dripping dramatically down the sides, too.

"We're supposed to give *you* the cake," Tess says, her face a combination of gratitude for the gesture and annoyance that they've made her cry again. She leans in, her tears twinkling in the candlelight, and whispers to them, "Thank you, guys. And please know, I'd go back for you if you tripped in a horror movie."

As Leo's party draws to a close, he spots his dad off by himself, farther into the garden, admiring the landscaping and gravel work. They haven't talked much the past few days, wrapped up in the excitement of Tess's success. But this could finally be the right moment. He takes a calming breath and, as he walks over, he laughs to himself, too, thinking back to Gabe's romance novel and its secret gardens.

"Getting any ideas for the yard back home?" Leo asks, walking up behind Johnny as he takes a too-close photo of a patch of brilliant red and pink sweet peas.

"Leo, the only thing I have ever been able to grow back home is weeds," he says with a chuckle. "So, did you enjoy your party?"

"I did," Leo says. "Thanks for all this. It's been great."

"Good, good," Johnny says. "That was nice of you guys to get a cake for Tess. She's something, isn't she? Your mom and I are so glad you've kept up with her and Ollie. And Gabe now, too. Who would've thought?"

"Yeah, right?" Leo asks, his heels digging into the gravel walkway. Okay. He can do this. It's time. "Um, speaking of—"

"Speaking of—" his dad says at the same time.

"Oh, go ahead," Leo says.

"Well," Johnny says, "I was just going to say, speaking of your mom, before we fly out, I wanted to tell you that I'll be sticking around Delray with her for a bit when we get back home."

"For a couple weeks, right? Until Atlanta?" Leo asks.

"Um, no, actually," Johnny says. "Until New York."

"Wait, what? You're not doing the summer swing? Is everything okay?"

Johnny brushes his hand against the white dahlias beside him. A sudden cackle from Tess erupts in the background. She'll probably have a funny story to tell him later.

"Leo, you deserve a consistent coach. You need a stable team. I can't be up and down like this. I know it threw you off in the quarters when I couldn't be there last minute, and—"

"No, it—"

"Leo, you don't have to do that. I know it affected you, bud. I could see it in your game. So, if it's okay, I'll come to the Open, but I should skip the warm-up tournaments. I should just rest up, crank the AC, watch from home. And if it makes sense, I'll rejoin you guys in New York. We'll figure the rest out from there."

"Are you sure? Maybe we could—"

"I'm sure," Johnny says, and puts his hand on Leo's shoulder.

"Okay but, Dad, you have to come to the Open," Leo pleads, knowing that this is likely his last shot for them to win it together. He suddenly feels much younger than thirty. "We need you there. We . . . I can't imagine doing that without you. So, I need you to take care of yourself this summer. I'll come home when I can. But be ready for New York. Okay? Please?"

"Okay," Johnny says, nodding. "I'll be ready. And you will too, right? Keep practicing hard with Brian. This is your year. But, Leo, have fun, too. I want you to have fun. I do."

Leo gives him a hug, hoping for some stability amid the emotional turbulence. He can practically hear the clock ticking—on his dad's career and his own.

"Now, what were you going to say?" Johnny asks.

"Oh, um," Leo says, sputtering. "You know what? I don't even remember now."

"Ah, I'm sorry. You sure?"

"Yeah," Leo says, waving his hand, "slipped my mind. Must not have been anything important. Let's get back to the party before everybody takes off."

"Yeah, let's go enjoy what's left," Johnny says, walking back to the group with Leo. "Happy birthday, bud."

The summer swing ahead of the US Open is always steamy. Over the next month, the players will make their way through a swampy American circuit—from Atlanta to DC to Cincinnati—as temperatures climb higher, an oppressive heat radiating off the hard courts, practically melting their sneakers. But Leo's dad is always quick to remind him, "It's not the heat that gets you, it's the humidity." Leo sort of misses those dad-isms as he inches closer and closer to the US Open without him there.

What distracts him from the anxiety that his dad might miss their last Open together, though, is that this summer swing is even steamier than usual. Playing the same tournaments, Leo and Gabe are inseparable, their bodies constantly finding their way to each other.

One night, in the Cincinnati locker room, Gabe walks past Leo in nothing but a white towel, which he briefly opens as he passes, flashing him. "Let's go," he says, nodding toward the showers.

"Excuse me?" Leo panic-whispers back, unable to take his eyes off Gabe, who's slowly getting hard. "We have to be careful!"

Stolen touches, quick kisses. That's as far as they've let themselves go in public. They've been good about keeping things clandestine. Really, they have. But did Leo actually think it would stay that way? Come on.

"Nobody's here right now," Gabe says, looking around at the empty locker room, then back at Leo with a mischievous glint in his eye. "Practices are done for the day."

Leo does another scan of the room as he bites his lower lip. "Okay, fine!" he whisper-yells as Gabe walks away. He pulls off his shorts, yanking them over his own dick that's now growing, wraps a towel around his waist, and scurries after him.

The curtain on each shower stall is pulled shut, except for one. Leo can see steam wafting out of it farther down the row. He glances over his shoulder one last time and walks toward it. Inside, he finds a scene that may actually strike him dead. A naked Gabe is facing him, fully hard, hair slicked back, soaping himself up.

"Get my back?" Gabe asks nonchalantly, that smirk of his slowly emerging, clearly aware that he's causing Leo's entire body to malfunction. Well, not his *entire* body. He's now poking out of his towel as he stands there, trying to grasp how he's found himself at a tennis tournament, in a locker room, gazing at Gabe in a shower stall. It's like a waking wet dream.

"Get in here," Gabe says, hands moving in circles over his chest and stomach, spreading around the suds.

Leo drops his towel, steps into the stall, and pulls the curtain shut behind him. He knows this is risky. He knows this is the opposite of what Esme told them to do. But holy fucking hell, this might be worth ruining his career.

There is no speaking in the minutes that follow. Leo couldn't find the words if he tried. He can only focus on muffling his own moaning. One hand is steadying himself against the white tiled wall, the other is getting himself off. Gabe's hands grip Leo's waist as he thrusts, slick thighs slapping against slick thighs. Leo turns his head to glance back, and Gabe leans forward, kissing Leo deeply. It's a little sloppy and a lot wet, and he loves it. He never wants this to end, but he can't hold back, and releases onto the wall.

After Gabe finishes, Leo faces him, and pulls him in gently, arms wrapping around his back, hands pressing into his firm shoulders.

As Leo holds onto him under the water, watching dozens of drops slide down the curves of Gabe's body, he senses it. A feeling that's been working its way to the surface over the past several months. Over the past several years, really. And now it's here. He pulls his head back to look into Gabe's eyes, and he's sure of it now. He can come clean, to himself at least. He smooths out Gabe's hair and quietly admires how beautiful this man is, while water streaks down both of their faces, steam swirling around them.

Yes, he's sure of it now. Leo is in love with Gabe.

Grand Slam: US Open
Surface: Hard
Where: Queens, New York
When: August 26–September 8, 2024

CHAPTER NINETEEN

Four days before the US Open begins, Leo is stuck in traffic in the back of a black Escalade on his way to practice, watching a clip on Instagram of *What a Racket*'s latest episode, featuring Brad Gilbert, who coached Andy Roddick to his US Open victory in 2003.

"Leo Chambers has been one of the most consistent players on tour this year. He's knocking on the door of the top ten again after his quarterfinals run at Wimbledon and after a solid swing around the United States this summer. He's the number one American player again and the number eleven seed at the Open. I don't know, Paul, I think this could finally be Baby Rod's year."

"Here's the thing, Brad. If you look at his results at the Slams this year, he made the third round at the Australian Open, fourth round at Roland-Garros, and quarterfinals at Wimbledon. So, yeah, he's trending up. The next step in that pattern would be semifinals at the US Open. But he's been there before, two years ago. Does he really have it in him to go all the way? Especially with his dad's health weighing on him? Having a coach in and out of your box all season can affect your mentality, and I think it has with Chambers."

"I hear you. And, of course, all our best to Johnny. One of the best guys I know. But with Brian Wilkins at the helm this year, he's had such a positive effect on Leo. Has it gotten sloppy at times? Sure. But he's gotten Leo to loosen up and understand that even if he's not in fifth gear, he can drop down to fourth gear and still play lights-out tennis. He can throw in some variety to supplement when his shots maybe aren't firing on all cylinders. I wouldn't count him out, Paul. Leo hasn't gotten any titles this season, but he's still got that champion's mindset."

"You make some good points, my friend. And yes, we're hoping Johnny is feeling well. We've seen glimpses of him practicing with his son on the grounds this week, so that's a positive sign. So inspiring to see him still out there. One thing I'll say: Leo just turned thirty this year, so the clock's tickin'. Only time will tell if he still has it in him to fulfill that prophecy everybody had for him from the beginning—to be the next American man to win the US Open. We'll just have to wait and see if he can find his form in New York again. It's going to be an exciting two weeks either way. I'll be keeping you updated on all things Leo Chambers and US Open. Thank you, Brad, for hoppin' on here with me. Let's get a round of golf in soon, yeah?"

"Always a pleasure, Paul. Sounds good to me, buddy."

"And hopefully I'll see some of you, my listeners, around the grounds soon. This is Davis, Paul Davis, signing off."

Three days before the US Open begins, Leo is stuck in traffic in the back of a black Escalade on his way to practice, checking out Serving Looks' post about his upcoming first-round match.

> **servinglooks** Y'all, now that the draw is out, Leo Chambers must be *rejoicing* that he's not up against Gabe

> Montoya in the first round of the US Open like last year. (But tbh, I would've loved to have seen that rematch now that they're besties. I'm still not over those shirtless photos of them practicing together in DC!!!). Instead of his kryptonite, he's up against a Croatian qualifier he's beaten handily before, so let's hope this is the launching pad he needs to find his form in New York again. I want to see my favorite guy go all the way, don't you? Side note: So, so happy to see his dad back on the team, too.

Two days before the US Open begins, Leo is stuck in traffic in the back of a black Escalade on his way to practice, overhearing a clip on a sports radio channel the driver is playing.

"He's gotten some good results this year, but his dad has been on and off his team, he's been trying to shift his game from counter-puncher to aggressor, and he's gotten closer with his former nemesis, Gabe Montoya, who's been a lightning rod for press this year. That's a lot on Chambers's plate. Can he balance it all?" one of the radio hosts asks.

"We know he's a resilient player. And the proof is in the pudding. We've seen him get to the semis in New York before. Let's hope he can find that form again."

The day before the US Open begins, Leo is stuck in traffic in the back of a black Escalade on his way to practice, listening to his Queen pump-up playlist while he locks every social media app on his phone.

CHAPTER TWENTY

Leo Chambers has found his form in New York again. With his dad back on the team after a month of rest and now showing support for the creativity Brian has been fostering in his game, Leo has been feeling confident, instinctual, fluid. He also looks damn good in his retro kit: a white polo with black and light-blue stripes down the sleeves, white short-shorts, tube socks with black and light-blue stripes around the top, and white sneakers.

In the first three rounds, he has proven that he can rely on the basics of his game while peppering in the unexpected. He has bossed his opponents around the court with his forceful forehands and graceful backhands, while surprising them with his much-improved drop shots and volleys. Not to mention, his ace count is already leading the men's field at the US Open this year. There's an added power behind his serve—ahead of the tournament, he announced that for each ace, he's donating $1,000 to the National Multiple Sclerosis Society. The fans are feeding off his winning performance and his winning smile in his post-match interviews, their roaring approval echoing through the grounds. He feels how proud he's making the home crowd already.

The only thing missing is Gabe.

With more headlines and cameras and expectations on Leo this year—and the increased attention on Gabe, too, as he competes at his first US Open as a publicly gay player—they've decided to heed Esme's warning and keep a low profile in press-heavy New York. They've stuck to their usual knowing smiles and furtive fingertip brushes in the locker room, but they aren't meeting at each other's hotels or attending each other's matches. Leo wishes he could look up to his player's box and see Gabe there, and vice versa. Merely sending texts to Gabe as he's made it through each of the first three rounds of the Open hasn't felt nearly special enough.

So, even if Leo can't shout to the rafters of whatever stadium he's playing on that he's in love with Gabe, he wants to show him that he's thinking of him during every one of his matches. After he wins and shakes hands with his opponent and the ump, he picks up the marker to write his message on the camera screen, and he sends Gabe a secret note, there, in plain sight. The fans watching at home around the world might not understand his messages yet, and he's certain Serving Looks is enlisting its followers to try and decode them, but until Leo is ready to share that part of himself on his own terms, he can start with this. He can tell Gabe exactly what he means in front of everyone, and if the fans—and his dad, who still doesn't know—think it's about the New York crowd, so be it.

After his first-round match, he simply wrote, "Couldn't do this without you."

After his second-round match, he wrote "You make me so proud" and drew some flowers, calling back to the romance novel they read to each other and giving Gabe his flowers as he breaks barriers at the tournament.

After his tough third-round match, he referenced their bartending gig at Delray, where their own romance began to blossom: "Could use an Orange Slice after that one."

When he heads back into the locker room after his matches to cool down, shower, and attend the post-match press conference, he first checks his phone and there's always a text waiting for him from Gabe, who must have been watching to see what the latest secret message to him would be. Each time, he sends Leo a red heart emoji.

If the first week of the US Open was smooth sailing for Leo, the second week is sure to be choppier seas. The competition will only get stiffer from here to the final, and the round of sixteen has already thrown him for a loop. In an all-American matchup, his current opponent is Chris Robinson, the sixteen-year-old teen titan. Last year, Chris got into the main draw here with a wild card, but this year, he's in on his own, having staked his claim in the top one hundred, which secures players their spot in a Slam. This past week, he's been lighting up the crowds with his youthful fearlessness, ensuring the fans and his opponents won't forget his name.

In the first set of their match, Chris came out guns blazing. He couldn't miss, and the wheels on this kid are out of this world. He's everywhere on the court. In a blink, he won the set 6–2, leaving Leo feeling bewildered in his chair afterward. He stared straight ahead, taking measured sips from his electrolytes as his mind went over each point, assessing what he could have done differently. He's never played Chris before, so he's had to figure out where the weaknesses are, and like Chris told him when they met at BP last year, his backhand is just like Leo's, too. With both of them leaping into the air, their bodies stretching open as they swing out to a flowing backhand, it looks as if they're performing a ballet at Lincoln Center, not a tennis match at Louis Armstrong Stadium. The fourteen thousand-person crowd has been rapturous.

It's been unnerving for Leo to see this next-generation superstar on the other side of the net—the kid who will surely succeed him at the top of American tennis—with the very same backhand Leo has mesmerized crowds with for years. Make no mistake, he wants to see Chris do big things in his career, and he'll be there to mentor Chris whenever he wants. But he's also here to take him down. He's not here to roll over. He's not here to pass the torch. He's here to win. This is Leo's year.

Over the course of the next two sets, the weakness becomes clear. In the first, Chris was running on the pure adrenaline of being in the round of sixteen at the US Open. Still acclimating to the tremendous endurance it takes to play round after round at a Slam—physically, mentally, and emotionally—the teenager's stamina simply doesn't match his opponent's. Leo takes the second set 6–4 and the third 6–3, Chris's level dropping as the match progresses, Leo's rising. By the fourth set, Chris is stretching out his legs and going to his towel box between every point, and attempting to end every point early by going for risky winners and drop shots. Leo knows this can only mean one thing for a young player: cramping. While he empathizes, having been there before, he knows this is his moment to pounce. This is his moment to expose the weakness. Standing firm on the baseline, he gets Chris on the run, sending him back and forth with a relentless stream of forehands and backhands. By the fourth shot, Chris can't keep up with the pace, forcing him to watch Leo's winners whiz by him. Leo's plan to tire him out is working—and it earns him a match point. In a one-two punch, he sends a 140 mph serve careening out wide, which Chris reaches out for, bunting a backhand that lands right in Leo's strike zone. His forehand punishes the weak return, sending it flying past Chris in the opposite direction.

"Game, set, and match: Chambers," the ump announces, "2–6, 6–4, 6–3, 6–1."

The Honey Deuce-soaked voices of the crowd howl for Leo, American flags waving around the stadium as he looks to his box and shakes a clenched fist. His team, including his mom, are up on their feet, celebrating Leo booking his ticket to the quarterfinals.

Leo smiles as he approaches the net, where Chris is nodding his head like, *You got me.*

"Too good," Chris says as he clasps Leo's hand. "I ran outta gas."

"I have a feeling I'll be seeing you in the final here someday," Leo says, and pats him on the back as they walk toward the ump to shake her hand.

"Thanks," Chris says with a half-smile. Before turning for his bench to gather his gear and bid farewell to this year's Open, he bumps Leo's fist and tells him, "I'm rooting for you."

After the fans cheer their heads off for Chris as he exits the stadium, they direct their applause to Leo, who's taken the court to speak with one of the announcers.

"Leo," the announcer says, and that's all he can get out before the fans raise the noise level even higher. "You know the New York crowd loves you, obviously. They had two Americans to cheer for tonight, though. What did it take to get the win on Robinson tonight?"

"I mean, it took a lot of patience. He came out swinging for the fences, and I thought it was curtains for me the way he was playing. But I knew if I waited, got him on the move as much as I could, I would get the momentum in my favor, and that's what I was able to do. It was the fans, too, like you said. You all give me the energy I need to keep pushing. This is my favorite tournament every year. There's nothing like this New York crowd."

The announcer interjects another round of applause and whistles. "There was a lot for the American fans to cheer for tonight. I'm sure you know, but Gabe Montoya wrapped up just before your match. I don't know if you're the type of player to look ahead at the draw, but you're taking on the winner of that match. And in his first-ever quarterfinal appearance here at the US Open, you'll be facing Montoya!"

It's a good thing the crowd has gone berserk again, because Leo needs a moment to collect himself. He knew, of course, that Gabe was still in the tournament, but just like he's kept away from social media this year, he's also kept away from the draw. So, this news is breaking for him right now. He knows that somewhere among the feelings racing around his body is excitement for Gabe over this momentous achievement for him. There's no doubt they're both motivating each other to bring their best this year. Leo's trying not to jump for joy on the court. But he's also, well, panicking.

"That's going to be, um, quite a rematch from last year," he manages to say through his dizzying emotions. "I better go start warming up now." He fakes a laugh, knowing this is probably going to be the toughest match he will ever play.

"Well, I'll let you get to it," the announcer says excitedly. "A rematch between two Americans, and between two friends, awaits! Give it up one more time for Leo Chambers!"

Leo packs up his stuff, slings his big red Wilson bag over his shoulder, and walks over to the camera. A neon-pink Sharpie in hand, he writes on the screen: "See you soon."

As Leo walks into the locker room, he checks his phone, and there's the red heart. He sends back, *Better bring your A game.*

Gabe responds, *Never needed to before.*

Leo sends back his own red heart.

It's the last time they speak before their rematch.

CHAPTER TWENTY-ONE

When Leo used to play matches against Gabe, the man on the other side of the net was two-dimensional. He was a flattened, simplistic rendering. All Leo could see was the teenager who burned him back at BP. Buried underneath that, of course, was Leo's affection for Gabe, manifested through the breath that would catch in his throat without fail. So focused on his resentment, so committed to the denial of his attraction to Gabe, so unbalanced by Gabe's style of play, there was no way Leo could find it in himself to win a match against him.

But tonight, in the quarterfinals of the US Open, under the lights of the largest tennis arena on the planet, Arthur Ashe Stadium, Leo sees a three-dimensional man across the net from him. He now sees Gabe for who he really is, in all his kindness, gentleness, and vulnerability. He now understands their shared struggle to belong within a sport that has never carved out space for queer men. He now feels solidarity with him.

Leo thinks about the odds of them finding their way to each other, in this sport, in this world. The odds of two queer men who have shared their full selves with each other playing a match on tennis's biggest stage. The odds feel infinitesimal. Certainly, they are far, far slimmer than the odds that this coin the ump has just tossed will land on heads, the side Leo has called.

"It's heads," the ump says, gesturing to Leo to choose whether he'll serve or receive first.

"I'll serve," Leo says, and he can barely look at Gabe, knowing what they're both thinking: *"Tell me, Chambers, who serves and who receives?"* It wasn't okay when Sascha said it! Fuck that guy! But okay, fine, it's a little funny. He can also barely look at Gabe because he's so goddamn hot in his tight white shirt and red shorts.

"Stay as we are," Gabe says.

"Good match, gentlemen," the ump says before taking his place up on his chair.

American, Peruvian, and Pride flags wave in sections around the stadium. Leo and Gabe sprint back to their respective sides to warm up for a match unlike any other in tennis history.

Leo's emotions during this match are entirely different from the one they played a year ago in the first round. He now feels as if he's playing in tandem with Gabe, rather than in spite of him. They have grown together this season, and it shows in the free-flowing exchange between them tonight. They are pushing each other to bring their best every point. Both of them are refusing to give up any ground in the first set. They respect each other too much to give anything but their all. And just like when he played Chris Robinson in the previous round, even though Leo cares about his current opponent, he isn't here to roll over. (He'll save that for the bedroom.) He won't let Gabe end his run to the final. Not this time.

From the moment the match starts, it mirrors their meeting at last year's Open. The first set is a stalemate, both of them holding serve each game, and as the fans' voices already grow raspy from their constant cheering, the ump's voice comes over the microphone to announce where this set is headed.

"Six games all," he says. "Tiebreak."

Through the noise of the crowd, Brian and Johnny shout out encouraging words.

"Right here, LC, right here!"

"Point by point!"

There is no letup in the tiebreak. It's a litany of aces and forehand winners and perfect volleys from both sides of the net. There are no bedroom eyes to be found, only unwavering focus. Finally, at 5–5, Gabe hits a slow second serve and Leo spots his opportunity, snapping into position and sending the ball screaming back over the net, right past Gabe.

"6–5, Chambers," the ump says, the crowd hollering with excitement. Leo doesn't take any time to celebrate. He has to remain focused. He has to get the job done now.

He steps up to the line. *Bounce, bounce, bounce, bounce, bounce.* He tosses the ball up, his body following, his arm rotating around, and he smacks it across the court. It lands long. Okay. He shakes out his body. He looks across the court at Gabe, who's moving in and keeping his eyes locked on Leo, prepared to pummel his second serve, to show no mercy for his man.

Don't get the yips. Don't get the yips. Don't get lost in his eyes. Don't get lost in his eyes.

Leo's toss goes up. His arm comes down. The ball flies over the net and slices out wide. Gabe lunges for it—and smacks it into the net.

"Game and first set: Chambers," the ump announces. "7–6."

The parallel with last year's match has split.

Leo shuts his eyes in utter relief as the crowd goes wild. When he opens them and looks to his box, they're cheering like he just won the whole tournament. He shakes a clenched fist at them. While Johnny claps furiously, Brian yells to him, "Let's go, LC! Let's go!" His mom looks like she can breathe again—for now, at least.

Leo doesn't look at Gabe as he walks by to his bench. He can't break his concentration.

"Second set," the ump says as Gabe steps up to the line. "Montoya to serve."

Shifting his weight from left foot to right foot, Leo prepares for the next point. He barely blinked during the changeover, determined to bring the same intensity into this set. If he can clinch this one, he will only have to win the third to be in the semis. It's a tall order, but the momentum is with him and he plans to keep it that way.

Gabe lifts his shirt a little as he bounces the ball before his serve, the habit that has always driven Leo to lustful distraction. He does his best to resist.

The serve comes flying down the T. Leo shifts to his left, getting out on his front foot, and flings the ball through the middle of the court with his backhand. Gabe smacks the ball back to Leo's left, targeting his backhand like he's been doing all match, avoiding his lethal forehand.

Leo sends a strong backhand crosscourt.

Gabe hits a curving slice.

Leo slices it back.

Gabe slices it again.

Leo hits a sloping drop shot.

Gabe slides into it and slices it to Leo's right.

Leo slides into and lobs it up and over Gabe's head.

As Gabe runs sideways to try and position himself under the lob for a smash, his feet get tangled up in each other—and he rolls his right ankle. His racket flies from his hand and makes a cracking sound as it falls onto the court.

"Carajo!" Gabe groans, wincing.

Leo and the ump both immediately run over to where he's sitting on the ground, clutching his ankle. Behind them, the medic standing by rushes out to treat him.

"I can barely walk on it," Gabe says, sitting on his bench with Leo, the ump, and the medic huddled over him.

"It looks like it's just a sprain," the medic says. "Stay put. We'll get you crutches and take a closer look off court."

When the medic leaves to get the crutches and a temporary wrap for Gabe's ankle, the ump gives Leo and Gabe some space.

"I am so sorry," Leo says. He tries to ignore the incessant clicking of the cameras on the sidelines, snapping their images for the wires.

"Why?" Gabe asks, looking genuinely confused. "You didn't push me. I tripped. Like a fucking idiot. Puta." He rubs his temples.

"You're not an idiot," Leo says, and he wants to put his arms around him, kiss him on the forehead. "This happens to players all the time. I'm just glad it's not broken. But this does fucking suck. I really wanted to beat you fair and square."

He hopes it's not too soon for teasing.

After a beat, Gabe glances up at him. "Guess it takes me spraining my ankle for you to get through me."

"Um, okay, short-term memory," Leo says. "Who won the first set?"

"I would've made a comeback," Gabe says.

"I guess we'll never know," Leo says, and turns as he sees the medic coming back out of the corner of his eye. "Hey, I know tonight didn't exactly go as planned, but um, I've never been so proud to play you. Just want you to know that."

Gabe gives a half-smile.

"Actually, I've never been proud to play you," Leo jokes. "Tonight was a first for me, really."

"Oh, fuck off, Leonardo," Gabe says. "Look, I'm probably going to be lying low for a little while as I get my ankle treated. There's a lot of physical therapy coming my way. So, keep those camera notes coming, all right? I'm really sorry."

"What are *you* sorry for?" Leo asks.

"That I won't be here to watch you win the whole thing," Gabe says.

"All right, I've got your crutches," the medic says as she approaches. "Let's get you back to the locker room."

The stadium gives Gabe a standing ovation as he walks off the court and into the tunnel, Leo watching on, gritting his teeth so his tears don't fall.

As he steps up to the camera screen, he wonders if people will make the connection that all his messages have been for Gabe, not just this one. But he doesn't care. He's just happy it doesn't have to be a secret this time.

He writes "Get well soon" and draws a heart.

CHAPTER TWENTY-TWO

The semifinals. The final four. Leo is the only American man remaining, so all hope for someone to succeed Andy Roddick now rests with him. Though, "rests" is a generous word, considering the obnoxious amount of a photographers outside his hotel, the gigantic photo of him clenching a fist in victory now splashed across a Nike ad in Times Square, and the indelicate questions from reporters after the quarterfinals, such as, "Do you feel ready to redeem yourself from your semifinals loss two years ago and go all the way this time?"

And he does. He does feel ready.

The thick night air is absolutely *buzzing* in Arthur Ashe Stadium as it fills to the brim with spectators, their murmurs echoing like distant thunder in Leo's ears. The stage is set: In a rematch from the Australian Open, he will be taking on the Australian Jack Hughes, the fiery, tattooed sk8r boi. But this time, it's on Leo's home turf.

Under the blaring floodlights, the tension is already palpable, crackling like static around the court. After their warm-up, the ump struggles to get the fans to quiet down.

"Ladies and gentlemen, please," he says. "Players are ready."

When they finally settle—some stray cheers and whistles still wafting down from the upper levels—the ump continues.

"First set. Leo Chambers to serve," he says. "Ready? Play."

Leo continues to bounce his body to keep his blood flowing and wriggle through the nerves. Then, he bounces the ball five times. This is it. He lets his racing thoughts recede to the back of his mind. He tosses the ball up.

From the moment Leo's racket touches the ball, the first set unfolds with blistering pace. Both of them unleash thunderous serves and piercing forehands. Leo's precision and agility keep Jack on the defensive, but the Australian refuses to yield an inch. Game after game, they battle fiercely, neither willing to concede ground. The score seesaws back and forth, drawing gasps and cheers from the crowd with every stroke of their rackets.

"5–4," the ump announces after Leo holds serve yet again. The fans' volume increases. The home crowd is desperate for their player to win.

As the tension mounts, Leo digs deep, tapping into the variety Brian has helped him develop. With a series of blistering forehands and perfectly placed drop shots, he manages to seize the momentum—and he breaks Jack's serve to take the first set.

"Game and first set: Chambers, 6–4," the ump declares.

"Come on!" Leo yells, and the stadium meets his excitement with its own echoing roar, the fans on their feet, their cheers rocking the stadium.

Unfortunately for Leo, even though Jack has a stick-and-poke tattoo on his wrist that says *fuck this*, he's proving to be anything but a quitter. He fights back in the second set, throwing a barrage of powerful serves and punishing groundstrokes at Leo. For a while, Leo is able to match him shot for shot, their duel remaining intense, their rallies defying the laws of physics as they push each other to the limit. It's a nail-biter of a second set, each of them refusing to break. But as the clock ticks on and the pressure mounts, it's Jack who manages to find that extra gear this time. As Leo serves at 4–5, it's like Jack is reading his mind. Everywhere Leo sends the ball, Jack is there. Leo can't get a single ball past him. He's like a brick wall. He's like Roger the Buff Kangaroo. Leo is struggling to find answers, feeling his body tighten with stress and, at 30–40, Jack breaks his serve, clinching the second set with a forehand winner down the line.

"Game and second set: Hughes, 6–4," the ump says.

"Let's go!" Jack screams to his box, though it sounds more like, "Let's gaur!"

For now, he's silenced the crowd.

Okay. Third set, reset. Leo needs to let the previous set go and focus up before Jack runs away with this match.

From the jump, there's no letup. Like in the first two sets, the games in this one fly by in a dizzying blur of lightning-fast serves and gravity-defying volleys, each point a miniature epic in its own right. Leo finds himself going to his towel box whenever possible just for some reprieve from the pace. He looks to his box for encouragement, using their positivity to keep his tank full. He lets the fans' support wash over him.

As the set wears on, Leo finally finds himself with the edge—a break point at 6–5—his relentless aggression and pinpoint accuracy proving too much for Jack to handle. With the crowd ready to burst, the tension reaching a fever pitch, Leo seals the deal with a stunning backhand crosscourt, securing the third set 7–5 and inching closer to his place in the final.

Leo knows he shouldn't be thinking about the final yet, but there's a voice in his head that desperately wants to. *All you need is this set*, it tells him. *Just one more. Don't get scared now. Don't crash out in the semis again. And don't fuck it up.* Wait, RuPaul?

As the set marches on, Leo fights back against the voice in his head. He fights back against Jack, too. They trade blows like heavyweight prizefighters in the ring. Leo was hoping to see Jack's level drop, but he knows his opponent wants this badly, too. How could he not? Revenge against Leo for knocking him out of his home Slam—at *Leo's* home Slam? And to reach the final? What could be better?

But a New York crowd is a New York crowd. Leo can feel their energy charging him, allowing him to hit shots without fear. He harnesses the sound of their support to find an extra spark of brilliance, his forehands and backhands carving through the air like uppercuts.

Jack is serving at 5–6, 30–all. If Leo could push himself to win the next two points, the match would be his. There would be no tiebreak. He stops going to his towel box. He stops looking at his player box. He forces himself into tunnel vision. *Hold your own*, he thinks.

This is a pressure point, and there's nowhere for Jack to hide. All twenty-four thousand people in Arthur Ashe Stadium are willing him to make a mistake, willing him to flop. And then, he does. Leo sees that his ball toss is off, an undeniable sign of nerves, and watches as Jack's next two serves fly clumsily into the net. It's a double fault. Jack throws his racket to the ground in frustration.

"30–40," the ump says. But what Leo and the crowd hear instead is, "Match point."

As Leo crosses the back of the court to position himself for Jack's next serve, he clenches his fist and pumps it, psyching himself up, muttering, "Come on. Come on. Come on."

The crowd is practically untamable.

"Please," the ump pleads. "Players are ready. Thank you."

Leo summons every ounce of strength and determination left in his body for this one point. He lets the fans refill his resolve. The stadium falls silent, holding its collective breath. Wide and wild, his eyes home in on Jack's next serve—the ball careening down the T—and he lunges to his right. His first step proves quick enough. His timing is perfect. He rockets a forehand to the back left corner. It catches Jack off guard, soaring past his desperately outstretched racket, and landing square on the line.

He can just barely hear the ump announce it. "Game, set, and match: Chambers. 6–4, 4–6, 7–5, 7–5."

Leo instantly drops his racket and buries his head in his hands in disbelief. He's nearly shaking. He's done it. For the first time in his career, he is into the US Open final.

He's stunned into silence, but the home crowd is not. He can hear whistles at a pitch that must be waking up dogs across the city, applause that must be shaking the entire stadium.

When he finally removes his head from his hands, he looks over to his box, where his parents are hugging and Brian is gripping the railing as he lunges forward, ready to fling himself onto the court as he shouts, "Let's go, LC! Let's go!" He can't help but wish Gabe were there.

Speechless, he picks up his racket, and the simplicity of this thing in his hand suddenly strikes him. Just some strings and a metal frame. But look what it's unlocked for this crowd, for his family, for himself. He spins it in his hand. There are goosebumps up and down his arms.

During the on-court interview after the match, it's the announcer's turn to struggle to quiet the stadium down. It's like a teacher trying to settle their class on the last day of school.

"Leo, I don't know if you can hear me," she says, "but I think this noise says it all. The New York crowd has been waiting for this moment for a long time. An American man in the finals of the US Open. And an American man we've been watching on these courts for over a decade now. Congratulations!"

"Thank you so much," Leo says, still feeling stunned. "I've been dreaming of making this final since I was a little kid. I wasn't sure I'd ever get here."

"Let it sink in," she says. "You made it. And what a way to kick off your thirties. You just celebrated the big 3–0 this summer, so this is a pretty sweet belated birthday gift, huh?"

"You have no idea," he says.

"Let's talk shop for just a second: What helped you get the win tonight in this tough match against Hughes? He's a tricky opponent. The entire night felt with you two felt like, 'Anything you can do, I can do better.'"

"I mean, you're looking at it," Leo says, and gestures around to the crowd, who sends the love right back to him, jumping up and down, spilling what's left of their Honey Deuces.

After the interview, he steps up to the camera screen and takes the hot-pink marker. He writes "This one's for you." He winks.

CHAPTER TWENTY-THREE

"I'm really glad you guys are still here," Leo says, sitting between Tess and Ollie, his back against the cushioned headboard of his hotel bed.

"Um, duh," Tess says, popping a bite of a chocolate chip muffin in her mouth. "You're in the final girls club now. Like I would miss this."

"Tabarnak," Ollie says, "I'm actually trying to watch."

It's the day before Leo plays none other than the White Walker himself, Sascha, in the final. The three of them are watching *The Golden Girls* before Leo's practice session this afternoon. Tess and Ollie asked him what he'd like to do to unwind before the mayhem begins, and this is obviously what he chose. They ordered room service: a brunch spread of coffees, juices, fruits, eggs, croissants, muffins, the works. It's all splayed out on the bed across several silver trays. They're watching the episode where the girls are in a local pairs bowling competition. Dorothy and Blanche are facing off against Rose and Sophia for the championship. And it's heated.

As it comes to a close, Rose bowls a strike, giving them the lead.

"I did it! I did it! We're gonna win!" she shouts, jumping for joy.

"Rose, aren't you forgetting something?" Dorothy asks confidently. "We haven't bowled our last frame yet. We can still win. And we will."

"Oh, I don't think so," Rose says. "You see, I've bowled with Blanche before. Maybe this isn't the best time to mention it, but when the chips are down, Blanche chokes. Don't you, sweetheart?"

Blanche pauses, then glares at Rose. "Eat chalk, Nylund."

"Oh, shit," Tess says.

"I know, Rose is so intense, I love it," Leo says.

"No," Tess says, scrolling on her phone. "Shit. Leo. You and Gabe. It's you and Gabe. A photo of you together. Kissing. It's all over Instagram."

Fuck.

Fuck.

Leo feels cold and clammy and short of breath.

Fuck.

Who would have a photo of them? Who would have posted it? It must have been Sascha. Of course. That fucking homophobe would want to screw Leo over right before their match. Or, no, it must have been Serving Looks. They're always posting the latest photos of players. They've basically become the Deuxmoi of tennis.

"Who? What? Where?" Leo asks, eyes bulging, hovering over Tess to see the photo. Ollie pauses the episode as Blanche bowls her last shot.

"It looks like *What a Racket* posted it first," Tess says, and she hands the phone to Leo, her face wincing in sympathy pain.

There it is. A zoomed-in photo of Leo kissing Gabe in the hallway outside Gabe's hotel room in Paris, saying goodbye after their first night spent together.

His stomach drops.

The caption reads: "Has Gabe Montoya, the first homosexual player on the ATP Tour, met his match in US Open finalist Leo Chambers? We got our hands on this photo of the pair getting close in Paris during this year's Roland-Garros. A major distraction as Chambers looks to win his first major title. We'll get into all of it during our next episode, coming ASAP!"

Fucking. Paul.

Leo hands Tess her phone back and picks up his own. His hands are shaking so much, he can barely hit the right buttons as he calls and texts Gabe. He calls. He texts. He calls. He texts. But the calls go to voice mail and the texts turn green, undelivered. Where *is* he? Has he gone into hiding?

He looks at Tess and Ollie, all of them unsure what to say.

"I think I have to go," Leo says abruptly, then turns to leave, hands still shaking.

"Leo, maybe we should—" Tess starts to say, but he's already halfway out the door.

"Sir, you can't just go back there," the security guard yells as Leo marches toward the lobby's turnstiles, making his way to the elevators.

Leo stops in his tracks and looks over to the security desk. Above the guard, he sees Sascha on the giant TV mounted on the wall.

"Can you turn that up, please?" he asks the guard.

The guard raises an eyebrow in confusion, but after he glances up at the TV and sees the photo of Leo kissing Gabe, he glances back at him, grimacing. "Oh, uh, yeah," he says, and turns up the volume.

Next to the enlarged photo of Leo and Gabe, Sascha is being interviewed outside his hotel, a mic in his face.

"This is what I am talking about," Sascha is saying angrily, throwing his hands up. "This is what I have been saying from the beginning. Knowing about homosexual players is distracting. It is not right. Now that I have seen this photo, how do I concentrate on practice? How will fans concentrate on our match tomorrow? What do they tell their children? We should not have to see this. Chambers should forfeit."

Leo stands there, fuming.

"Okay, yeah, you can go on through," the guard says, looking embarrassed as he hits a button to unlock the first turnstile.

Leo bites his lip the entire elevator ride up to the floor of the podcast studio, obsessively running a hand through his hair and tapping his foot on the floor. He doesn't want to lose his nerve, feeling as if he's about to serve out a match.

As Leo enters the studio, he first spots Jesse, who looks rightfully shocked to see Leo standing before him.

"Where is he?" Leo asks. "Where's Paul?"

"I think he's in the restroom," Jesse says. "But wait, Leo, can we talk—"

Before Jesse can continue, Leo finds the restroom in the hall and stands outside it.

What should he do? Trip Paul as he comes out of the bathroom? Punch him squarely in the nose? No, he doesn't want to resort to violence. Or risk an assault charge. Or, worse, risk hurting his right hand before the final. Yes, priorities.

"Leo," Paul says, measured, as he pushes open the swinging door. "What are you doing here?"

He can tell Paul is doing his best not to seem guilty, but the growing reddish tint to his normally pale cheeks betrays him.

"What am I *doing* here?" Leo asks incredulously. "Are you serious?"

"All right, that was a stupid question," Paul says, still giving his best shot at a calm demeanor. He adjusts his glasses. "I can see you're angry. But listen, Leo—"

"No, *you* listen," Leo says, and the strange taste in his mouth, a metallic one, is still there. "You had no right to post that photo.

And I'm assuming you're going to put out an episode about me and Gabe now?"

"Well—"

"Fuck you," Leo says, shaking his head. "How dare you? This was *my* thing to share. It's *my* decision when to tell people. And you robbed me of that. And now . . . now the whole world knows. Now I have no control over any of this. Everyone just knows now. It's going to be total chaos, as if the final wasn't already going to be wild. What made you think this was okay? What made you think you could take this away from me?"

Paul doesn't speak right away, just stands there. For the first time, after all his appearances on Paul's podcast, swallowing Paul's inane comments, Leo has finally shut him up.

"I, well," Paul begins. "I'm sorry, Leo, but look, I'm just trying to save the show here. It's not what it used to be. Nobody's listening like they were before. It isn't keeping up with all the new podcasts and Instagrams and TikToks, and I thought this might be it. This might be my shot at keeping it alive. I had this photo of you and Gabriel, and all your generation seems to want is gossip, so that's what I gave them. Leo, it's not that big a deal, is it? Gabriel's already the first homosexual player. People knew that. This will blow over."

"What the fuck do *you* know?" Leo yells, refusing to let the hot tears behind his eyes flow. "It is a big deal! And it's *gay*. Just say *gay*. Fuck! Where did you even get that photo? Were you just creeping around that hotel? The one in Paris?"

Paul looks even shiftier than before. "You might want to talk to Jesse."

Back in the studio, Leo finds Jesse in a swivel chair, biting his nails and bouncing his leg.

"Leo, we really need to talk," Jesse says, standing up as Leo storms into the room.

"Ya think?" he says. "Why did Paul just tell me to talk to you about the photo? Please, enlighten me."

"Okay," Jesse says, and gulps. Leo has never felt this threatening in his life. "We ran into each other at the hotel during Roland-Garros. Do you remember that?"

"Yes, I remember that."

"Well, I was staying on the same floor as Gabe. That's why I bumped into you that day. And, the next morning, while I was heading out to get coffee, I saw you. Leaving his room. Kissing him in the hallway. You were saying goodbye, I think."

Leo's head spins. He sits down, but Jesse remains standing.

"I took a quick photo when I saw it. It was like a reflex or something. I don't know."

"Why?" Leo asks, looking up at him wildly. "To jerk off to? Why?"

"No!" Jesse says. "I guess I thought—well, I just thought maybe it would work for Serving Looks."

"You were going to send it to Serving Looks? Seriously? Who cares? I know they're big now, but what the fuck?"

"Not *they*," Jesse says. "Me."

"I don't follow."

"I . . . run Serving Looks," he says hesitantly. "And, well, you do follow."

Leo is glad he's sitting down.

"It's just a side hustle," Jesse says frantically. "I never thought it would take off. Paul didn't even know I was running it. But it did take off. It keeps gaining more followers. And I guess I got carried away. I knew the podcast was fizzling out, and you know how I feel about Paul. The account has been an escape for me. I thought maybe it could turn into an actual gig. When I saw you kissing Gabe, I didn't even think. I just took the photo. But I didn't post it! I never would! It's been months, and I still haven't. I would never out someone. I know what that feels like."

"Then how the fuck is it all over the internet?" Leo asks sternly. He still hasn't logged back into his social accounts, but he doesn't need to. He knows it's everywhere. He knows what everyone must be saying.

Told you so.

What a fag.

This is bad for tennis.

How can he win the final now?

I don't want him to win the final now.

"I never deleted it," Jesse says ashamedly, "so I accidentally uploaded it to the cloud on my work computer with the rest of my Roland-Garros photos. I always take some in case we want to use them on our Instagram. Paul was going through our Slam photos from the year with our social manager, you know, to post a bunch of photos of you ahead of the final tomorrow. He came across it and, well, he shared it on our account."

All Leo can do is stare at the floor.

"The social manager is quitting. I am, too. I'm sure Paul's going to get fired before he can even release an episode about this. They've been talking about replacing him as it is. I know that's not any consolation," Jesse says, and then sighs heavily. "Look, Leo, I know you hate me for this. And you have every right to. But before you never speak to me again, I just have to tell you this. Ever since I started Serving Looks, the posts that have brought people together the most are the ones of you, and not just the thirst traps. The ones of you and your dad, you and your friends, you and Gabe. Your relationship with him has been so good for tennis. Gabe coming out and then you getting closer to him, it's shown people that tennis can be a welcoming place. You should see the amazing DMs I get. Even if they didn't know the whole story, they're drawn to what you have. They can see it. I'm sure you're worried about getting on court tomorrow. But people love you. They still do."

Leo is still staring at the floor, unable to look at Jesse. "I hope you're right," he says. "God, I really wish you hadn't taken that photo. Or you'd deleted it. Anything."

"I know," Jesse says somberly. "Me too."

"Because your posts, they've actually been great," Leo says, finally looking back up at him. "You've actually been kind to me, to my dad, to my friends. And to Gabe. It's not always like that online. I can't believe I'm saying this, but I've really enjoyed following you. So, if you do keep Serving Looks going, just please don't invade people's privacy. We don't need another fucking Perez Hilton."

"The thought of becoming him will keep me up at night, I can promise you that," Jesse says. "And I can promise you I would never out anybody. Fuck Paul."

"Pass," Leo says. He stares at Jesse for a moment. He's ready to get out of here now. "I'll see you around."

"Yeah," Jesse says quietly. Before Leo turns to leave, he says, "Leo, I—I'm sorry. I hope you win tomorrow. I really hope you win."

Where the hell is Gabe? Why isn't he responding to Leo's calls or texts? Leo knows he was flying back to Miami this morning to rest and rehab from his ankle injury, but shouldn't he be there by now? Shouldn't he be frantically trying to get in touch, too? They FaceTimed last night after Leo got home from his semifinals win and Gabe was practically jumping through the screen to congratulate him. Then he was practically jumping through the screen to apologize that he couldn't stay for the final. Gabe attempted all the convincing and persuading he could muster in order to stay and receive treatment in New York, but it was no use. His team insisted he return to their home base in Miami if he's going to recover from this injury as swiftly and smoothly as possible. Plus, Gabe couldn't exactly make the case that he had to stay in New York because he's, well, sleeping with one of the finalists.

Leo continues to call him, but still nothing.

What if this post from Paul has scared Gabe off for good? The thought jabs at Leo's insides. Gabe has faced enough media scrutiny this year as it is, and now his secret relationship with Leo has thrust him into the spotlight yet again. Surely, he's done with Leo now. This is Leo's worst fear realized. Gabe would prefer to be with someone who's already out and proud. Why would he want to be with a closet case? With a project like Leo? He could be with anyone he wants. He should be with someone who's openly queer, someone who doesn't complicate his life further, someone who moves through the world exactly as they are. Even Esme made it clear to them that tennis fans wouldn't be ready for their relationship. After all, they've never seen one like it before. She urged them not to share this news, and now it's dropped just days after they played each other in the quarters and the day before Leo plays the final. Superb timing. Just excellent. Really. Beyoncé couldn't have planned a better surprise release herself.

With exactly zero calls from Gabe and seventeen missed ones from his own agent, Leo decides to shut his phone off. He knows this is probably not the wisest choice, but he's desperate to settle his racing mind and eject himself from this hellish situation for a while, and it's at least a better move than tossing his phone into the East River, which was his first thought.

"Do you mind just . . . driving around for a bit . . . before we go to the grounds?" he asks the man driving the black SUV that he's basically called home for the last few weeks. He should be taking Leo to his practice session at this point, so Leo is relieved when he replies, "Of course."

The driver ignores the exit he usually makes for the US Open and instead keeps driving through Queens, leaving Leo to ponder his countless thoughts in the backseat.

"Excuse me, you can't go in th—oh, oh, um, sorry, can I, um, help you with anything?" a security guard at Arthur Ashe Stadium says upon realizing that the man trying to enter the stands isn't some drunk spectator loitering after the women's final, which ended a couple hours ago.

"Sorry, I know this is weird," Leo says, rubbing the blisters on his fingers, "but would it be okay if I just . . . sat for a little while? I promise I won't, like, vandalize the court or anything."

"Oh, yeah, yeah, go for it," the security guard says, visibly flustered. "No problem. Sit wherever you want. And, you know, good—good luck tomorrow."

"Thanks," Leo says, smiling gently.

He takes a seat in one of the last rows of the 100 level, not far, if he isn't mistaken, from where he and his dad sat when they watched Andy Roddick win in 2003. The stadium is almost perfectly clean again in preparation for the men's final tomorrow, but there are still some lingering sticky spots from spilled Honey Deuces and some pieces of red, white, and blue confetti from the celebration stuck to them. When he moves his legs under the seat, crossing his ankles, he hears something plastic knock over and bounce on the concrete. He feels around and picks it up. It's the souvenir cup that Honey Deuces come in, the names of each year's champions printed on it in blue. He aches to see his name there instead of Sascha's, but right now it doesn't seem possible.

As his eyes scan the stadium and its thousands of empty blue seats, it's the quietest he's ever heard it in here. His mind, however, is thumping with noise. This is far from how Leo imagined the weekend of his appearance in a US Open final would look. From such a young age, he had daydreamed in striking color about how celebratory it would be, how joyous, how triumphant. He pictured it just like Andy's. But now, as it lay before him in sullen grayscale, the illusion of his daydreams has shattered. Being outed has left him feeling stripped of his own agency. There's always an element of vulnerability when he takes to the court in front of such an enormous crowd and shows them his abilities. Tennis can be a lonely sport, navigating the stress on your own, all eyes on your body, and whether the match is trending in your favor or slipping away from you, the tension is yours and yours alone to manage. But this time, he thinks, that anxiety will be heightened. It's not just his abilities that will be on display tomorrow, but his sexuality, his character, his personhood. The idea of what twenty-four thousand spectators will be thinking of him during the final sends him into a dizzy spell. He's spent his entire career ensuring that he flew under the radar, that he was a good kid, that he carried on his dad's legacy with no room for criticism. Where did it get him?

"Thought I might find you here."

Tucked away in the corners of his mind, Leo jumps when he hears a voice other than the one in his head. He whips around. Behind him, his dad is standing there, cane in one hand, a bottle of water in the other. He tosses Leo the bottle.

"Thanks," Leo says.

A few drops of condensation splash from the bottle onto Leo's gray Nike T-shirt. He takes a much-needed sip. As he realizes that he can't outrun this conversation with his dad any longer, he expects to be more panicked. But to his surprise, the nerves don't come. Maybe they're too fried after hours of activity. *No more*, his nerves tell him. *Just do it.* Or maybe that's just what his T-shirt tells him.

"Well, this has been . . . quite the year," Johnny says, and lets out a sigh as he takes the seat next to Leo.

"Why, what happened?" Leo says, deadpan, and waits a moment before turning to his dad. When they make eye contact, they burst out laughing, knocking their heads back, their cackles echoing in the stadium. Leo didn't think laughter was possible today.

"Leo—"

"No, wait, Dad, before you say anything," Leo starts. "I just want—well, I just want to tell you myself. That it's true." His shoulders rise a little. "I'm, um, I'm gay."

Leo turns his gaze down to his knees, and he listens for a response from his dad.

"This is about where we sat when we watched Roddick win, isn't it?" Johnny asks. Leo's brow furrows in confusion. He waits before saying anything back. "God, I remember that day so well. This place went ballistic when he won. Even Roddick was blubbering like a baby." He chuckles. "It's always strange to see it so quiet in here. Strange to see how this place still sits here even when there isn't anything happening inside."

"Dad—"

"I remember that day so well because it was the happiest I had been in a while," Johnny continues. "I wasn't always the happiest guy when you were a kid, and I regret that. But having MS was still so new to me. I still resented it so much then. I even resented tennis, if you can believe it. So many people saw me differently. I wasn't a successful player to them anymore. I was just my illness. It was a hard pill to swallow."

Leo's eyes are glued to the side of his dad's face, who's staring out at the stadium. There are more grooves and lines in it than he remembered.

"I had a relapse not long before that final with Roddick. I don't know if you remember that," Johnny says.

"I don't think so," Leo says.

"Good. I'm glad you don't," Johnny says. "I started to feel better physically, but I was having a hard time finding my way out of that funk. You and I had already been hitting together for a few years at that point, and I thought, *What if someday I can't play with Leo anymore?* I was so angry with tennis, with the world. But that afternoon, watching Roddick win with you, it brightened things for me. Yeah, I was over the moon to see an American guy win, but seeing how excited you were . . . man. You were high fiving people around you, smiling so big, telling me how it was the best day of your life."

Johnny chuckles again.

"Sharing that with you kind of snapped me out of it," he says. "I think I forgot what it felt like to root for something. I remembered why I fell in love with tennis in the first place, and I loved seeing it happen for you, too. Even if I couldn't play like I used to, I knew I could still share this sport with you, and maybe you don't want to hear this right now, but I knew I would be watching you win it someday, too."

Leo's lower lip is quivering a bit. He's staring at his knees. "I don't know if I can," he says. A couple tears fall onto his legs as he remembers Gabe's shorter line when they bartended in Delray, the sponsors Gabe lost, the online comments, the hate from Sascha. "What if people don't want to root for me anymore?"

"Just indulge your old man for a little longer," Johnny says. "Even while I started to feel some symptoms of MS, I kept playing. I would lose my balance during a match or forget it was time for a changeover, stuff like that. Every day, I hoped nobody noticed, hoped it would go away. But it didn't, and so eventually I went to the doctor and I was diagnosed. I tried to hide it for a bit longer, but it was getting harder and harder. I thought announcing my diagnosis and my retirement would be the worst thing in the world, and of course it hurt like hell, but to be honest with you, I felt free. I felt like I was on a tightrope before that. It was this balancing act, trying to hide my symptoms from everybody. I was happier and more relieved to leave that part of my life behind than I'd expected, even if it did come with new challenges."

Before Leo can speak—though, he's not even sure what to say—Johnny turns to him and puts a hand on his shoulder.

"You might not feel it right now, but Leo, you'll feel that happiness, too, that relief. I know it's not exactly the same thing, what I went through and what you're going through now. But you don't have to hide anymore, either. You get to be honest about who you are. You'll get to connect with people and know that they're with you, the real you, one hundred percent, not just who they think you are. That's not something everybody gets to have," Johnny says. "I'm with you, one hundred percent. I love you. You know that, right?"

Leo nods as more tears stream down his cheeks.

"You could've told me," Johnny says.

"It's not that easy," Leo says.

"I know. God, I just hate that you had to deal with all this while worrying about me, too."

"No, no, that's not a big—"

"Leo, it is. It is a big deal. You don't have to sugarcoat it for me anymore. You told me yourself that you worry about me. And that isn't fair," Johnny says, and he lets out another sigh. "I guess I've tried to protect you from it as much as I could. I tried to shove the MS aside, and then the stroke. That's what I was doing when we were on the podcast together, too. Trying to be strong in front of you, in front of Paul." He grimaces. "Fucking Paul. I tried to keep my distance from you early in the season. But that didn't really work, did it?"

Leo shakes his head.

"We've both kind of been suffering in silence, huh?" Johnny says.

"I never wanted to make you feel different or like I didn't want you there," Leo says. "I know how people have treated you. But I do worry about you. You push yourself so hard sometimes, and I guess it—it just feels like you don't see how that affects me."

"I'm so sorry, Leo," Johnny says. "I never wanted that for you. But I'm telling you, it's not on you to take care of me, okay? You don't have to tell me what to do when it's hot or—"

"But I do have to!" Leo shouts.

"You don't," Johnny says, shaking his head. "I know what's best for me. I know how this body operates pretty well by now. If you're really worried, just ask me if I need anything. When you tell me what to do, it's not good for either of us. Does that make sense?"

"Yeah," Leo says sheepishly. "I'm sorry."

"Nothing to apologize for," Johnny says, waving him off. "This is on me. You've had to be an adult for too long. I think Brian's helped you be a kid again, though, hasn't he?"

Leo's cautious not to be too eager about how much he's loved his one-on-one time with Brian this season. "I guess so."

"We had a little talk after you and I got into it back in London," Johnny says. "I think he could tell I was having a hard time letting you go, seeing you succeed with another coach. I was so desperate to get back to how things were while I still could. I know I was putting too much pressure on you. Brian told me I needed to lighten up. I'm sure you could tell I was having a hard time."

"No, I—"

Johnny shoots him a look that says, *Don't even try.*

"He's helped you find the joy in this sport again. That joy you had when we watched Roddick. I've seen that in you this season. That was another hard pill for me to swallow. But it's a good thing," Johnny says, and he turns back toward the stadium. "Especially because it'll just be you and him next season."

"So, you're definitely going to"—Leo hesitates before saying it—"retire, then?"

"I think it's time to hang up the racket. Not for good. Don't think I won't be coming to some of your matches and practices still. But yeah, you and Brian are a damn good team. And I'm, well, I'm really fucking tired, to be honest."

A laugh jumps out of Leo unexpectedly. "It's going to be weird doing this without you next year," he says.

"I know," Johnny says.

"What do you think you'll do?"

"Not sure yet," Johnny says. "Maybe get a dog."

"I know a guy," Leo says, smiling. "Ever heard of Pawsitive Futures?"

"That's right!" Johnny says, his eyes lighting up.

After a beat, Leo needs to say it. "I hope I don't let you down. I hope I haven't."

"Leo," Johnny says, "you could never let me down. Okay?"

Leo swallows. "Okay."

They sit in silence for a minute.

"So, what are you gonna do when you get out there tomorrow?" Johnny asks as he stands.

"Uh, I don't know, try not to puke all over the court?" Leo asks.

"Hold your own," Johnny says. "You're gonna hold your own."

Leo looks out at the stadium. He nods.

As they ascend the steps to leave, Johnny says, "That's for you, by the way."

Leo looks up, peering through the gap in the stadium where there's a clear view of the Manhattan skyline in the distance. The top of the Empire State Building is lit in rainbow colors.

CHAPTER TWENTY-FOUR

Tennis is one of the most physically demanding sports in the world. It requires an endless amount of strength and speed and endurance and control. By the time a player reaches the final of a Grand Slam, six long matches behind them, their body is aching and covered in blisters. And yet, if you were to ask any player what makes a champion, they would tell you it's mentality. Any player can have an amazing forehand, backhand, or serve. But only the greats have the mental power to succeed at the highest level.

So, yes, Leo is rubbing the blisters on his hands and feet in the locker room as he prepares for the finals of the US Open, but the discomfort of those is nothing compared to the discomfort of the anxiety rattling around his mind. He's trying to breathe through it, relax his shoulders, unclench his jaw, listen to the words Brian is speaking to him.

"This isn't how you pictured this moment, LC," Brian says, standing over Leo, who's lacing up his sneakers. "I know that. What happened yesterday was fucked up."

"Yeah, remind me to deck Paul," Johnny says from behind Brian, taking a step forward as he continues. "You know, he's the reason we didn't win doubles at Wimbledon in '87, because he never really—"

"But," Brian says, remaining focused, drowning out Johnny, "that's life, my friend. No matter how hard you try to have everything go your way, you can't control it all. Life laughs at your best-laid plans. What you can control is how you react, what kind of person you're going to be in the face of it."

"Thanks, Brian," Leo says. He stands, looking him in the eye. "For helping me get here."

"It's been a privilege, LC. I'm not going anywhere. I'll be in your box whenever you need me," Brian says. "Play without fear."

He bumps fists with Leo and steps out of the locker room and into the hall, leaving father and son to talk.

"I think you've heard enough from me," Johnny says with a wink. "You've got this."

"Thanks," Leo says, managing only a whisper, desperate not to cry anymore. "For everything."

Johnny gives Leo a last look of confidence before turning to find Brian in the hall. It's time for them to take their places in Leo's player box for the match.

With that, Leo is on his own. But only for a moment.

As Sascha passes by, he gives Leo a wry, judgmental glance and a few murmured words in Russian, then huffs out a laugh and says, "What a joke." He leaves the locker room before Leo can even search for a response.

It shouldn't matter. Leo has all the support in the world from his team, his family, and his friends. That's what he thought about as he struggled to fall asleep last night. He hopes he still has Gabe in his corner, too. Tess and Ollie showed up at his hotel room last night to comfort and encourage him after what was truly one of the strangest days of his life. But with Gabe in Miami and Leo's phone off, they still haven't connected. Maybe that's a mistake. Maybe Leo's hiding, putting a wall up, tucking into his shell to protect himself. Either way, his compartmentalization has taken over. He's approaching the Gabe situation the same way his agent, who also appeared at his door last night, told him they'll approach the whole you're-now-an-openly-gay-player situation: Win the final, then they'll figure out the rest.

Still, it does matter to him. He can't help but wonder if more scrutiny is waiting for him out in the stadium. An entire arena full of rejection could be outside the tunnel he now finds himself walking down. He takes his place in front of Sascha, who's stretching out his hips and doing some last minute lunges. Leo puts on his headphones and turns up the volume on "Don't Stop Me Now" even higher than usual to drown out the sounds of the packed stadium. Whatever is waiting for him out there, he can lose himself in the music. He can stay calm and ready. But his palms are sweaty. Knees weak, arms heavy. He wants to vomit the spaghetti he ate last—wait.

Okay. This is it. The announcer is waving him forward, signaling that it's almost time for his walkout.

What will you be thinking about as you head onto the court?

Paul's question from the podcast last year pops into Leo's head. He wishes it hadn't, but it has. And he is, of course, thinking about that big blue piece of confetti that landed on his shoulder after Roddick won the final. The moment that made him want to win the goddamn US Open in the first place. He holds the image in his mind—the confetti, his dad by his side, the fans around him applauding and high fiving. Only faintly, over Freddie Mercury's voice, he hears the announcer call his name. He walks through the final portion of the tunnel, and his hand is shaking as he lifts it to touch the large bronze plaque hung there, engraved with the words of gay tennis legend Billie Jean King: "Pressure is a privilege."

As he stares at the quote, he knows it to be true. It's a privilege to play this match, and to play it as his full self, like Billie. Like Gabe. He wasn't sure he would, but before he walks out, he takes the rainbow ribbon that he stuffed into his bag just in case, and he pins it to his shirt collar.

Stepping into the electrified air of Arthur Ashe Stadium, he keeps his headphones on and his eyes fixed on his player bench.

But something grabs his attention out of the corner of his eye. Many somethings, in fact. *Don't look around. No distractions.* He tries to keep to his tunnel vision, but he breaks it. He allows his eyes to look up into the great vortex that is Arthur Ashe Stadium, and there they are.

Signs. Hundreds of them. Cardboard signs, white posterboard signs, pink signs, yellow signs, blue signs, green signs. A mosaic of them around the stadium. And as he looks across the sea of fans, he realizes that they all say the same thing.

HOLD YOUR OWN

HOLD YOUR OWN

Hold your own!

hold your own

HOLD your OWN

Hold. Your. Own.

HOLD YOUR OWN!

How is this happening? How could everyone have these? How could they know what his dad has always told him when he's feeling down and out? The jumbotron is showing the signs, at least when it's not zooming in on the celebrities in attendance: Taylor Swift, the Obamas, Laura Dern, Nicole Kidman, Zendaya, Andy Roddick. The stars are out in New York. Leo whips his head around to look at his box, and standing next to Brian, his dad, his mom, his agent, his physio—the whole team—is Gabe, holding a large Pride flag above his head that has "HOLD YOUR OWN" painted across it in white. One of his cardboard cutouts is standing next to him. Leo's mouth hangs open. The joy of seeing Gabe surges through his body.

Leo takes off his headphones, which are still blasting "Don't Stop Me Now" on repeat, and what he hears then is somehow even louder than his music—a thundering roar of applause, whistles, and cheering. He sees fans holding Pride flags and American flags. If anyone in the crowd is booing or sneering, he can't hear or see them. He's too overwhelmed by the standing ovation. He's too overwhelmed by the sight of Gabe. There are goosebumps forming down his body, each little blondish hair rising on his limbs.

He doesn't know how they pulled this off, but he will use every ounce of the love on display to get through this final match, the most important one of his career.

"Ready?" the ump says into the mic after their warm-up, during which Sascha appeared stone cold, unmoved by the crowd, a sinister look fixed in his eyes. As the fans and sideline camera shutters finally fall silent now, Leo takes a deep breath and bounces the ball five times. With nowhere to hide now, with everything on the line, he hears the ump say, "Play."

Let it be known that Leo really is sinking his teeth into this match. He's hitting some stellar shots, landing some impressive aces. The stadium loses its collective mind every time he wins even the simplest of points. They're desperate for him to win today. The scoreline, though, doesn't quite show his quality. Sascha settled into the match immediately, while Leo was still getting his sea legs, and he broke Leo's serve in the opening game. Ever since, Leo has been playing catch-up. He feels like he's running in deep white sand, moving forward without much distance to show for it. He's held his serve each time after, but Sascha is still up that single break, which has put him in position to serve for the first set at 5–3.

Leo wins the first point of the game, a fourteen-shot rally that gets him and the crowd pumped up. He clenches a fist. Maybe he can break back, get back on serve, still claim this first set.

But his brief glimmer of hope is wiped out by two consecutive aces.

"30–15," the ump says.

Sascha hits another massive serve, but Leo's able to chip it back. Sascha pummels it to the opposite corner, leaving Leo scrambling to it. He doesn't reach it in time.

"40–15."

Set point. The crowd is cheering louder now, urging Leo on, hoping their voices and hands will lift him to stay in it.

They get into another clash, smacking forehand after forehand at each other. Leo sees the next one coming toward him, and in the split second he has to make a choice, he decides he's ready to go for the winner. He pulls the trigger, hits the ball even harder this time, groaning as he makes contact. It flies down the line. It just misses.

"OUT," the system calls.

"Game and first set: Volkov," the ump announces.

For a moment, Leo wants to throw his racket to the ground. The factors that separate brilliance from disaster in this sport are so minuscule—the slight tilt of a racket, a single step, the speed of a swing, a ball out by millimeters—it can drive a player mad. But Leo decides to keep his racket in his hand and breathe through it.

There's applause from the crowd, but it doesn't reach anywhere near the octave they hit for Leo. He glimpses Sascha's smug grin, as if he believes he's already won the whole thing. Leo needs to move on from this set as quickly as possible. He was playing better toward the end, and the next one is a chance to steal the momentum. He's not going anywhere yet. He makes his way over to his towel box so he can dry off and talk to his team before set two begins.

"Reset, LC," Brian says. "You're winning the longer points. Be patient. Don't go for the big shot too soon. And don't be afraid to show him more variety in the next set. You can't let him stay in his rhythm."

He's listening to Brian, but he's staring at Gabe. All he wants to do is climb up to his player box and hug him and kiss him and tell him how relieved he is to have him here.

Gabe stares at him intently for a moment, then winks.

"How did you do—" Leo starts to ask.

"I'll tell you later," Gabe says.

"But how are you even—"

"I'll tell you later!" Gabe shouts.

To his surprise, Johnny, who's always encouraged Leo to play within himself, tells him, "Use the crowd. They're here for you, not him."

"Remember to really put your legs and hips into that drop shot," Gabe adds. "Yeah?"

"Yeah," Leo says.

He could stay and talk to Gabe for hours—about everything that's happened this weekend, about where they go from here—but set two is waiting.

Every time Leo glances into the stands between points and sees a Pride flag waving in someone's hands, it recharges him. He typically keeps his eyes fixed to the court to avoid distraction, but he's following his dad's advice now, looking to engage with the fans whenever he can. And they're loving it.

When he gets into a twenty-one-shot rally with Sascha, using every inch of the court to get him moving, he doesn't miss this time. He goes for a down-the-line winner again, this time with his backhand, and the ball glides perfectly into the corner, gliding right past Sascha. Leo doesn't just go for his usual clenched fist afterward, but turns toward the crowd and waves his arms up and down, signaling them that he sees them, he hears them, and he wants more.

They give it right back to him, raising their voices even louder, raising their hands in the air, giving him all the adrenaline he needs to take this second set.

And he does.

With an ace of his own, he evens the match.

"Game and second set: Chambers," the ump says. "One set all."

As he walks toward his bench to cool down, Leo wants the fans to continue heating up. He taps a finger to his ear, telling them to keep the noise going. Sweat dripping down his face, he takes a seat, looks to his box, and finds Gabe smirking at him.

Leo's body is holding up, but he can tell that after two weeks of, frankly, emotional terrorism—not to mention, extreme physical exertion—his battery is running low. He tries to slow down between points, go to his towel box as often as he can, conjure any kind of queer power from the Pride flags all around him. But after winning the third set, his level drops slightly, and like a shark smelling blood in the water, Sascha takes the fourth.

This match is going all the way. A fifth and final set will decide it.

The things Leo would give just for Sascha to dip. Please, for fuck's sake, just let this man's level dip. But it simply won't happen. He continues to play ruthlessly, patiently. Fortunately, so does Leo, even if his legs hate him right now.

Like a pendulum, the score ticks back and forth, each player holding their serve. The set inches toward its conclusion, and there's nothing between them.

"Five games all," the ump says after Leo secures yet another hold.

Steadying his breath, Leo picks up his towel and wipes his face as Brian shouts instructions down to him like a boxing coach talking into the ear of his player, a bloody and bruised man leaning back on the ropes of the ring.

"He keeps going down the T on his second serve," Brian says, "because he's missing the one out wide too often. If you get a look at a second serve, I want you to step in and cheat over a little. Punish that shit, LC."

Leo nods and looks to his dad, who's nodding, too.

In the next couple points, Leo still can't find a way into Sascha's service game. He's hitting him with the one-two punch: a huge first serve followed by a winner to the opposite corner. There's nothing Leo can do.

"30–love," the ump says.

"Next one, LC," Brian yells, clapping.

He breathes out. *Reset.* He watches as Sascha tosses the ball up. His arm comes down, and the ball comes careening toward Leo.

"OUT," the system calls.

Finally. A look at a second serve. Okay. Step in. Cheat over.

Like clockwork, Sascha sends his second serve down the T, and Leo is ready for it. He rips a forehand and it whizzes by his opponent before he can even recover from his service motion.

"30–15."

The next point, it happens again.

"Let's go!" Leo yells after his bullet of a backhand.

"30–all."

He sees Sascha talking angrily with his player box. A crack in the ice.

As his opponent steps back up to the line, Leo is feeling pumped up. He's bouncing from foot to foot, spinning his racket, ready to return before Sascha even bounces the ball. He wants to get in Sascha's head, show him that he should be afraid to send the next serve Leo's way.

The two of them get into another rally, dashing from side to side, sliding into their shots, sneakers screeching on the court.

Leo isn't thinking, only moving. With each ball, he inches closer to the baseline, then inside of it. He's taking control. When the next one comes to him, his instinct takes over—and he goes for it. He sees that Sascha is deep behind the baseline now, and he sends a drop shot floating over the net. Sascha sprints for it, but as he stretches out his racket, the ball hits the ground for a second time.

Leo launches his fist into the air and roars up to the heavens, "Come on!"

The fans are out of their seats, screaming and jumping. It's a break point.

"30–40," the ump says.

He doesn't go to his towel box. He gets back into position, putting the pressure right back on Sascha. When his next serve misses, Leo knows this is an opportunity he can't miss. A second serve on a break point. He steps in. Sascha drags out his preparation, bouncing the ball several extra times. Leo's pressure is working. He's in his opponent's head. Sascha will know that this second serve has to be good or Leo will return it with interest again.

The ball goes up—and it flies into the net. Sascha's racket flies out of his hand and onto the ground. The fans fly out of their seats.

"Game: Chambers," the ump attempts to announce, competing with the noise of the crowd, which has reached an earth-shattering level. "Chambers leads six games to five."

A fist in front of his face, Leo stops and turns toward his box, straight-faced. He means business now. He's about to serve for the championship. His mom is about to faint.

During the changeover, sitting on his bench, Leo stares straight ahead to maintain any semblance of concentration, a true feat given the volume of the fans, who are now singing along like a choir to Jay-Z and Alicia Keys's "Empire State of Mind," the song blasting in the stadium.

Leo feels like he's breathing manually.

This is it.

The moment he's worked for nearly every day of his life.

He's a game away from winning the US Open. For his dad. For himself. With four more points, he could cement himself in tennis history. The dream that's fueled him since he first picked up a racket at five years old. Would that little boy even believe it?

This is it.

"Time," the ump calls.

Leo jogs over to the baseline, mostly because he's forgotten how to walk, and nods to the ball boy to toss him the tennis balls. He feels for the newest ones, tossing one back to the ball boy. He steps up to the line, unable to hear himself think as the crowd grows wilder and wilder.

He bounces the ball five times. He tosses it up. His body explodes upward as his arm comes around. He sends the ball speeding out wide.

It's an ace.

"15–love."

He can barely feel his limbs.

He bounces the ball five times. He tosses it up. His body explodes upward as his arm comes around. He sends the ball speeding out wide.

It's another ace.

"30–love."

He's blacking out.

He bounces the ball five times. He tosses it up. His body explodes upward as his arm comes around. He sends the ball speeding out wide.

Sascha smacks it back and it lands at Leo's feet. He can't position himself right and hits a mistimed forehand that sails wide.

"30–15."

Okay. That's okay. That's fine.

He bounces the ball five times. He tosses it up. His body explodes upward as his arm comes around. He sends the ball speeding down the T.

Sascha whacks it into the net. "Fuck!" he screams, and he smacks his racket against the court. "Fucking piece of shit."

Leo doesn't know if Sacha's talking about himself or Leo. He doesn't care anymore. "40–15," the ump says loudly. "Code violation, audible obscenity, Mr. Volkov."

Sascha screams again, but Leo ignores him. Because it's here. Championship point. He's arrived at championship point.

He feels like he's underwater.

He's forgotten how to swim.

The crowd is feral.

His team shoots him almost psychotically encouraging looks and applaud with force to keep him amped up.

He bounces the ball five times. He tosses it up. His body explodes upward as his arm comes around. He sends the ball speeding out wide.

"OUT," the system shouts, cutting off the fans, who expected another ace and began to scream in celebration.

With some near-begging from the ump, the crowd settles again. The stadium is now the most silent it's been today as Leo prepares to hit a second serve. He can't hear anything but the blood pumping in his ears. He can't double fault. He won't.

He bounces the ball five times. He tosses it up. His body explodes upward as his arm comes around. He slices the ball down the T.

It lands in.

Sascha returns it.

Back and forth, they smack each other's shots with power and precision. Leo is in animal mode now, letting go of all thought, relying only on instinct. He's making it to every shot coming his way. He's pushing his body to its limits. Sascha sends a forehand careening down the line, and as Leo runs toward it, he's not sure he'll make it in time. He slides into it, stretching out his racket at an angle that will pop the ball high into the air.

He's there. The ball flies above Sascha's head, who's squinting to locate it in the sun. He finds it, and smashes it back. The sun in his eyes, it's not as powerful as it should be. Leo lunges for the ball. Sascha's coming toward the net, ready to smash or volley whatever is about to come his way. But Leo sees an opening. He sprints up to the ball and whips his arm around, hitting a forehand that curves past Sascha, who sticks his racket out but can't make contact in time. The ball soars past him and Leo watches as it hangs in the air, spinning closer and closer toward the line. He squints his eyes to see the ball. He stops breathing.

It drops in.

All at once, each part of his body relaxes, and he falls to the ground, splayed out like a starfish on the court. The stadium erupts louder than he's ever heard it.

"Game, set, and match: Chambers," the ump yells into the mic, barely audible over the crowd. "3–6, 6–4, 6–4, 3–6, 7–5."

He's done it.

Leo Chambers has won the US Open.

His body shakes as he begins to sob, putting his hands over his eyes.

This can't be real. This can't be real. This can't be real.

But he can hear the stadium roaring, so it must be. When he pulls his hands from his eyes and sits up, his eyes confirm it, too. Across the stadium, people are applauding, jumping, yelling, hugging, taking photos of him. The Pride flags and American flags are billowing. He's still crying as he stands up.

He sees Sascha waiting at the net, a stern look on his face, and jogs up to him. Sascha puts his hand out and offers an emotionless, "Congratulations."

Playing with the rainbow ribbon on his collar, Leo is sure to look him square in the eye as he grips his hand. "Thank you," he says. "You just lost the US Open to a fairy." He then takes pride in gesturing for Sascha, as the runner-up, to shake the ump's hand first. Sascha, for maybe the first time ever, is speechless.

And with that, the moment is all Leo's.

He stumbles onto the court as if he's drunk, his hands like windshield wipers for his tears. He runs to the other side of the court, waving to the fans, and with security tailing him, he makes his way up the stairs and jogs down the landing, the crowd like a thousand-armed monster, limbs sticking out every which way to take photos and touch the champion.

Before he can even reach the next set of stairs and run down to his box, he meets his dad on the landing. Johnny drops his cane and pulls Leo into a hug, his hand on the back of Leo's head like he's holding a baby. Leo's tears are now draining onto Johnny's shoulder. The noise of the crowd is still thundering, cameras clicking all around them, but he can hear his dad tell him, "I'm so proud of you. My boy."

With Johnny guiding him down the landing, Leo finds his way to his box, where everyone is waiting for him. He hugs his mom, whose cheeks are stained with mascara, as she whispers, "You did it, you did it, you did it."

The moment he pulls away from his mom, Tess and Ollie bombard him, shaking him and hugging him and taking a million selfies with him.

"All right, my turn," Brian says, squeezing in to bump fists with Leo and, before giving him a hug, says, "I knew you'd do it, LC. Never a doubt in my mind."

When Brian steps aside, there's Gabe, standing in awe of Leo. He steps up to him, and Gabe wraps his Pride flag around Leo's shoulders. Before Gabe can even say anything, Leo takes his face in his hands and pulls him into a kiss that's deep and salty from the tears still streaming into his mouth. There's a chorus of *WOOOOO*s and *AHHHHH*s from the crowd.

"Congratulations, Leonardo," Gabe whispers, tears in his eyes.

"Thank you," Leo says. "Oh my God, you have a boot on. Is your ankle okay? Should you even be here? How are you here? Tell me about the signs! Please!"

"Jesse," Gabe says. "He messaged me saying he wanted to make it up to you and asked if I had any ideas. I told him about 'hold your own,' he put out a call on Serving Looks for people to show up with signs, and, well, it kinda went viral. Considering you had your phone shut off, I knew you wouldn't see." He raises an eyebrow.

"Thank you, thank you, thank you," Leo says. "You have no idea how much it meant to me. And I'm sorry. About my phone. About going into my shell. I just—when I didn't hear from you after the leak, I panicked. I thought you didn't want to talk to me or needed space or—"

"Leo, I was in physical therapy all day for my ankle, and Esme hijacked my phone so I couldn't do anything rash," Gabe says. "To her credit, I probably would have. By the time she gave it back to me, none of my messages would go through to you and my calls went straight to your voice mail. So, I booted up and hopped on a late flight to New York."

There are no words that Leo can find to tell Gabe just how unbelievable he is, so he just kisses him again. The *WOOOOO*s and *AHHHHH*s return.

"So, what are you going to write on the camera screen this time?" Gabe asks.

"I think I'd rather tell you to your face this time," Leo says. "I love you."

Gabe's eyes widen.

"You don't have to say anything," Leo says. "I just—"

"I love you, too," Gabe says, a smile stretching across his cheeks.

"I can't believe this is happening," Leo says, shaking his head.

"It's happening, Leonardo," Gabe says. "Hey, before they honor you on court and shit, go talk to Jesse. He's right there." He nods to the section just above Leo's player box.

Leo moves up a few rows, gesturing for Jesse to come forward, too.

"Hey," Leo says. "Thank you."

"Congratulations," Jesse says, his eyes shining. "It's literally the least I could do. I'm so happy for you, Leo."

"Thank you," Leo says. "I'm glad you could be here."

"I wouldn't have missed it," Jesse says. "I also wanted to tell you that I'm, um, starting my own podcast. No bullshit gossip. Definitely no outings. Just real stories about all kinds of players, a real pulse on everything going on in the tennis world. It'll be called Serving Looks. Actually, I'm looking for a host. Any ideas?" Jesse gives him a knowing look.

"Hmmm," Leo says, feigning deep thought. "Have you met my friend Tess?"

Leo yells for Tess to come over.

"I'll let you two talk," Leo says, putting his hand on Tess's shoulder. "I think they need me down there."

"It is my honor to present to you," the USTA president announces on the stage that's just been built on the court, "your US Open champion, Leo Chambers!"

Leo shakes his hand and takes the mic, expecting that when he looks down, he'll be naked, and this will all be a dream. But he's clothed, and it's not.

"Thank you so much," Leo says as the crowd refuses to stop roaring. As the volume comes down, he continues, knowing he has to get the polite part over with, stomach it as best he can. "First, I . . . have to say congratulations to Sascha and his team."

The fans applaud him, many still loyal to the twenty-time Slam champion. They keep the clapping going as Leo then thanks the people who make the US Open happen—the crew, the ball kids, the food workers, everybody.

"I'll keep this short because I know you want to keep the party going, and so do I. Everyone who cheered for me today, who held up a sign, you have no idea what you've done for me. You've shown me and so many other people like me that they belong here. That phrase, 'hold your own,' that's something my dad used to tell me growing up. He'd tell me to be strong, to be proud, to stand my ground, no matter what," Leo says.

He tries to swallow the giant lump in his throat, but it's no use.

"I guess I should address the gay elephant in the room. There have been a lot of people who've tried to derail me on my way here. But look where we are," he says, gazing up at the highest seats. "We're in Arthur Ashe Stadium, on the grounds of the Billie Jean King National Tennis Center. History is on the side of people who dare to show that you can become a champion while remaining true to yourself. I stand on the shoulders of giants, and that includes Gabe Montoya. Gabe, you've changed my life this year, and even though it wasn't anybody else's news to share, I'm proud to stand here and say that I love you."

Their eyes meet, blurry with tears.

Leo has to wait a full minute for the stadium to get all the cheering out of their system. The rainbow flags are shaking faster and faster.

"My dad was a finalist here back in 1990. He taught me how to play tennis, but he also taught me so much more about perseverance, life, and love. Thank you, Dad. For showing me the way."

The entire stadium is on their feet now, clapping for Johnny, whose face is awestruck and being recorded closely by a weepy Sheryl.

"Okay, so I didn't keep it short. I'll stop there, but just one more thing—I'm gay and I just won the US Open!" Leo shouts into the mic, and the crowd keeps the noise going.

The USTA president hands Leo his spectacular trophy—handcrafted by Tiffany's, no less—and as Leo takes it from him, he sees his reflection in the shiny silver, and it starts to sink in. He's really done it. He kisses the trophy as dozens of cameras flash, and then hoists it into the sticky September air, confetti cannons going off behind him.

As Leo looks around Arthur Ashe Stadium, at all twenty-four thousand people whistling and applauding, he sees it out of the corner of his eye—a big piece of blue confetti that's landed on his shoulder. He shuts his eyes, smiling to himself.

He knows that no matter what happens from here, no one can take this title, this achievement, this triumph from him. He will always have this moment.

After all, time never runs out in tennis.

ACKNOWLEDGMENTS

Thank you to everyone who has been in my player's box, cheering me on as I brought *Thirty Love* to life.

To my agent, Bibi Lewis, I'll never forget the day I got your email during the 2024 US Open, saying you loved this book and wanted to talk about its future. I almost fell off the couch. Thank you for championing *Thirty Love* from the very beginning.

To my editor, Jess Verdi, I can't thank you enough for your belief in this story and in me. My book is better for your immense talent and passion. You've made my dream come true.

Thank you to everyone at Alcove Press and Crooked Lane who had a part in getting this book out the door, including Julia Abbott, Rebecca Nelson, and Thai Fantauzzi Pérez.

Can we talk about the cover? I couldn't have imagined a more beautiful one if I tried. Thank you to Débora Islas for perfectly capturing the love, tenderness, and magnetism between Leo and Gabe.

To Gabriela Barrantes, thank you for taking the author photo of my dreams. Thank you for screaming with joy every time I gave you an update about the book. I wrote Gabe's Peruvian story for you.

To Megan Soria, thank you for never once doubting that I'd get here. Thank you for our endless talks about writing, style, music, and tennis—since we were teenagers. I wrote Tess's Filipino story for you.

Thank you to all my friends and family for believing in me—with a special shout-out to Jeff, Georgia, Emma, Greg, and Doug for being there throughout the writing process, lifting me up whenever I needed encouragement.

To my dad, whose journey with MS, like Johnny's, has taught me what it means to find your place in a world that wasn't built for you. You passed your love of writing down to me, and I could never thank you enough.

To my mom, who was the first person to play tennis with me as a kid, whether it was at our local park or against the giant wall of the JoAnn Fabrics at the shopping center up the street. Thank you for all your love and support.

To Dorothy, Rose, Blanche, and Sophia, thank you for being a friend.

Thank you to Autumn and Arthur, my ridiculously cute rescue dogs, for keeping me company while I wrote and edited. Good girl! Good boy!

To Danny, this book is for you. Thank you for listening to all my comments and questions during the months I was writing—from "I just realized that Leo needs to be a bottom" to "Do you think people will even want to read this?" You are my ideal reader, my dream husband, my best friend. I love you more than words can say—and I wrote 100,000 of them.

I've been playing and watching tennis for most of my life, but my love for this sport deepened during the pandemic. When tennis matches were allowed to begin again—a socially distant sport by nature—I watched, stuck at home, every day. Match after match after match. Thank you to all the players whose power, perseverance, and fearlessness on the court gave me something to root for when the world felt directionless. I truly believe tennis is the most difficult and most beautiful sport in the world. I'm in awe of it, and I wanted to capture even an ounce of its glory here.

Throughout those years I was watching, I waited to see someone like me step onto the court. But he never came along. That's what inspired me to write *Thirty Love* in the first place. When I started writing this book, there had never been an openly gay man on tour. Hell, when I started writing this book, *Challengers* hadn't even come out yet. I wanted to write a story where a gay man in tennis could find love and find himself in the process. I want that for all queer people. I want a world where we can all do what we love as our full selves. I want a world where we can all find our happily ever after. For now, I hope this book brings you some joy, laughter, and comfort.

Hold your own.